CATHI UNSWORTH moved to London's Ladbroke Grove in 1987 and has stayed there ever since. She began a career in rock writing with *Sounds* and *Melody Maker*, before co-editing the arts journal *Purr* and then *Bizarre* magazine. Her first novel, *The Not Knowing*, was published by Serpent's Tail in 2005, and her next novel, *The Singer*, will be published in 2007.

LONDON NOIR

CAPITAL CRIME FICTION

EDITED BY

CATHI UNSWORTH

First published in 2006 by Akashic Books, New York

First published in the UK in 2006 by Serpent's Tail,
4 Blackstock Mews, London N4 2BT
www.serpentstail.com

London map by Sohrab Habibion

ISBN-13: 978-1-85242-930-0
ISBN-10: 1-85242-930-5

Printed by Mackays of Chatham, plc

10 9 8 7 6 5 4 3 2 1

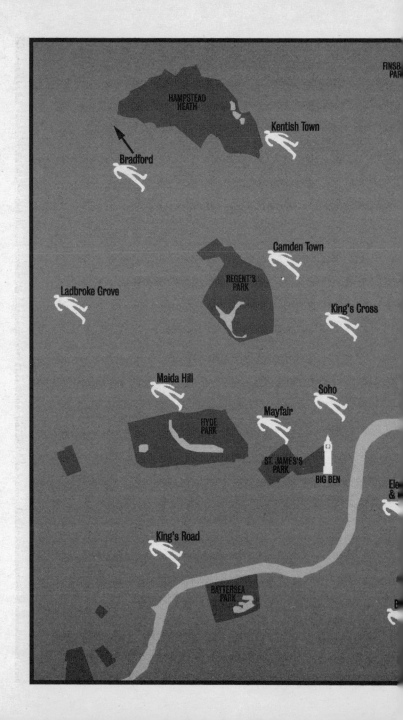

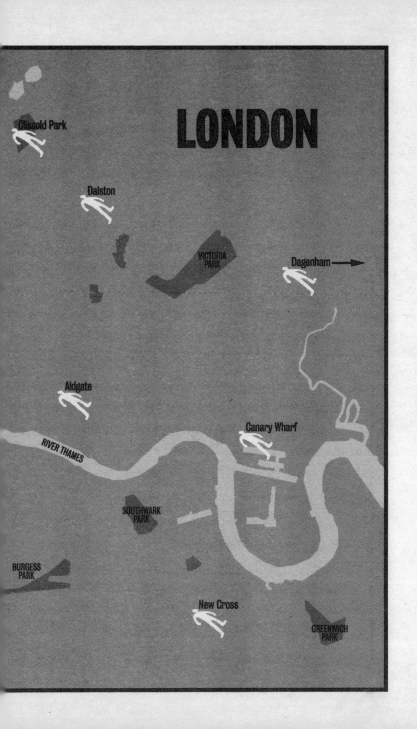

TABLE OF CONTENTS

Sic gorgiamus illos subiectatos

INTRODUCTION

Crime and Establishment
BY CATHI UNSWORTH

W hat you have in your hands is not a collection of crime stories set in London. This is rather a collection of crime stories that *are* London. The things that happen within these pages would not be unfamiliar to those who have come before to render the city's psyche in words, art, music, theatre, or magic. It's not that this *was* the city of William Blake, Charles Dickens, Dr. Johnson, Samuel Pepys, Daniel Defoe, Oscar Wilde, George Orwell, Dylan Thomas, Francis Bacon, Joe Strummer or Johnny Rotten. It's that it still very much *is*.

London needs illumination from its own darkness, from its perpetual cycle of crimes. This is also the city of Newgate Prison, Bedlam, Amen Corner, Tyburn Cross, the London Monster, Spring-heeled Jack, Jack the Ripper, Jack the Hat, the Blind Beggar, the Baltic Exchange and 10 Rillington Place. The most famous detective in the world, Sherlock Holmes, stepped out of the smog of a London night, shouted, "The game's afoot!" and conspired to send his creator Arthur Conan Doyle, along with every actor who tried to make him flesh, mad.

London always extracts its price.

The keys to the city are contained in a line you'll find in Patrick McCabe's story "Who Do You Know in Heaven?" "Consciousness," his know-it-all café-owner spouts, "prompts you to hypothesize that the story you're creating from a given set of memories is a *consistent history*, justified by a consistent narrative voice . . ."

London's stories seep out of its walls, rise up from the foundations laid by the Romans two thousand years ago, up through its sewers, buried rivers and tube tunnels, and out through the pavements. They wind their way through twisting alleyways that formed themselves long ago, before the order of the grid system could be placed upon them. They whisper their secrets through the marketplaces where every language on earth is and has been spoken; every measure of trade haggled over, from fruit and veg to children's lives. They drift up at night from the currents of Old Father Thames, through the temples of commerce that form the Square Mile, across the halls of Parliament, the cathedrals laid by Norman kings, the tunnels dug by Victorian engineers.

Listen to London for long enough and the city will impart in you your own notion; your own form of navigation through the maps laid down over centuries; your own heart's topography of the metropolis. Your soul blends with the walls and pavements, the tunnels and spires, the street markets and the stock exchanges. But is that notion really your own, or has the suggestion been planted, the story already written long ago?

The stories in this collection form maps of the city you will not find in the A – Z. Already, the city has exerted its collective subconscious over this creation without the authors being aware of it, so that the bohemian West, the iconic East, the melancholy North and the wild South are linked. By lines of songs from the same jukebox; angles in the heads of priests, coppers, witchdoctors, lawyers, pornographers, psychopaths, con men and terrorists; even the trajectory of a skein of wild geese.

Every kind of crime has been committed here; most of them never solved. London is responsible for all of them. London confuses the mind: Pat McCabe's IRA man comes to the mainland on a mission and gets seduced by a black-and-white photo of a London only felt in his blood, of a haunted '40s dancehall. Jerry Sykes's lonely pensioner dreams of '50s Camden Town even as he is mugged by its twenty-first-century offspring. Sylvie Simmons's psychiatrist talks to a ventriloquist's doll. Joe McNally sees London's ectoplasm form into grotesque, mythological shapes as he traverses the labyrinth of Elephant & Castle.

Some can see through the veils more clearly than others. For Joolz Denby, the Great Wen is an even Greater Con, a grey eternity without a soul, beckoning you into its clip-joint belly for more addictions you can never beat, more itches you can never scratch. For Barry Adamson's Father Donaghue, the Maida Hill community of losers and bruisers he serves are all souls worth fighting for, so that he may even redeem his own. But for Stewart Home's dead-eyed policeman, the souls of the neighbouring parish of Ladbroke Grove are mere commodities, investments for his pension scheme.

London favours the entrepreneur. London thrives on the violence it incites. London built its Parliament on a bramble-riddled mire known as Thorney Island a thousand years ago. It is policed by villains, ministered to by the damned, carved up by Masonic market traders.

London's perennial themes rise to the surface in relentless waves. Martyn Waites stirs up the mob mentality in the mean estates of Dagenham, the traditional dumping ground of the city's poor, manipulated and united by self-destructive hatred. Daniel Bennett places a Ripper in Hackney's Clissold Park, just slightly north of his old stomping grounds. The city's most infamous bogeyman takes on a new shape here, no longer an eminent Victorian surgeon or the wayward offspring of the Queen but a disturbed adolescent, pulsing with the red rage of the city's demented heat. Mark Pilkington gets down among the traders of lost souls to record human trafficking and child sacrifice in Dalston, where John Dee reincarnates himself as a Nigerian *sangoma*, in the opposite end of the city from where he started in the reign of Elizabeth I. Michael Ward reminds us of the Establishment, those bewigged members of the Temple, and the closet of the Cabinet: They Who Are Really Pulling the Strings, and always have been.

London's Burning, London Calling, Waterloo Sunset, the Guns of Brixton. London pulses to the music of the world, each district retelling its own folk legends through bhangra, reggae, ska, blues, jazz, fado, flamenco, electronica, hip hop, punk – pick your own soundtrack. John Williams's ageing punk rocker finds the man he could have been, lying wasted and dribbling at a gig in a New Cross bar. Like the lines from a song, the past comes back to haunt Desmond Barry's would-be filmmaker, through a wormhole in time and out in the middle of Soho.

London is a siren, calling you to the rocks of your own destruction, taunting and teasing and offering you a flash of its flesh as you teeter drunkenly in the doorway. Ken Bruen's gangster finds her on a Brixton dancefloor. My own creation, private eye Dougie, tries to spirit her out of the city through the portal of King's Cross.

That London has survived so long comes down to its foundation in the root of all evil. The river, as the Romans knew, meant the riches of the world could be shipped directly to its ravenous mouth. London has controlled the world for many of the years of its existence. London is the Grand Wizard. It's no coincidence that Ken Hollings writes a future projection for the city from the gleaming towers of Canary Wharf, the monument to capitalism laid down on the ashes of the working-class East End by the Wicked Witch of Westminster, Margaret Thatcher.

So again, this is not really a collection of crime stories. This is a compass for the reader to chart their own path through the dark streets of London, to take whatever part chimes most closely with their soul and use it as a talisman.

London is shadows and fog. London is haunted. London is the definitive noir.

PART I

POLICE & THIEVES

PART I

BACKGAMMON

BY DESMOND BARRY

Soho

At three o'clock, on Thursday, September 5, I was supposed to be at Soho House on Greek Street to meet with Jon Powell, the film director. Jon was interested in a script I'd written called *Rough House* about nasty goings-on in Soho in the late '70s. He'd had a top-ten box office success with his last film, *Anxiety* – a horror flick with reality TV overtones – so sitting on the tube train from Kilburn down to Piccadilly Circus, I don't mind admitting that I was well gassed up and a bit nervous because I really wanted it all to go well. The thing is, I had to eat something fast, both to silence the juices gurgling away in my stomach and to deal with the lack of blood sugar making me more nervous and edgy by the second. I was lucky. I still had an hour and a half to kill before the meeting, and the Ristorante Il Pollo, which serves the best lasagne in Soho, was close to the corner of Greek Street where the meeting would take place. The Pollo was definitely going to be my first stop.

I jostled up the packed escalator of the tube station, pushed my way up the stairs, and I was out onto the Dilly – Eros, lights, action. I dodged a couple of taxis and ducked up Great Windmill Street. It could have been a scene from the film script: beautiful girls on the doors of the strip joints, all with flashes of cleavage, coy smiles or lewd words to tempt me inside. But I wasn't biting, was I? I had work to do. I turned right onto Brewer Street and then jagged right and left onto Old Compton Street, where I got the eye from the pretty boys sitting at the tables of the cafés and leaning in the doorways of the hip gay boutiques. Everybody wants something in Soho. I wanted lasagne.

I pushed through the glass door into Ristorante Il Pollo and breathed in the rich meat and tomato smells oozing out of the kitchen and the whiff of coffee from the Gaggia machine that roared behind the counter. The Pollo had been selling the same lasagne in steel dishes for at least thirty years and probably longer, and I was really counting on that béchamel and meat sauce and a nice glass of wine to sort me out before the meeting with Jon. The waitress seated me at a little table in the front.

That's why I didn't see Magsy at first. Not until after I'd dug my way through the crusty cheese and into the soft green pasta and scraped the brown and crispy bits off the edge of the steel dish. It was a shock to see the old bastard come walking down between the booths from the back of the café. Twenty-six years ago. How did he happen to be in here right at this moment when I hadn't seen him in twenty-six years? We had a bit of a history, me and Magsy, I got to admit. I pushed the steel dish back and smiled at him, but my shoulder muscles got tight and my knee started bouncing as if somewhere inside me I was all ready to run for it. Like a lot of people who'd gone bald these days, Magsy had shaved his head.

But then there was that old mickey-taking smirk on Magsy's face when he saw me. He wasn't a tall bloke, about 5'8", still five inches taller than me though. He looked well enough off in his cord jacket, checked shirt and jeans. I'd heard he'd gone to live in Spain after he'd come out of prison.

Twenty-two years back that must have been. But he didn't look at all tanned. He'd been through some real damage, I reckoned: the tiredness around the eyes, the deep wrinkles, the greyness of the skin of a long-time smoker.

"What are *you* doing here?" he said.

I got up from the table and I even gave him a hug. It was a bit stiff to tell the truth, but he still had that pleased-to-see-me grin on his face when we stepped back.

"I got a meeting," I said. "Business thing in about . . ." I jerked my sleeve so the watch showed on my wrist, "ten minutes."

"What business you in, then?"

"I'll tell you about it later, if you like, if you're gonna be around."

"Half past four in Steiner's," he said.

"Right," I said.

Steiner's, yeah. One of our old haunts.

We came out of the Pollo and into the sunshine on Old Compton Street, walked the few yards to Greek Street in the glare, and then crossed the road to the shady opposite corner.

"You working down here again?" I said.

I hoped he wasn't.

"Nah, I live in Bridgwater now."

"Bridgwater?" I said. "What you doing in Soho, then?"

"Meeting Richie when he gets off his shift."

Richie was one of Magsy's oldest mates, though I didn't know him that well myself.

"He still work here?" I said.

"Yeah. Manager of about four Harmony shops."

"Corporate porno."

"Fully licensed and legit," Magsy said. "New Labour, son. As long as it makes money, it's all right. Liberal attitude, innit?"

"Fair play," I said.

"So I *will* catch you in Steiner's?" Magsy asked.

"Yeah, right," I said.

He just walked off then. I watched him as he headed west. Weird that I ran into him in the Pollo after all those years. It gave me the wobblies a bit. But I checked my watch. I was bang on time for the meeting. I had to get Magsy out of my head for now. I rang the bell on the door of the club and then went up the stairs to meet Jon Powell.

On the roof of Soho House, in the bright sunshine, over a couple of bottles of sparkling mineral water, the meeting went okay. Not great, but okay. It would appear that trying to get a film made is a process that requires a lot of patience. I told Jon that I wasn't sure how the producers who'd got the soft money for me to write the script planned on coming up with the hard cash to get this thing into production but they did have some serious co-production interest. That's films-peak for a lot of hot air that might one day float a balloon. Jon said that he really liked the script and promised he would pass it on to someone he knew with Pierce Brosnan's company who might well be interested in the project, and that he would do that as soon as he came back from the Toronto Film Festival and a trip to L.A. This was all very positive. But no one had, as yet, signed on the line, or was eating a bacon sandwich on the set of the first shoot. This was either a great way to make a living, or I was chasing a total mirage. Still, I'd been paid for the script and I'd get more money if the film got made, and the sun was shining. It was not a bad way to make a living. I swallowed the last of the mineral water and we went down about five flights of stairs to the street. Mineral water? Christ, I'm losing my identity. I can't even drink much coffee these days.

I shook hands with Jon and he set off north towards Soho Square while I went west along Old Compton Street towards Steiner's. I *was* going to meet Magsy – if he was there. Me and Magsy had been mates together in the mid-'70s and I'd spent long hours back then in his flat, just lying around and listening to music. He'd lived there with his girlfriend, Penelope. I was in their flat in Camden so often that I practically lived there. I *did* live there when the lease ran out on my own little gaff in Chalk Farm. Then, after I'd crashed there for six months, him and his girlfriend found a place for me in Dalston, "through a mate of Penelope's," they said.

So they didn't have to officially throw me out. We had some times, me and Magsy. Incredible times. Like . . . just before I was due to move into the new gaff on a hot July afternoon in 1975 . . . me and Magsy decided we'd celebrate my last night in the flat. We bought a 100-gram bag of salt and half a dozen lemons from a corner shop, and three bottles of tequila from the offy on Camden High Street. Then we picked up Penelope from her job at the Royal Free Hospital. She was standing outside the gate with this petite long-haired girl, Angela. We hadn't expected this at all – we *had* just planned on going back to the flat and getting blasted on the tequila – but Angela invited us all to dinner at her place on Cornwall Gardens, just off the Gloucester Road. Cornwall Gardens – now that is a class-A address, mate. And it was a bright and lovely summer's day, and we had the salt and lemons and tequila to donate to the proceedings, so I felt okay. We drove down Haverstock Hill and through the West End and into Kensington in Angela's car, and Angela said that her boyfriend, Ted, owned the flat that I was just about to move into in Dalston.

Ah, I thought, the flat connection.

So we turned onto Cornwall Gardens. Angela had a permit to park on the street and she opened this big Georgian door for us and took us up in a lift to a lovely three-bedroom flat with all these Persian carpets in the lounge. It was gorgeous. And the balcony overlooked the fenced-in private gardens.

Angela started cooking a vegetarian dinner in the open-plan kitchen. She said she always ate macrobiotic food, but she kept having a break from the kitchen every now and then so she could smoke a cigarette, which didn't seem somehow kosher to me, her being macrobiotic and that. Ted arrived home about half an hour after she'd begun preparing the dinner. He wasn't that big, a bit skinny with wire-rimmed glasses and a ponytail. A bit of an old-time hippy. He'd been out doing business, according to Angela. What with the sunshine and the shooters and the fresh taste of the lemons, by this time we'd already finished the first bottle of tequila: at least, me and Magsy had; the girls had been chatting most of the time in the kitchen.

So then we all sat down around a tablecloth that Angela spread over the Persian carpet in the lounge and we polished off the brown rice, pickles and veggies. I was feeling really healthy after that meal. We slumped back against the giant cushions and started on more shooters of tequila, and Ted brought out this lovely pearl-inlaid backgammon board. We all tried to concentrate on the game. That was when Ted produced a large mirror and laid out five enormous lines of white powder that he said was Colombian cocaine. Ted vacuumed up a line of powder and took the tails off the other lines and handed the rolled-up note to Magsy. Magsy dug into it and then Penelope had a line. I had a sense of relief when Angela said she didn't want any. It made me feel a little less like a dork when I said, "Thanks, but I'll stick with the tequila." I'm not a prude – but I get these terrible asthma attacks if I breath hostile flower pollen, let alone cocaine, and I didn't want to risk anything at all, given the state I was already in. The black and red and white triangles on the backgammon board already had a glow all their own after we'd finished the second bottle.

So we threw the dice and moved a few counters and then Ted laid out another set of lines of the Colombian coke and I downed another three shots of tequila and I felt a lot less nervous about the heavy drugs the boys on my right kept snorting and we threw the dice some more and we finished the third bottle of tequila and I was feeling all sunny even though it was dark and time to go home and I stood up and my knees didn't seem to work so good and I thought, well, it's all right because I'm going to go home now, and I really hadn't realized just how good I was at backgammon. I thought, I really wouldn't mind meeting Ted again, even if he *is* a bit of cokehead. I really wanted to play another game with him.

But you know what? I never did get to go back to that flat . . . not ever again, did I? I'd been there by chance, really, I suppose. I mean, it was Magsy and his girlfriend who Angela had meant to invite and I'd just happened to be along with Magsy after we bought the tequila. So I had no real business being there, did I?

Just as we were about to leave, Ted grabbed Magsy by the arm, all friendly.

"Hey, Magsy," he said. "Think you can shift some coke for me?"

Magsy's face lit right up. A business opportunity . . . Magsy liked that . . . and no doubt he really had enjoyed all that marching powder, and Ted liked him so much that, right there and then, he laid a couple of ounces on Magsy and told him to pay it back in a week. Even with all that liquor in me, I knew that this was probably a bad idea, but Magsy was dead thrilled. Fair play, I know for a fact he paid Ted back on the fronted coke two days before the week was up.

Ted, of course, was now my landlord. That made me feel a bit uncomfortable, but after a month or so a lovely woman of thirty-one by the name of Sheri moved in with me and I was glad I had my own gaff. Sheri was a real cockney. I met her when I got a job as a shipping clerk in Mile End. I had to pay the rent somehow. I took her round to see Magsy. He was still my mate, wasn't he? By now he was doing a brisk trade. What I felt though . . . when we were around there . . . was that Magsy seemed a lot happier to see his clients than he did to see us. I thought, well, he's my mate. I'll confront him, like.

"What's going on?" I said. "You know, really going on?"

He knew what I was talking about, when you're mates, you do; but he just said, "I'm doing fine, son. Doing well. Just the sniffles, like. It's just like having a cold, really. No bother at all."

The sniffles? What the . . . ? I wanted to push him on it, but right then Ted walked in. He had this bloke with him called Danny. Danny had a very good haircut, a very expensive suit, a black crew-neck cotton pullover, and a camel's-hair coat. He was not an old-time hippy at all. He was very definitely an old-time villain – even if he was only about twenty-eight or so. Danny oozed charm.

"Magsy," he said, "how would you like to make a very sound investment, my son?"

"What's that?" Magsy replied.

"How would you like to take out a lease on a small pornography outlet on Dean Street? Reckon it might be the perfect front for your proper business."

Magsy's proper business was now, very definitely, hard-core narcotics.

"Yeah," Magsy said, big smile on his face. "I could get into that – a finger in every pie, innit? Sex and drugs and rock and roll."

I laughed along with him. He was charmed. I was charmed. But I still didn't know if this investment was a good idea at all. I didn't know the financial details, of course. But who was I to know, anyway? At that time I had a shit job in a shipping office on the Mile End Road while Magsy was about to move up to the West End with all the villains. And he did. After he opened up the porn shop, I used to go up to Soho every Friday night to have a drink with him after work.

To tell the truth, I enjoyed meeting all those strippers and hookers and pimps and hustlers – who all seemed to be his mates – especially after I'd just spent the previous five days filing bills of lading. I felt like I was a very well-connected desperado . . . Well, not exactly . . . just a sort of desperado by proxy, really, wasn't I? Magsy moved with the big fish like Ted and Danny, and, more and more often, the time came when we were out for a drink and he'd say, "Sorry, Dex, I got to push off. There's a party at Ted's flat."

I used to go home to Sheri then.

"He's leaving you behind, love," Sheri would say. "He don't give a damn about you, does he?"

"No, he's just busy with all that business," I'd respond. "Ted probably don't want him bringing his mates around there, does he? Got to keep a low profile and that."

But it hurt, I tell you that.

I still met Magsy every now and then for a drink. I still liked it when he'd spin all those yarns about all the gangster stuff.

So this one Friday night we were on the cognac in Steiner's and Magsy said, "Hey, Dex, remember that flat on Gloucester Road?"

"Yeah," I said.

"Me and Penny are moving in next week."

"Get away," I said.

"Ted got tipped off, didn't he? The Old Bill are looking for a major bust, so him and Angela got to leave the country in a hurry. He asked me and Penelope to house-sit for him."

"Ace," I said.

The weird thing was . . . Magsy never – ever – invited me round to the flat in Cornwall Gardens . . . not once.

"Why d'you keep meeting up with that bastard?" Sheri said. Meaning Magsy.

"Well, a mate's a mate, innit?" I said. "He'll come round . . ."

But I didn't see him for about three months after he moved into Cornwall Gardens. Then I met him on Old Compton Street one weekend.

"What happened to you?" I said.

Magsy's face was swollen on both sides. And the skin was all swirls of green and yellow and purple.

"Let's have a drink," he said.

He had his jaw wired shut so he spoke through clenched teeth. We went into Steiner's.

"Ted sent me this blotter acid from the States," Magsy sort of hissed and gurgled. I think he was all coked up so he kept on talking. "Mr. Natural tabs. Pure acid. One drawing of

Mr. Natural perforated into four parts. Ted fronted it all, didn't he? Told me to sell it on for a pound a go and he'd collect when he came home. A few months later, Ted did come home – very sudden. And when he came home, he came to collect. Fair enough, I thought. But he went berserk. Claimed I was giving him only a quarter of the money I was supposed to. I said that he told me to sell the Mr. Naturals for a quid apiece. Ted said I should have sold them for a quid per perforated square."

I wondered if Magsy was bullshitting me. How much was this a genuine misunderstanding with Ted and how much of the money might have gone up his nose?

"So he did you over?" I said. I found that hard to believe. Ted didn't look that hard.

"Not just Ted. His family and all . . ."

"Ah," I said.

"They're all old-time villains – just like Danny. So I had to leave the flat, didn't I? Under some duress . . . with the aid of all of Ted's brothers and father and uncles and Danny, who, when they were finished with the duress, like, threw me down the stairs, didn't they?"

He hissed a bit as he laughed. I was glad he could laugh about it.

"How's Penny?" I asked.

"They didn't touch her. She's with some mates of hers out near Epping."

"Where you staying?" I asked.

"Sleeping on the floor of the shop."

"Come back to my flat."

I thought, well, those bastards have done him over, maybe he'll drop all the gangster crap and get back to normal. He shook his head.

"Nah, gotta stay in Soho," he said.

We arranged to meet the following Sunday at Steiner's, and in those few days the swelling on his face had gone down a bit, though the bruises had started to take on some very spectacular greens and blues. I got us in a couple of pints of Stella Artois.

"I gotta meet someone here," he said.

Ah, shit, I thought.

This curly-haired bloke with a squashed nose and a lot of gold chains came through the door. He went down to the gents and Magsy followed him. Then they came back out and Curly left.

"Got to pay off the debts to Ted," Magsy said. "Had to borrow some money."

Ah, no, I thought.

Magsy was practically bouncing all of a sudden – his fingers drumming on the bar, the shift of his shoulders. And he was probably low on coke, which gave him a sort of added drive. Magsy necked his lager in three large swallows.

"Sorry, Dex," he said to me. "Gotta score. Adios, amigo."

So off went Magsy to buy a load of coke and I went home to Sheri.

And, truth to tell, that was the last I saw of Magsy. Not that I didn't think about him. The police must have been watching him for ages and they decided to pay a visit to his Dean Street porno shop very early the next morning. They found about an ounce of coke and a weight of grass. Magsy got four years in Brixton. I never went near him in there.

Twenty-six years later and I bump into him at Ristorante Il Pollo in the heart of Soho and we were going to meet in Steiner's, the last place we'd seen each other before he went down. I took a breath and pushed through the door into the saloon bar. There was Magsy, standing at the bar with Richie Stiles, an old mate of his, who was as tall as ever but plump now, with a receding hairline and fuller cheeks. He *was* in an Armani suit though.

"Dexie!" Magsy said. "Good to see you, son."

He and Richie were already three sheets to the wind on the shots of tequila and Corona beers that were lined up on the bar. I couldn't resist it. Blame it on old time's sake, or maybe because I was a bit nervous, but I had a lick of salt, a shot of tequila, bit on the lemon, and then soothed the burn in my throat with a cool slug of the Corona.

"Rich!" I said. "Corporate bigwig now, son."

"Still a party," Rich said. "But government-licensed now, innit? Make more money being legit these days. No police raids or nothing."

"So what are *you* doing with yourself?" Magsy said.

If I said I was a writer, it would have had this stink of me being a bit of a braggart – which I am, really.

"I'm a writer."

"A writer?" Magsy said. "You make money at that?"

"I got to hustle to make a living," I said. "But it's okay. Better than any other job I've had . . . and I've had a lot since working in the shipping trade: labouring on building sites, bookkeeping, library assistant, then I decided to get a real life."

I could see that I'd stung him a bit with that. I hadn't meant to. What was he doing? Brickie? On the dole? I knew he wasn't dealing.

"God, how long has it been since I seen you?" Magsy said.

I was sure he knew well enough.

"Twenty-six years," I said.

I was buzzed but not drunk.

"Yeah . . . right . . . since just before the trial," he said.

I nodded. "Yeah, right."

What he meant was: *You didn't come to see me in prison, you gutless shit.*

And I didn't, it was true, because when Magsy was sent down – call it total paranoia if you like – I was thoroughly convinced that if I *had* gone to see Magsy, I would be on a police list of known consorters with convicted drug traffickers and that within a very short time I would receive a similar dawn visit from the police just as Magsy had. And if the police needed to make up their arrest rate and decided that a consorter with known traffickers was worth fitting up, then I would be on the inside with him – with a criminal record and fighting off anal rapists. I just couldn't face even the remotest possibility of it.

Now he wanted me to feel guilty for it, which he had definitely succeeded in doing, and that made me really mad. What he was doing, you see – what he was really doing – was trying to return me to that position I'd been in back then: him as Jack the Lad and me as the shipping-firm employee dogsbody. Knock me back to square one. He'd always thought of me as a bit of a wimp for not having the balls to do what he'd done: ducking and diving right into the thick of the coke dealing and the porn business. But he'd had his life and I'd had mine, and I wasn't sorry at all with the way mine had gone. I wasn't any shipping clerk any more, was I? And what was he? What was he? Tell me that.

And then it dawned on me . . . a slow creeping-up kind of dawn. I'd never forgiven him for treating me the way he did when he was all coked up with the Soho dope dealers and porn traders, had I? He'd been in the middle of the trade, and I was just a nobody, and our being mates hadn't counted for a thing in his eyes back then. And all that shame and rage I felt over being dissed by Magsy, of being dissed by someone I thought was a mate, and, yes . . . all right . . . the guilt of my not visiting him in prison . . . it was that which had driven me to use the story of Magsy's rise and fall in Soho for the script of *Rough House*. I hoped he'd like what he'd see when his life story would be all up there on the big screen in glorious Technicolor. If we got the money it would be me who put him there. Magsy on the big screen. *Now* who was the hot shot? What was he doing – in Bridgwater of all places – while I was on the roof of Soho House drinking expensive gassy water? Well, I thought. Well, the truth is . . . really, the truth is . . . it really didn't matter what *he* was doing – or what *I* was doing – because we were both here in Steiner's breathing the same air and drinking the same tequila, and sucking the same fucking lemons, and nothing was ever going to put the clock back to the time before he went to prison, before his trial, before the cops, before the loan shark, before the coke, before Ted, and before that fucking game of backgammon in Cornwall Gardens. And the truth is . . . the truth is . . . I was sorry. I really was. And that was just the fucking end of it.

LOADED

BY KEN BRUEN

Brixton

Blame the Irish.
I always do.
The fuckers don't care, they're used to it, all that Catholic guilt they inherit, blame is, like, habitual. Too, all that rain they get? Makes them amenable to bad shit. I've known my share of micks – you grow up in Brixton, they're part of the landscape. Not necessarily a good part but they have their spot. Worked with a few when I was starting out, getting my act together. I didn't know as much as I thought I knew, so sure, I had them in my early crew.

Give them one thing, they're fearless, will go that extra reckless yard, laugh on the trip, and true, they've got your back, won't let you get ambushed. But it's after, at the pub, they get stuck in it, and hell, they get to talking, talking loose. Near got my collar felt cos of that. So I don't use them any more. One guy, named, of course, Paddy, said to me: "Not that long ago, the B'n'Bs . . . they had signs proclaiming, *No coloureds, no dogs, no Irish.*"

He was smiling when he told me and that's when you most got to worry, the fucks are smiling, you're in for the high jump. Paddy got eight years over a botched post office gig, he'd torn off his mask halfway through the deal, as it itched. I'd driven to the Scrubs, see if he needed anything, and he shook his head, said, "Don't visit any more."

I was a little miffed and he explained, "Nothing personal but you're a Brit."

Like that made any sense, he was in a *Brit nick*. Logic and the Irish never gel, but he must have clocked my confusion, added, "In here, I'm with my countrymen. They see a Brit visiting, I'm fucked."

Let him stew.

Life was shaping up nice for me. Took some time but I'd put it together real slow. Doing some merchandise, a little meth, some heroin, and, of course, the coke. Didn't handle any of the shit my own self, had it all through channels, lots of dumb bastards out there will take the weight. I arranged the supply, got it to the public, and stayed real anonymous, had me a share in a pub, karaoke four nights a week, the slots, and on Sunday, a tasty afternoon of lap dancing. The cops got their share and everyone was, if not happy, reasonably prosperous. None of us getting rich but it paid for a few extras. Bought into a car park and, no kidding, serious change in that.

Best of all, I'd a fine gaff on Electric Avenue, owned the lease, and from outside, looked like a squat, which keeps the burglars away. Inside, got me Heal's furniture, clean and open-plan living room, lots of wicker furniture. I like it, real laid-back vibe. No woman, I like my freedom. Sure, on a Friday night I pick up some fox, bring her back, but she's out of there by three in the morning. I don't need no permanent company. Move some babe in and that's the end of my hard-bought independence.

Under the floorboards is my stash: coke, fifteen large and a Glock. The baseball bat I keep by my bed.

Then I met Kelly.

I'd been to the Fridge to see a very bad hip hop outfit who

were supposed to be the next big thing. Jeez, they were atrocious, no one told them the whole gangsta scene was, like . . . dead. I went down to the pub after, needed to get the taste out of my mouth. I ordered a pint of bitter and heard, "To match your mood."

A woman in her late twenties, dressed in late Goth style, lots of black make-up, clothes, attitude. I've nothing against them, they're harmless, and if they think the Cure are still relevant, well, it takes all kinds . . . better than listening to Dido. Her face wasn't pretty, not even close, but it had an energy, a vitality that made it noticeable. I gave her my best London look with lots of Brixton overshadow, the look that says, *Fuck off . . . now.*

She felt an explanation was due, said, "Bitter, for the bitterness in your face."

I did the American bit, asked, "I know you?"

She laughed, said, "Not yet."

I grabbed my pint, moved away. She was surrounded by other Goths but she was the centre, the flame they danced around. I'd noticed her eyes had an odd green fleck, made you want to stare at them. I shook myself, muttered, "Cop on."

On my second pint, I chanced a glance at her and she was looking right at me, winked. I was enraged, the fuck was that about? Had a JD for the road – I'm not a big drinker, that shit becomes a habit and I've plans, being a booze hound isn't among them. Knocked it back and headed for the door, she caught up with me, asked, "Buy me a kebab?"

Now I could hear the Irish lilt, almost like she was singing the words. I stopped, asked, "What the hell is the matter with you?"

She was smiling, went, "I'm hungry and I don't want to eat alone."

I indicated the pub. "What about your fan club, won't they eat with you?"

She almost sneered. It curled her lip and I'd a compulsion to kiss her, a roaring in my head, *What is happening to me?*

"Adoration is so, like, tiresome, you fink?"

The little bit of London – *fink* – to what? To make me comfortable? "I wouldn't know, it's not a concept I'm familiar with."

She laughed out loud, and her laugh made you want to join in. She said, "Oh, don't we talk posh, what's a *concept,* then? Is it like a condom?"

I'm still not sure why, but I decided to buy her the bloody kebab – to get rid of her, to see what more outrageous banter she'd produce? She suggested we eat them in the park and I asked, "Are you out of your mind? It's a war zone."

She blew that off with: "I'll mind *you.*"

The way she said it, as if she meant it, as if . . . fuck, I dunno, as if she was looking for someone to mind. So I said my place was round the corner and she chirped, "Whoo . . . fast worker. My mammie warned me about men like you."

I'd just taken a bite of the kebab, it was about what you'd expect, tasteless with a hint of acid. I had to ask. "What kind of man is that, a stranger?"

She flung her kebab into the air. "No, English." Then she watched the kebab splatter on the road, sang, "Feed the birds."

Bringing her back to my place, the first mistake – and if it were the only one, well, even now, I don't know what was going on with me, like I was mesmerized.

She looked round at my flat, and yeah, I was pretty damn proud, it looked good.

"Who lives here, some control freak, an anal retentive?"

Man, I was pissed, tried: "You have some problem with tidiness, with a place being clean?"

Fuck, you get defensive, you've already lost.

She was delighted, moved to me, got her tongue way down my throat, and in jig time we were going at it like demented things. Passion is not something I've had huge experience with – sure, I mean, I get my share, but never like that.

Later, lying on the floor, me grabbing for air, she asked, "What do you want?"

She was smoking. I didn't think it was the time to mention my place was smoke-free, so I let it slide, not easily, bit down. I leaned on one elbow, said, "I think I just had what I want."

She flicked the butt in the direction of the sink; I had to deliberately avert my eyes, not thinking where it landed. She said, "Sex, sex is no big deal. I mean in life, the . . . what do they call it . . . the *bigger picture?*"

I wanted to be comfortable, not go to jail, keep things focused. I said, "Nice set of wheels, have my eye on – "

She cut me off, went: "Bollocks, fecking cars, what is it with guys and motors? Is it like some phallic symbol? *Got me a mean engine.*"

Her tone, dripping with bile. Before I could get my mouth going, she continued, "I want to be loaded, serious wedge, you know what I'm saying?"

I nearly let slip about my stash, held back and asked, "So, you get loaded, then what?"

She was pulling on her clothes, looked at me like I was dense. "Then it's *fuck you, world.*"

She was heading for the door, I asked, "You're leaving?"

That's what I always wanted, get them out as soon as possible. Now, though . . .

Her hand was on her hip and she raised an eyebrow. "What, you think you're up for another round? I think you shot your load, need a week to get you hot again, or am I wrong?"

That stung, I'd never had complaints before, should have told her to bang the door behind her, near whimpered, "Will I see you?"

Her smile, smirk in neon, said, "I'll call you."

And was gone.

She didn't . . . call.

I went back to the pub, no sign of her. Okay, I went back a few times, asked the barman. I knew him a long time, we had, as they say, history, not all of it bad. He was surprised, said, "The Irish babe, yeah?"

I nodded miserably, hated to reveal a need, especially to a frigging barman, cos they talk to you, you can be sure they talk to others, and I didn't want the word out that I was, like . . . bloody needy, or worse, vulnerable. That story goes out, you are dead, the predators coming out of the flaming woodwork. He stared at me. "Matt, you surprise me, hadn't figured you for a wally."

Bad, real fucking bad.

I should have slapped him on the side of the head, get the status established, but I wanted the information. I got some edge into my voice, snapped, "What's that mean?"

He was doing bar stuff, taking his own sweet time, stashing glasses, polishing the counter, and I suppressed my impatience. Finally he straightened, touched his nose, said, "Word to the wise, mate, stay clear, she hangs with that black guy, Neville, you don't want to mess with that dude."

Neville, story was he offed some dealer, did major trade in crystal, and was serious bad news. I moved to leave, said: "I knew that."

He didn't scoff but it was in the neighbourhood. "Yeah, right."

Fuck fuck fuck.

The bitch, playing with me, I resolved to put her out of my head, get on with my business. Plus, I had to get a new carpet, the cigarette had burned a hole right where you'd notice.

A week later, I was in the pub where we had the karaoke nights, nice little earner, punters get a few on, they want to sing, did brisk sales those nights. I was at the back, discussing some plans with the manager, when I heard a voice go, "I'd like to sing 'Howling at Midnight'."

It was her, Kelly, with the Lucinda Williams song, one of my favourites, she no doubt saw the CD in my gaff. I looked quickly round, no sign of Neville, the pub hushed as she launched. Her voice was startling, pure, innocent, and yet, had a hint of danger that made you pay attention. When she finished, the applause was deafening. The manager, his mouth open, whispered, "Christ, she's good."

Then she hopped off the stage, headed in my direction, small smile in place. I resolved to stay cool but to my horror whined, "You never called."

Even the manager gave me an odd look.

"What happened to *hello, how have you been?*" she asked.

I moved her away, touching her arm lightly, and just that small gesture had me panting. She said: "Yes, thank you, I would like a drink."

I ordered two large vodkas, no ice, and tonics. She took the glass. "I'd have liked a Bushmills, but shit, I just can't resist the alpha male."

The touch of mockery, her eyes shining, that fleck of green dancing in there. I was dizzy, decided to get it out in the open, asked, "What do you want?"

She licked the rim of the glass, said, "I want you inside me, now."

Never finished my drink, never got to mention the black

guy either. We were in my place, me tearing off my shirt, her standing, the smile on her lips, I heard: "White dude is hung."

She'd left the door ajar. Neville standing there, a car iron held loosely in his hand. I looked at her, she shrugged, moved to my left. Neville sauntered over, almost lazily took a swipe at my knee. I was on the floor.

"Cat goes down easy."

Kelly came over, licked his ear. "Let's get the stuff, get the fuck out of here."

He wanted to play, I could see it in his eyes. He drawled, "How about it, Leroy, you want to give us that famous stash you got, or you wanna go tough, make me beat the fucking crap outta you? Either is, like, cool with me. Yo, babe, this mother got any, like, beverages?"

I said I'd get the stash, and he laughed.

"Well, get to it, bro, shit ain't come les' you go get it."

I crawled along the carpet, pulled it back, plied the floorboard loose, Kelly was shouting, "Nev, you want Heineken or Becks?"

I shot him in the balls, let him bleed out. Kelly had two bottles in her hands, let them slide to the floor, I said, "You're fucking up my carpet again, what's with you?"

I shot her in the gut, they say it's the most agonizing, she certainly seemed to prove that. I bent down, whispered, "Loaded enough for you, or you want some more? I got plenty left."

Getting my shirt tucked into my pants, I made sure it was neat, hate when it's not straight, ruins the sit of the material. I looked round, complained: "Now I'm going to have to redo the whole room."

RIGOR MORTIS

BY STEWART HOME

Ladbroke Grove

I 've been in the Met all my adult life and I've spent most of that time pounding the mean streets of West London. After the war the area around Ladbroke Grove was known as the *Dustbowl*. This was where smart property developers came to make their mint. Back in the '50s and '60s, during those thirteen glorious years of Tory rule, anyone who wanted to could make a bomb from the slums. Houses changed hands over and over again, with their values being inflated on each sale. Before the introduction of ridiculously strict controls on building societies at the start of the '60s, it was common for property speculators to offload properties to both tenants and other parties with one hundred per cent mortgages which the seller had prearranged. Despite the prices paid under such arrangements being above market value, ownership still proved cheaper than renting. Unfortunately, it was all too common for the new owners to take in lodgers to cover the costs of their mortgage, rather than working to earn their crust like a free-born Saxon. The resultant overcrowding bred crime and this law-breaking stretched police resources to the limit.

The investigation I've just completed took me back nearly twenty years to the early '60s. I knew Jilly O'Sullivan was dead before I arrived at 104 Cambridge Gardens, and in many ways I considered it a miracle she'd succeeded in reaching the age of thirty-five. I'd first come across Jilly in 1962 when she was a naïve young teenager and I was a fresh-faced police constable. I'm still a PC because rather than striving to rise through the ranks, I long ago opted to take horizontal promotion by becoming a coroner's officer. This job brings with it substantial unofficial perks, and I'm not the only cop who's avoided vertical advancement since that makes you more visible and therefore less able to accept the backhanders you deserve.

Returning to O'Sullivan, when she arrived in Notting Hill she rented an upstairs flat on Bassett Road for five years before moving to nearby Elgin Crescent in 1966. The bed in which Jilly died was but a few minutes' walk from her Notting Hill homes of the '60s. I'd first called on her at Bassett Road after the force was informed that one of her brothers was hiding out there. My colleagues and I knew parts of the O'Sullivan clan like the backs of our own hands. The family was involved in both burglary and protection. Jilly and her brother had grown up in Greenock, but headed for the Big Smoke as teenagers. Jilly was doing well back in the early '60s, making good money in a high-class Soho clip joint, and at that time she even had a pimp with a plummy accent and public school education. Jilly's brother was eventually nicked alongside a couple of his cousins while they were doing over a jeweller's shop and that's how I learned he'd actually been hiding out with his gangster uncle in Victoria. After he'd served his time in a civil prison for burglary, Jilly's brother was sent to a military jail for being absent without leave from the army. By the mid-'60s, when her brother was finally let out of the nick, Jilly was the black sheep of the family. It wasn't prostitution but an involvement with beatniks, hippies and drugs that alienated O'Sullivan from her kith and kin.

If Jilly had been smart she'd have married one of her rich johns and faded into quiet respectability. She worked with a number of girls who had the good sense to do just that. Jilly was a good looker, or rather she'd been a good looker back in the day – anyone seeing her corpse would think she was in her late forties. That said, right up to her death O'Sullivan's eyes remained as blue as a five-pound note. When Jilly was a teenager, these baby blues had men falling all over her petite and innocent-seeming self. O'Sullivan's eyes looked like pools of water that were deep enough to fall into, and naturally enough, she made sure her carefully applied make-up accentuated this effect. O'Sullivan lost her looks through hard living, and since I knew the story of her life, I didn't need to take many details about her from the woman who'd found the body.

I didn't even bother to ask Marianne May how she'd got into Jilly's flat; I'd already heard from Garrett that he'd left the door to the basement bedsit open after finding O'Sullivan dead in bed and making a hasty exit. Being a dealer and a pimp, Garrett considered it wiser to disappear than inform the authorities of his girlfriend's death. Even if he wasn't fitted up for his Jilly's murder, Garrett figured he'd get busted for something else if he stuck around. After I'd gotten the call to go to the back basement flat at 104 Cambridge Gardens to investigate a death, I'd headed first for Observatory Gardens, where I found Garrett nodding out with Scotch Alex. Garrett lived with Jilly, and since only one death had been reported, I'd figured that either one or both of them would be in "hiding" at Observatory Gardens. Before I got to Scotch Alex's pad I hadn't known who'd died, and I'd entertained the possibility it might have been one of their heroin buddies.

Garrett told me what he knew, which wasn't that much. He'd gone home after cutting some drug deals and found Jilly dead in bed, so he'd left again immediately. Garrett was inclined to think O'Sullivan had accidentally overdosed, although he considered it possible she'd been murdered by some gangsters, who'd threatened to kill her after she ripped them off during the course of a drug deal. I told Garrett not to worry about a court appearance, since I wasn't about to drag him into my investigation if he was cooperative. He got the idea and handed me a wad of notes, which he pulled from his right trouser pocket. I patted down the left pocket of Garrett's jeans and he realized his game was at least partially up. He removed another wad of notes from the second pocket and gave them to me. After I'd prodded his abdomen he stood up and took more bills from a money belt that was tied around his waist. I then made Garrett take his shoes and socks off, but he didn't have any cash secreted down there.

Satisfied with my takings, I told O'Sullivan's pimp that in my report I'd state that Jilly was living alone at the time of her death. I didn't tell him that I'd have done this even if I hadn't succeeded in shaking him down, since recording that O'Sullivan lived with a heroin dealer would make matters unnecessarily complicated for me. Although Garrett was scum he wasn't stupid, so I didn't need to tell him it would be a good idea if he found a new place to live. Likewise, I had absolute faith in his ability to find some fool to rip off in order to provide PC Lever with his cut from the drug money I'd purloined and cover various other debts he simply couldn't avoid meeting if he wished to remain alive and in reasonable health. While I was in Observatory Gardens I also took the opportunity to touch Garrett's junkie host and co-dealer, Scotch Alex, for a few quid.

Marianne May, the woman who'd called the authorities to report Jilly's death, was middle-class and respectable. What Marianne had in common with Jilly were some bizarre New Age religious interests. Aside from this she was the ideal person to have found the body since she created the impression that O'Sullivan's friends at the time of her death were middle-class professionals. In all likelihood, prior to Marianne's arrival, a stream of junkies had called at the flat hoping to score, and having found the door open and Jilly dead in bed, departed without telling the authorities there was a corpse stinking up the bedsit. Garrett wouldn't have left his drug stash in the pad, and there probably wasn't anything else worth stealing. If there had been it would have disappeared long before my arrival.

There wasn't much I needed to ask May, but for the sake of appearance I had to make it look like I was doing my job properly. I told her to wait upstairs with Jilly's neighbours while I made some further investigations. I was able to go through the flat and remove used needles and various other signs of drug use before the medics arrived. I then examined Jilly's body. As you'd expect it was cold to touch. O'Sullivan was lying on her side, naked on the bed.

After the corpse had been loaded into an ambulance I went upstairs and told May she could go home, saying I'd contact her if there was anything further I needed to ask. I had no intention of troubling Marianne again, but since she was a middle-class professional, I had to make it look like I was doing everything by the book. May had fine manners and excellent verbal skills, so there was an outside chance that if she was moved to make a complaint about my investigation, what she had to say would be taken seriously.

Because Jilly certainly had traces of heroin in her body, it was important I arranged things so that any need for toxico-logical analysis was avoided. That said, since I knew O'Sullivan was an intravenous drug user, there was nothing to worry about in terms of a purely visual inspection of the body. Indeed, even in instances of suicide brought about by the ingestion of pills, evidence of a drug overdose is only visu-ally detectable in fifty per cent of such cases. Likewise, there is necessarily a good deal of mutual understanding between all those involved in the investigation of a death, one which is sometimes greased by the circulation of used fivers. I have many good reasons to request a particular result from a pathologist, and the croaks I work alongside know this with-out my having to spell it out. Aside from anything else, I don't have time to properly investigate the circumstances surrounding every death that occurs on my beat. It would waste a considerable amount of taxpayers' money and my time if the circumstances in which every miserable junkie overdosed were fully investigated. Every pathologist under-stands, regardless of whether or not a fistful of fivers are being pressed into their greasy palms, that the police know what's for the best.

Given that I wished to avoid an inquest into Jilly O'Sullivan's death, it wasn't much to ask of medical science that it should back up my false contention that she'd died from natural causes. Something will invariably be found in the lungs after death, so bronchopneumonia would provide a suitable explanation of Jilly's passing, as it had in so many other instances where I found it imperative to avoid a full-scale investigation. Death, of course, is always the result of the failure of one of the major organs, and according to the legal rule book, what matters is the chain of events leading up to such a failure. In practice, the letter of the law can be safely ignored in favour of its spirit. Only the elderly and homeless die from bronchopneumonia in truly unsuspicious circumstances. Bronchopneumonia is often brought on by a drug overdose, but my colleagues and I will nonetheless routinely treat it as a natural cause of death in a young addict. We see no point in arriving at an accurate conclusion that will only upset and confuse the family of some wastrel who didn't deserve the loving home she grew up in. Grieving is a difficult process and I've done countless decent parents a huge favour by making it possible for them to avoid facing up to the fact that their child was a good-for-nothing junkie degenerate.

To shift the focus once again to the particular, there wasn't much in O'Sullivan's basement flat. Jilly and her pimp Garrett had only lived there for a few weeks. They'd occupied an equally spartan Bayswater bedsit over the autumn. Junkies mainly use possessions as a form of collateral, they rarely hang onto stuff, personal items tend to be stolen and sold as required. However, Jilly's diary was in the flat and the final entry was dedicated to Garrett:

COMPUTER IN PURSUIT OF A DREAM

You lie there, legs straddled, an easy lay
Like some "gloomy fucker" (your words)
For hours you have put me through mental torture
Because I desired you
Sure I wanted love anyway I could
But you denied me both fuck & fix
And then dropping a Tuinal, like an over-the-hill whore
You became an easy lay

I knew this piece of nonsense was merely one of many pieces of proof that Jilly's drug use had been ongoing. That meant fuck all to me because my considered professional opinion was that O'Sullivan's death was entirely unsuspicious and solely due to natural causes. Any police officer worth his or her salt knows that to lie effectively one must stick reasonably closely to the truth. Therefore, in my official report I wouldn't gloss over the fact that Jilly had been a long-term drug addict. Aside from anything else, the pathologist couldn't ignore the track marks on her arms. All I needed to do was claim that her addiction was well in the past.

After acquiring some cash from Jilly's landlord in return for overlooking the fact that drug dealing was taking place in his gaff, I phoned my chum Paul Lever to acquire suitable evidence to back up the fictional content of the report I was in the process of compiling. PC Lever had a thick file on Jilly and this included several of the fraudulent job applications he'd directed her to make. Back in the mid-'70s Paul had wanted to know exactly what was going on in various local drug charities, so he'd sent Jilly into them as a spy. He provided me with a copy of a successful application she'd made for a job as a social worker at the Westbourne Project. In this Jilly claimed to have a degree and postgraduate qualifications in philosophy from UCL, despite the fact that she'd left school at sixteen and had never attended a university. Something else that made the document Lever handed me fraudulent was Jilly's claim that although she'd been a smack addict, she'd cleaned up in 1972. While I knew this was untrue, it placed her long-term drug addiction seven years in the past, which was good enough for my purposes.

Since the general public is blissfully ignorant of the problems police officers face, people are often surprised to learn of my working methods, should I choose to speak openly about them. What needs to be stressed in relation to this is that since it is impossible for the police to completely suppress the West London drug scene, the next best thing for us to do is control it. Only dealers we approve of are allowed to carry on their business, and cuts from their profits serve to top up our inadequate pay. Likewise, Paul Lever and various other police officers, including me, had been getting our jollies with Jilly during the early '70s.

Lever had the evidence, both real and fabricated, to get O'Sullivan banged up for a very long time. To avoid jail, Jilly had made a deal with him. O'Sullivan had to sell drugs on Paul's behalf and provide him with information about anyone who set themselves up as a dealer without his approval. She also agreed to see us once a week at the police station where we had a regular line-up with her. Jilly wasn't the only junkie Paul had providing us with sexual favours, all of which might give the impression he's a hard man. Certainly this is the appearance he cultivates, but actually he's somewhat sensitive about his macho self-image. Back in 1972, Jilly had the singular misfortune to be around just after a colleague made a crack about Lever always taking last place in our gang-bangs.

Paul, like any virile male, enjoys slapping whores around while he's screwing them, and on this particular occasion he was determined to prove through sheer ultra-violence that he didn't harbour any unnatural sexual desires. As I gave Jilly a poke, Lever grabbed her right arm and broke it over his knee. O'Sullivan was in agony, but Paul took great pleasure in amusing himself by making the bitch indulge him with an extended sex session before allowing her to go to the hospital. On the surface this might sound somewhat sick, but Paul is basically a good bloke, and he genuinely believes that being a bit psycho is the most rational way to deal with whores and crims. After all, the only thing these reprobates respect and understand is brute force. Indeed, what other way is there to deal with someone like O'Sullivan? In the early '60s she had offers of marriage from more than one of her upper-class johns, but she turned them down and became a junkie instead.

It was Jilly's decision to live the low life and what she got from us was no more than she had coming for choosing to subsist, as her extended Irish family have done since before the days of Cromwell, beyond the pale. Jilly wasn't just a junkie and a prostitute, she was also a pickpocket, a thief, and she engaged in chequebook and other frauds. Any reasonable person will agree that without laws and police officers prepared to carry out a dirty job vigilantly, society would collapse into pure jungle savagery. That said, there are still too many do-gooders who love besmirching the name of the Metropolitan Police, and an inquest into Jilly's life and death would in all likelihood bring to light the type of facts that fuel the enmity these bleeding hearts feel towards us.

Police officers like me deserve whatever perks we can pick up, providing this doesn't impinge upon the rights of law-abiding citizens. Bending the rules goes with the territory of upholding the law; if I stuck to official procedures my hands would be tied with red tape. Punks and whores really don't count as far as I'm concerned, nor do the pinkos who bleat on about police oppression. In a sane society criminals wouldn't have rights, and the police wouldn't have to break the law to protect decent folk.

MAIDA HELL

BY BARRY ADAMSON

Maida Hill

Above the sound of sirens, my view is as always: stark, sullen and eldritch. I'm prone to believe that it's a vile and disgusting world below.

Where I stand, the Harrow Road police station is to my right, and Our Lady of Lourdes and St. Vincent de Paul Catholic Church is to my left.

Crime and redemption carved into each set of knuckles.

I catch myself on the turnaround – reflected in stained glass. I am at once as black as night and yet somehow as white as a sheet.

Moiety me!

I hang my head and lean on a knee that sways gently. The smell of tumble dryers and fried food piques my hunger for something more than the reminders of a not so comfortable existence.

Beneath me: the Harrow Road. This is the main artery that divides (at this juncture) Notting Hill and Maida Vale into an area uncommonly known as Maida Hill.

More commonly known as Maida Hell.

If it were a pen it would be broken. The scribe's grasp sullied by an unthinkable, irremovable liquid; marking him forever as the guilty one.

If it were a book it would be stolen. Pushed into a dark alley; fingers around its throat; gasping and bleating for its very existence to be ratified before being hauled over the coals and the very life beaten out of it.

Sucked in.

Chewed up.

Spat out.

Stepped on.

MAIDA HELL.

I spy with my little eye; the red, white and blue blood vessels that jam their way through this darkened grey conduit we'll refer to as the "Harrowing Road". The number 18 bus domineeringly crawls the entire length of it like a fat, hideous tapeworm; its red and shining sixty-foot body bulging with sweating parasites. This *Dipylidium caninum* heads as far west as one can imagine, taking in "Murder Mile" Harlesden, where you could very well be "starin' down de barrel of a 'matic", as though you were merely being greeted by an old friend. Then forever you'll sit on your backside next to some undesirable with few manners, as the nauseating carrier snakes its way through Wem-ber-ley and finally sets in Sudbury. Which is as far west as one can imagine.

Or: it heads north-east, over Ballard's Concrete Island; ceremoniously known as the Paddington Basin (which, in my opinion, is as good a place as any to let go of the contents of a now infested stomach!). Scolex-features then slithers up the Marylebone Road, and finally breaks itself down by Euston railway station to complete its life cycle and let everybody get the hell out to the rest of the country. Which is precisely what I intend to do when all this is over.

Not a hundred yards from where I stoop, the Great Western Road jumps over the lazy Harrow Road and becomes Elgin Avenue. This is also the sector where

Fernhead Road comes to an end, along with Walterton Road, creating a psychic wasteland of sorts. This circumambience consists to my mind of five corners. (Traditionally four. Nineteenth-century Ordnance Survey maps will forever testify that Walterton and Fernhead came much later. However, bananas to all that.) These *five* corners shall become evinced and bring into our very consciousness the indurate domain of:

THE SPACE BETWEEN.

I'll take you there.

On one corner: the bank.

Always full and with few tellers, most of who are off shopping in Somerfield and grabbing all the reduced-price stock before it goes out of date later that day. Outside the bank, they'll flirt with the locals they looked down upon not a moment earlier. (Don't kiss her, she's a teller!) Then stroll lazily back to the jam-packed treasury, where one guy is now screaming the place down.

"YOU KNOW ME! *NIG NOG.* WHERE DID HE GO?"

The toothless, yellow-eyed man with the pee stains on his coat then begins to cry, and shamefully leaves.

"Tosser. Jennifer, will you buzz me in?"

The teller then shirks in to stuff her face with tuck and gossip, before slipping into a dream of tonight's date with the new business manager, Clive. Twenty-two. Looks a bit like Ronaldo without the skills.

He'll part my lips with first and third and slip in the second. He'll stare into me. Through me . . .

Cream oozes from the doughnut she scoffs and lands on her skirt, and she wipes it off with her hand. The rest of us? Well, we just lose another day silently practising the art of queuing; bemoaning a self-confidence we just don't seem to have been born with.

On the other corner: the mobile phone shop.

"Mobile phone, please?"

A skinny girl in a tight sweater hands out flyers, which nobody takes, except this one bizarre-looking guy who lurks ominously, scratches his crotch, and then approaches her with a greasy smile.

"Oh, this is the new Ericsson, right?"

"Yes. Please. To take. My boss . . ."

"It's the flat-top, isn't it?"

"Please, just take."

"Yeah. It's got those buttons that really stick out. You could play with them all night. What are you, love? Polish? Latvian?"

"Please, I don't . . ."

He gives her the killer's stare.

"Mark my words, love. You fucking do. And you fucking will. All right?"

He holds her gaze before leaning away and into the distance. Feeling exposed by the coruscating sunlight, she pulls her coat together, mumbles an idea of faith while thinking about her mother and the friends she left behind, and moves onto the next.

"Mobile phone, please?"

On the other corner: the public toilets.

Usual set-up. Standard, heading underground. Disabled, at floor level. Toilet of choice for drug addicts.

"The animals went in two by two, hurrah, hurrah."

"Fuck off. Give me the gear."

"You make me feel like dancin', gonna dance the night away."

Lucy takes the first boot. The backs of her knees fold and immediately she's scratching like a monkey.

"Gimme that."

Sandra, not singing for the first time since these two scored, squirts Lucy's blood into the sink and then rinses the syringe in the toilet bowl before drawing up the heroin, tying up, shooting up, tying off, and time ending and trouble saying goodbye. She looks to Lucy who now slides down the wall like a lifeless doll, smashing her head on the toilet bowl in the process.

"Get up, you stupid bitch."

Nothing.

Sandra gets the hell out of there. She makes a fuss to an oncoming guy who's wheelchair bound.

"They're broke, love. You should try downstairs."

The guy looks at her. "Un-fucking-believable." Finally she notices the wheelchair; scratches her face in slow . . . motion.

"Sorry, love. You must have done all right though, eh? Couldn't lend me a fiver, could you?"

On the other corner: Costcutter. *The* most expensive twenty-four-hour supermarket in the world.

What the fuck are they on about? Nine pounds sixty for a couple of newspapers, some fags and a drink?

"Nine pounds sixty."

Someone bursts through the door.

"Give me a single, you get me?"

The shopkeeper (*There're six of them. Remember the time some posh kid walked in followed by fucking Crackula himself, wielding a crook-lock and swinging at the poor cunt, whose only crime was to point out that the Count could take a piss in the bogs instead of in the road?)* responds with, "No more singles. Out. Get out."

A couple of stray Australians, believing themselves to be in the warmer reaches of Notting Hill, wander in. Seeing a chance to exercise an act of old-country benevolence, the Aussie guy pulls out a smoke and gives it to this arsehole. Now this idiot's all over him.

"Nice one, bruv. SEEEN. Let me carry you shit for you."

"I'm good, thanks."

"I WASN'T TALKING TO YOU. I WAS TALKING TO THE LADY."

"It's cool, buddy, just er . . ."

"Just what?"

He stares hard into the Aussie guy's eyes and presses his head against him, the poor sod now reeling; purblind; red in the face and his girlfriend is starting to really get the shits.

"Tell him to go fuck himself, Dobbo."

Dobbo decides to wade in, kakking himself.

The shopkeepers surround the scene and the guy walks, lighting the smoke; grinning and staring between the Aussie girl's legs as she puts some breakfast stuff, eggs and the like, on the counter.

"Nice nice nice nice nice."

"Rack off, numb-nuts."

"Lay down, gal, let me push it up, push it up."

"Look, mate, just fuckin' . . ."

"Leave it."

"Twenty-four pounds thirty-eight."

"What?"

* * *

On the final corner: the pub.

Well. I wouldn't know about that any more, would I? Be the last place I could afford to be seen in. I mean, what if they decide to reopen the case? Then what?

When Mary tells me that it's "the best craic in town", I undoubtedly always agree with her that it just might be, and change the topic as fast as I can, save that she might see me faltering.

The ways of W9 lives are reflected in the otherwise preposterous comparisons with the South Bronx.

The five corners.

The five boroughs?

Preposterous.

Henceforth, the tradition of tolerance for the rights of ordinary fucked-up people, a communal tradition that was fought for in the '70s right on this spot by the one and only Joe Strummer and company, intertwines and combines to make up the disfigured landscape.

Truth is, there's no shrugging off the fact that these folk are forever condemned to scrape around like lunatics, sucking for dear life on yesterday's rotten air, cast over hill and vale.

Hanging over W9, Mr. Goldfinger's Trellick Tower watches as the nuclear sun sets down. This architectural abomination stands creaking, turning a blind eye to Japanese photographers, while at its roots, skulls are caved in and crack rocks are sold to whoever the hell wants, by dealers who freewheel the nearby Grand Union Canal on stolen bicycles.

Meanwhile Gardens is also apparent as it skirts both canal and tower and is the divider and last breathing space before visitors to this hellhole say goodbye to common logic. Forever.

On the canal itself, most are as oblivious to the Canada goose; grey heron; mallard; kestrel; coot; moorhen; black-headed gull; wren; robin; song thrush; whitethroat; chiff chaff; willow warbler; starling; greenfinch; goldfinch; wood-pigeon; grey wagtail; dunnock; and blackbird, as the birds are to them.

Best keep it that way.

Meanwhile.

Gardens.

The underdeveloped.

The youth.

The hood rats and the squeaks.

Hood rats (mainly black), who like any young voluble yet asinine revolutionary guise themselves and any sign of vulnerability in a uniform of oversize sports clothes; hoods pulled down low over cap even lower, with one hand always down the trouser front. *Listen listen listen listen. I do what the fuck I want. Don't arsk. A gun is a gun and I DO have one. Next to my blade. Live at my mum's, innit. My sister's got three kids and she's younger than me, innit. My dad? Don't know, mate. Don't fuckin' know. Three guys, right. Chase me in my car and I get mashed, innit. Don't want no fuckin' hospital though, innit.*

Squeaks (mainly white), who like any terrified young revolutionary guise any sign of vulnerability by wearing a uniform of tight-fitting sportswear which also doubles as a mask for the lack of a soul. Obsessive about their appearance to the point of perfection, their goal is to have you believe that the projection of superiority is indeed true. *Nice trainers. Gleaming. I do the right thing by me mum. If you (dirty filthy fucking animal) do anything to hurt any one of my family or their kids, I'll fuckin' kill you. I'll clump you with a fuckin' hammer. I'll cut your fuckin' heart out (after I've cleaned the house for me mum and taken me gran up to the hospital). All right? Have you been fuckin' smokin'?*

A community of chagrins and fighters set against a world of cheap booze and even cheaper promises.

Fighters against a war they started.

Fighters for peace.

Second-hand peace.

A community of losers and bruisers.

A community nonetheless.

Life made difficult is practical by default, with little room for the spiritual.

Even less room for the likes of me.

My mobile rings.

"Hello?"

"Johnny."

"Yes. This is . . ."

"I fuckin' know all about you, you cunt. You won't get away with it this time."

Then the line goes dead.

I look at the last caller to find the number withheld and flick a somewhat tentative snarl into the eye of my fear.

Loud pangs begin in my temples. My throat tightens, and remembering to breathe, I look around to see where I might fall if I were to pass out. The world begins to swim around me and the deafening sound of an ambulance threatens to pop my right ear. As though a six-foot tuning fork has been struck at the core of my very being, I vibrate from the inside out. Then I stumble to a chair and clench my eyes as a million pinpricks pepper my forehead, squeezing out tiny beads of alternating hot and cold sweat. I don't know if I will ever see again as I open my eyes and hear a high-pitched wail that accompanies the darkness. A backward scream travels into my chest, and as though a light has just exploded, I begin to make out solarized shapes in front of me. I can also hear my heartbeat and I know I'm back. After a few deep breaths, I manage to look out of the window from behind drawn curtains. Fade up to a rat and a squeak and a Mazda. Music so, so loud.

> *Back from the dead*
> *Back from the dead*
> *To put a fucking hole in your motherfucking head.*

Their own heads bop up and down together, as though choreographed like two ornamental dogs that people used to place in the back window of their cars in days gone by.

Arseholes.

Easy now.

Remember the foundations of morality and grace.

Hovering on Johnny's lowest periphery, Colleen O'Neill staggers along Harrow Road towards Our Lady and curses those *red-nose buggers* in Alcoholics Anonymous.

Her bright red hair ambuscades the crowd; the stench of sperm keeps them at bay. She is literally dying for another drink. She now sweeps aside her blazing locks to reveal a face that resembles a weather-torn cliffside, as she sniffs an air not quite good enough for her and surveys the space with a condemnation reserved for the damned. Her goal is to head out of the space for Westbourne Park Road, where she just might get lucky with a punter, preferably three.

Since the age of eleven, Colleen has been fucked into one bad situation after another. At the age of twelve, when she realized she could get paid for getting laid, there was no looking back. There were also no trips to the seaside. No hopscotch. No crushes on boys. No *Bunty* or *Judy* magazines with cut-out dresses and little tabs attached to place on figures that you could also cut out and keep. No bedroom where she and her friends could practise kissing on their arms. No "what's for tea today, mam?" Just no one. When the boxer said he'd take care of her, he kept his promise: beating her to a pulp, using her as an ashtray, and raping her daily. The drink became her only means of protection from a world that offered ineffectual amounts of faith, and little by little the price of that protection got higher and higher and higher.

I walk around my own little "space between" and straighten everything, catching parallel lines and matching them up to other lines, like the edge of the carpet with the sideboard, the table with the edge of the carpet and the sideboard. Crouch down. Oops! That's got to be out by two millimetres. I dust and vac just to make sure and straighten the cushions. Then I wash all the dishes. Well, they need it and you never know, do you? I dry them and put them away and wipe down the sink. Polish it? Go on, then. Wow. What a smell. The guy who makes Cif or Jif or whatever they're calling it now is a genius. *Removes even the most stubborn of dirt.* That's the truest statement I've heard today. I breathe in synthetic alpine drives and here I am.

Back from the dead.

Kelly Mews.

Kelly's eye. Number one.

Ready?

As I'll ever be.

I wash my hands and face several times so I can only smell the soap and brush my teeth again. Then I decide on a shower, where I'm tempted into an act of turpitude, but no. Come on. We all know that the devil makes work for idle hands. Cleanliness is next to Godliness. Next to! Alongside!! The very next thing in line!!! I towel down and look at my lean body. Not an ounce of fat. I iron five shirts and lay out several tracksuit tops and stand before them.

Days off always did throw me into a spin.

How to blend in? Achieve total stasis?

No. Freedom. Freedom of choice. That's the key.

I pick my clothes for the evening and after several changes of mind (real freedom) I agree on smart but casual and decide I will roam into the open before catching up on some paperwork at the office.

Into the open.

Into the space.

I double-lock the door and then unlock both locks and re-enter to straighten out a couple of the cushions that seem to be slightly sagging at their corners. I then stand still. Quite still. I can't see or hear any dust and breathe yet another sigh of relief. I double-lock the door and bounce down the stairs but the smell and the din of human life begin to take a hold of me, sending my guts into a whirl.

Here comes Manny. I know him but I don't know him so neither of us trades any goodwill.

Best keep it that way.

In fact, I quickly decipher that he thinks I am not me! That, for all intents and purposes, I am somebody else. He gives me a *You're not who you say you are, are you?* kind of a look, and since, truth be told, I *am* in all earnest pretending to be somebody other that who I really am, I have no argument with the man. At all.

I turn onto Harrow Road, past the "bus stop of doom". Twenty people on mobile phones, waiting for a number 18, piled on the pavement and not moving as I approach. The signal of an oncoming bus sends everyone into a frenzy and I just get past before possibly ending up a victim of a human stampede.

I cross the corner of Woodfield Place and Harrow Road and a 4x4 speeds up to get around the one-way system; it could have all ended right there. Luckily I glanced down to where his indicators are and, seeing no light flickering and knowing that the art of indication has been lost forever, guessed he was going to turn right. I jumped back as the deafening sound of throbbing bass covered the sound of my own aorta. He missed me by an inch. I imagine his face behind the blacked-out glass panel and give him the stare. He stops the car dead in the middle of the road with a screech.

Suddenly I'm the people's choice, Mr. Fiduciary!

I continue to stare at the blacked-out window, letting him know that if someone has to die, let it be me. The door is about to open and I raise the stakes as I spread my arms in a gesture of fearlessness.

Time stops.

The light goes on.

He pulls away with another screech and I cross the road next to an old West Indian gent, in a *très chic* outfit from Terry's Menswear. He sees an old flame on the other side of the street; her stockings falling down by her ankles; her stained pinafore billowing in what he perceives to be a *lucky gust*.

He calls out, "Old stick a fire don't tek long to ketch back up!"

She laughs out loud. "Tiger no fraid fe bull darg!"

He takes his time crossing.

Nobody minds. Except for a Prammie (*Eighteen and born pregnant, with a hand extended to the council. Hair scraped back, causing a do-it-yourself, council-house face-lift meant to reverse the ageing process. Cigarette extending from an expensive manicure. Two kids and another on the way. Shell-shocked and suicidal seventeen-year-old boyfriend carrying a maxi pack o' nappies*), who pushes out in front of the old guy and kisses her teeth in disdain.

I hit the five corners.

Situated here, circus performer and audience participation reach their mutual understanding.

Crossing at the lights, I see seven drunken Bajans cussing and laughing outside the bookie's. They pass the bottle from plastic cup to plastic cup. Close your eyes and you might think you were listening to a bunch of Dorset farmers discussing the price of beef and Mrs. Mottle's lumbago.

I see a drunken redheaded woman and walk into the beginnings of a bad dream.

Sancta Maria, Mater Deu, ora pro nobis peccatoribus, nunc, et in hora mortis nostrae. Amen.

A performer runs out into Harrow Road, just in front of where I'm positioned. He cajoles his potential crowd.

"You tink me nah got money?" Everybody turns and laughs.

Within a moment.

A lean *yoot*, one jeans leg rolled up to the knee but not the other, chews on a matchstick and stares into the eyes of potential protagonists.

A woman in her sixties – jeans emblazoned with the

words *Foxy Lady* across the buttocks, swinging her hips vera-
ciously – blows a bubble from too much gum and bursts it
loudly, laughing and adjusting her bra.

A man in tracksuit bottoms, too short, no socks, beaten-in
shoes, and unshaven forever, stands rooted to the spot and dribbling.

A guy selling scratch cards and methadone is able to pick
someone's pocket as she turns to see what the fuss is about.

Someone asks for change.

Someone asks for a cigarette.

Two crackheads: "See my fucking solicitor?"

"See my fucking selector?"

Somebody screams.

The performer stops the traffic dead.

A couple of hood rats, left hands disappearing down
tracksuit bottoms as though hiding some obscene disfigure-
ment, steel themselves.

"If yuh no ketch me a moonshine, yuh nah ketch me a
dark night."

Someone's mobile pipes up with an unrecognizable series
of beeps meant to be the popular tune of the day.

The guys outside the bookie's carry on arguing about irri-
gation, feigning oblivion to *dis stupidness*.

A Fiat Punto's tyres screech as the driver just misses the
performer, who is now hitting himself on the head and throwing tens and fives into the air. He then sets about grabbing an
aluminium chair from outside Jenny's bad food restaurant
and throws it at the window.

Loud smash.

Applause.

I enter the chemist's opposite the commotion and feel a
slight nausea as I automatically smile at the dirty-blonde

transvestite who works at the sales counter. She knows I know she knows, and I enjoy watching her hoodwinking the locals, our secret tryst sending me into a childish bout of rubescence.

The chemist's is like Doctor Who's Tardis, as from where I came in; I now stand in a huge space filled with the cheapest goods possible. A queue forms in front of the pharmacist, who's stationed in the top left corner. Mr. Pill for every ill. He's got the purple rinses and the overweight hooked into his whole world and is dazzling in his diagnoses.

I stare at Mishca's hands, and catching me (as she's telling some old bat with a mole that's sprouting more hair than is on my head), she seemingly mocks us both: "Yes. It will work on you every time."

She quickly rubs the crotch of her jeans to guide my eye towards her. I over-stare and feign arousal before looking at the various '70s shaving foams and after-shaves that I remember seeing in Mike's bathroom at the home.

My knees begin to knock and I want to fight somebody.

I approach the counter, not sure what I'm to say.

"Pack of Wrigley's, please."

"What flavour?"

Everything grinds to a halt. Freezes, and the natural sound fades out.

What flavour? How about fucking . . . COQ AU VIN, eh, Johnny? Be there at six; bring the van round the back or I'll fucking kill your sister, all right?

"Er. Spearmint . . . ? No, freshmint."

The chemist's now seems small. Dirty. That pharmacy guy should be shot.

So much for providence.

Mishca licks her lips. "Any time, sugar."

She then turns and reaches up to the shelf for the gum and I'm taking myself out of this place fast.

I move quickly so that she imagines me to have been merely an apparition.

I'll deal with her later.

I walk back towards Kelly Mews.

Looking skyward and seeing red, I remember it all.

Red sky at night, Shepherd's cottage on fire.

Cops are clearing the place out, as that idiot who threw the chair is being pushed, shirtless, into the back of a van. One slimy copper is talking to a girl of about fifteen and asking her where she lives, with a grin.

I'll deal with him later.

The redhead is talking to some old woman and nodding her head as though she is a kid being told where bad girls go, and catching a ray of hope reflected in my eye, looks to me like the ghost I might have just become. She makes towards me but the woman holds her arm, pulling her back.

"Just listen to me, Colleen, and you might learn something."

I dip my head and keep moving. Someone bumps into me, he's about seventeen and I can just make out his eyes beneath that hood. I think twice as I know he is armed. He recognizes me. His face widens as I get in first.

"How's your mum?"

"Yeah. She's good."

I'll have to deal with him later.

I cross the road by the bank, or at least try to. The lights are on red but the cars just keep coming, afraid that if they were to stop, someone would drag the driver out and beat him to death. I walk out anyway, knowing I've got the law on my side. Hit me and I'll sue you for everything you're worth, after I've dragged you from your vehicle and beaten the life out of you, of course!

Haven't been in a gym for a while, but you never lose it. Right cross. Uppercut. Jab. Pow. Pip. Pow. Super-middleweight title-holder from '74 to '77. Mike said he'd never seen a lad like me. Said I had the "killer's gaze".

I get to the other side. Away from the din. I cross again and dip between east and west, keeping an eye on Woodfield Place in case the 4x4 has found his stomach and decided to come back and face me.

No one.

I'm on the home stretch thinking about later, now I've made my decision.

A drunk is relieving himself against the bins outside the futuristic Science Photo Library next door to mine. A *trustafarian*, some spill from the Hill seeking a cheap thrill, opens the door from one of the flats upstairs, and seeing what the drunk's up to, pretends, *It's all good in da hood, bro.*

"Don't mind me."

The guy spits, "I fucking won't, cunt."

After dumping his rubbish, *I'll fucking dump him in a minute*, he shuffles off back to where he came from, counting out his father's money, no doubt, in his ironic "chav" Burberry pyjamas and fluffy slippers.

He glances, the guy still peeing, and he gives me a limp smile before hopping back indoors.

Life on the edge of a very plush cushion.

Indeed.

Something in the air catches me and sends me spiralling back through time.

Bernadette: Diorella.

Eileen: Diorissimo.

Margaret: Chanel No. 5.

In the distance, a crackhead screams for all she's worth, maybe for all *we're* worth.

"THE WHORE OF BABYLON! THE WHORE OF BABYLON!"

Blood songs coagulate in the black currents of a cold cold night.

The need to believe.

Credo in unum Deum, Patrem omnipotentem.

Ready?

Ready as I'll ever be.

I approach the mews and should I go in and change or just get on with it? I decide to perform the latter and go to the office. I skip around the back of the building and turn the key, walk in and head for my desk. Mary approaches me with a smile.

"Father Donaghue?"

"Yes, Mary?" I toss my keys onto my desk. "What is it?"

"Well, Father, I know you're very busy, but I was wondering if you might be able to add a few prayers tomorrow for my sister. A remembrance, if you would."

"How long has it been now?"

"It's been five years, Father. Five years since he took her away from us." She begins to cry.

I put an arm round her and remind her that the Lord is with us. And to call me by my first name, which is Johnny.

She begins to feel a little uncomfortable, questioning my grasp ever so slightly with her eyes, and so I let her go and then offer her a drop, which she accepts.

"Father. I didn't know."

I stare at my glass.

"Neither did I, Mary. Neither did I."

Mary takes a sip as I put my glass down onto the desk and pick up my crucifix.

We both laugh now and chat about the bargains to be found at Iceland and Somerfield and how the new pound shop is really quite amazing. Mary lowers her now empty glass back onto the tray by the whiskey decanter.

"Thank you, Father, I feel so much better now. Yourself? Settling in? Getting used to our little neighbourhood? I know it seems a bit on the rough side, but . . ."

"Oh, I've seen worse, Mary, believe me. Now. I've plenty to do, as you can understand?"

"Oh, forgive me, Father, for taking up your time."

"Not at all, Mary. And I'll be sure to mention . . ."

"Molly."

"Molly. Yes. I won't forget."

"Goodbye, Father."

I sit and wait. For an hour. I fill my glass as tears begin to well up in my eyes and roll down my face.

Poor me. Poor me. Pour me a drink.

Believing in Him. Not believing in Him.

Deus Meus, ex toto corde poenitet me omnium meorum peccatorum, eaque detestor, quia peccando, non solum poenas a Te iuste statutas promeritus sum, sed praesertim quia offendi Te summum bonum ac dignum qui super omnia diligaris. Ideo firmiter propono, aduvante gratia Tua, de cetero me non-peccaturum peccandique occasiones proximas fugiturum . . .

The phone rings and the glass smashes in my hand, just as I bring it to my lips.

"Johnny. You know I will have to kill you."

A smile widens across my face. "How can you kill what's already dead?"

Twelve Canadians were the first to welcome the next day as they took off from the Grand Union on their way to the much gentler climate of Kew. Their wings making a terrific, terrifying noise. Pete, the cleaner of the Grand Union pub, was mopping up the beer garden; lost in the fight with his wife, who'd said before he left at five in the morning, "Panic, stupidity and withdrawal. That's all you've got to fucking offer."

"Fuck away from me."

When he first heard the noise, he almost dropped dead believing, *This is it*, expecting Osama himself in a Harrier jet, with eleven henchmen in tow.

Pint and eleven white wines for the ladies?

Pete was mysteriously taken by the magnificence of those beasts and marvelled in slow motion when they, first down low and then rising up under the Halfpenny Step Bridge, yelled out as they made their ascent, "What a beautiful sight!"

He looked around to see if Carmel was about.

"Carmel, you should see this. Come here."

Carmel shook her head from inside the pub, and thinking about her eldest daughter's latest abortion, snapped, "What is it now? Don't you fucking play games with me, because I'm in no mood."

Carmel threw a rag down and turned again to see Pete standing there like a frozen statue. She laughed to herself and walked out toward him. "What's got you all fucking excited?"

Pete was still motionless, as though aliens had taken his soul. He was now white as a sheet. "Jesus."

"Oh yeah? And I suppose the fucking holy Virgin Mother of Mary, too . . ." Carmel's voice trailed off, as *now* she understood.

Tied by the wrists to the railing under the bridge.

Black tights pulled tight around her white neck.

Eyes, nose, ears, fingers and lips removed.

Half-submerged in the canal.

Dead as a fucking doornail.

Legs severed at the thighs.

Red hair ablaze.

Senseless.

Legless.

Beneath the sound of sirens, my view is as always: stark, sullen and eldritch. I'm prone to believe that it's a vile and disgusting world above.

Where I'll die, the Harrow Road police station, now a hive of cordoned-off activity – choppers and coppers setting the landscape on fire – is to my right. Our Lady of Lourdes and St. Vincent de Paul, where in less than half an hour I will asseverate Mass before a shaken community, is to my left.

A community brought together by God only knows whom.

A community of chargrins and fighters.

A community no less.

Fighters for peace.

Second-hand peace.

Crime Time West Nine.

Meanwhile.

Gardens.

Animals.

Birds.

Amen.

PART II

I Fought the Law

PART II

I FOUGHT THE LAWYER

BY MICHAEL WARD

Mayfair

I pressed PLAY and the screen on the dinky digital camcorder came to life. Vanya's face the only thing in view, gurning and sticking her tongue out as a kind of visual "*testing, testing . . .*" before disappearing.

Good girl.

From where the camera was positioned on top of the wardrobe, it takes in about half the room. In the far right-hand corner is a bed with a large mirror next to it, to the left a small chest of drawers, and in between, against the far wall, a coat stand with a French maid's outfit, a leather basque and a nurse's uniform with a white cap; a pair of black thigh-length boots is slumped in front.

Two seconds later Vanya reappears into view, carrying the chair she's just used to reach the top of the wardrobe, and placing it in its usual position next to the chest of drawers. She looks in the mirror, makes a cursory adjustment to her hair and smoothes her hands down her slip before exiting the frame stage left to the door that leads to the sitting room.

Ten seconds of stillness, then back to moving pictures as he enters the room. Four slow, graceful strides bring him to the mirror, where he stops to take in his reflection. A tall, slim, handsome man in his early fifties wearing a tastefully expensive dark grey suit offset by a weighty flop of silver hair. The epitome of conservative English style. He runs an index finger over each arched eyebrow, taming any rogue hairs, then turns and unwittingly strikes a face-on, screen-test pose for the camera.

Perfect.

Vanya's back in the room now, her heels wobbling slightly on the squishy carpet as she walks to the chest of drawers and finds a condom. The gentleman takes off his jacket and hangs it on the back of the chair, then places his shoes neatly underneath. By the time Vanya has rolled the condom over her index finger and greased it thoroughly with Vaseline, the man is naked but for his calf-length thin black socks and has positioned himself on the bed, facing away from the camera, bearing his arse to it.

Vanya kneels behind him on the bed, still in her slip and shoes, and gently greases the QC's rectal area, accompanying the finger strokes with a softly murmured Croatian lullaby. *Picka. Mamu ti jebem u guzicu.* She gently eases the digit inside and begins finger-fucking the man, her Serbo-Croat mantra rising in volume as the pace of the thrusts quickens. *Picka, picka. Mamu ti jebem u guzicu* . . . About one minute later the silver-haired gentleman, wanking furiously now, reaches his climax and the transaction is complete.

I press STOP.

Got the cunt.

Time to rewind.

The previous week – the previous millennium, in fact – I'd been at the River of Fire. The government had organized the Thames to be set on fire on the stroke of midnight. It was going to be an almighty twenty-storeys-high flaming surge of orange-and-red pyrotechnic power bursting through the heart of the city at 800 miles an hour. *PM Turns Water into Fire; Elemental Alchemy on the Grandest of Scales.* But all anyone got were a few oversized candles fizzling away on some barges along a muddy river.

Not that I gave a fuck. Fabrication, fabrication, fabrication. I knew those sloganeering cunts would never deliver. I wasn't there for the show. I was there to steal stuff from unsuspecting thick cunts. And unsuspecting thick cunts do deliver. Copiously.

I wasn't doing it for the money – though some of the stuff I nicked did come in handy later. It just needed to be done. With all that sense of hope and expectation for the dawning of a new millennium, someone had to restore the balance. Inject a bit of reality into the situation. These people were supposed to be slick city folk, weren't they? Experts at the urban experience. *Come to London.* Where the people are such cunts they piss and shit and vomit on their own streets while a bunch of incompetent failed lawyers-turned-slogan-peddlers fuck them up the arse and make them pay for the pleasure.

So I put on my own show. Illegal performance art. A one-off special for a discerning audience of – me. Creative theft. Taking and giving. No one else would've got it anyway. It was a world away from the ham-fisted gippos and hood rats who worked Oxford Street and the tubes. Banging into tourists with an awkward fumble into their pockets and coming away with the odd one-day travel pass to sell on for two quid. The occasional mobile. No sense of style, no originality. No drama. Mine was a virtuoso performance – just me, my ruck-sack and my pair of dextrous pals: Right-hand Man and his partner, Leftie. Dab hands, the both of them. Digitally precise, you might say. Got to keep them at arm's length though. You see? It's called style, cunt. Wit! Something those fucks will never have. I take and I give. It's art, fucking art.

True, the actual pickpocketing was pretty much the same as I'd done in my act a hundred times before. Same technically, anyway. And I'd picked pockets for real before, illegally that is, a couple of times. But it hadn't given me quite the buzz I'd expected it to. No sense of occasion. This was different though. The river bit might have been shit but there were still two million happy, stoned, drunk singing people all squashed up together. All mesmerized by a few colourful lights in the sky. And everyone happily embracing their fellow man, getting up close and hugging, like they didn't actually hate each other, like they weren't all cunts for one second. I'll give you "Auld Lang Fucking Syne", you twats. "Should auld acquaintance be forgot . . ." *Forgot to keep an eye on that, mate, thanks very much.* "And never brought to . . ." *Mind if I take that off you, sir?* "Should auld acquaintance be for . . ." *Gotcha!* "For the sake of auld lang . . ." *Signing off now, gotta go!*

All in front of about a zillion boys in blue. It was a good night. A new beginning. The way forward.

After the show I figured I'd go for a celebratory fuck. Vanya would still be working. I'd been going to her for about six months – since she'd come over from Croatia. She was very good value for money – extremely pretty face and a good body, but still reasonable rates. If she were English she'd probably have charged twice as much. Maybe three times. But then I guess that's one of the benefits of immigration. Cheap, efficient labour.

I started slowly working my way through the throng. Up the Strand, past Trafalgar Square and on towards Piccadilly and Shepherd Market. Made up a little song on the way, to the old Robin Hood theme tune: *He steals from the thick/And gives to the whore/Robbing's good!/Robbing's good!/Robbing's good!* Sometimes, Jonathan Marcus Tiller, I thought, you really are the wittiest fucker in the world. In the fucking world.

I was just taking in Piccadilly Circus – the glitz of Burger King, the glamour of Dunkin' Donuts – when I was approached by an American tourist: "Hey, there. Could you direct me to Piccadilly Circus?" He said the last two words uncertainly, as if no such place with that name could possibly exist.

I didn't reply, just announced the thing with outstretched arms, then turned to him with an expression I'd hoped conveyed: *What the fuck do you think that is, cunt? Now fuck off.*

It didn't work.

"Only, I'm kinda here to make this movie and I was told Piccadilly Circus was where to look."

I glanced up and down his face as he spoke.

"Look for what?" I said, mildly intrigued.

"To meet actors. Only, I'm filming the thing in my hotel tonight and I thought you might like to . . ."

Suck your cock? "Don't think so, mate. But yeah, this is the right area – just a decade or so too late . . ."

I left the Yank fruit to it and carried on up Piccadilly. Walked along the north side. It's lined with imposing grey-stoned edifices, like gigantic doormen keeping an eye on things, keeping the undesirables out. Raising a suspicious eyebrow at anyone who dares venture near the promised land of Mayfair. *Perhaps sir would be more comfortable taking a different thoroughfare? A street more suited to sir's . . . position, shall we say?*

Not tonight though. Tonight I wasn't being hassled by them. It was as if I'd passed some kind of test. Like I was okay now. They hadn't exactly handed me the keys, but at least they were going to turn a blind eye while I picked the locks for a while. It was definitely a new beginning.

I took a right down White Horse Street and into Shepherd Market, a twisty-turny little red-lit corner where all Mayfair's dirt had been swept to, out of sight. Like a mini Soho but better-spoken and wearing a blazer. By day, the place wasn't really that special – a bit too twee for my taste. But come night – proper night, that is, once the after-work lager's been drunk and the late-night diners have fucked off – that's when it happens. When it reveals its true identity. The perfect place for a discerning maverick street thief artist.

I stopped to hitch my rucksack up, then turned left, then right into Market Mews. Stopped at the open door marked *Model 1st Floor* and made my way up the stairs. Up the wooden hill to Shagfordshire. *Another good one, Jonny boy.* On the way up I waved at the CCTV camera on the wall and pressed the plastic doorbell helpfully labelled *Press*. Rita opened up. A short round woman with enormous sagging tits, bald but for a few patches of yellowy-grey hair. She was sporting worn-out pink slippers and a loose-fitting cream-coloured tracksuit topped with an off-pink towelling dressing gown. Rita is Vanya's maid, the woman who welcomes the punters.

"Hello, Jonny, love, she's with a gentleman at the moment, be about ten minutes, that all right?"

"Fine," I said, unhitching the rucksack and plopping myself on the foam two-seater sofa in the living room. The only other rooms in the flat are a tiny kitchen with a kettle and microwave and a small bedroom.

The TV was on so Rita and I sat watching the ITN news report of the millennium celebrations. I broke a Marlboro open to pad out a joint while Rita puffed on her B&H.

"Looks bitter out," she said, nodding at the TV images of the crowds along the Thames. She got up to turn the thermostat to one hundred.

"Yes," I said, twisting the end of my newly constructed joint before lighting it up.

"Aren't you playing a show tonight, love? Thought you'd be busy tonight of all nights."

"Nah. I could've had a gig but I wanted to check out the River of Fire," I said, watching the end of my joint glow as I toked on it.

I'd often chat with Rita while Vanya was otherwise engaged. She thought I was a bit glamorous cos I was a magician.

"Been busy?" she asked.

I told her about the last gig I'd done – a Christmas party for an accounting firm in the city. I'd been booked with an illusionist called Damon Smart to entertain the staff before dinner. I'd worked with Smart before. His real name was Dave Smith. He was a cheesy cunt, but skilful.

We would approach a group of five or six of the accountants as they enjoyed some pre-prandial quaffing and introduce ourselves as so-and-so and so-and-so who'd just joined the firm. After a while Smart would start behaving oddly, grimacing and rubbing his stomach, complaining of indigestion. Then he'd do some pretend-retching and – this is the particularly cuntish bit – start pulling a thread of razor blades from his mouth. Yes, it was that shit. Shitter, in fact, cos once his shtick was over I would then produce a selection of items I'd lifted from them while they were busy watching Smart hamming it up. "And I believe this watch is yours, sir . . ." I fucking hated it. I fucking, fucking, fucking hated the fucking fuck out of it.

Not that I let Rita know this though. She was happy to think of me as some kind of Paul fucking Daniels, so I figured, why upset her? Nothing to be gained.

"So, yeah, it was a good night," I lied, and took another draw on my spliff.

"You'll be on the telly next," she said, nodding towards the box.

We watched the news coverage for another minute or so, then Rita nodded towards the bedroom door. "That'll be it, then, love," she said.

She meant it was time for me to step into the kitchen – out of sight so the punter could leave without the embarrassment of seeing another male in the place. I don't know how the fuck she knew it was time – I hadn't heard a thing from the other room – but her orgasm-detector was spot on. I went into the kitchen and shut the door, leaving it open a tiny crack so I could see who was coming out without him seeing me. I always liked to get a look at the bloke Vanya had been with immediately before me. Just natural curiosity, I suppose.

Half a minute later Vanya appeared from the bedroom and left the flat for the communal toilet on the landing.

Then out he came.

I knew I knew him as soon as he came into view. Someone famous, but I couldn't think who. A newsreader maybe? No, not that well-known. An MP? Not sure, but someone . . .

He picked up the overcoat he'd left on the settee, then pulled out a tenner and handed it to Rita.

Rita smiled and took the tip. "Safe journey now, it's bitter out."

"My overcoat will guard me against the cold, my dear," he said. "And I shall savour your delicious non sequitur the length of my secure passage home."

The name hit me.

I waited till I heard his footsteps disappear down the staircase before coming back into the room.

"Do you know who that was?" I didn't wait for an answer. "Nicholas Monroe. The lawyer. He's . . ."

Vanya teetered back in from the toilet.

"He's famous. Well, for a lawyer anyway . . ."

"Fahmous? Fahmous who? Frederick?" Vanya asked, taking the £60 I had ready for her.

I followed her into the bedroom.

"No, yes – no – his name's Nicholas Monroe. He's always on the news. He got that gang off who killed that black kid in East Ham a couple of years ago. And that gangster from where you're from . . ."

"From Croatia?"

"Somewhere like that, I don't know. Albania maybe, it doesn't matter," I said, shutting the bedroom door. "The point is, he's fucking well-known, got shitloads of money."

"He's not from Croatia, silly, he's English," she said. "Very fine English man. Now what shall we do? Talking or fucking?"

"I mean, what the fuck's he doing here?" I said, ignoring the question.

Vanya plopped herself down on the bed and started inspecting her fingernails.

"If he wants a shag he could go to some discreet high-class place in Kensington or somewhere. What's he doing coming here?"

Her eyes narrowed. "He like me," she said. "He like the way I speak and how I – "

"What, has he been here before? He's a regular?"

"Yes, of course." She said it as if it was obvious, as if I was the stupid one. "He come to here every week nearly. I speak to him in Croatian and put my finger up his arse and he . . ."

Fuck me. "You put your finger up his arse?"

"Yes, of course, this is normal, what's wrong with this?"

"Fucking hell, Vanya – it's not what's wrong with it, it's what's *right* with it. He's rich. He can't afford this to get out. He'll pay us not to tell anyone."

Vanya had a habit of being a bit "kooky", like she wasn't quite all there. Like everything was a game, everything was happening in some surreal Eastern European kiddie film. But now she became more serious, more real. I felt a rise of something in my belly.

"Pay us? How much pay us?" she said.

"Dunno. Ten grand. Maybe more." *Fifty, at least.* "It's nothing to him. He can earn that in a week probably . . ."

"In a week? *Nemoj me jebat!*"

"Exactly." I spoke calmly now, took the tempo down a notch. "We just have to do it properly. Plan it right . . ."

I didn't know a lot about Vanya, but I knew she wasn't a whore by choice, that she hadn't known this was what she'd be doing when she was brought to England. And I knew that, like Anna and Katarina in the flats upstairs, she wasn't seeing much of the five grand or so a week she was earning for the management. She listened carefully as I went through the plan, nodding slowly as I showed her how to work the camcorder, where the record button was, and how to tell if it was on or not. Then I marked the exact spot on the wardrobe where she should put it next time Monroe visited. She would phone me as soon as he'd gone and I would come and collect the camcorder and tape and put Phase 2 into operation.

Ten minutes later I left. We hadn't even fucked but it didn't matter. This was better, I thought. Much better. As I left the place I became aware of the warmth again. Only now it was spreading, up through my chest and arms and down into my groin. This was proper, I could feel it happening now. The real thing. The way forward. The night's earlier performance was a mere prelude. A toccata to the fugue I was composing. I went home but couldn't sleep. Six spliffs and a bottle of wine later, I could . . .

I spent the next few days in my flat in Kentish Town planning Phase 2 and thinking about what to do with the cash. And afterwards too, the next job. Maybe some type of con. It had to be something elegant, stylish. After a few years I'd retire and write my memoir, get it published anonymously. Reveal myself to a select few, my own little magic circle.

The call finally came on Monday night, about eleven. I left the flat and hailed a cab for Market Mews. Rita let me in and Vanya was there on the settee eating a Pot Noodle.

"Did you get it? Did it come out okay?" I said.

"Yes, of course."

"Where is it?"

Vanya put the plastic pot down on the carpet and pulled the camcorder out from under the sofa.

"Brilliant." I took it off her. "I'll give you a call. Gotta go. See you."

I left her to her MSG-flavoured processed soya and caught a cab on Piccadilly.

"Kentish Town, please, mate."

The cabbie nodded and I got in and hit the PLAY button. It was all there. *Good girl. Perfect. Got the cunt.*

Back at the flat I fired up my Mac and started working on the blackmail letter. The title – *Blackmail Demands* – in twelve-point size, centred on the page. I used italics in the first draft but decided it was a bit too soft so opted for plain text. Then the font. That proved more difficult. Gothic Bold seemed like a good choice but it looked too melodramatic. I liked the sound of Chicago, a bit gangsterish, but it came across too friendly on the page. Then Typewriter. Quite sinister-looking, but more of a ransom-note font, I thought. In the end I went for Times New Roman. Simple. Serious. Businesslike.

Then the text itself. I spent a good few hours on this and was pretty satisfied with the results:

I have in my possession a videotape of you, Mr. Nicholas Monroe, QC, engaging in an act of depravity with a prostitute. The tape is three minutes and twenty-six seconds in length and you are clearly identifiable in it. I am prepared to sell this tape to you for a price of no less than £50,000 in cash. Otherwise I will take it to the newspapers. The fee is non-negotiable and there is only one copy of the tape. You will have to trust me on that last point. Bring the cash, alone, to the Printers Devil public house in Fetter Lane, 4 p.m. on Wednesday the 12th of January, and in return you will receive the tape, which will be in the video camera so you can see what you are getting. Looking forward to doing business with you, Jon X

After a couple of spell-checks I printed it out on a clean piece of white A4. It looked good but the vertical position of the text wasn't quite right so I moved it down slightly, then printed it out again. That was it. I folded it into thirds and sealed the letter in an envelope. *Strictly Private and Confidential. Nicholas Monroe, QC*, it said. I used my left hand to write it, just in case, then deleted the document from my Mac.

I looked over at the TV. *Countdown* was on – the early-morning repeat. It was about half an hour before the tubes started running so I watched the last fifteen minutes, waiting for the nine-letter conundrum bit at the end. I wanted to see if it would be *BLACKMAIL*. I had a feeling it would be. It wasn't.

At that time of day, it only took thirty minutes to get from Kentish Town to Chancery Lane, where Monroe's chambers were. I slipped the letter through the letterbox and went back to the flat to get some sleep.

It was two in the afternoon when the alarm woke me up. Wednesday. I shaved, took a shower, put my suit and overcoat on, and headed back down Chancery Lane to the Printers Devil. I got there at 3.30 and the place was about half full, which was good. Bought a G&T and found a table with a clear view of the door. While I waited I went over what I was going to say to Monroe. He would walk in alone; I'd gesture for him to come and join me at the table and offer to buy him a drink. He was bound to be nervous and I wanted to keep it friendly. When I'd brought his drink back from the bar I'd say my piece: *Well, Mr. Monroe, I think we both know why we're here, don't we, so let's get down to business, shall we?* He'd probably just nod, I figured, be happy for me to do the talking so he could get the fuck out of there as soon as possible. After the exchange we'd shake hands and I'd leave him there and go and see Vanya to give her her five grand.

Except it didn't quite happen like that. For a start, Monroe was late. Very late. So late in fact that he didn't actually fucking bother to turn up. I phoned his office and was told he was in meetings all afternoon but would I like to leave a message. Would I like to leave a fucking message? What the fuck was going on here? Monroe was in no position to fuck with me. I had the tape; I was in control of the situation. My instructions were clear. The letter. He couldn't just ignore this. It wasn't going to go away. I had him by the balls and he had to deal with it. He had to. The arrogance of this cocky fuck – I couldn't believe it. Like I was some prick of a client he could keep on hold while he plays golf or gets finger-fucked or whatever else the cunt does in his spare time.

I needed to calm myself, so I had another drink and considered my options. There was only really one. Dominic. We'd been at Ampleforth together and had kept in touch since. Dom had taken up journalism and was working as a news sub-editor at the *Sunday* where his dad had worked. I'd sell the tape to them. It wouldn't fetch quite the same price, but what else could I do? If this cunt thought he could ignore me, he could think again. He'd been warned. It was all in the letter.

I phoned Dom from the pub and set up the meeting, a drink after work at the Prospect of Whitby in Shadwell, near the *Sunday*'s offices. I got there at around 6.30 and he introduced me to his workmate.

"Jon, this is Stuart," Dom said. "He's up for the Young Journalist of the Year award next month."

Really? Looks like a cunt to me.

"Nice to meet you, Stuart," I said. He looked in his late twenties. Had a shaved head and wore a black suit with a dark shirt, no tie. And his handshake was too firm.

"I've brought Stu along cos this is more his kinda thing," Dom explained. "I'm more on the editing side of things, not really a reporter, but Stu here – "

Is a cunt. "Brilliant," I interrupted, keen to get things moving. "Can I get you guys a drink?"

They both wanted lagers.

When I got back from the bar I launched straight into it. "So, what do you know about Nicholas Monroe, the QC?" I threw the question firmly at Young Cunt of the Year.

"Monroe, yeah, mate, what about him?" Shave-head said, picking up his pint for a gulp.

"Well, what if I were to tell you I have a video of him getting finger-fucked by a £60 whore in Shepherd Market?"

He put his pint down. "Have you?"

"How much would the *Sunday* pay for it?" I asked.

"Have you got it with you?"

I played them the tape. A minute in and I could tell he was impressed – with the tape and with me. Once he'd seen Monroe's face on the vid, he shot me a look that said: *Okay, cunt – I can do business with you.* When it was over I pressed STOP and put the camera back in my overcoat pocket. Stu spoke first.

"It's good but we'd need the girl," he said bluntly.

"The girl? Why? It's all there . . ." I looked at Dom for some back-up. It didn't come.

"It's all there, yeah, yeah," Stu said, "but it's more complicated than that. He's a very powerful guy, old Monroe. He knows half the fucking cabinet. Probably worked with them when they were still practising."

"Stu's tried to do pieces on Monroe before, Jon," Dom chipped in.

"Yeah, but they always get spiked," the cunt continued. "He knows everyone. His old flatmate from law school is tipped to be the next DG of the Beeb." He took another gulp and held my gaze. *My move.*

"But he couldn't sue you when you've got him there on tape, clear as day," I said.

"Look, the guy likes to take chances, likes to think he's a bit dangerous. But he's smart, he's fucking smart, covers his tracks. As I say, friends in high places. He's supposed to be on the Queen's birthday list for a knighthood."

"So what? He's untouchable?" I said. I could feel it slipping away.

"Mate, I'm not saying it's impossible. But I know Neil and he's going to be very wary of this."

"Neil's our editor, Jon," Dom said.

"And he wouldn't even consider it without the girl," Stu continued. "We'd need her, on the spread, telling her story – and prepared to testify, if necessary."

"I see. But how much – What's the story worth if I get her?"

"That's not really my call. Dunno, probably five figures though," he said.

Five figures, that's at least ten grand. It was still good, I thought. I downed my G&T, then made my excuses and left, as the tabloids say. Cabbed it to Shepherd Market, up the wooden hill, and pressed *Press*.

Rita answered the door. But this time there was no cheery hello. She would only keep the door ajar, wouldn't let me in. She just said: "Vanya's gone. She won't be back. You're not to be let in." And then shut the door.

What the fuck?

"What do you mean *gone*?" I said through the door. "Rita? Gone where? Rita?"

"Go on, hop it now or I'll have to call him," she said.

She meant Davor, the gangster who owned the place.

I walked slowly back down the stairs, trying to make sense of what had just happened. I'd never seen Rita look stern before. It was odd. And to threaten me with Davor or one of his thugs . . .

I went home and spliffed myself to sleep. Woke up in my clothes around noon the next day and started getting ready. The camcorder was still in the pocket of my overcoat. I put it on and left the flat to find a payphone. Dialled the number.

"Put me through to Nicholas Monroe," I said.

"Mr. Monroe is in a meeting with a client at the moment, he can't – "

"It's urgent. He's expecting me to call."

"Sir, Mr. Monroe hasn't mentioned a – "

"Just tell him it's John X. It's extremely urgent."

The line went quiet, that electric nothingness you get when you're in phone-line limbo. Then a man's voice.

"Ahhh, Mr. X . . ."

He sounded relaxed, jovial even.

"This is your last chance, Monroe," I said. "I've been to the *Sunday* and they are very interested in the tape. They're prepared to run the story . . ."

"The *Sunday*? I see."

What the fuck is it with this twat? I was talking, you rude cunt.

"So the situation we find ourselves in, Mr. X," he said, each word measured, calm, "is that you have a firm financial offer from the *Sunday* newspaper and you're wondering whether I'm prepared to beat that offer. Am I correct?"

"Yes."

"Good. And may I ask how much their offer is?"

Five figures, Shavey had said. "Ten grand."

I regretted the words as soon as I said them. He would have expected me to come up with a figure twice what I was being offered. And why did I tell him which paper it was? I was fucking this up, I knew it. He was too calm and I couldn't deal with it. It wasn't what I was expecting.

"Mmm," Monroe said. "I can probably lay my hands on five thousand by this afternoon – will that do you?"

I suppose it'll fucking have to. Five grand. It was an insult. But I didn't really have a choice.

"Six o'clock in the Printers Devil on Fetter Lane – and don't be late." I put the receiver down.

I killed the rest of the afternoon in my local, trying to drink away what had happened, and left at five to meet Monroe. The platform at Kentish Town was fairly full when I got there – trouble on the Northern Line, as usual – but it was completely rammed by the time the train finally arrived. I fought my way onto the tube, southbound for Tottenham Court Road where I'd change for the Central Line and Chancery Lane. I managed to defend my own little corner by the doors as far as Camden Town, where about a billion people squeezed on and I was thrust into the middle, both hands holding onto the bar above to keep balance. I rarely got the tube, but even I knew that this was worse than normal. Pensioners, office workers, hood rats, tourists – almost every type of low-life London scum was pressed right up against me.

I felt the first risings of a panic attack coming on but pushed it away with a happy thought. I closed my eyes and relived my New Year's Eve performance, then Monroe, the tape and the letter, the money, the next job, the memoir . . . then what? . . . Monroe not turning up, the shavey-head cunt trying to make me look stupid, getting turned away by Rita . . . Davor . . . and then Monroe laughing at me on the phone, the arrogant fuck. How dare the cunt? Me with video proof of this fucker – this QC, no less, who knows the cabinet, is in line for a knighthood – getting finger-fucked up the arse in his stockinged feet by a whore he's probably managed to have chased out of the country, and all I can get for it is a stinking £5,000, if the cunt shows up at all. He just didn't seem to give a fuck. It was a minor detail in another week's work. Hadn't he grasped the situation? I was in charge here – I was the blackmailer – I had the power.

I opened my eyes. Tottenham Court Road – needed to get off and change. I slowly pushed my way through the pensioners and hood rats, still gripping the bars for balance, and made it to the open doors, squeezing myself out of the carriage just in time before they shut behind me and the train moved off, leaving two dozen or so pissed-off commuters to wait for the next one. A moment of *schadenfreude* consolation for me. I started moving towards the *Way Out* sign, patted my coat pocket for the camera. Nothing there. I checked the other outside pocket, then the lining one, panic surging through my body, then my trouser pockets, and back to the pocket where I knew I'd put it. Empty. Gone. I started running after the train as it moved along the platform, swearing, screaming at it as it disappeared down the tunnel. I covered my face with my hands.

"You all right, mate?" a voice said.

I let my hands drop to my sides and opened my eyes. It was a station guard.

"No. I've been pickpocketed."

That was five months ago now. I've never been back to the flat in Shepherd Market. But I did go to the Printers Devil – that same day, in fact. I don't know why exactly. Just to see Monroe there, I suppose. See without being seen. Thought I might be able to come up with another plan there and then. I waited till seven. He didn't turn up.

I got a text message from Dominic the next day, Friday, saying sorry but they couldn't go ahead with the story, girl or no girl. He didn't say why.

I've been doing more gigs since then. My agency has got me a cruise thing lined up, starts in July, next month.

The funny thing was, though, a few weeks after it all happened I was looking on the web for porn when something caught my eye – a video clip. The description said: *Sexy brunette finger-fucks old guy up the arse – in his socks – funny*. I downloaded it, sent it out on a group e-mail – to the Law Society, three cabinet MPs and the Lord Chancellor's office. No text, just *Nicholas Monroe, QC* in the subject field.

Monroe didn't make it onto the Queen's birthday honours this year. He must be very disappointed.

I HATE HIS FINGERS

BY SYLVIE SIMMONS

Kentish Town

That's what she said. "I hate his fingers." I tugged open the freezer door – iced up, as usual; who the fuck ever had time to defrost a freezer? – and when I managed to pull the box out, it too was encased in solid ice. I stabbed at it a few times with the bread knife – more because it felt good than for any effectiveness it was having – then threw it into the microwave and put it on defrost. I opened a bottle and poured a large glass.

"You're supposed to let wine breathe."

I lit a Dunhill – only ten so far today, not bad.

"And you might consider letting me breathe as well." Dino coughed. He sounded like an old, gay Jack Russell with emphysema.

"Nice try," I said, "but I never did get the knack of emotional blackmail."

"Shame, or Kate might still be here and we might have something decent to eat."

"Fuck you." I smiled.

"In your dreams. A dangerous line to use on a Freudian." Dino giggled like a girl. "So, this patient of yours, I take it you thought of asking whose fingers and what she had against them?"

"I told you, that's all she said."

"*I hate his fingers?* For fifty minutes?"

"Apart from the forty spent saying nothing at all and the two spent telling me she was only here because her GP told her she was getting no more temazepam until she took some sessions with the practice shrink."

"Who's her GP? Philip?"

"Yeah. His letter said his best guess was OCD – obsessive-compulsive disorder – but it could be a weird phobia. He said he knew what a hard-on I got from those." Since I moved out of general practice into psychiatry – long story, and one I'd prefer not to go into here – I'd made a name, if I say so myself, with my papers on unusual phobias.

"Hating being touched is not unusual. Having your hand up my arse gives me the heebie-jeebies and I'm a hardened pro."

I chose to ignore him. "Yeah, haphephobia's pretty commonplace, but if it's fingers, per se – well, dactylophobia's a new one on me. But I don't know, from the look of her she might well have some kind of body dysmorphic disorder. She looked borderline anorexic. Like she weighed all of seven stone."

She was the kind of girl who leaves no footprints when she comes into a room, but makes a big impression, you know what I mean? She was small and delicate, looked about sixteen years old. Wore one of those little girl dresses, bare legs, short-sleeved cardigan. And big Bambi eyes, like one of those little urchin paintings the tabloids always say are cursed. Burn your house down the second you go out. Maybe they're right. Her medical records said she was thirty-five and married.

"Would it help if I sat in on a session?" Now and again I'd take Dino along – mostly when I was treating children. They seemed to relax around him. Opened up more. The microwave dinged. The cardboard box was wet and steaming. Smelled disgusting. I tore it off and put the plastic tray back in the oven. Dino was right about the food.

"I don't know," I said. "I'll see."

"I'll tell you what I see: a lump in your trousers." Damn if the little fucker wasn't right again. "Takes wood to know wood. And what I know I see is a man who wants this little girl all to himself."

When Dino got excited his voice became unbearably camp. Now he was chanting in a high, sour voice, "Doc has got a stiffie, Doc has got a stiffie."

"Right, that's it." I strode across the kitchen and put my hand around his throat, lifting him clean out of the chair. I carried him like that into the living room, and hurled him against the wall. Legs splayed, bow tie skewed, his jaw hinged open like a snake getting ready to swallow a rabbit, the dummy lay propped up against the TV set, staring at space.

For the first half hour of the second session she didn't say a word. Just chewed the hangnail at the side of her thumb and looked up and sideways at me through her eyelashes. That little-girl-lost look. It was like she was waiting for me to tell her what to do. I found myself reaching across the desk to comfort her, make it all right. Fortunately I stopped myself in time; that was all I needed, another incident. If it wasn't for my old friends at the practice – or more to the point, if it wasn't for what I had on my old friends at the practice – I would have been out on the street. Which is where Kate and her fucking lawyer wanted me. At the last minute, I pretended to swat an imaginary bug off the Kleenex box on her side of the desk.

Since she wouldn't talk, I did. I told her not to worry.

That she'd come to the right place. Phobias, I said, like American T-shirts, came in all different colours but just one size, extra-large. There's no such thing as being a little bit phobic. It's like being pregnant, you either are or you aren't. As I said that, in reflex, her knees pressed together tight. They were pink and rosy, like a little girl left out in the playground too long, but there was nothing at all childlike about the rest of those legs. They ended in a pair of expensive, black, strappy stilettos, with a half-moon cut out of the end of each one where her red lacquered toenails peeped through.

I found myself, and I don't know why, talking about myself, telling her about my automatonophobia. Fear of ventriloquist dummies. When she didn't seem that impressed, I admitted that it wasn't, of course, as socially debilitating as being finger phobic, since you're likely to run into more fingers on a daily basis than ventriloquist dummies. But the effects, I said – the panic, the terror, that black-ice, deep-gut nausea – they were exactly the same. A few years ago, I told her, I was in the Oxfam shop buying coffee when I saw an old wooden dummy staring down at me from the shelf behind the till. In the past I would have frozen in fear. But I was so over my phobia that I bought it and took it home. Since then we'd become something of a double act, at least in medical circles, me and Dino. Kate of course would have put it differently, but Kate wasn't here. Kate was fucking her lawyer, and she was colder to me than a Marks & Spencer microfuckingwave meal.

I assured her that she too could feel the same way about fingers.

"It's not all fingers I hate," she said. "Just my husband's."

Her husband's? We were getting somewhere. If I'd only

known where, I'd have run straight out of that door, down to Kentish Town station, and jumped on the first train going anywhere else.

My other half is a bitch. Did I tell you that? I'm sorry. I've been obsessing a lot lately, going over and over the notes. These are from our third session – the one where I looked across the desk at her and fell uselessly, impossibly, in love. It was raining like a dog that day. A typical black, filthy London day, I remember. Sunny when I left home at 7.30, though, or I would have taken the car. But I walked down the street and into a climate change. You'd think I'd be used to that trick by now, wouldn't you? The one God plays on the English almost every single fucking day: an hour of sun first thing in the morning to wake you up and get you off to work, then pissing on you mightily. I'm a slow learner, I guess.

It's a short walk to the surgery but not a pretty one. It gets uglier still the closer you get to Kentish Town Road. Shabby, shapeless old buildings, oddly bent, like they're about to collapse, though no one seems to notice or care. And those garish shop signs. The whole street looks like an old tart with osteoporosis. London's full of shabby old buildings, but you can look at them and see that once in their lives they looked grand. On Kentish Town Road, they look like they were built to look that shabby. And the people on the street have grown to look just like the buildings, the way people start to look like their dogs. It's no wonder half of Camden is on SSRIs; the other half are just too fucking depressed to go and fill their prescriptions.

It was still raining hard when she arrived at three that afternoon. Her bare legs were so badly splashed by passing cars they looked like Rorschach tests. Her short skirt was soaked right through. It stuck to her so tight you could see she wore no underwear. When she sat down, she tried pulling the thin fabric over her thighs, but realized it was hopeless. She covered her lap with her bag and gave me the sweetest, saddest smile. Then she furrowed her brow. I didn't have to say a word. She started talking right away.

"Doc," she said, "I'm telling you this because I think you're the only person who would understand. I feel like a stranger in my own life."

I'd heard this before, of course, or a thousand different variations, but coming from her, it shot through me like electricity. She told me she'd been married for eight years – I felt another stab, jealousy, envy, loss? – to, well, let's just say a famous rock musician. Or as famous as bass players are likely to get. Bass players are the overlooked band members. I've had a few of them sitting in that same seat in the past, trying to deal with not getting enough attention, not getting enough love. With nothing ever being quite big enough.

"Have you ever looked at a bass player's hands?" she asked. I couldn't say I had. She was looking at my hands now, so intimately it felt like a touch. "You have elegant fingers. Artistic. I'm sure a lot of people have told you that. Bass players' fingers are repulsive. They don't have joints like regular fingers. They bend at the knuckle and that's it. When they play the bass they just kind of throw themselves at the strings and bounce off – *thwack*. Like pork sausages on a grill. Like pigs throwing themselves at an electric fence." She illustrated it with an air bass guitar solo. It made me smile, which made her frown again. "I hate his fingers," she said.

The rest of him, apparently, was all right. He was ten years older than she was, but that wasn't a problem. He had money and was happy to let her spend it. He spent most of his time in the studio he had near King's Cross. Their sex life had always been good, though it had tapered off in the past six months. She thought the reason for that was her bringing up the idea of children, but really she didn't care either way. Kate didn't want children – my children anyway. Though I got hold of her medical notes through one of my contacts and, what do you know, she's four months gone. Did she and her thieving-cunt lawyer think I was dumb enough to just sign it over to them? She said the only reason she'd mentioned babies was because for a while she thought she might be pregnant. She would throw up every morning, usually when he tried to touch her. It had got to the point where all she could think of were the pigs. His fingers even smelled porky. They revolted her, to the point where she could barely eat . . . or sleep, worrying about the morning coming and the fingers. That's why she needed the temazepam. It wasn't so bad if she took a couple of those.

The desk clock chimed. I couldn't believe fifty minutes had gone so fast. I didn't want to send her out into the rain and ugliness of Kentish Town. I wanted to make things all right for her. Somehow it felt like this was my one last chance to make things right for anybody – me in particular. That night I told Dino I felt there was a voice that wasn't mine inside me that kept on saying, *Drop it. Send her back to her GP. Give her the number of the divorce lawyer. It's not too late. Stop now.* I expected Dino to say something sarcastic about how he knew he had a voice inside him that wasn't his. But he realised how serious I was and didn't say a word.

I'll tell you what it was like. Like I'd dreamed about this so often that I wasn't sure what to make of the reality. One thing's for certain, it wasn't so real. Surreal, certainly, especially after our fifth session – but I'm getting ahead of myself.

It was session four when she came in, picked up her chair and carried it around to my side of the desk. She sat down next to me, close enough that the smell of her shoulder made me light-headed. She opened up a large school satchel and said, "I've got something I want you to see."

It was a folder containing several sheets of A4 paper. Pictures printed from a computer. The first was a photograph of her husband. She looked at me expectantly, seeing if I recognized him. I didn't. Like I said, he was a bass player. Good-looking though. Tall, thin, angular, unkempt in a studied sort of way. A lot of hair for a man in his mid-forties. Very English face, upper-class; it had that distracted, vaguely inbred look. He stood by the front door of a house – theirs, I imagine – with his hands in his pockets, smiling. In the second picture he was onstage. The third was the same photograph zoomed in on his fingers, playing the bass guitar. She was right. They were ugly. Thick, pink and rigid, like a glove-puppet's. The last picture was the most disturbing. It was another close-up, but this time so close up and so fuzzy as to be almost impossible to make out. It appeared to be his fingers, or the bottom half of them anyway. The top half had disappeared into something white and mottled like cottage cheese and at the same time dark and fleshy like meat.

"He's cheating," she said, and then she started to cry, loudly, like someone was gutting her. So loudly one of the practice nurses came in and put an arm around her. For the rest of the session I sat there helplessly, watching her sob. When I got home, Dino asked me if I'd seen the package under the front doormat. I hadn't, though I must have stepped on it coming in. It was an envelope, which I opened right up. Inside was a DVD. I poured a glass of wine while my laptop booted up. We spent the whole night, me and Dino, watching that DVD over and over on the computer screen. And again, not a single word of sarcasm. Not even about the cigarettes.

She turned up for session five in a pair of black jeans and an oversized Red Hot Chili Peppers T-shirt – mine, I recognized the bloodstain on the front, but that's another story. This one's about fingers. It was funny how boyish she looked. Beautiful though. Especially when she blushed, which she did when I told her that Dino had watched the DVD with me. Dino sat in this time. She told me she wanted to meet him. I asked her if it was shot in her husband's studio. She said she supposed so but she'd never been inside. If he wasn't on the road or with the band, he went there at two every afternoon, returning home at eight. He told her he was working on a "solo project" and didn't want to be disturbed.

In the film, the place had the look of a well-appointed office. A wood-panelled front room was hung with gold and platinum albums. There was a large, leather-top desk, an upright bass, three or four electric bass guitars on stands. A trestle table, almost as wide as the room, was packed with an assortment of computer and recording equipment. There must have been webcams everywhere, since you could pretty much see every corner. He selected one of the electric basses, and with that in one hand and a carrier bag in the other, he walked along a corridor that led to another room at the end.

This room was even larger. Most of the space was taken up by an enormous mattress stacked on two, maybe three divans. It was very high for a bed. Lying on top was an old woman. She must have been seventy years old if she was a day. It takes more than sixty-nine years to get that ugly. She was stark naked. And the fattest woman I had ever seen in my life.

He put the carrier bag on the bed and sat beside her. Out of the bag he took a cardboard box which was stuffed with cakes, the sort they sell in cheap bakeries, yellow sponge, bright pink icing. Tenderly he slotted a whole cake into her mouth. As soon as she finished one, he fed her another, until the box was empty. Every time a piece fell from her lips he would guide it back in with one of those broad fingers. When she was all done, he kissed her mouth, which was puffy and purple, haemorrhoidal. Then he tried moving her – with difficulty, but not unkindly – to the foot of the bed. One hundred and ninety kilos of human being, shifted centimetre by centimetre. He got her upright somehow and propped her against a mountain of cushions. She looked like a melting Buddha blancmange. He kissed her face, her breasts – the folds on her body made every part of her look like breasts – then eased her thighs apart. He aimed a remote control at the doorway. Recording equipment clicked on. Facing a camera, he began to speak. I was wrong about him being upper-class English, he was American.

"The music of the spheres. We've all heard that expression. Some of us – the true artists – have spent our lives trying to capture the mysterious, terrifying beauty of that siren sound, only to be dashed on the rocks. It was the scientists that discovered its source. It's the sound waves made when a black hole sucks in and swallows a star." At these words the old woman licked her lips and grinned. He thrust his right hand between her legs.

"There is no gain without pain. Nothing survives the black hole other than this hum, which is the deepest note ever recorded – a B-flat, oscillating to a B, but six hundred octaves deeper than anything my bass guitar can play." He pulled his hand out abruptly, grabbed his guitar and started to play, wet fingers slapping the thick strings. The look on his face was ecstatic.

So. Her husband was a feeder. And a gerontophile. Married to a tiny woman who looked like a child, and whose face, on our sixth and last session, I had touched with my own finger, tracing the thin bones and the delicate chin, down her neck and across her beautifully corrugated sternum, all the while whispering that I was going to help her. The question, as I asked Dino when we got in the car, was, who was going to help me?

"A *bass* solo? And that sniffing business? Yee-uk! This *dude*," Dino stretched the word out to a good six seconds long, "doesn't make snuff films. He makes *sniff* films. Snuffing them would have been kinder than a bass solo." Dino's eyes swung wildly from side to side. "What is *wrong* with Americans? Do you remember that couple Kate brought here for dinner who said they didn't think the statue on Nelson's column looked much like Nelson Mandela at all? And that *creature* – when he has a *princess* at home. It's Charles and Camilla, all over again." He rolled his eyes back in his head.

"You'd need far more sessions with a shrink than you'll get on the NHS to figure that out," I replied. "What was it Clint Eastwood said in *Unforgiven*? It's got nothing to do with deserves. It's all about betrayal and double-cross – my work, my life, her husband, my wife . . ." Maybe she'll betray me too. Burn the whole house down like one of those big-eyed urchin paintings until there's nothing left but a pile of ash. But if I wasn't going to get as iced up as that freezer, right now I needed that flame. Which is why, instead of heading home after my last appointment, Dino and I were in my car, inching along Leighton Road. I parked on Lady Margaret, picked up Dino and my briefcase, and walked around the corner to the tube. By the station, as always, there was a clutter of winos perched on the benches under the glass-and-iron canopy. It always struck me that there was something theatrical about this spot. Like it was some kind of project Camden Council had for out-of-work actors. Putting those insane uplighters in the pavement to illuminate the puddles of puke and piss only added to the effect.

As I approached, one of the men looked up. "I'm working hard," he said, "although I appear to have the air of a holiday-maker." He patted the space on the bench beside him. "Take a load off, doc. How's it going?" I recognized him. Back in the day when I worked as a GP around the corner, he had been one of my patients. I sat down and took out the cropped headshot I'd printed from the DVD. A man at the next bench with a can of Special Brew eyed me suspiciously.

"Are you a cop?"

My old patient cut in with, "How many cops have you seen with a ventriloquist's dummy? I know him, he's all right," he said, and the man with the Special Brew came over.

"I know her too." He pointed at the picture. "It's Fat Mary."

"Oh, my love," his companion laughed. "That it is, and in the prime of health. And I thought she was dead. She's not dead, is she?"

Mary, he told me, used to work King's Cross; she had a handful of regulars who'd come to her for years. The cops left her alone mostly, but then they brought in all those community officers who shifted the girls along York Way up to the park by the astroturf football pitch. Her clients stopped coming and the younger girls gave her a rough time. Around a year ago she disappeared. Which must have been when the bass player took her in. They told me they had no clue where she was, but I already had an idea. I picked up Dino and headed for the car.

It was easy. Surprisingly easy. All you need is a computer and the medical profession behind you. The hardest part was changing the appointments; patients, psychiatric ones particularly, don't like change. My secretary put a few of them off and crammed the real crazies into the mornings. That way I had the afternoons to myself. I didn't spend the whole of that time with her, even though her husband was at his studio and we could work on her problems at her place, undisturbed. Like I said, I had other things to do, people to track down, plans to make. I'd lost contact with David and Malcolm many years ago, but here we all were, e-mailing each other like old friends.

I'd worked with both of them closely, way back when. It was before I started specializing in phobics. My interest back then was fetishists. David was an accountant. He was also my first feeder. Jailed for locking up and fattening up an underage girl from Poland who had answered his ad for an au pair. He said she lied to him about her age and, already on the chubby side, she looked much older than she was. He believed that she was happy with the set-up. Maybe she was. It was clear he worshipped her; he waited on her hand and foot. When they sent me to see him, all he did was ask if I would look out for her and make sure she was all right. At some point after his release, when the Internet started to catch on, he set up a site for fellow fat-admirers; it might even have been the first in the UK.

He knew about Fat Mary – her picture had been posted

in a number of places. Feeders took pride in their work, and there was a lot of Mary to be proud of. Most of the feeders were possessive of their gainers, but not the bass player. According to David, Mary had asked the bass player to let her bring customers in once in a while so she could make some money of her own. She said she didn't want to spend his; the bass player apparently found that amusing. So he lent her out to some of the FA network; probably filmed them too. David told me to give him a week and he'd come up with an address and a key. He did. I left a message with the secretary to book me two days' leave.

It's only polite to take a gift when you visit a woman. I took four. I hadn't realized I would be so spoiled for choice in Kentish Town. Since she came along, I had been taking more interest in my immediate environment than I had in years, if ever. I'd even defrosted the fridge. Though I hate to say it, and it's still no excuse, there might have been something in Kate's accusation about my work taking over everything. I bought flowers, of course, then I crossed the road to the bakery and bought her some of those cakes. I swung back over to Poundstretcher, which Lord knows how but I'd never noticed before, and came out of the place with two huge jars of chocolates and, while I was at it, a child's silver shell suit for Dino. The tux definitely neeed a trip to the dry cleaner's.

On the way back home I made another find. A couple of blocks past the station there was a weird old ladies' underwear shop – you'll know it if you've ever seen it. It's like the place that time forgot. The main feature of its window display is an absolutely colossal pair of knickers, almost as big as the window itself. Too small for Mary, though. Still, things might change.

When rush hour was over I picked up Dino and got in the car. I knew precisely when the bass player would be leaving.

Sitting outside on a yellow line, I pretended to examine the A-Z when I saw him come out the door. He walked a few paces to the residential parking bay, aiming a device on his keychain at a gleaming Range Rover. It chirped and he stepped in. I waited another ten minutes after he'd driven off before I got out and walked up the front steps.

Apart from the cars, the street was empty, or as empty as any Central London street can be. I tried the first key in the lock, then the second. Neither seemed to fit. I dropped them, cursing, just as someone walked out of the building next door. He did not so much as look in my direction. When I picked them up and tried again, it worked.

The front door opened into what appeared to be a storage space. Other doors, all unlocked, opened onto rooms crammed with boxes and packing crates. On the left there was a fairly narrow staircase. There must have been a lot less of Mary when she first came here. I climbed the stairs until they stopped at a locked door at the top. The second key opened it without trouble and I stepped inside.

I knew this room so well from watching that DVD over and over. It was as preternaturally clean and tidy as it appeared in the footage. Not so much as a finger smudge on the panelled walls. I spotted the webcams and wondered if they were filming me. I must have considered, subconsciously at least, the possibility, since I knew I was looking pretty good. Kate didn't know what she'd thrown away.

And there was the corridor. I walked along it. I noticed another door off to the side that I didn't remember from the film. I opened it: a large bathroom, also spotless. The mirrors that covered every wall looked like they'd been rubbed harder and more often than a teenager's dick. I walked on to the end of the corridor and pushed open the door.

"Hello, doc," she said. "You got a little something for me?"
I opened my bag.

I didn't feel like going home. Malcolm wouldn't be here until morning, but I just wanted to sit a while, take a load off. My shoes were hurting me so I kicked them off. We left her lying there, she looked so peaceful, and went back into the other room. When I passed by the upright bass I felt a compulsion to give the strings a twang, but I resisted. There was a chair by the window, and we sat there, me and Dino, just listening to the traffic go by. Did I tell you about Malcolm? My memory's been getting fuzzy lately. Maybe it's the temazepam.

Malcolm was a surgeon, another of my patients from the old days. An acrotomophiliac. Though Dino used to argue with me that he was actually an apotemnophiliac by proxy, didn't you, Dino? Either way, Malcolm took a keener than usual interest in amputation and amputees in and out of the hospital. Like I said, I know things about people; it's interesting work. Malcolm is still a surgeon, but it's all private practice now. Gets paid a fortune. His patients love his work. Mary's going to love it too. And the bass player – why can't I remember his name, I'm sure she told me. He's going to look so much better without those fingers. Mary first in the morning, and then the bass player's appointment at two. Shame I didn't think of asking Kate to come along, there's plenty of time. Maybe I should call her. What do you think, Dino? Shall I call Kate? Tell her I've signed the papers and she can come by and pick them up? Tell her I don't need her. That I don't need anyone any more? What do you say, Dino?

Dino's awfully quiet tonight.

PARK RITES

BY DANIEL BENNETT

Clissold Park

The black-haired lady jogger beat her way around the concrete path that circled the western edge of Clissold Park, passing the brick shed near the entrance. Enzo watched her come. He stood in his place by the bushes where the path forked up towards the pond. He'd known she'd be here: it was 4 p.m. and she was always here. The lady jogger had her routines.

She ran towards him, the way she always ran, with her elbows pushed out wide, her head bent to the ground, so she couldn't see anyone in front of her. She ran like she was the only one in the world. Once, when Enzo had been watching, she'd been so far away in her head, she'd jogged right into a woman with a pushchair, fallen over and hurt her knee on the tarmac. Enzo had walked past as she staggered to her feet, a tear in her leggings showing a large gash. She had touched it gently, wincing, while the woman with the pushchair had asked her if she was okay. Enzo had forced himself to keep on walking, his head down, his hand steady in his pocket. But he was unable to resist one quick glance, a theft, thinking to himself, "Yeah, and one day, lady, *I'll* be there."

The jogger made her way onto a stretch of path opposite the estate. She was very close now. Enzo breathed in and smelled the air. He was waiting for a sign that things were ready, that the time was right. The sky was a pale grey above the green of the trees, the air smoky from a fire on the other side of the park, the ground reeking of wet earth. A triangular pattern of geese crossed the sky, and suddenly Enzo knew that this was the final piece that defined the moment: the sign that the time was right. The lady jogger reached the straight track that led right down towards him. Enzo's left hand worked inside the torn pocket of his tracksuit, his hand squeezing his prick. It was time.

Enzo stepped from the bushes as the jogger approached. He felt very calm. He gave himself one more grasp and then removed his left hand, and placed his right into the pocket of his hooded top. The jogger was almost on top of him now, and Enzo could see the words on her blue T-shirt, *University of Kent*, stretched over her small breasts, the black Lycra tight on her legs, her huge white trainers with fat tongues. She was such a *small* woman, she was perfect for him, with her black hair in long bangs that flapped as she ran, like the limp beat of blackbird wings.

Enzo tensed, his right arm ready. Suddenly, on the road beyond the railings, a car pulled up, a blue Ford. Enzo looked up to see a man step from the passenger door, saying loudly, "Yeah, well, maybe later, but I'm not sure about it," to whoever was driving the car. He was wearing a football shirt, red and white. It was all too much for Enzo: he glanced quickly at the woman jogger, thinking maybe, maybe, when the man beyond the railings turned and looked over and stared Enzo fully in the face.

Enzo wasn't scared, but it caused the slightest delay in his movement. It was enough to spoil everything (the birds had gone from his eyeline now and the lady jogger was just a few steps too close) and make the moment lose its rhythm. Enzo let his hand drop from his right pocket. He looked down at the ground, kicked at a stone, sucked his lips against his teeth. The jogger pounded past him, the soles of her trainers squeaking slightly as she took the turn up towards the pond. The man slammed the passenger door shut and stood waving as the car pulled away. The moment had sailed away from Enzo, and it was exactly like that.

"Yeah, but I seen you!" Enzo called out to the jogger's back. "I seen you running, lady. I'll catch you maybe on the next time round."

The jogger didn't hear him. Enzo watched her run up the slight hill that led towards the pond and the white house at the centre of the park. He wondered if today was one of the days she'd decide to run another circuit, or if she would leave by the entrance on Church Street, making her way back through Stoke Newington, through the cemetery. It didn't matter to him anyway. It was spoiled. He put his hand back into his left pocket and squeezed himself a couple more times, his prick sore and hard and hot. But he didn't let himself finish, although he was so close now, he was ready. To finish now would spoil things even more. That wouldn't be right. Instead, he set out walking up the path the jogger was running along, although he wasn't following her now. Instead, he headed over to see the deer.

On the grass by the side of the path, a group of boys were playing football, imitating the game that was going on right now in the Arsenal stadium over on the other side of Blackstock Road. Enzo recognized a few of the kids on the football pitch, a couple from school, a couple from his estate. Almost all of them were wearing the red-and-white shirts. Sometimes on match days like this when Arsenal scored, you could hear the crowd screaming in unison, like a choir. It haunted you, but could thrill you too: make you want to be the one that could make a crowd scream like that. It was what all the boys on the park were imitating, and in his way, it was what Enzo was working towards himself. As he walked in the direction of the deer enclosure, the ball squirmed from the playing field and rolled across the path in front of him, but no one shouted for him to kick it back. Enzo let the ball roll into the gully by the side of the path. It didn't concern him.

Enzo hadn't been back to school since some black kid, some tall Somali, had called him a freak at break, and who knows what *he* had been trying to prove? Enzo had stewed on it for the rest of the day. They met up at the gates after school, and when the Somali kid came towards him, Enzo had sliced a split Coke can across the kid's eyeball, judging it just right. The kid had dropped onto his knees, no time to say anything, not even enough time to put a hand to his eye. He squatted on all fours, staring down at the ground. He couldn't stop himself from blinking and his eyeball parted with a slice that grew wider every time his eyelid flicked over it, yawning into wet blackness. This disappointed Enzo. He'd hoped it would bleed more.

Not much school for Enzo after that run-in: not many calls of freak either. No calls at all. Enzo spent a lot of time alone. He spent most of it in the park, because it was better than being at home. Back there, Ma stayed in the kitchen, Dad on the living room sofa, the Virgin beaming down at everyone from the picture above the TV, Jesus wherever you wanted to go looking for him. That was life back in the flat. But sometimes Ma and Dad didn't stay in separate rooms, and for whatever reason, it was a bit more violent. That was home.

The park was a mess this afternoon. During the week,

London had suffered under record storms, blowing the TV aerials and skylight covers from the roof of Enzo's estate, and shredding the heads of the trees. The grass all around was covered with small branches and twigs, as well as rubbish from the bins. Those storms had made Enzo feel crazy; he'd been able to feel them in his prick, like a pulse. He'd come three times the night the winds had shrieked at his window, telling himself no, no, no, have to save it for the park, have to look out for the lady jogger with the black hair. He'd been unable to hold himself back. And all he saw when he was touching himself were the fangs of a wolf piercing raw red meat, blood on white fur, on teeth.

It didn't take him long to walk around to the deer enclosure, but when he reached it, he found a father and son standing by the rails. A deer stood close by on the other side. The little boy was offering the deer a handful of grass, the father bent low over him, the shape of him spooned around the little boy. Enzo gave the father a look that said, *Yeah, and don't think I don't know what* you'll *be doing when you get the chance.* The man must have seen the way Enzo was staring, and he must have known that Enzo knew, because, you know, Enzo had that power too, he had all kinds of power. Eventually, the man got the message and gathered the little boy up in his arms. "Come on, let's go," he said. "Let's go and find Mum."

The first time he heard there were animals in the park, Enzo had been disappointed when he'd found there were only deer and goats. He wanted wolves. When he was a kid, Ma and Dad had taken him to the zoo. This was not long – a few months – after *that* day. Enzo had seen the wolves at feeding time. He'd watched as they gnawed on raw meat, the blood flicking over the white fur and teeth, and suddenly it all made sense to him. Enzo understood. That night, Enzo pulled himself raw thinking about the wolves. He pulled himself raw, even before anything could happen, thinking of white teeth plunged into red flesh, blood splashed on fur. He pulled himself raw until one night the sperm came, and then he knew he was ready. He rubbed it over his fingers, gummy and warm. Finally he was close. He'd been waiting for years.

Now Enzo was finally alone. He squeezed himself a couple of times before he pulled his left hand away, and again he pushed his right hand into the pocket of his hooded top. He moved close to the fence. The deer raised its head for a moment, surveying him with a large, bland, steady eye, a black ball. If the light changes, Enzo said to himself, I will be in that eye. It will shine and I will be inside the deer. He breathed deeply, quivering as he exhaled. The deer bent its head and nibbled at a patch of grass by the fence. Enzo pulled his right hand from his pocket and flashed it into the flank of the deer, two, three, four times, the knife sliding in like a dream, the metal not catching the light at all. The blood burst from the fur, over the blade, and it was all Enzo could do to hold himself back and not finish right there. The deer brayed and kicked up its back legs, bucked away from the fence, and ran over to the rest of the herd, the wound leaking into the grey fur on its side. If I could just go *there*, Enzo thought, if I could just finish in there it would end everything, I know it. He stayed, despite himself, despite everything he had to get busy with, he stayed staring at that hole in the flank of the deer until it trotted behind a fallen log and disappeared from his sight.

Enzo started walking away from the enclosure quickly, and once he was far enough away, he broke into a run. He headed across the concrete in front of the bandstand, skater punks practising moves, kids spinning around on bikes. He ran down beyond the pond, to the hedges that lined the northern edge of the park, bordering on a stretch of white houses. Every step that Enzo took made his prick bounce against his tracksuit bottoms, bounce dangerously. The bloody knife was hot in his hand. Enzo dashed around a wooden bench facing the duck pond and pushed himself between a green-barked ash tree and the hedge. He was careful, even though it was the last thing he felt like being. He checked the road behind the hedge first, and the path leading down by the pond. No one was approaching.

He fell down on his knees and rested his head against the bark of the tree, his cheek bitten by the weight of his body. The wood smelled green and bitter. (*That day, a man wearing a hooded parka dragged him into a small copse, pushed him up against a tree.*) Enzo touched the bark with his tongue, the way he had the first time, tasted the bitter green against his lips, flakes of it dirty on his teeth. (*"You keep it quiet now, you keep your mouth tight and shut or I'll open your throat."*) Enzo screwed up his eyes tight and closed his lips, his left hand moving to his pocket. (*And the fur on the man's hood brushing against the back of his neck as he pushed into him.*) His eyes were screwed tight, his mouth closed, the way he'd been told to keep it, his breath whistling down his nostrils. (*And the feel of the man inside him, pushing against his insides, stretching and pushing, an ache that seemed to rise up through his guts, out of his mouth.*) Enzo hardly had to touch his prick to come, it lashed out into his palms, a hot slap that seemed to explode from behind his eyes. (*"You turn round, I'm gonna come and get you, cut your throat. Do you understand?"*) He stayed for a moment, breathing through his nose, his cheek bitten by the green wood. He opened his eyes. That first time, he'd seen a couple of birds beating steadily in the sky. This time, there was nothing but a cloud.

He sat back on his heels and gently, carefully, pulled his left hand from his pocket and his right from his hooded top. Both palms were wet: the left with the white of his sperm, the right with the red of congealing blood. He looked down at them for a moment, feeling the power of what lay in his hands, all of birth and life right there for him to hold. He saw the red and white of the boys at Mass and the football strip of the boys in the park. He saw the white of the wolf's teeth in the flesh. He weighed them in his hands and then slowly squeezed them together. He looked once more at his palms, and the white lay on the red like a blister, a pinkish tinge in the place where they had mixed. Life was this colour. It caused things to be born.

That day, when the man had gone, Enzo had reached behind him to touch where he'd been hurt, and his hand had come back covered with the white and the red. He'd wiped his hands in the earth to bury it. Now, he bent down to the ground and wiped his palms over the dirt at the base of the tree. He pushed his hands hard into the mud, his fingers clawed at the earth, coming up black under the nails. He tried to bury it again, but this time he was planting it in the earth of the park, making it grow.

Enzo sat back, breathing heavily. The mud was caked onto his hands. Beyond the pond, the routine of the park was continuing. The boys were still playing football. Dogs chased the cyclists. A kite of red silk throbbed in the sky. Enzo watched it, thinking how good it would have been if he'd been able to open his eyes to this afterwards, how it would have been almost perfect. It had become his place now, this park, he ruled it like a kingdom. It didn't matter that it wasn't this park where it had happened, that first time. It didn't matter that Enzo didn't really know where he'd been, that it was all in pieces, all sharp and bright in his head, like the upturned broken bottles they cemented into the walls to stop the kids climbing over. It didn't matter that Enzo didn't really understand the ritual of it. All he knew was that he had to do this, and keep on doing it, because if he fed the land with the red and the white, then maybe he'd grow stronger and one day *he* would be the wolf.

Later, Enzo walked around to cross the stream and head back over Church Street, back home. He passed the aviary as he crossed the bridge by the side of the house, and another lady jogger came pounding towards him, her blonde hair wound up tight on her head. Enzo didn't even look at her, but the birds started shrieking in their cage. Enzo smiled. The birds knew that he was close to them. They knew what was about to come.

A tree had blown down. It had fallen over from the churchyard at the back of the park, bringing with it a section of the cemetery wall. Enzo stopped for a moment and looked down at the top of the tree, the leaves and shoots and buds. He felt like only a god could, seeing the tree like that, he felt like a giant. One day, he knew, it wouldn't be the storm that would blow down the trees. Enzo would tear through the city like a wolf, a great white creature the size of a storm. Trees and houses would fall in front of him, and all the people would scream, a great noise rising towards him like a choir. And they would feel his breath upon them, and it would burn with the heat of the red, it would stink with the heat of the white.

TROUBLE IS A LONESOME TOWN

BY CATHI UNSWORTH

King's Cross

Dougie arrived at the concourse opposite the station just half an hour after it had all gone off. He'd had the cab driver drop him down the end of Gray's Inn Road, outside a pub on the corner there, where he'd made a quick dive into the gents to remove the red hood he'd been wearing over the black one, pulled on a Burberry cap he'd had in his bag so that the visor was down over his eyes. That done, he'd worked his way through the mass of drinkers, ducked out another door, and walked the rest of the way to King's Cross.

The Adidas bag he gripped in his right hand held at least twenty grand in cash. Dougie kind of wished it was hand-cuffed to him, so paranoid was he about letting go of it even for a second that he'd had trouble just putting it on the floor of the taxi between his feet. He'd wanted it to be on his knee, in his arms, more precious than a baby. But Dougie knew that above all else now, he had to look calm, unperturbed. Not like a man who'd just ripped off a clip joint and left a man for dead on a Soho pavement.

That's why he'd had the idea of making the rendezvous at the Scottish restaurant across the road from the station. He'd just blend in with the other travellers waiting for their train back up north, toting their heavy bags, staring at the

TV with blank, gormless expressions as they pushed stringy fries smothered in luminous ketchup into their constantly moving mouths. The way he was dressed now, like some hood rat, council estate born and bred, he'd have no trouble passing amongst them.

He ordered his quarter-pounder and large fries, with a supersize chocolate lard shake to wash it all down, eyes wandering around the harshly lit room as he waited for it all to land on his red plastic tray. All the stereotypes were present and correct. The fat family (minus Dad, natch) sitting by the window, mother and two daughters virtually indistinguishable under the layers of flab and identical black-and-white hairstyles by Chavettes of Tyneside to match the colours of their footie team. The solitary male, a lad of maybe ten years and fifteen stone, staring sullenly out the window through pinhole eyes, sucking on the straw of a soft drink that was only giving him back rattling ice cubes. On the back of his shirt read his dreams: 9 SHEARER. But he was already closer to football than footballer.

Then there was the pimp and his crack whore; a thin black man sat opposite an even thinner white woman with bruises on her legs and worn-down heels on her boots. Her head bowed like she was on the nod, while he, all angles and elbows and knees protruding from his slack jeans and oversize Chicago Bulls shirt, kept up a steady monologue of abuse directed at her curly head. The man's eyes where as rheumy as a seventy-year-old's, and he sprayed fragments of his masticated fries out as he kept on his litany of insults. Sadly for Iceberg Slim, it looked like the motherfuckingbitchhocuntcocksucker he was railing at had already given up the ghost.

Oblivious to the psychodrama, the Toon Army had half of the room to themselves, singing and punching the air, reliving moment by moment the two goals they'd scored over Spurs – well, thank fuck they had, wouldn't like to see this lot disappointed. They were vile enough in victory, hugging and clasping at each other with tears in their eyes, stupid joker's hats askew over their gleaming red faces, they might as well have been bumming each other, which was obviously what they all wanted.

Yeah, Dougie liked to get down among the filth every now and again, have a good wallow. In picking over the faults of others, he could forget about the million and one he had of his own.

Handing over a fiver to the ashen bloke behind the counter, who had come over here thinking nothing could be worse than Romania, Dougie collected his change and parked himself inconspicuously in the corner. Someone had left a copy of the *Scum* on his table. It was a bit grubby and he really would have preferred to use surgical gloves to touch it, but it went so perfectly with his disguise and the general ambience of the joint that he forced himself. Not before he had the bag firmly wedged between his feet, however, one of the handles round his ankle so if anyone even dared to try . . .

Dougie shook his head and busied himself instead by arranging the food on his plastic tray in a manner he found pleasing: the fries tipped out of their cardboard wallet into the half of the Styrofoam container that didn't have his burger in it. He opened the ketchup so that he could dip them in two at a time, between mouthfuls of burger and sips of chocolate shake. He liked to do everything methodically.

Under the headline "STITCHED UP", the front page of the *Scum* was tirelessly defending the good character of the latest batch of rapist footballers who'd all fucked one girl between the entire team and any of their mates who fancied it. Just so they could all check out each other's dicks while they did it, Dougie reckoned. That sort of shit turned his stomach almost as much as the paper it was printed on, so he quickly flipped the linen over, turned to the racing pages at the back. That would keep his mind from wandering, reading all those odds, totting them up in his head, remembering what names went with what weights and whose colours. All he had to do now was sit tight and wait. Wait for Lola.

Lola.

Just thinking about her name got his fingertips moist, got little beads of sweat breaking out on the back of his neck. Got a stirring in his baggy sweatsuit trousers so that he had to look up sharply and fill his eyes with a fat daughter chewing fries with her mouth open to get it back down again.

Women didn't often have this effect on Dougie. Only two, so far, in his life. And he'd gone further down the road with this one than anyone else before.

He could still remember the shock he felt when he first saw her, when she sat herself down next to him at the bar with a tired sigh and asked for a whisky and soda. He caught the slight inflection in her accent, as if English wasn't her first language, but her face was turned away from him. A mass of golden-brown curls bobbed on top of her shoulders, she had on a cropped leopardskin jacket and hipster jeans, a pair of pointy heels protruding from the bottom, wound around the stem of the bar stool. The skin on her feet was golden-brown too; mixed-race she must have been, and for a minute Dougie thought he knew what she would look like before she turned her head, somewhere between Scary Spice and that bird off *Holby City*. An open face, pretty and a bit petulant. Maybe some freckles over the bridge of her nose.

But when she did turn to him, cigarette dangling between her lips and long fingers wound around the short, thick glass of amber liquid, she looked nothing so trite as "pretty".

Emerald-green eyes fixed him from under deep lids, fringed with the longest dark lashes he had ever seen. Her skin was flawless, the colour of the whisky in her glass, radiating that same intoxicating glow.

For a second he was taken back to a room in Edinburgh a long time ago. An art student's room, full of draped scarves and fake Tiffany lamps and a picture on the wall of Marlene Dietrich in *The Blue Angel*. This woman looked strangely like Marlene. Marlene with an afro. *Black Angel*.

She took the cigarette from between her red lips and asked: "Could you give me a light?" Her glittering eyes held his brown ones in a steady gaze, a smile flickered over her perfect lips.

Dougie fumbled in the sleeve of his jacket for his Zippo and fired it up with shaking fingers. Black Angel inhaled deeply, closing her bronze-coloured eyelids as she sucked that good smoke down, blowing it out again in a steady stream.

Her long lashes rose and she lifted her glass to him simultaneously.

"Cheers!" she said, and he caught that heavy inflection again. Was he going mad, or did she even sound like Marlene too? "Ach," she tossed back her mane of curls, "it's so good to be off vork!"

"I'll drink to that," Dougie said, feeling like his tongue was too big for his head, his fingers too big for his hands, that he was entirely too big and clumsy. He slugged down half his bottle of Becks to try and get some kind of equilibrium, stop this weird teenage feeling that threatened to paralyse him under the spell of those green eyes.

She looked amused.

"What kind of vork do you do?" she asked.

Dougie gave his standard reply. "Och, you know. This an' that."

It pleased her, this answer, so she continued to talk. Told him in that smoky, laconic drawl all about the place she worked. One of the clip joints off Old Compton Street, the ones specifically geared up to rip off the day-trippers.

"It izz called Venus in Furs," she told him. "Is fucking tacky shit, yeah?"

He started to wonder if she was Croatian, or Serbian. Most of the girls pouring into Soho now were supposed to be ones kidnapped from the former Yugoslavia. *Slavic* was a word that suited the contours of her cheeks, the curve of her green eyes. But how could that be? Dougie didn't think there was much of a black population in Eastern Europe. And he couldn't imagine anyone having the balls to kidnap this one. Maybe she was here for a different reason. Images raced through his mind. Spy films, Checkpoint Charlie, the Cold War. High on her accent, he didn't really take the actual words in.

Until at some point close to dawn, she lifted a finger and delicately traced the outline of his jaw. "I like you, Dougie." She smiled. "I vill see you here again, yes?"

Dougie wasn't really one for hanging out in drinking clubs. He was only in this one because earlier that evening he'd had to have a meet in Soho and he couldn't stand any of the pubs round there. Too full, too noisy, too obvious. This was one of the better places. Discreet, old-fashioned, not really the sort of place your younger generation would go for, it was mainly populated by decaying actors skulking in a dimly lit world of memory. It was an old luvvie who'd first shown him the place. An old luvvie friend of a friend who'd been ripped off for all his Queen Anne silver and a collection of Penny Blacks by the mercenary young man he'd been silly enough to invite back for a nightcap. Dougie had at least got the silver back, while the guy was sleeping off what he'd spent the proceeds of the stamps on. He really didn't come here often, but as he watched the woman slip off her stool and shrug on her furry jacket, he felt a sudden pang and asked, "Wait a minute – what's your name?"

She smiled and said: "It's Lola. See you again, honey." And then she was gone.

Dougie found himself drifting back to the club the next evening.

It was weird, because he'd kept to himself for so long he felt like his heart was a hard, cold stone that no one could melt. It was best, he had long ago told himself, not to form attachments in his line of work. Attachments could trip you up. Attachments could bring you down. It was better that no one knew him outside his small circle of professional contacts and the clients they brought. Safer that way. He'd done six months' time as a teenager, when he was stupid and reckless, and had vowed he'd never be caught that way again.

He was mulling over all these facts as he found himself sitting at the bar. He didn't quite know what he thought he was doing there, just that he felt his heart go each time the buzzer went and a new group of people clattered down the steps. Lola had come into the place alone. He supposed he could ask the guvnor what he knew about her, but that didn't seem very gentlemanly. After all, he wasn't a regular himself, who knew how long she'd been making her way down here after the grind of an evening "huzzling the schmucks" under Venus's neon underskirts?

At half past one she had wound her way down the stairs towards him. A smile already twitching at the corners of her mouth, she was pleased to see him. One look up her long, bare, perfect legs to her leather miniskirt and that same leopardskin jacket and he felt the same.

"Hel-*looo*, Dougie," she said.

Dougie felt drunk, as he had ever since.

Gradually, over whisky and sodas with the ice crinkling in the glass, she'd told him her story. It was all very intriguing. Her father was Russian, she said, ex-KGB, who since the fall of communism had managed to create an empire for himself in electronic goods. He was a thug, but a charming one – he had named her after a character in a Raymond Chandler book that he'd read, contraband, as a teenager.

They had a lot of money, but he was very strict. Made her study hard and never go out. There was not a lot of emotion between him and her mother.

Her mother was an oddity, a Somalian. Lola didn't know how they met, but she suspected. Back in the old days, it was quite possible her father had bought her out of semi-slavery in a Moscow brothel. Her mother always claimed she was a princess, but she was also a drunk, so what was Lola to believe? She was beautiful, that was for sure. Beautiful and superstitious, always playing with a deck of strange cards and consulting patterns in tea leaves. She might have mastered dark arts, but never managed to speak Russian – probably she never wanted to. So Lola grew up speaking two languages, in one big, empty apartment in Moscow.

Right now, she was supposed to be in Switzerland. She

looked embarrassed when she told Dougie this. "At finishing school. Can you believe? Vot a cliché." Lola had done a bunk six months ago. She'd crossed Europe, taking cash-in-hand work as she did, determined to get to London. She wanted to escape while she was in the "free West" rather than go back to what she knew would be expected of her in Russia. Marriage to some thick bastard son of one of her father's ex-comrades. A life of looking nice and shutting up, just like her mother.

But she feared her father's arm was long. There were too many Russians in London already. Someone was bound to rat her out, the reward money would be considerable. So she had to get together a "travelling fund" and find somewhere else to go. Somewhere safe.

"Vere are you from, Dougie?" she purred. "Not from round here, eh?"

"What do you reckon?" he said archly. "Where d'you think I got a name like Dougie from, heh?"

Lola laughed, put her finger on the end of his nose.

"You are from Scotland, yes?"

"Aye," nodded Dougie.

"Where in Scotland?"

"Edinburgh."

"Vot's it like in Edinburgh?"

A warning voice in Dougie's head told him not to even give her that much. This story she had spun for him, it sounded too much like a fairy tale. She was probably some down-on-her-luck Balkans hooker looking for a sugar daddy. No one could have had the lifestyle she described. It was too far-fetched, too mental.

The touch of her finger stayed on the end of his nose. Her green eyes glittered under the optics. Before Dougie knew what he was doing, words were coming out of his mouth.

She had given him the germ of an idea. The rest he filled in for himself.

Venus in Furs was not run by an established firm, even by Soho standards. Its ostensible owners were a bunch of chancy Jamaican wide boys whose speciality was taking over moody drinking dens by scaring the incumbents into thinking that they were Yardies. Dougie doubted that was the case. They could have been minor players, vaguely connected somehow, but Yardie lands were south of the river. Triads and micks ran Soho. He doubted these fellas would last long in the scheme of things anyway, so he decided to help Lola out and give fate a hand.

Trying to help her, or trying to impress her?

It helped that her shifts were regular. Six nights a week, six till twelve. Plenty of time to observe who came and went on a routine basis. Maybe her old man really was KGB cos she'd already worked out that the day that the Suit came in would be the significant one.

There was this office, behind the bar, where they did all their business. Three guys worked the club in a rotation, always two of them there at the same time. Lynton, Neville and Little Stevie. They had a fondness for Lola, her being blood, so it was usually her they asked to bring drinks through when they had someone to impress in there. She said the room had been painted out with palm trees and a sunset, like one big Hawaiian scene.

Like everyone, Dougie thought, *playing at gangsters — they're playing* Scarface.

Once a week, a bald white guy in a dowdy brown suit

came in with an attaché case. Whichever of the Brothers Grimm were in at the time would make themselves scarce while he busied himself in the office for half an hour. One of them would hang at the bar, the other find himself a dark corner with one of the girls. Then the bald man would come out, speak to no one and make his own way out of the club.

Every Thursday, 8 p.m., punctual as clockwork he came.

That proved it to Dougie. The lairy Jamaicans were a front to terrify the public. The bald man collected the money for their unseen offshore master. With his crappy suit and unassuming exterior, he was deliberately done up like a mark to blend in with the rest of the clientele.

Dougie had a couple of guys that owed him favours. They weren't known faces, and it would be difficult to trace them back to him – their paths crossed infrequently and they moved in different worlds. On two successive Thursdays, he gave them some folding and sent them in as marks. They confirmed Lola's story and gave him more interesting background on the Brothers Grimm. Both weeks, it was the same pair, Steve and Neville, little and large. Large Neville, a tall skinny guy with swinging dreads and shades who was always chewing on a toothpick, sat behind the bar when the bald man showed up. He practised dealing cards, played patience, drank beer and feigned indifference to the world around him, nodding all the while as if a different slow-skanking soundtrack was playing in his head – not the cheesy Europop on the club's PA.

Little Stevie, by comparison, always grabbed himself a girl and a bottle and made his way over to the corner booth. While Neville looked like a classic stoner, Little Stevie was mean. He wore a black suit and a white shirt, with thick gold chains around his bulldog neck. A porkpie hat and thick black shades totally obscured his eyes. Occasionally, like when the girl slipped underneath the table, he would grin a dazzling display of gold and diamond dental work. Neville always drank proper champagne – not the pear fizz served to the punters as such – and both Dougie's contacts copped the telltale bulge in his pocket.

Neville's booth was the one from which the whole room could be surveyed, and even while receiving special favours, he never took his eye off the game. The minute the office door clicked open and the bald man slipped away, he would knee his girl off him, adjust his balls and whatever else was down there, and swagger his way back over to the office all puffed-up and bristling, Neville following at his heels.

Yeah, Stevie, they all agreed, was the one to watch.

While they were in there playing punters, Dougie was watching the door.

The Venus was based in a handy spot, in a dingy alley between Rupert Street and Wardour Street. There was a market on Rupert and all he had to do was pretend to be examining the tourist tat on the corner stall. The bald man went the other way. Straight to a waiting cab on Wardour. Each time the same.

On the night it all happened, Dougie felt a rush in his blood that he hadn't felt since Edinburgh, like every platelet was singing to him the old songs, high and wild as the wind.

God, he used to love that feeling, used to let it guide him in the days when he was *Dougie the Cat*, the greatest burglar in that magical city of turrets and towers.

But now he was Dougie Investigates, the private eye for the sort of people who couldn't go to the police. He had changed sides on purpose after that first prison jolt, never wanting to be in close proximity to such fucking filth ever again. If you couldn't be a gentleman thief these days, he reckoned, then why not be a Bad Guys' PI? His methods may have differed from those used by the Old Bill, but Dougie had kept his nose clean for eighteen years, built up his reputation by word of mouth, and made a good living from sorting out shit without causing any fuss. Filled a proper gap in the market, he had.

His blood had never sung to him in all that time. He supposed it must have awakened in him that first night he met Lola, grown strong that night she'd finally allowed him back to her dingy flat above a bookie's in Balham, where she had so studiously drawn out the map of the Venus's interior before unzipping his trousers and taking him to a place that seemed very close to heaven.

Bless her, he didn't need her map. He didn't even need to know what Neville and Stevie got up to, only that they were good little gangsters and stayed where they were, in that little palace of their imagination where they could be Tony Montana every day.

He wasn't going to take them on.

All he needed was the thirty seconds between the Venus's door and Wardour Street. And the curve in the alley that meant the taxi driver wouldn't be able to see. All he needed was the strength of his arm and the fleetness of his feet and the confusion of bodies packed into a Soho night.

At the end of the alley he slipped a balaclava over his head, put the blue hood over the top of that, and began to run.

He was at full sprint as the bald man came out of the door, fast enough to send him flying when he bowled into his shoulder. The man's arms spread out and he dropped his precious cargo to the floor. Dougie was just quick enough to catch the look of astonishment in the pale, watery eyes, before he coshed him hard on the top of his head and they rolled up into whites. He had another second to stoop and retrieve the case before he was off again, out of the alley, across Wardour Street, where the taxi was waiting, its engine running, the driver staring straight ahead.

Dougie was already in the downstairs bogs of the Spice of Life before the cabbie was checking his watch to make sure he hadn't turned up early. Had pulled out his sports bag from the cistern where he'd stashed it and busted the lock on the attaché case by the time the cabbie turned the engine off and stepped out of the car to take a look around. Dougie's deftness of touch was undiminished by his years on the other side. He counted the bundles of cash roughly as he transferred them into his sports bag, eyebrows rising as he did. It was quite a haul for a weekly skim off a clip joint. He briefly wondered what else they had going on down there, then chased the thought away as excess trouble he didn't need to know.

By the time the cabbie was standing over the crumpled heap in the alleyway, he had put the attaché case in the cistern and taken off the blue hood, rolling it into a ball when he nipped out the side door of the pub. He junked it in a bin as he came out onto Charing Cross Road and hailed himself a ride up to King's Cross.

Dougie looked up from his racing pages. As if struck by electrodes, he knew Lola was in the room. She walked towards him, green eyes dancing, clocking amusedly his stupid cap and the bag that lay between his feet. Sat down in front of him and breathed, "Is it enough?"

"Aye," nodded Dougie. "It's enough."

He hadn't wanted there to be any way in which Lola could be implicated in all this. He'd had her phone in sick for two days running, told her just to spend her time packing only the essentials she needed, and gave her the money for two singles up to Edinburgh.

The night train back to the magic city, not even the Toon Army could ruin that pleasure for him.

"You ready?" he asked her.

Her grin stretched languidly across her perfect face.

"Yes," she purred. "I'm ready."

Dougie gripped the Adidas bag, left his floppy fries where they lay.

As they stepped out onto the road, St. Pancras was lit up like a fairy-tale castle in front of them. "See that," he nudged her shoulder, "that's bollocks compared to where we're going."

His heart and his soul sang along with his blood. He was leaving the Big Smoke, leaving his life of shadows, stepping into a better world with the woman he loved by his side. He took her hand and strode towards the crossing, towards the mouth of King's Cross Station.

Then Lola said: "Oooh, hang on a minute. I have to get my bag."

"You what?" Dougie was confused. "Don't you have it with you?"

She laughed, a low tinkling sound. "No, honey, I left it just around the corner. My friend, you know, she runs a bar there and I didn't want to lug it around with me all day. She's kept it safe for me, behind the bar. Don't vorry, it von't take a minute."

Dougie was puzzled. He hadn't heard about this friend or this bar before. But in his limited experience of women, this was typical. Just when you thought you had a plan, they'd make some little amendment. He guessed that was just the way their minds worked.

She leaned to kiss his cheek and whispered in his ear: "Ve still have half an hour before the train goes."

The pub was, literally, around the corner. One of those horrible, bland chain brewery joints heaving with overweight office workers trying to get lucky with their sniggering secretaries in the last desperate minutes before closing time.

He lingered by the door as Lola hailed the bored-looking blonde bartender. Watched her take a small blue suitcase from behind the bar, kiss the barmaid on each cheek, and come smilingly back towards him.

A few seconds before she reached him, her smile turned to a mask of fear.

"Oh shit," she said, grabbing hold of his arm and dragging him away from the doorway. "It's fucking Stevie."

"What?"

"This vay." She had his arm firmly in her grasp now, was propelling him through to the other side of the bar, towards the door marked *Toilets*, cursing and talking a million miles an hour under her breath.

"Stevie was standing right outside the door. I svear to God it was him. I told you, he is bad luck that one, he's voodoo, got a sixth sense – my mama told me about *sheiit* like him. Ve can't let him see us! I'm supposed to be off sick, the night he gets ripped off – he's gonna know! He's gonna kill me if he sees me."

"Hen, you're seeing things," Dougie tried to protest as she pushed him through the door, down some steps into a dank basement that smelled of piss and stale vomit.

"I'm not! It vos him, it vos him!" She looked like she was

about to turn hysterical, her eyes were flashing wildly and her nails were digging into his flesh. He tried to use his free hand to extricate himself from her iron grip, but that only served to make her cling on harder.

"Hen, calm down, you're hurting me . . ." Dougie began.

"There's someone coming!" she screamed, and suddenly began to kiss him passionately, smothering him in her arms, grinding her teeth against his lips so that he tasted blood.

And then he heard a noise right behind him.

And the room went black.

"Fucking hell." Lola looked down on Dougie's prone body. "That took long enough."

"I told you he was good," her companion pouted, brushing his hands on his trousers. "But I thought you'd enjoy using all your skills on him."

"Hmm." Lola bent down and pried Dougie's fingers away from the Adidas bag. "I knew this would be the hardest part. Getting money out of a tight fucking jock."

The slinky Russian accent had disappeared like a puff of smoke. She sounded more like a petulant queen.

"Come on." She stepped over her would-be Romeo and the pile of shattered ashtray glass he lay in. "Let's get out of here."

The car was parked near by. As Lola got into the passenger seat, she pulled the honey-gold Afro wig off her head and ran her fingers through the short black fuzz underneath.

"I am *soooo* tired of that bitch," she said, tossing it on the back seat.

Her companion started the car with a chuckle.

"He fucking believed everything, didn't he?" He shook his head as he pulled out.

"Yeah . . . and you said he was a private detective. Well, let me tell you, honey, you wouldn't believe what I suckered that dick with. My dad was a Russian gangster. My mother was a Somalian princess. I was on the run from Swiss finishing school. Can you believe it?"

Lola hooted with derision. "Almost like the fairy tales I used to make up for myself," she added. "You know, I thought he might fucking twig when I told him I was named after a character in a Raymond Chandler novel. But I couldn't resist it."

"Well," her companion smiled at her fondly, "you certainly made up for the loss of that Queen Anne silver. We've got enough to keep us going for months now. So where do you fancy?"

"Not back to Soho," Lola sniffed, as the car pulled into the slipstream of Marylebone Road. "I've fucking had it with those poseur thugs. I know. I fancy some sea air. How does Brighton sound to you?"

"The perfect place," her companion agreed, "for a couple of actors."

Dougie came around with his face stuck to a cold stone floor with his own blood. Shards of glass covered him. He could smell the acrid stench of piss in his nostrils, and from the pub above he could hear a tune, sounding like it was coming from out of a long tunnel of memory. He could just make out the lyrics:

"*I met her in a club down in old Soho/Where you drink champagne and it tastes just like cherry cola . . .*"

CHELSEA THREE, SCOTLAND YARD NIL

BY MAX DÉCHARNÉ

King's Road

Chelsea, July 1977.

They found him in the pedestrian underpass beneath the northern end of the Albert Bridge, a short walk down Oakley Street from the King's Road. He'd obviously been given a thorough kicking, and there was an orange shoved in his mouth, completely blocking the passage of air. Tied up like something in a butcher-shop window.

Didn't look like he was bothered, though. He'd been dead for a good few hours already.

There wasn't much about it in the local papers, but you could tell the police thought they were onto something. They'd been seen nosing around at Seditionaries the following afternoon, flicking through the racks, checking out the *Cambridge Rapist* T-shirts, clutching copies of the *NME* as if they were going to stumble over a clue in among the usual snarky jokes and record reviews. Who knows, maybe they thought they had, because there they were again later that day, looking very out of place at the rear of the spiky-haired crowd in the Man in the Moon watching Adam and the Ants.

Nosed around. Asked a few questions. Lowered the tone of the place. Something about bondage. Yeah, well, officer, what can I tell you? There's a lot of it about . . .

Didn't look like the gig was their kind of scene. They left halfway through the headliner, X-Ray Spex.

The following Saturday it was hot as hell. Usual collection of punky scufflers hanging around outside Town Records. Watching the passers-by. Opening cans. Wandering off to check out the stalls at Beaufort Street Market. Keeping an eye out for the Teds or the Stamford Bridge boys. Regular King's Road scene that summer, ever since the Jubilee violence had flared up – *Punk Rock Rotten Razored*, all the tabloid column inches stoking the flames. "Pretty Vacant" was heading up the charts while "God Save the Queen" was just on its way down, but Boney M and ELP were both in the top ten, and the papers were saying that Warner Brothers had just issued a single featuring a group made up of the *Sun*'s page three girls. Finger on the pulse, as always . . .

Davis got out of the tube at Sloane Square, picked up a copy of the *Standard* at the stall outside, and headed up past Smiths in the direction of the Chelsea Potter for a lunchtime pint. No word on that stiff they'd found the other week at the Albert Bridge, but now some posh woman had been discovered smothered to death in her bed in Cheyne Walk, just a few hundred feet away from the site of the last killing. Done in with a pillow. *Police are refusing to comment on possible lines of enquiry.* Yeah, sure. Unconfirmed reports of a message of some kind pinned to the body.

Davis looked out from his window seat and watched the nervous out-of-town kids heading for Boy a few doors away, heads down, expecting trouble.

Two killings in as many weeks. Not unusual for the Lower East Side, but this was Chelsea.

He rolled up the *Standard* and put it in his pocket, digging out the tatty copy of the *NME* he'd been dragging around for the past couple of days. Front page headline all about violence in the punk scene: *This* Definitely *Ain't the Summer of Love*. Turned to page forty-six and scanned the gig guide, looking for likely shows. Nothing much doing tonight. Pub-rock no-hopers in most of the clubs. Monday looked better – Banshees/Slits/Ants at the Vortex, or Poly Styrene's lot on Tuesday at the Railway in Putney. All good research material. Getting an article together on the upcoming rash of punk films currently in the planning stages. Russ Meyer farting about in Scotland with the Pistols, trying to get *Who Killed Bambi* off the ground. Derek Jarman rounding up his mates for something called *Jubilee*. Then there was the bloke who'd put some money into the last Python film and was now backing a disaster-in-the-making called *Punk Rock Rules OK*.

"Get out there and see what's happening," said his editor. Five thousand words on the punk film scene. Throw in a sidebar about Don Letts's 8mm footage they'll be showing at the ICA. Have a look round the clubs. Keep your eyes open. Nice little feature with a few shots of some of these punkettes in fishnet stockings and ripped T-shirts. Play up the punch-ups with the Teddy Boys as well. Sex and violence. *Must we fling this filth at our kids? Blah, blah, blah* . . . Get a quote from that GLC nutter, Brooke-Partridge, the one who reckons most punk rockers would be improved by sudden death. *Is this the future of the British film industry?* The usual bollocks, you know the form . . .

So there he was, knocking back a few pints in the Chelsea Potter, waiting to interview some idiot who claimed to be getting a script together about punk, but whom none of the bands or the managers on the scene that he'd spoken to had ever heard of. Probably a wasted afternoon, but what the hell. Even if the guy turned out to be a complete dingbat, he might provide some comic relief. A few stupid quotes. Ten years of interviewing some of the "giants" of European cinema for the magazine and listening to all their pompous arty bull-shit had taken its toll. Egomaniacs, the fucking lot of them. Fellini's 8, Fellini's *Roma*, Fellini's talking out of his arse . . . Give him an out-and-out chancer or a total loser any day of the week. At least they might be funny.

In any event, the guy was a no-show. Two hours late and nothing doing, he was three pints down and had read both papers cover to cover, winding up back at that murder report in the *Standard*. Smothered to death some time yesterday? Let's check out the scene. Mildly pissed but coherent, he pushed through the door and headed west along the King's Road. Turned left at Oakley Street, down past Scott's old house, with someone playing *Unicorn* by Tyrannosaurus Rex out of an upstairs window near by, then round the corner to where Rossetti had kept wombats and peacocks in his Cheyne Walk back garden a decade before they even built the Albert Bridge.

Bored-looking copper on guard outside, bolting the door after half of Aintree had scarpered. Davis dug through his wallet and pulled out the press card he hardly ever used, knowing full well that it meant damn-all to most people. Still, you never knew.

"Afternoon, officer . . . Nothing much left to see, eh?" Offered the copper a fag but he turned it down. "Heard there was a note pinned to the body . . ."

"That's right. Not that it helps much."

"Guess he's hardly likely to have left his home phone number . . ."

"Sounded like a quote from a book or something."

"Oh yes?"

"They'll be putting out a statement this afternoon, so there's no harm in saying . . ."

"Saw it, did you?"

"Some people think little girls should be seen and not heard . . ."

July 21. Hadn't been a bad week. He'd seen the Only Ones at the Speakeasy on the Saturday. The Adverts and 999 at the Nashville on Monday, then that new bunch of Australians, the Saints, down in Twickenham at the Winning Post. Talked to a lot of people – punters, groups, managers. Bernie Rhodes refusing to let him talk to the Clash. Miles Copeland trying to convince him that some desperate bunch of ageing hippies calling themselves the Police were actually a punk band. Same old story. He'd also gone back to Chelsea again, to the Royal Court this time. Alberto y Los Trios Paranoias and their punk rock musical *Sleak!* with the annoying bloody exclamation mark on the end. The coppers were still sniffing around the scene, chasing some supposed connection with the two murders. As if killers are so eager to be caught they go around leaving clues, just like in the films.

Davis was wandering up the King's Road with a photographer in tow, looking for likely faces in the right gear who could help decorate the article. Fishnet stockings, the man wanted. Ripped T-shirts. Okay, then. Sure, they'd already been down to the Roxy, but that was full of tourists – not like in Czezowski's day back in the spring. Ever since the Roxy live album had come out a few weeks back, you couldn't move down there for bandwagon-jumpers. Mind you, if today was any indication, the King's Road was suffering from the same disease. It was like a lot of people had been telling him at shows all week: half the real punks had already bailed out of the scene, and the plastics were moving in. Still, the editor wanted photographs . . .

Saw a couple of likely-looking prospects outside the Chelsea Drugstore, on the corner where Royal Avenue met the King's Road. Bought them a can of beer, slipped them a quid each, and they said it was cool to photograph them for ten minutes or so. Davis let them get on with it and wandered off a few yards away to sit in the sun. Before you knew it, more police, uptight about the camera.

Asking for ID. Getting aggressive. The photographer couldn't see what the fuss was about. Wasn't as if she was the first person trying to get some shots of punks on the King's Road that summer. Turned out it wasn't that at all. They'd found another body. Right there on Royal Avenue, early that morning. Milkman practically tripped over it.

When he came over to see what the fuss was about, Davis noticed that it was the same policeman he'd talked to outside the Cheyne Walk house.

"Aren't you the press man who was asking me questions about the previous murder?" said the copper.

He admitted that he was. Somehow, being seen taking photos a few yards away from the latest crime scene started the constable's antenna twitching. Davis agreed that he had a few minutes spare in which to come along and talk to the detective sergeant.

"Bit of a coincidence, isn't it? What's your interest in all this?"

"In the first one, pure curiosity. I'm a journalist. I read about it in the paper. I was round the corner having a drink. Thought I'd take a look."

"And today?"

"Shooting pictures of punks for a feature I'm writing. It's for a film magazine. They want coverage of some upcoming punk movies. I've been going around checking out the scene."

The sergeant thought about that for a while.

"So would you describe yourself as an expert on this type of music?"

"Not an expert, no. I'm way too old for this. Most of the punters are about sixteen. But I've been at a lot of the shows these past couple of months. Talked to some of the bands involved. Research. Building up a picture. Why, is there a connection between the punk scene and the murders?"

"That's one possible line of enquiry."

The sergeant produced a clear plastic evidence bag and held it out for inspection. Visible inside was a sheet of paper with the usual blackmail lettering cut out from newspapers which had fast become a punk cliché through overuse. There was just one short phrase written on it:

I wAnNA Be a sLAvE FoR yOU aLL

"Mean anything to you?" asked the sergeant.

"Found on the body, was it?"

"If you'd just answer the question, sir . . ."

"Yes, actually, it does."

"I see. And why might that be?"

"X-Ray Spex."

"X-Ray Spex?"

"The band . . ."

"I know who they are, sir. I had the *pleasure* of seeing them perform several songs at the pub up the road a couple of weeks ago . . ."

"All right, then. Go down to Town Records, 402 King's Road. Get a copy of a new album called *Live at the Roxy*. X-Ray Spex track called 'Oh Bondage Up Yours', I think you'll find it's part of the lyrics."

Early August. "I Feel Love" by Donna Summer blasting out from every pub jukebox. Pistols still at number four with "Pretty Vacant", just one place down from "Angelo" by Brotherhood of Man. Check out the record reviews in the *NME* and the two main albums featured were the new ones from the Grateful Dead and Soft Machine. These were strange times. Davis was finishing up his evening getting plastered at the Roebuck. Usual mixed crowd. A couple of the staff from Seditionaries getting the evil eye from some of the older geezers who took exception to the swastikas on their clothes. Francis Bacon wandering in, looking for who knows what. Two famous actors in the corner, saying nothing, seemingly miserable, and a smattering of underage drinkers keeping their heads down. Davis spotted a few of the punks he'd interviewed at a Rezillos show in the Man in the Moon a few days previously, then went up and bought them a drink on expenses to see if they had any likely tips for the coming week.

"How's it going, lads? Still getting hassled by the boys in blue?"

"Now and then. They were at the Spex gig at the Hope & Anchor the other day. Taking people outside. Going through your pockets. The usual crap."

"Did they say what it was about?"

"Nah. Don't need an excuse, do they?"

Apparently not. He went off to get some more cancer sticks and then pushed his way out through the doors and into the street. It was still bloody hot, but at least the tubes would still be running.

Now it was September. He'd finally finished that bloody punk films article, not that the editor had been particularly impressed. Easy to see why, really. The Pistols film with Meyer was shaping up to be a total fiasco and no one would even let him *near* that shoot – a sure sign of trouble. Nice idea on paper, but what would a director like that know about punk? Or care, for that matter . . . As for *Jubilee* – God help him – if he had to listen to much more of Jarman droning on about his plans to have some of the actors speaking in Latin, like his fucking unwatchable previous effort, then Davis would personally pay a group of King's Road Teds to show up on the set and batter people to death with copies of the script. At least that German bloke who'd shown up in town from Munich making a punk documentary a week or so back seemed to have the right idea. Go to the clubs, talk to the fans, talk to some of the music papers and shops. Capture it as it's happening.

Still, what the fuck, the article was done now.

As for the cops, they had rounded up some poor sod who was now "helping them with their enquiries". Three killings in four weeks. Must have made all the happy little rate-payers in their Chelsea Mews houses start screaming bloody murder at their local MP. No wonder somebody's been arrested. Can't have that sort of behaviour in the neighbourhood. The *Standard* didn't have much in the way of details, as per usual. Seemed like the guy had been picked up after a show at the Nashville, following "information received". According to the way it played in the press, it sounded like they were hoping that they'd taken some kind of dangerous lunatic off the streets. Innocent until proven guilty, of course . . .

What the hell. After a summer in which all the tabloids had spent their time running stories which claimed that the Sex Pistols cut up dead babies onstage and that your average punk was just as likely to bottle you in the face as say hello, hardly surprising that the cops would believe almost anything of someone who wore all the bondage gear. Was he guilty? Well, it seemed like he was their best bet . . .

Davis turned on the television, but there wasn't anything on the news about the killings. *New Faces* on LWT. Couldn't stomach that so he turned it over and got the last ten minutes of *Dr. Who* on BBC1, followed by Bruce Forsyth and the bloody *Generation Game*. Still, at least in the film slot there was a double bill later on of *House of Dracula* and Corman's *Fall of the House of Usher*, kicking off just after 10 p.m. Saturday night, though. What did they expect? Sometimes it looked as if they felt that anyone over the age of about fourteen or under the age of sixty would definitely be out and about having a wild time, so why bother?

He turned off the TV. All right, then, if all else fails, do some work. Went to the fridge, dug out a beer, and sat down in front of the Olivetti manual typewriter. The neighbours never liked hearing the clatter it made, but then fuck 'em; their kids had been playing the sodding *Muppet Show* album all week at huge volume on what appeared to be continuous repeat, and when the father ever succeeded in commandeering the record player it changed to the fucking Allman Brothers and *The Fucking Road Goes On For*-fucking-*ever*. All of it. Several times. In the same evening.

Jesus wept.

No, a little typing at 7 p.m. was hardly enough to repay

them for that kind of abuse.

The punk film article was done and dusted, due to hit the news-stands in a week or so, but he still had a piece to write for some arty French cinema magazine which was right up itself but paid surprisingly well. He supplied them with stuff written in English, which they then translated and printed in French. Who knows if they did a good job or not. He didn't care, and no one he knew ever saw the stuff. Mostly they wanted pretentious toss of the worst kind, and he was happy to oblige, under a pseudonym. This time, though, he'd sold them on the idea of a subject that actually interested him. Still, better not run this one under his real name either, all the same. Okay, the magazine only sold about 20,000 copies a time, virtually all of them across the Channel, but you never quite knew who might be reading it, putting two and two together.

Another swig of beer. Light up a fag. In with a new sheet of paper. Here we go:

CHELSEA ON FILM

Next time you're in London on holiday, take a walk down the King's Road. Now notorious for the exploits of some of Britain's new "punk rockers", it also has much to interest the student of film history.

Did you know that Stanley Kubrick shot parts of A Clockwork Orange *right here in the neighbourhood? Try catching the underground to Sloane Square station, then walk down the King's Road until you reach number 49, the Chelsea Drugstore. Malcolm McDowell's character, Alex, picks up a couple of girls in the record shop here before taking them back to his flat for an orgy. Then, if you continue in the same direction up the road, turning left onto Oakley Street, you'll come to the Albert Bridge. It's here, in the pedestrian underpass which runs beneath the northern end of the bridge, that McDowell is given a severe beating by a gang of tramps towards the end of the film.*

While you're there, look back along the Chelsea embankment about a hundred feet and you'll see an imposing Georgian house which is number 16 Cheyne Walk. It was in one of the upstairs bedrooms that Diana Dors was smothered to death with a pillow in Douglas Hickox's hugely entertaining 1973 horror film, Theatre of Blood, *starring Vincent Price as a homicidal Shakespearean actor.*

Retracing your steps back to the Chelsea Drugstore, turn off at the road leading down the side of it called Royal Avenue. Another fine Georgian house, number 30 Royal Avenue, was used as the location for Joseph Losey's 1963 film The Servant, *in which Edward Fox treats his manservant Dirk Bogarde almost like a slave, until the latter starts to get the upper hand . . .*

He paused and sat back in his chair, consulting his notes. *Blow Up, Killing of Sister George, The Party's Over* . . . Yeah, there were enough other ones to pad out the article. Shame to waste all that research.

And anyway, how many coppers could read French?

PART III

GUNS ON THE ROOF

LOVE
BY MARTYN WAITES
Dagenham

Love it. Fuckin' love it. No other feelin' in the world like it.

Better than sex. Better than anythin'.

There we was, right, an' there they was. Just before the Dagenham local elections. Outside the community centre. *Community centre*, you're 'avina laugh. *Asylum-seeker central*, more like. Somali centre.

June, a warm night, if you're interested.

Anyway, we'd had our meetin', makin' our plan for the comin' election, mobilizin' the locals off the estate, we come outside, an' there they was. The Pakis. The anti-Nazis. Shoutin', chantin' – *Nazi scum, BNP cunts*. So we joined in, gave it back with *Wogs out* an' that, *Seig heillin'* all over the place. Pakis in their casual leathers, anti-Nazis in their sloppy uni denims, us lookin' sharp in bombers an' eighteen-holers. Muscles like taut metal rope under skin-tight T-shirts an' jeans, heads hard an' shiny. Tattoos: dark ink makin' white skin whiter. Just waitin'.

Our eyes: burnin' with hate.

Their eyes: burnin' with hate. Directed at us like laser death beams.

Anticipation like a big hard python coiled in me guts, waitin' to get released an' spread terror. A big hard-on waitin' to come.

Buildin', gettin' higher:

Nazi scum BNP cunts

Wogs out seig heil

Buildin', gettin' higher –

Then it came. No more verbals, no more posin'. Adrenalin pumped right up, bell ringin', red light on. The charge.

The python's out, the hard-on spurts.

Both sides together, two wallsa sound clashin' intaya. A big, sonic tidal wave ready to engulf you in violence, carry you under with fists an' boots an' sticks.

Engage. An' in.

Fists an' boots an' sticks. I take. I give back double. I twist an' thrash. Like swimmin' in anger. I come up for air an' dive back in again, lungs full. I scream the screams, chant the chants.

Wogs out, seig heil

Then I'm not swimmin'. Liquid solidifies round me. An' I'm part of a huge machine. A muscle an' bone an' blood machine. A shoutin', chantin' cog in a huge hurtin' machine. Arms windmillin'. Boots kickin'. Fuelled on violence. Driven by rage.

Lost to it. No me. Just the machine. An' I've never felt more alive.

Love it. Fuckin' love it.

I see their eyes. See the fear an' hate an' blood in their eyes. I feed on it.

Hate matches hate. Hate gives as good as hate gets.

Gives better. The machine's too good for them.

The machine wins. Cogs an' clangs an' fists an' hammers. The machine always wins.

Or would, if the pigs hadn't arrived.

Up they come, sticks out. Right, lads, you've had your fun. Time for us to have a bit. Waitin' till both sides had tired, pickin' easy targets.

The machine falls apart; I become meself again. I think an' feel for meself. I think it's time to run.

I run.

We all do; laughin' an' limpin', knowin' we'd won.

Knowin' our hate was stronger than theirs. Knowin' they were thinkin' the same thing.

Run. Back where we came from, back to our lives. Ourselves.

Rememberin' that moment when we became somethin' more.

Cherishin' it.

I smiled.

LOVED IT.

D'you wanna name? Call me Jez. I've been called worse.

You want me life story? You sound like a copper. Or a fuckin' social worker. Fuckin' borin', but here it is. I live in the Chatsworth Estate in Dagenham. The borders of East London/Essex. You'll have heard of it. It's a dump. Or rather, a dumpin' ground. For problem families at first, but now for Somalis an' Kosovans that have just got off the lorry. It never used to be like that. It used to be a good place where you could be proud to live. But then, so did Dagenham. So did this country.

There's me dad sittin' on the settee watchin' *Tricia* in his vest, rollin' a fag. I suppose you could say he was typical of this estate (an' of Dagenham, an' the country). He used to have a job, a good one. At the Ford plant. Knew the place, knew the system, knew how to work it. But his job went when they changed the plant. His job an' thousands of others. Now it's a centre of excellence for diesel engines. An' he can't get a job there. He says the Pakis took it from him. They got HNDs an' degrees. He had an apprenticeship for a job that don't exist no more. No one wants that now. No one wants him now. He's tried. Hard. Honest. So he sits in his vest, rollin' fags, watchin' *Tricia*.

There's Tom, me brother, too. He's probably still in bed. He's got the monkey on his back. All sorts, really, but mostly heroin. He used to be a good lad, did well at school an' that, but when our fat slag bitch of a mother walked out, all that had to stop. We had to get jobs. Or try. I got a job doin' tarmackin' an' roofin.' He got a heroin habit. Sad. Fuckin' sad. Makes you really angry.

Tarmackin' an' roofin'. Off the books, cash in hand. With Barry the Roofer. Baz. Only when I'm needed, though, or seasonal, when the weather's good, but it's somethin'. Just don't tell the dole. I'd lose me jobseeker's allowance.

It's not seasonal at the moment. But it's June. So it will be soon.

So that's me. It's not who I am. An' it's not WHAT I AM.

I'm a Knight of St. George. An' proud of it. A true believer. A soldier for truth.

This used to be a land fit for heroes, when Englishmen were kings an' their houses, castles. A land where me dad had a job, me brother was doin' well at school, an' me fat slag bitch of a mother hadn't run off to Gillingham in Kent with a Paki postman. Well, he's Greek, actually, but you know what I mean. They're all Pakis, really.

An' that's the problem. Derek (I'll come to him in a minute) said the Chatsworth Estate is like this country in miniature. It used to be a good place where families could live in harmony and everyone knew everyone else. But now it's a run-down shithole full of undesirables an' people who've given up tryin' to get out. No pride any more. No self-respect. Our heritage sold to Pakis who've just pissed on us. Love your country like it used to be, says Derek, but hate it like it is now.

And I do. Both. With all my heart.

Because it's comin' back, he says. One day, sooner rather than later, we'll reclaim it. Make this land a proud place to be again. A land fit for heroes once more. And you, my lovely boys, will be the ones to do it. The foot soldiers of the revolution. Remember it word for word. Makes me shiver all over again when I think of it.

An' I think of it a lot. Whenever some Paki's got in me face, whenever some stuck-up cunt's had a go at the way I've done his drive or roof, whenever I look in me dad's eyes an' see that all his hope belongs to yesterday, I think of those words. I think of my place in the great scheme, at the forefront of the revolution. An' I smile. I don't get angry. Because I know what they don't.

That's me. That's WHAT I AM.

But I can't tell you about me without tellin' you about Derek Midgely. Great, great man. The man who showed me the way an' the truth. The man who's been more of a father to me than me real dad. He's been described as the demigog of Dagenham. I don't know what a demigog is, but if it means someone who KNOWS THE TRUTH an' TELLS IT LIKE IT IS, then that's him.

But I'm gettin' ahead. First I have to tell you about Ian.

Ian. He recruited me. Showed me the way.

I met him at the shopping centre. I was sittin' around one day wonderin' what to do, when he came up to me.

"I know what you need," he said.

I looked up. An' there was a god. Shaved head, eighteen-holers, jeans an' T-shirt – so tight I could make out the curves an' contours of his muscled body. An' he looked so relaxed, so in control. He had his jacket off an' I could see the tats over his forearms an' biceps. Some pro ones like the flag of St. George, some done himself like *Skins Foreva*. He looked perfect.

An' I knew there an' then I wanted what he had. He was right. He did know what I needed.

He got talkin' to me. Asked me questions. Gave me answers. Told me who was to blame for my dad not havin' a job. Who was to blame for my brother's habit. For my fat slag bitch mother runnin' off to Gillingham. Put it all in context with the global Zionist conspiracy. Put it closer to home with pictures I could understand: the Pakis, the niggers, the asylum-seekers.

I looked round Dagenham. Saw crumblin' concrete, depressed whites, smug Pakis. The indigenous population overrun. Then back at Ian. An' with him lookin' down at me an' the sun behind his head lookin' like some kind of halo, it made perfect sense.

"I feel your anger," he said, "understand your hate."

The way he said *hate*. Sounded just right.

He knew some others that felt the same. Why didn't I come along later an' meet them?

I did.

An' never looked back.

Ian's gone now. After what happened.

For a time it got nasty. I mean REALLY nasty. Body in the concrete foundations of the London Gateway nasty.

I blamed Ian. All the way. I had to.
Luckily, Derek agreed.

Derek Midgely. A great man, like I said. He's made the St.
George pub on the estate his base. It's where we have our
meetin's. He sits there in his suit with his gin an' tonic in
front of him, hair slicked back, an' we gather round, waitin'
for him to give us some pearls of wisdom, or tell us the latest
instalment of his master plan. It's brilliant, just to be near
him. Like I said, a great, great man.

I went there along with everyone else the night after the
community centre ruck. I mean meetin'. There was the usu-
als. Derek, of course, holdin' court, the foot soldiers of which
I can proudly number myself, people off the estate (what
Derek calls the concerned populace), some girls, Adrian an'
Steve. They need a bit of explainin'. Adrian is what you'd call
an intellectual. He wears glasses an' a duffel coat all year
round. Always carryin' a canvas bag over his shoulder. Greasy
black hair. Expression like he's somewhere else. Laughin' at a
joke only he can hear. Don't know what he does. Know he
surfs the Internet, gets things off that. Shows them to Derek.
Derek nods, makes sure none of us have seen them. Steve is
the local councillor. Our great white hope. Our great fat
whale, as he's known out of Derek's earshot. Used to be
Labour until, as he says, he saw the light. Or until they found
all the fiddled expense sheets an' Nazi flags up in his livin'
room an' Labour threw him out. Still, he's a true man of the
people.

Derek was talkin'. "What you did last night," he says,
"was a great and glorious thing. And I'm proud of each and
every one of you."

We all smiled.

"However," Derek went on, "I want you to keep a low profile between now and Thursday. Voting day. Let's see some of the other members of our party do their bit. We all have a part to play."

He told us that the concerned populace would go leafletin' and canvassin' in their suits an' best clothes, Steve walkin' round an' all. He could spin a good yarn, Steve. How he'd left Labour in disgust because they were the Pakis' friend, the asylum-seekers' safe haven. How they invited them over to use our National Heath Service, run drugs an' prostitution rings. He would tell that to everyone he met, try an' make them vote for him. Derek said it was playin' on their legitimate fears, but to me it just sounded so RIGHT. Let him play on whatever he wanted.

He went on. We listened. I felt like I belonged. Like I was wanted, VALUED. Meetin's always felt the same.

LIKE I'D COME HOME.

The meetin' broke up. Everyone started drinkin'.

Courtney, one of the girls, came up to me, asked if I was stayin' on. She's short with a soft barrel body an' hard eyes. She's fucked nearly all the foot soldiers. Sometimes more than once, sometimes a few at a time. Calls it her patriotic duty. Hard eyes, but a good heart. I went along with them once. I had to. All the lads did. But I didn't do much. Just sat there, watched most of the time. Looked at them. Didn't really go near her.

Anyway, she gave me that look. Rubbed up against me. Let me see the tops of her tits down the front of her low-cut T-shirt. Made me blush. Then made me angry cos I blushed. I told her I had to go, that I couldn't afford a drink. My job-seeker's allowance was gone an' Baz hadn't come up with any work for me.

She said that she was gettin' together with a few of the lads after the pub. Was I interested?

I said no. An' went home.

Well, not straight home. There was somethin' I had to do first. Somethin' I couldn't tell the rest of them about.

There's a part of the estate where you just DON'T GO. At least not by yourself. Not after dark. Unless you are tooled up. Unless you want somethin'. An' I wanted somethin'.

It was dark there. Shadows on shadows. Hip hop an' reggae came from open windows. The square was deserted. I walked, crunched on gravel, broken glass. I felt eyes watchin' me. Unseen ones. Wished I'd brought me blade. Still, I had me muscles. I'd worked on me body since I joined the party, got good an' strong. I was never like that at school. Always the weak one. Not any more.

I was kind of safe, I knew that. As long as I did what I was here to do, I wouldn't get attacked. Because this was where the niggers lived.

I went to the usual corner an' waited. I heard him before I saw him. Comin' out of the dark, along the alleyway, takin' his time, baggy jeans slung low on his hips, Calvins showin' at the top. Vest hangin' loose. Body ripped an' buff.

Aaron. The Ebony Warrior.

Aaron. Drug dealer.

I swallowed hard.

He came up close, looked at me. The usual look, smilin', like he knows somethin' I don't. Eye to eye. I could smell his warm breath on my cheek. I felt uneasy. The way I always do with him.

"Jez," he said slowly, an' held his arms out. "See anythin' you want?"

I swallowed hard again. Me throat was really dry.

"You know what I want." Me voice sounded ragged.

He laughed his private laugh. "I know exactly," he said, an' waited.

His breath was all sweet with spliff an' alcohol. He kept starin' at me. I dug my hand into my jacket pocket. Brought out money. Nearly the last I had, but he didn't know that.

He shook his head, brought out a clingfilm wrap from his back pocket.

"Enjoy," he said.

"It's not for me an' you know it."

He smiled again. "Wanna try some? Some skunk, maybe? Now? With me?"

I don't do drugs. I hardly drink. An' he knows it. He was tauntin' me. He knew what my answer would be.

"Whatever," he said. "Off you go, then, back to your little Hitler world."

I said nothing. I never could when he talked to me.

Then he did somethin' he'd never done before. He touched my arm.

"You shouldn't hate," he said. "Life too short for that, y'get me?"

I looked down at his fingers. The first black fingers I'd ever had on my body. I should have thrown them off. Told him not to touch me, called him a filthy nigger. Hit him.

But I didn't. His fingers felt warm. And strong.

"What should I do, then?" I could hardly hear my own voice.

"Love," he said.

I turned round, walked away.

I heard his laugh behind me.

At home, Dad was asleep on the sofa. Snorin' an' fartin'. I

went into Tom's room. Empty. I left the bundle by his bedside an' went out.

I hadn't been lyin' to Courtney. It was nearly the last of me money. I didn't like buyin' stuff for Tom, but what could I do? It was either that or he went out on the street to sell somethin', himself even, to get money for stuff. I had no choice.

I went to bed but couldn't sleep. Things on me mind but I didn't know what. Must be the elections. That was it. I lay starin' at the ceilin', then realized me cock was hard. I took it in me hand. This'll get me to sleep, I thought. I thought hard about Courtney. An' all those lads.

That did the trick.

The next few days were a bit blurry. Nothin' much happened. It was all waitin'. For the election. For Baz to find me some more work. For Tom to run out of heroin again an' need another hit.

Eventually Thursday rolled round an' it was election day. I went proudly off to the pollin' station at the school I used to go to. Looked at the kids' names on the walls. Hardly one of them fuckin' English. Made me do that cross all the more harder.

I stayed up all night watchin' the election. Tom was out, me dad fell asleep.

Steve got in.

I went fuckin' mental.

I'd been savin' some cans for a celebration an' I went at them. I wished I could have been in the St. George with the rest but I knew us foot soldiers couldn't. But God, how I WANTED TO. That was where I should have been. Who I should have been with. That was where I BELONGED.

But I waited. My time would come.

I stayed in all the next day. Lost track of time.

Put the telly on. Local news. They reported what had happened. Interviewed some Paki. Called himself a community leader. Said he couldn't be held responsible if members of his community armed themselves and roamed the streets in gangs looking for BNP members. His people had a right to protect themselves.

They switched to the studio. An' there was Derek. Arguin' with some cunt from Cambridge. Least that's what he looked like. Funny, I thought people were supposed to look bigger on TV. Derek just looked smaller. Greasy hair. Fat face. Big nose. Almost like a Jew, I thought. Then felt guilty for thinkin' it.

"It's what the people want," he said. "The people have spoken. They're sick and tired of a government that is ignoring the views of the common man and woman. And the common man and woman have spoken. We are not extremists. We are representing what the average, decent person in this country thinks but doesn't dare say because of political correctness. Because of what they fear will happen to them."

I felt better hearin' him say that. Then they turned to the Cambridge cunt. He was a psychologist or psychiatrist or sociologist or somethin'. I thought, here it comes. He's gonna start arguin' back an' then Derek's gonna go for him. But he didn't. This sociologist just looked calm. Smiled, almost.

"It's sad," he said. "It's sad so few people realize. As a society it seems we base our responses on either love or hate, thinking they're opposites. But they're not. They're the same. The opposite of love is not hate. It's indifference."

They looked at him.

"People only hate what they fear within themselves. What they fear themselves becoming. What they secretly love. A fascist," he gestured to Derek, "will hate democracy. Plurality. Anything else," he shrugged, "is indifference."

I would have laughed out loud if there had been anyone else there with me.

But there wasn't. So I said nothing.

A weekend of lyin' low. Difficult, but had to be done. Don't give them a target, Derek had said. Don't give them an excuse.

By Monday I was rarin' to get out of the flat, was even lookin' forward to goin' to work.

First I went down the shoppin' centre. Wearin' me best skinhead gear. Don't know what I expected, the whole world to have changed or somethin', but it was the same as it had been. I walked round proudly, an' I could feel people lookin' at me. I smiled. They knew. Who I was. What I stood for. They were the people who'd voted.

There was love in their eyes. I was sure of it.

At least, that's what it felt like.

Still in a good mood, I went to see Baz. Ready to start work.

An' he dropped a bombshell.

"Sorry, mate, I can't use you no more."

"Why not?"

He just looked at me like the answer was obvious. When I looked like I didn't understand, he had to explain it to me.

"Cos of what's happened. Cos of what you believe in. Now don't get me wrong," he said, "you know me. I agree, there's too many Pakis an' asylum-seekers over here. But a lot of those Pakis are my customers. And, well, look at you. I can hardly bring you along to some Paki's house and let you work for him, could I? So sorry, mate, that's that."

I was gutted. I walked out of there knowin' I had no money. Knowin' that, once again, the Pakis had taken it from me.

I looked around the shoppin' centre. I didn't see love anymore. I saw headlines on the papers:

Racist Councillor Voted in to Dagenham

Then underneath:

Kick This Scum Out

I couldn't believe it. They should be welcomin' us with open arms. This was supposed to be the start of the revolution. Instead it was the usual shit. I just knew the Pakis were behind it. An' the Jews. They own all the newspapers.

I had nowhere to go. I went to the St. George, but this was early mornin' an' there was no one in. None of me people.

So I just walked round all day. Thinkin'. Not gettin' anythin' straight. Gettin' everythin' more twisted.

I thought of goin' back to the St. George. They'd be there. Celebratin'. Then there was goin' to be a late-night march round the streets. Let the residents, the concerned populace, know they were safe in their houses. Let everyone know who ruled the streets.

But I didn't feel like it.

So I went home.

An' wished I hadn't.

Tom was there. He looked like shit. Curled up on his bed. He'd been sick. Shat himself.

"Whassamatter?" I said. "D'you wanna doctor?"

He managed to shake his head. No.

"What, then?"

"Gear. Cold turkey. Cramps."

An' he was sick again.

I stood back, not wantin' it to get on me.

"Please," he gasped, "you've got to get us some gear . . . please . . ."

"I've got no money," I said.

"Please . . ." An' his eyes, pleadin' with me. What could I do? He was me brother. Me flesh an' blood. An' you look after your own.

"I'll not be long," I said.

I left the house.

Down to the part of the estate where you don't go. I walked quickly, went to the usual spot. Waited.

Eventually he came. Stood before me.

"Back so soon?" Aaron said. Then smiled. "Can't keep away, can you?"

"I need some gear," I said.

Aaron waited.

"But I've got no money."

Aaron chuckled. "Then no sale."

"Please. It's for . . . It's urgent."

Aaron looked around. There was that smile again. "How much d'you want it?"

I looked at him.

"How much?" he said again. An' put his hand on my arm.

He moved in closer to me. His mouth right by me ear. He whispered, tickling me. Me heart was beatin' fit to burst. Me legs felt shaky.

"You're like me," he said.

I tried to speak. It took me two attempts. "No I'm not," I said.

"Oh yes you are. We do what our society says we have to do. Behave like we're supposed to. Hide our true feelings. What we really are."

I tried to shake me head. But I couldn't.

"You know you are." He got closer. "You know I am."

An' kissed me. Full on the mouth.

I didn't throw him off. Didn't call him a filthy nigger. Didn't hit him. I kissed him back.

Then it was hands all over each other. I wanted to touch him, feel his body, his beautiful black body. Feel his cock. He did the same to me. That python was inside me, ready to come out. I loved the feeling.

I thought of school. How I was made to feel different. Hated them for it. Thought of Ian. What we had got up to. I had loved him. With all me heart. An' he loved me. But we got found out. An' that kind of thing is frowned upon, to say the least. So I had to save me life. Pretend it was all his doing. I gave him up. I never saw him again. I never stopped lovin' him.

I loved what Aaron was doin' to me now. It felt wrong. But it felt so right.

I had him in my hand, wanted him in me body. Was ready to take him.

When there was a noise.

We had been so into each other we hadn't heard them approach.

"So this is where you are," they said. "Fuckin' a filthy nigger when you should be with us."

The foot soldiers. On patrol. An' tooled up.

I looked at Aaron. He looked terrified.

"Look," I said, "it was his fault. I had to get some gear for me brother . . ."

They wasn't listenin'. They was starin' at us. Hate in their eyes. As far as they was concerned, I was no longer one of them. I was the enemy now.

"You wanna run, nigger-lover? Or you wanna stay here and take your beating with your boyfriend?" The words spat out.

I zipped up me jeans. Looked at Aaron.

They caught the look.

Now run, the machine said, hate in its eyes. But from now on, you're no better than a nigger or a Paki.

I ran.

Behind me, I heard them layin' into Aaron.

I kept running.

I couldn't go home. I had no gear for Tom. I couldn't stay where I was. I might not be so lucky next time.

So I ran.

I don't know where.

After a while I couldn't run any more. I slowed down, tried to get me breath back. Too tired to run any more. To fight back.

I knew who I was. Finally. I knew WHAT I WAS.

An' it was a painful truth. It hurt.

Then from the end of the street I saw them. Pakis. A gang of them. Out protectin' their own community. They saw me. Started runnin'.

I was too tired. I couldn't outrun them. I stood up, waited for them. I wanted to tell them I wasn't a threat, that I didn't hate them.

But they were screamin', shoutin', hate in their eyes.

A machine. Cogs an' clangs an' fists an' hammers.

I waited, smiled.

Love shining in me own eyes.

SIC TRANSIT GLORIA MUNDI

BY JOOLZ DENBY

Bradford

We put six black plastic bin bags of stuff in that Rent-A-Wreck transit van; that's what we took, and we left another twelve or so of rubbish in the house. We'd cleaned up too – or at least what we thought of as cleaning; though it's no good excuse, you'd have needed an industrial steam-cleaner to shift the muck in that kitchen. And we left a note, taped to the spotted mirror in the front room:

> *Dear Mr. Suleiman,*
>
> *We are very sorry to run away and not pay what we owe you for the rent. One day we will come back and settle up, we promise.*
>
> *Yours sincerely,*
> *The tenants at no. 166*

And we set off in the middle of the night, an old transistor radio and tape deck wedged on the filthy dashboard, the rain smearing the windscreen as the wonky wiper jerked spastically across the glass and we put "Babylon's Burning" on at full distort and we laughed and you floored the pedal until the engine howled.

Oh, man; running away from Bradford in the lost, gone

and sadly, not forgotten '80s. Running into the great spirit gold of the rising sun and the hot rush of cutting loose at last from the viscous, clinging mud of small-town England; every weekday the dole and just enough coarse cheap food to keep you alive, every Saturday night the same round of drinking, fighting and dreaming, every Sunday a long smashed afternoon of everyone droning on about how shit it was and how if only they had the breaks, cha, just watch 'em, they'd be rock stars and axe heroes and *somebodies*.

If they had the breaks, yeah. If some god on high did it all for them and made it all for them, they'd be off to London in a trice, because that, we all knew, was where everything was. That's where über-cool parties were a dazed haze of glitter-floating beautiful people with clothes from boutiques so hip even their names were a transgression, where even the lowliest shop-girl was such a counterculture punkette pin-up she got her pic in *Sounds*, and the streets were paved with cocaine and the gutters ran with Jack in a fumey vapour of sweet decadence; rich boy's piss, the blood of rock 'n' roll. We all knew this to be 110 per cent true because what journalist ever wrote paeans to the punk night at Queen's Hall, Bradford, or eulogies to some dark-time niterie in say, oh, Chester? No, it was London; everything, everyone, every luminous, lush and longed-for treat was stashed in the belly of that old beast. It was a fact. We'd read it in every newspaper, Sunday arts supplement, music journal and fashionable novel since forever. It was the way it was and we were the huddled peasant masses crouching on our savage hills gazing up in the torch-lit dark at the divine superstar that was London, London, London.

So we sat in the van as it hurtled down the M1, wired out of our skulls with adrenalin and burning with messianic passion, white hot and calamitous. We weren't kids, oh no; we weren't teen escapees, you see; we were genuine artists, gone twenty-five and *almost* possessing a record contract with EMI; cash-poor we might be, but we'd worked like dogs and earned our turn at the table – so no pallid, plump, dumb fuck of a corporate recording executive was going ruin our Big Chance. We would be there in the thick of it, in London, in control. We weren't going to be throwaway tinsel two-bit popstrels, oh no – we were going to change the face of music, of literature, of art, of life, *forever*. Those decadent, air-and-arse kissing Londoners would be forced to welcome us with open arms because we were the future, we were the *Warriors of the New*. Strapped into our armour of hand-stitched leather and raggedy black, we looked in my tattered old tarot cards and saw rapture rising behind us like a prophecy.

It had to be that way. We'd told everyone it would be. We'd been princes and princesses in Wooltown, now we were going to live like kings and queens in the Big Smoke. We'd chanted the spell, we'd invoked the gods. It was a done deal.

All that winter six of us slept on the spare bedroom floor of our singer's sister's shoe-box flat in the Northerner's ghetto of London, Highbury New Park. Done up like chrysalides in our stinking doss-bags, we waited for spring when we'd be turned into butterflies. At night the floor heaved like a living carpet and the air was sucked clean of oxygen, but it was too cold and grimy to open the window. They'd never said how tumble-down, litter-strewn and dirty London was in those magazines and on the telly; the muck was terrible. Put on a clean T-shirt and it'd be black-bright in ten minutes of being exposed to the exhaust-fume leaden reek of the monstrous crawling traffic. Blow your nose and the snot was black; clean your make-up off and the grease was shot with gritty grey that wasn't mascara. The dirt had its own smell too, sour and rank, hanging in the unmoving air like a filthy veil.

Back home, we'd think – each to ourselves and not letting on for fear of being thought soft – the cold, fresh wind off the moor unrolled through the canyons of gothic sandstone buildings, embroidered with the faint scent of heather and the sweet dust of the craglands, scouring the crooked streets and lighting wild roses in your cheeks.

But it was no use thinking like that. We were here to stay, to make our mark. So we'd shake ourselves back to the now and think, hey, who cares about *Wuthering Heights* when we can go to Heaven, guest-listed on the strength of the last article in the *NME* about our meteoric rise to cult stardom, or my snarling mask adorning the front cover of *Time Out* – kabuki-style, rebel-girl eyes sparkling incandescent with unreason and fury. Fame, we thought, never having been taught to think otherwise, was better than bread – and infamy was preferable to anonymity. We didn't have to stand in line with the other runaways outside whatever nightclub was in that week, listening to the chopped vowels and singsong drawl of the North, the West or all the other great cities that netted the country – what Londoners called "the provinces" in that particular tone of voice that made you want to spit in their eyes.

So we walked past the Liverpool whine or the Brummie choke of the queuing hordes, and strode in a cloud of patchouli, crimper-burnt hair and Elnett into the dreamland they could only hope for. A London nightclub; wow. The carpets patinated with muck, spat-out gum, and marinated in beer slops and puke. The glasses plastic and the watered-down drinks a fortune, the toilets a slick tsunami of bog-water and busted, stinking, scrawled-on, paperless cubicles flapping with broken-locked doors. You never really got anything for nothing in London, see; proved how sharp they were, proved no one got anything over on a real Londoner.

Not that we ever met a real Londoner. Not one born and bred, like. Maybe they were out there somewhere, but we never found them. Certainly not one who could truly say he'd entered this vale of tears to the cheery clamour of Bow bells, the coarse comforting din of the old pub pianner belting out "Miybe It's Becorse I'm a Lunnoner", and the smiles of pearly royalty handing out platters of jellied eels and cockles. No, folk said they were from London, but there was always somewhere else hidden in the dusty folds of their fast-forgotten past; they'd lived in London, oh, now, you know, God, forever. But they came from Leicester or Bristol or Glasgow or Cyprus or Athens or Berlin or Ankara. They came to be famous, but until that bright day they washed dishes, threw plates of greasy nosh about in caffs, or struggled round the heart-and-soul-breaking savagery of the infamously brutal London dole offices.

Oh, aye, it was a cold coming we, and many like us, had, and no mistake. But what did we care? If we felt heartsick or homesick, we stood ourselves up straight, wiped our eyes if we were girls, unset our rock-hard jaws if we were boys, and commenced afresh our sure-to-be-stellar careers in the world of art. We would show them, we would not be broken and crawl off home like yellow, sag-bellied curs – we had a meeting with EMI tomorrow where we'd tell 'em how it was, and tonight there was a *happening* at an old warehouse by the river, promising an installation featuring a naked model-girl embedded in a tank full of jelly created by the latest cutting-edge performance art duo, a clutch of ranting skin-punk poets, and a couple of hot new London bands cobbled together from the tatterdemalion remnants of last year's hot new London bands.

How many of those *happenings* did we go to, expecting the dark whirligig of cruelly brilliant excess and getting instead a half-cocked mock-up in a rickety-rackety draughty squat where some anorexic pilled-up slapper was toted round in a rusty wheelbarrow slopping with lime Chivers by two public schoolboys whose aristo boho dads had been Hampstead artists in the '60s, and people we recognized from magazines cooed about authenticity and artistic daring as they wiped their coke-snotty noses and patted each other on the back? They always, always all knew each other from school and from their families and they didn't know us – but suffering Jesus, we knew them, because we knew what real really was and they. Did. Not. Still don't, as it goes. Anyway, all these evenings ended in fighting, in smack-and-thunder brawls driven by our frustration and our rage at those whited sepulchres and their great stitch-up. How we frightened them, the faux-Londoners, how we shook their skinny trees. Yeah, yeah, yeah – all that talk of voyeuristic ultra-violence and the thrill of the street evaporated like oily vapour off a stagnant pond when they saw the *lightning* we were. They never knew us, no, they never did. They never saw us weep.

Oh, it was all such a shill, a sell, a sham; while we ripped ourselves apart searching for the pure, beating heart of things, believing we could, by telling the truth, by tearing the old lies apart at the seams, set ourselves and all our tribe free, London rolled on, a tottering juggernaut of blind and desperate delusion, all the little mannequins trying to find the tailor who made the emperor's bee-yoo-ti-ful new clothes, so they could ape the great cockalorum and maybe, maybe grab a tiny bit of reflected glory. It was a non-stop dance macabre and we didn't realize how bone-tired we were becoming.

Then, for us, it all came down in twenty-four hours.

First, we woke up and knew that yet again we wouldn't be able to see the sky. Might not sound like much but it finally got to us, hemmed in and overshadowed as we were by the ugly grey buildings crouching over us, the exhalations of air-cons and extractor fans panting rancid fast-food farts into the starving air, choking us. In Bradford, you see, the skies constantly scroll above us in a massive cloudscape, as free and ever-changing as the wild pulse of nature – the sandstone of the city is buttery amber, lit from within by a million prisms when the light hits it at sunset. We live in a flame, in a painting by Turner, in Gaia's Lamp. In London, we were dying for lack of light.

That morning, well, we knew it would be another London day, and lo! It was. And that night it was my thirtieth birthday, and I wasn't a kid any more. I had decided to have a party. It was to be at the Embassy Club, private, just for the tribe, and it would be a suitable send-off for my dishevelled youth. I spent hours with the crimpers and the kohl pot and I looked like the priestess at Knossos, but I covered up my breasts out of modesty. The snakes, well, I had them tattooed on; easier that way.

How long did my birthday party last in that tatty mould-smelling red-velvet cellar before the scavenging liggers arrived, cawing over the booze they stole, screeching and cackling at us, the barbarians? How long was it before one of them abused the wrong soldier in our little army, and bang-bang it went? Not long, believe me. Then there were cracked noses, plum-black eyes, split lips swelling fat in an instant over sharp-chipped teeth, and the shrill screams of speed-skinny harridans egging on their leathery menfolk to try and "fuck that bitch up". *That bitch* stood as the maelstrom rolled around her in a sparkle of broken glass and the red stitch of blood, and thought, ah, *enough*. So that bitch – which was me, of course, naturally – picked up a tall bar stool and, raising it overhead, smashed the great mirror by the bar into a blossom of shards so I wouldn't have to see my reflection backdropped by that screeching mess.

Then it went quiet, and all you could hear was breathing and a fella coughing where he'd been whacked in the gut. And the mangy jackals slunk off as the bouncers – late as ever – bulked into the room and tried to get lairy and failed, no one having the energy left to take them seriously.

And I went to the bar manager and said I was sorry for breaking his expensive-looking glass, and he said I hadn't.

So I said, no, it was me, I'll pay for it, fair's fair, somewhat nervous though, as I was mortally skint as usual.

And he said, no, it wasn't you.

But it was, I said. It was.

No, he said, it wasn't, you didn't do it, it's nothing; you're famous, we all know you, *people like you don't have to pay for what you do.*

And an abyss opened up in front of me that reeked sulphurous of what I could become, of what was in me that rubbed its corrupted hands together and murmured about fame, power and hubris, which would be the end of freedom and the death of my spirit, and I knew too that a million wannabes would think me the biggest fool living for not pricking my thumb pronto and signing on the dotted line. So I threw some money on the bar – without doubt not enough – and walked out of that shabby shithole, my pretty golden boot-clogs crunching the broken mirror-glass, and I felt a great disgust at the sorry, sordid smallness of the sell-out offered me. For if I was going to trade my immortal soul, brothers and sisters, would it be for the entrée to crap clubs and pathetic parties in a slutty run-down frazzle of a city in a small island off the coast of Europe? Oh, I think not, I really think not, as it goes. Only the universe would be enough to satisfy my desire, and I'm still working on that.

So we left London and returned to Bradford double-quick before we had time to think too hard. We rented another stone house terraced on the slopes of our crazy secret city's hills and breathed the good air with profound relief and paid Mr. Suleiman what we owed, and more, and he said he knew we'd come back one day and we all shook hands, straight up. Then we set ourselves to write our own histories in songs and stories, make our own testaments in paintings and books, which we have done and are still doing and will do forever and ever, amen; stronger and stronger, brighter and brighter. And I'm grateful I saw what I saw when I did, before I was blinded by habit and despair, like so many I know who are lost now, beyond recall.

Twenty years have passed since that night, and I ask myself what it really was we all hated most about our sojourn in the Great Wen. What was the grit in the pearl in the oyster, the time-bomb ticking heart of it? I've heard all the stories of loneliness and fear, of self-harm and suicide, of madness and addiction, from others who finally limped home to lick their wounds – but it wasn't any of that for us. No. What finally, finally finished us with London wasn't the corruption or the scandals, nothing so interesting, nothing so bold, nothing so grand.

Sic transit gloria mundi – so passes away the glory of the world.

London, that braggart capital, passes away without glory, you see. Without greatness, without any kind of joy, without passion or fire or beauty. In the end, you see, London was such a pathetic bloody *disappointment*.

And you know what? It still is.

That's all.

NEW ROSE

BY JOHN WILLIAMS

New Cross

Years ago Mac had read this interview with a British soul singer whose career had had its share of ups and downs. The guy was asked whether he felt he'd been a success. "Well," he said, "I've never had to go back to mini-cabbing." It was a line that came into Mac's head quite regularly these days as he delivered a fare to the Academy or hung around the office playing cards with Kemal, the night controller.

Not that Mac minded cabbing particularly. There were a lot worse things to do, he was well aware. And it fitted pretty well with his lifestyle. Not just the working at night but the fact that you could drop it just like that when something better came along. Though it was a bit of a while since something better had come along. It had been three months since he'd finished a stint road managing for the Lords – a bunch of re-formed Aussie punks he'd known from back in the day. And it had been a good six months since anyone had asked Mac to get his own band back on the road. Mac had been in one of the original class-of-'76 punk bands but one that had somehow missed out on becoming legendary. They had a bit of a following in Italy, and most of the places that used to be Yugoslavia, but that was about it.

Five a.m. a call came in for a trip to the airport, Heathrow. Kemal looked over at Mac, who sighed then nodded. It was 7.15 by the time he made it home, a council maisonette in Gospel Oak. Jackie was just getting up, making some tea and yelling at the kids, teenagers now both of them, to get themselves out of bed.

"Hey," he said, flopping down on the couch, absolutely knackered.

"Hey yourself," said Jackie.

"Good time last night?" Jackie had been out with a couple of mates from the school.

"Yeah," said Jackie, "nice. Listen, there was a message for you when I got in. From someone called Etheridge. Wants you to call him. Sounds like it might be a job. Etheridge, why does that name ring a bell?"

"Used to manage Ross, you remember?"

Jackie pulled a face. "Oh, him."

"Yeah," said Mac, "him. He's doing all right these days, has his own label and management company. Did he leave a number?"

"Yeah, by the phone."

"Right," said Mac, stretching and heading for bed. "I'll call him later."

"So," said Jackie at teatime, her turn to sit on the couch looking knackered, after a day spent looking after special-needs kids at the school. "What did he want, this Etheridge?"

"Ah, he wants me to talk to someone."

"Oh yeah, any particular someone?"

"Yeah, someone he wants to do a gig, and he's heard I'm the man who might be able to talk this someone into doing one, or at least sober him up enough to get him on stage."

"Oh Christ," said Jackie, "not bloody Luke."

"Yeah," said Mac, "bloody Luke is exactly who he wants.

It's this label's twenty-fifth anniversary and they're having a whole series of gigs to celebrate and they really want Luke to be there, as he was the guy who started it all for them. There's some decent wedge in it for me and all, if I can get him on stage."

Jackie shook her head. "Well, just as long as you don't bring him round here again. Not after last time. Not if he's still drinking."

"Oh," said Mac, "it's a pretty safe bet he's still doing that."

Luke North was another old-timer, another feller who went all the way back to '76/'77, had played all the same speed-driven, gob-drenched gigs as Mac. Only Luke's crew had found favour with the all-important John Peel on the radio, and a bit of a cult had grown up around them over the years. Every decade or so a new band would come along and say their heroes were Luke and his mob, and then there'd be a feature in the NME about his dissolute genius or whatever.

All that dissolute genius stuff sounds fine when you read about it in the paper, of course. It tends to be a bit different when you get up close, though. The truth of it was that Luke was a fuck-up, and one who had the knack of fucking up anyone who came in his orbit. But to be fair, he had charm, charisma even, and, given that Mac wasn't planning on sharing his life with the bloke, he'd always got on with him okay. They'd been close for a while right back at the beginning, drifted apart as you do, then become mates again after they'd both been touring Slovenia at the same time a few years back, both of them at a low ebb. Since then, Luke would call up once a month or so and they'd go out, have a drink or whatever.

A few times Mac had brought him back to Gospel Oak

but Jackie wasn't too keen. Said she sort of liked him, you know, she could see what the attraction was, but there was something about him that creeped her out. Mac hadn't really known what she meant till the last time he'd come round. He'd been really drunk, maybe something else going on as well. He hadn't eaten a thing, stubbed his fags out in the food, all that kind of shit, which was bad enough, but this time Mac had really known what Jackie meant. There was something – not evil, that was overstating it – but rotten, something definitely rotten coming off him. And since then, that was three, four months ago, Mac had only seen him once.

But apparently that was more than anyone else had done, and if Etheridge was going to pay him a grand "consulting fee" just for getting him on stage, well, Mac was in no position to turn it down.

Calls to the couple of numbers he had for Luke proved fruitless, so Mac decided to cruise around a few of his known haunts in between fares. A run down to Soho gave him a chance to check out the Colony and the French; Luke liked those old-school boho hangouts. No sign of him though, which wasn't much of a surprise, no doubt Etheridge would have found him already if he was hanging around Soho. Same went for Camden Town. Mac checked the Good Mixer and the Dublin Castle just in case, but once again no sign, nothing but Japanese tourists hoping for a glimpse of someone who used to be in Blur. This was ridiculous, Mac decided, there had to be a million drinking holes in London and the odds of finding Luke at random were next to zero. Even if he was in a pub at all and not crashed out in some flat in Walthamstow or Peckham or God knows where else.

He'd just about given up on the idea when a fare took him to London Bridge station and he had a bit of an inspiration. Years ago, Luke had a kid with a woman who ran a pub just down the way. Well, she hadn't run a pub back then, but she did now. Luke had taken him in there a year or so back. He was from Bermondsey, was Luke, originally. Over the years, he'd become all international rock and roll, but scratch deep enough and there was a bit of barrow boy lurking in there. And for years, when he was starting out, he'd had this girlfriend who came from the same background as he, London Irish, Linda her name was.

The pub was tucked underneath the railway line, a real basic boozer with a pool table and jukebox and a bunch of old fellers sitting at the bar.

Linda was playing darts when Mac walked in. She was a tall woman, what you'd call handsome rather than pretty, chestnut hair and good bones, looked like she could sort you out herself, no problem, if you started any trouble. He waited till she finished her turn, then said hello.

"All right, darlin'?" he said, and she looked at him uncertainly for a second, then broke out a big smile, came over and hugged him. Women liked Mac, always had, he was big and solid and he kept his troubles to himself. Plus, in this particular case, there was a little bit of history. It was a long time ago, so long ago that Mac had kind of forgotten it till he felt her arms around him, but once, must be twenty years ago, they'd had a bit of a night. Nothing serious, just a bit of a laugh when Luke had been driving her crazy.

"So," she said, leading him over towards the bar, "what brings you down this way?"

"Well," said Mac, "pleasure of your company, of course."

"Oh, aye?" said Linda, and gave him a bit of a look, one

that said she didn't believe him for a moment, but she'd let it slide for now. "So how's the family?"

"Good. Growing up, you know. How's your boy?"

Linda shook her head. "In prison."

"Oh," said Mac, who wasn't inclined to rush to judgement, he'd done his own time in his wild youth. "Anything serious?"

Linda scrunched her face up. "Not really, just some Es and intent to supply."

"What? They sent him down for that?" He looked at Linda, saw the little shake of her head. "Oh, not a first offence, then."

"No," said Linda, "not exactly." Then she mustered up a bit of a smile. "Like father, like son, eh?"

"Yeah, well," said Mac, "he was always a bit of a boy, your Luke, that's for sure. You seen him recently?" Felt like a bit of a bastard slipping that in.

"Luke? Yeah, now and again, you know how he is." She paused, took a slug of the drink she had on the bar. Could just be Coke, though Mac wouldn't have bet on it. "You know what I used to think, back when?"

"No," said Mac, remembering her back then, a sharp girl in a ra-ra skirt, worked as a barmaid in the Cambridge. Ha, funny to think of it, but she was the only one of them who had managed to advance her career in the meantime, barmaid to landlady definitely had the edge on punk rocker to punk rock revivalist and part-time cabbie.

"I used to think you two were like twins. Like Luke was the good one and you were the evil one."

"Me?" said Mac, affecting an expression of mock outrage. "Evil?"

"Well," said Linda, "you had just come out of Strangeways when I first met you."

Mac shook his head. It was true. The band he'd been in, in Manchester, they were all proper little hooligans, got all their equipment by robbing music shops. Nothing subtle either. Just a brick through the window in the middle of the night and leg it with whatever you could carry. It was no wonder he'd ended up inside.

Linda carried on. "Then later on I thought I'd got it arse backwards, you were the good one and I'd picked the evil one."

Mac just looked at her, didn't say anything. The business they were in, you didn't play by the usual rules. You were in a band, no one expected you to behave properly. A woman went out with you, it was taken as read there'd be others. At least when you went on tour. Had Luke been worse than him? He didn't really know. He'd never really been one for judging other people. Certainly not back then.

"I chucked him in the end, you know. Well, of course you know. I just got tired of it. And I thought about you now and again. How I should have chosen someone like you."

Mac shook his head, started to say something. "You don't know . . ."

Linda waved his words away. "Yeah, I know. I realized it last time I saw you. A year or two back, when Luke brought you here. I saw you both then and I realized you were the same, just blokes. You just want what you want, all of you."

Mac had a sudden urge to protest. Was he the same as Luke these days? He didn't like to think so. Since he'd been with Jackie, God, getting on twenty years, he'd been a reformed character, responsible.

Well, up to a point. He'd tried to be responsible, he'd give himself that, but there were plenty of times he'd failed, plenty of times he'd strayed. Slovenia, where he'd met up with Luke again, that was a case in point all right. This girl called Anja. Yeah, Linda was close enough to the truth of it. Though he kind of hoped there was a sliver of difference in there somewhere, like the gap between Labour and Tory or something, tiny but just big enough to breathe in.

"So," he said, "you know where I might find my evil twin?"

Linda leaned forward, reached out a hand and took hold of Mac's chin, turned his face till he was looking right at her, and she at him. "See what I mean?" she said. Then she laughed and let him go and said, "Dunno, exactly, but you could try New Cross. He's got a new girlfriend, she's at Goldsmiths there."

"A student?"

"No, a bloody lecturer. What d'you think? Course she's a student. You think some grown woman's going to take Luke on?"

Mac put his hands up in surrender, then leaned forward and gave Linda a quick kiss right on the lips before heading back out to the car, where he could hear Kemal squawking on the radio.

"Hey," he said, "calm down, man. Look, I'm going off the radar now for a couple of hours, but I'll work through till morning. All right?"

He switched the radio off before he could hear Kemal's no doubt outraged reply and headed for New Cross.

Jesus Christ, Mac remembered when New Cross was a nice quiet place to drink, basically dead as anything with a bunch of big old Irish boozers. Now it was like a dank and ugly version of Faliraki, all-disco pubs with bouncers on the outside and liquored-up sixteen-year-olds on the inside. He'd tried

Walpole's, the New Cross Inn and Goldsmiths. No sign of Luke. He tried the Marquis of Granby, which was a slight improvement, a standard dodgy South London Irish boozer where you could at least hear yourself think. Tired and thirsty, he drank a quick pint of Guinness, tried to remember where else there was to drink in this neck of the woods, and was struck by an unwelcome thought. Luke had always been a Millwall fan.

Reluctantly he dragged himself back out to the car and drove round some back streets that had done a pretty good job of escaping gentrification till he got to the Duke of Albany. He'd been there once with Luke for a lunchtime pre-match session. Hard-core wasn't the word.

From a distance it looked as if it had closed down. The sign had fallen down and most of the letters of the pub's name had gone missing. But there was a light showing behind those windows that weren't blacked out, and Mac sighed and headed on in. He was rewarded by the sight of a dozen or so hard cases giving him the eye, England flags all over the place, and a carpet that immediately attached itself to his feet. He had a quick look round. No sign of Luke. The locals didn't seem to appreciate his interest. Still, Mac knew exactly how to handle these situations these days.

"Someone order a cab?" he said brightly.

"No, mate," replied the barman, and Mac shrugged and grimaced and got out of there.

Back in the car, he checked the time. Eleven, closing. He was about to turn the radio back on when he was struck by a memory. Years ago, he'd played a few gigs at a pub in New Cross. What the hell was it called? The Amersham Arms, that was it. Heading down towards Deptford. Maybe it was still there.

It was, and practically the first person he saw when he walked into the music room was Luke North – he was slumped on a banquette with his arm around a ghostly pale redhead.

"Hey," said Mac, "how you doing?"

"Hey," said Luke, his eyes taking a moment to focus, "big man. How you doing?"

Better than you, thought Mac. Luke looked ravaged. Way back when, he'd been tall and blond and slightly fucked-up looking. Now he was still tall and blond but more than slightly fucked-up looking: his hair was receding and thinning, his face, even in the light of the pub, was mottled and flaking, and his hard-drinker's belly was stretching his shirt underneath a black suit that looked like someone had died in it.

Luke pulled the girl to him, turning her attention away from the band, if that's what you called a bunch of art-student types hunched over record decks and laptops, silent films playing on a screen behind them. "Sweetie," he said, "this is Mac, an old mucker of mine. Mac, this is Rose, she's the best thing ever happened to me."

Christ, thought Mac, just how pissed is he? Rose smiled at him enthusiastically. She was very pretty in a Gothic sort of way. Extraordinarily pale skin, set off by hair dyed blood-red, skinny as a rake under a long-sleeved black top.

"Nice to meet you," said Mac. "You want a drink?"

"No," said Luke, standing up suddenly and banging the table as he did so, sending a glass tumbling to the floor. "Let me get them. Guinness, Mac, yeah? You sit down there and talk to Rose."

Mac nodded and watched Luke sway his way towards the bar, then seated himself across the table from Rose.

She smiled awkwardly at him and mumbled something. Mac gestured to indicate that the art students were making too much of a racket for him to hear, and she leaned forward. "You're a friend of Luke's?" she said.

"Yeah," said Mac, and paused for a second, then said what was on his mind. "Is he all right? He looks terrible."

Rose just gave him a look, like she had no idea what he was talking about, and leaned back and turned her eyes to the band. As she did so, her top rode up and Mac couldn't help noticing how terribly thin she was, not just skinny but full-on anorexic thin. Oh lord. Well, what sort of a girl did he think would want to go out with someone like Luke? She reminded him of someone. Anja the Slovenian. He'd fallen for her big-time. Typical midlife-crisis number, he supposed. Made him blanch to think of it now. He'd have given up Jackie for her, given up his whole life for her if she'd have had him. Thank Christ she hadn't been interested. He'd been an experience for her, that was all. A learning experience. Maybe that's all Luke was to this Rose. He hoped so, but her cuts gave him pause.

Moments later Luke hoved to, with a mineral water for Rose, a Guinness for Mac and a pint and a large whisky chaser for himself. Mercifully, the art students decided to pick that moment for a break in proceedings, and Mac figured he might as well make his pitch while the volume level permitted and Luke was still conscious.

He ran through the deal. The twenty-fifth-anniversary show. At the Festival Hall. Everyone was going to be there. All Luke had to do was twenty minutes. Could lead on to a whole lot of other stuff – Meltdown, All Tomorrow's Parties. Mac had no idea whether any of this was true or not, he was just spouting the same bullshit Etheridge had given him.

"He'll even sort out the band for you, if you want. Or you can use your own, if you've got one at the minute."

"Fuck that," said Luke, and slumped back in his seat. "Fucking wankers."

Mac wasn't sure who the wankers were – his band, Etheridge, the whole crew of post-punk entrepreneurial types with their post-modern music festivals in out-of-season holiday camps. Personally, he was quite happy to agree that the whole lot of them were, indeed, wankers. But that wasn't going to get the bills paid.

"There's good money in it."

Luke just shook his head, but Mac knew him well enough to see something feral appearing in his eyes.

"Five grand," said Mac, "twenty minutes' work. Not too shabby."

Luke rolled his eyes like five grand was neither here nor there. Then he leaned forward and grasped Mac's hands in his. "I don't give a shit about those wankers, Mac, you know that. But if you want me to do it, I'll do it. I love you, man."

Jesus Christ, thought Mac, wondering what chemicals Luke had imbibed along with the lake full of booze.

Mac hesitated for a moment. Say he delivered Luke to Etheridge, got him on stage with the right combination of chemicals inside him to impersonate sobriety – or at least sentience – for twenty minutes. What would be the upshot? Five grand for Luke – probably enough to kill himself. A grand for Mac – probably enough to pay off Jackie's credit cards.

Shit, why was he feeling guilty? They were all grown-ups, weren't they? Mac had enough to deal with in his own life, hadn't he? And anyway, we all had a few too many once in a while, didn't we? He looked at Luke trying to manoeuvre the pint of lager to his mouth without spilling it. It was blatantly obvious that he had passed the point of no return, social-drinking-wise. Dylan Thomas had that line about how an alcoholic was someone you didn't like who drank as much as you did. Well, Mac had been fond of quoting that in his time, but he could see the shallowness of it now. Thomas's drinking killed him, after all. Luke needed help. It was as simple as that.

"Look, I want you to promise me one thing. You do this gig, yeah? You'll spend the money on rehab."

"Sure," said Luke. "I love you, man."

Just then Rose got up to go to the loo. Luke watched her go, then leaned forward to Mac. "Isn't she gorgeous?"

"Yeah," said Mac, "she seems very nice, bit young though, eh?"

"Yeah," said Luke, "goes like a fucking firecracker, though." He knocked back his whisky, then leaned forward again, motioning Mac to do the same. "Got some nice friends and all, if you're interested."

Mac was appalled to find himself considering it, by the unwelcome knowledge that somewhere inside him was the capacity to say yes, set me up with an anorexic waif of my own. Linda's line about them being like twins was running through his head. It struck him now that it was the evil twin she liked, she wanted. It let her off the hook. Maybe he should just give in to his dark side, maybe that actually made it easier for everyone. No self-repression, no hypocrisy. Just get down in the dirt.

He looked at Rose, heading back from the toilet, stopping at the cigarette machine, all young and fresh and damaged, saw Anja in her place, remembered how much he'd wanted Anja the first time he saw her at that club in

Ljubljana. He saw Luke staring at Rose, eyes full of lust and lager, saw himself in Luke, embracing death. He felt like there was no air in the room. He took a deep breath, sucked in as much as he could. Then tilted his head back and stared at the ceiling, wondering how he got to this pass. Maybe he could retrain as a social worker or something. Something useful. Something that would stop him from taking his place in the tableau in front of him. He shook his head hard and the fog seemed to clear momentarily.

He became aware of the record that was playing, some old punk thing by the Damned, probably the art students were playing it ironically. It didn't sound ironic to Mac though, it sounded like his youth. It reminded him viscerally of what it had felt like being young then, nearly thirty years ago, playing this stupid fast music for no other reason than the sheer rush, the sheer pointless, joyous momentum of it.

And it reminded him that he wasn't young any more, and no matter how many Anjas or brand-new Roses he picked up, he would be nothing more than a vampire, not magically returned to the loud stupid kid he'd once been. He tilted his head back down and looked at Luke. Then it struck him, the difference between them. Luke was still the loud stupid kid he had been, still a selfish, pleasure-seeking child. Ah well, good luck to him, he supposed.

"Sorry, man," he said, shaking his head, "not my scene."

"Your loss," answered Luke. "I tell you, she's a fucking firecracker, that one. Another pint?"

"No thanks," said Mac, but Luke was already up and lurching barwards again. As he did so, Rose ran over to him, threw her arms round him and kissed him like she hadn't seen him for a week. He said something in her ear and she nodded and reached into her bag, took out her purse and handed him a twenty. Luke trousered it and turned towards the bar before suddenly seeming to convulse. And then, slowly and oddly gracefully, he collapsed on the floor, banging into the legs of a couple of his fellow drinkers.

"You fucking wanker!" shouted one of the drinkers, and wound up to throw a punch, before realizing that his opponent was already down and out.

Mac looked on transfixed, his attention entirely gripped by Rose, who calmly knelt down on the floor next to Luke and cradled him against her, stroking his head with one hand, a flame-haired, flat-chested Madonna and her debauched infant.

Later, sitting in the cab, resigned to being a grown-up, earning his money the hard way, he found the words "damned" and "blessed" jostling for space in his brain.

The following afternoon he was woken up by the phone. It was Etheridge on the line. Mac paused for a moment, wondering what to say. He wasn't sure he really cared what Luke did, but the thought of taking a finder's fee for tracking him down felt weirdly unclean, seemed to somehow make him complicit in Luke's grim debauch. On the other hand, it was undoubtedly an easy grand.

Before he could make the decision, Etheridge started talking. "Look," he said, "not to worry about tracking down old Luke."

"Oh," said Mac, "decided against risking him on stage, have you?"

"No, no, not at all," explained Etheridge, "people love a bit of drama, don't they? No, his manager's been in touch so it's all sorted out. I just thought I'd let you know."

"Manager?" said Mac.

"Oh yes, delightful young woman by the sound of her, name of Rose. Sounds like she's got him right under her thumb. So there we are. Well, thanks again."

"No trouble," said Mac and put the phone down.

The next morning he finished his shift deliberately early and got home in time to find Jackie still in bed. After they'd had sex he was happy to realize that for the first time in a long while he hadn't thought about Anja at all.

PENGUIN ISLAND

BY JERRY SYKES

Camden Town

Eamonn Coughlan had lived in Camden Town all his life, and from as far back as he could remember there had been packs of teenagers roaming the streets: from the wartime cosh gangs that had operated during the blackouts to the hippies in the '60s . . . from the punks of the '70s through to the . . . Well, he didn't know what they were called these days, but whatever they were called he had never come across a group of teenagers that had marked out their territories with as much determination as the current crop. Of course, he knew that graffiti had been around forever, ever since an unknown caveman had first picked up a piece of sharpened flint and scratched into the walls of his cave pictures of the animals that he had killed that morning. But it seemed that in the last few years almost every building in Camden Town had been marked with some kind of multicoloured lettering or sign. He knew that it had something to do with drugs, an ongoing turf war, and that the signs were forever changing because of the constant battle for the rights to deal drugs to the thousands of tourists who flocked into the area around Camden Lock each weekend, but the subtleties of the different signs were lost on him.

For the last eighteen months, the dominant piece of graffiti on the wall beside the lift in his building had been a large picture of a castle in red and blue. But as Coughlan pushed through the door that late spring morning, he saw that the castle had been covered over with black paint and that a couple of boys were now creating a new motif in its place. The new design was still little more than a sketch, he could just about make out three big letters outlined in red and orange – *YBT*, it looked like – but before Coughlan could see more, one of the boys caught him looking and turned and raised a hard chin in his direction.

"Yo, what d'you think you're lookin' at," snarled the boy, his neck stretching out of his collar. From the rest of his face he looked to be no more than thirteen or fourteen, but his eyes were cold and hard, aged before their time. He had a greased-down, straight-fringed haircut that made him look like a little Caesar, and the skin around the corners of his mouth was studded with cloves of acne. The other boy continued to paint, his head rising and falling to some music that no one else could hear.

Coughlan shook his head and let the door fall closed behind him. Averting his eyes, he shuffled across to the lift, Little Caesar following him with narrowed eyes, his breath loud and coarse through his mouth. As Coughlan pressed the button to call the lift, the other boy turned to see what his friend was looking at, and Coughlan recognized him at once as Pete Wilson, a boy from the building that he had known since he was a toddler. From what Coughlan could remember, he must have been about twelve now.

Pete's pupils went wide as he recognized the old man and his hands whipped behind his back, hiding the paint can.

"What do you think you're doing, Pete?" asked Coughlan, but as soon as the words were out of his mouth he felt his shoulders tense. He had never been one for making a fuss, and his outburst had scared him almost as much as it had surprised him.

Pete hesitated for a moment, torn between his childhood links and the new alliance of his fresh and future independence.

"I bet your mother doesn't know what you're up to," Coughlan persisted, brave now. "What do you think she'd say if she knew you were down here vandalizing your own building?"

Discovering that the decrepit old man in front of them knew his friend, Little Caesar's mood lightened and he sniggered and punched Pete on the arm. Pete grunted and punched him back, glad of the distraction. From further up the stairs the sound of someone cursing and kicking the lift door could be heard.

"I hope you're going to clean that mess up before you go home," said Coughlan, pointing a crooked finger at the wall.

"I was just painting over the castle," protested Pete.

"With black paint on a white wall? And what's with the red and orange letters? What's that supposed to mean?"

"That's YBT," replied Pete, smiling. "You Been Torched."

"I don't understand," replied Coughlan, frowning.

Pete opened his mouth to speak, but before he could do so, Little Caesar hit him on the shoulder again. "You know we're not supposed to tell no one about that."

"It's not a secret," protested Pete, holding his arm tight where Little Caesar had punched him.

"Fuckin' child," snapped Little Caesar, snatching the paint can from Pete's hand and storming out of the building. Pete watched him go and then, after taking a quick glance at the unfinished graffiti, followed him. At the door, Pete cast a look back at the old man, and Coughlan thought he detected the hint of an apologetic word in the nervous stutter of his lips.

Coughlan saw them disappear around the edge of the building, Pete trailing the other kid like a sibling desperate to please his elder brother. He waited a couple of seconds to make sure there was no return, and then felt a long hot breath leave his chest. He did not realize that he had been holding his breath. He turned back to the lift and pressed the button again.

A couple of minutes later, an old woman in a blue raincoat appeared at the foot of the stairs, panting as if she had just walked up them and not down. "I hope you're not waiting on the lift," she managed to gasp on a cloud of smoke, a cigarette burning in her fist, before she too disappeared through the door.

Coughlan took a deep breath and started up the stairs.

Back in his flat on the fourth floor, he filled the kettle and dropped a teabag into a mug. Waiting for the kettle to boil, he rested his hands on the edge of the sink and looked out over the estate towards Kentish Town Road, towards a couple of phone booths. Behind the booths was a low brick wall where it was common knowledge that a number of drug dealers practised their trade, their customers either walking up or pulling up on the street in their cars to pick up their goods. There was a dealer out there at the moment, and another one strolling up and down the street, gesturing with a pointed finger at the cars that passed. It had become such a common sight, part of the threadbare fabric of the estate, that it no longer triggered an emotional response in Coughlan. But as he let his attention drift across the rest of the estate, his heart filled with sorrow as he spotted Pete and his friend sitting on the back of a bench no more than fifteen feet from the phone booths, watching the drug dealers in silent fascination.

Later that night, stretched out on his bed, Coughlan listened with grim acceptance to the sound of his neighbours arguing, the rise and fall of drunken tongues and slurred insults. On the weekend it was like this most nights, along with the rumble of music through the wall that reminded him of the night during the war when a German bomb had reduced their neighbour's house to smoking ash and rubble. The bomb had buckled the foundations of their own house, and the front door had never fitted the frame after that, still letting in a draught when the council had moved them out of the house and into the Castle Estate the same summer he retired. And it was on nights like this that he wished his neighbours, his imagined enemies, could be bombed all over again.

A week later, Coughlan was walking across the estate to the newsagent's on Castle Road when he saw Pete with another boy at the side of the building. It was the first time he had seen him since the afternoon near the lift. The other boy was not the same one who had been with him that time. No, this one looked to be more like one of the lads that hung around the phone booths, older, all cold skin and hand jerks. The two of them were talking, but there was something odd about their body language. Pete was nodding and grinning as the older boy spoke, as if the older boy was telling him a long joke, although from the look on the older boy's face he seemed to be more annoyed than amused. Coughlan tried not to watch, but he kept glancing up as he walked past, and when Pete caught him looking, the grin fell from the boy's face and his once innocent cheeks flushed with something approaching shame. The other boy caught the change in his features and, after peering across at Coughlan, jabbed Pete on the shoulder and asked him who the old man was. Pete attempted to shrug off the question, but the other boy jabbed him again on the shoulder, harder this time, and Pete's mouth sprung open. Coughlan turned his head aside and hurried on, but not before he caught his name in the tumble of words that spilled from Pete's mouth.

The following afternoon, struggling home from the supermarket – since arthritis had calcified the knuckles in his hands, he was unable to load more than a few items into his bag at a time and so had to go shopping each afternoon – Coughlan ran into Pete again. As Coughlan was crossing the junction at the foot of the estate, a line of impatient cars pushing at the red light, Pete came rushing out of the greengrocer's with a loaf of bread under his arm and bumped straight into the old man. Coughlan stumbled but did not fall, though he did drop his shopping bag, and a tin of processed peas rolled into the gutter.

"Whoa, watch where you're going," squealed Pete, and then pulled up as he noticed that it was Coughlan he had bumped into.

Coughlan frowned at him and shook his head, and then stooped to pick up his groceries.

"Here, let me get that," said Pete, crossing to pick up the peas from the gutter. He held out the tin to Coughlan and the old man took it and put it in his bag with the other things.

"Sorry about that," Pete continued. "Look, why don't I carry your shopping home for you? The lift's not working again." Without waiting for an answer, he took the bag from Coughlan's hardened and aching hands and started walking.

Pushing through the door of the building, the boy holding

it open with the back of his heel, Coughlan noticed that Pete headed straight for the stairs without so much as a casual glance at the mess of graffiti on the wall. It had not been touched since Coughlan had stumbled across Pete and his friend with fresh paint on their hands, but he thought that Pete would have at least sneaked a look at it. Or perhaps that was the reason behind Pete helping him with his shopping . . .

Upstairs in the flat, Pete put the shopping bag on the kitchen counter, took out his own loaf of bread that he had put in there for safe-keeping, and then turned towards the door. But he appeared to be in no great rush to leave, his lips mouthing silent words as if he had something on his mind.

Coughlan thought he knew what it was. "Don't worry about it, son," he said, smiling. "I'm not going to tell your mum about the graffiti or anything, if that's what you're worried about . . ."

"Oh no, that's not the reason I helped you," insisted Pete, shaking his head. "No, that's got nothing to do with it. I just saw you struggling across the street and I thought . . ."

"I know, I know," Coughlan assured him, patting the air in front of him with his palms. "And I do appreciate it. It's just that . . . Look, can I get you a drink of squash or something?"

"No, that's all right," said Pete, shaking his head. "I better get this bread home or my mum'll be wondering where I am."

"All right," said Coughlan. "Well, thanks again, Pete."

The boy offered him a brief smile and then turned and disappeared back down the stairs.

The following afternoon, Pete was waiting for Coughlan when the old man came out of the supermarket, and once again offered to help him with his shopping. Coughlan was surprised to see him after the awkwardness of their last meeting, but he knew enough to keep his mouth shut if it meant that much to the lad. And on the walk back to the estate, it did seem that Pete had forgotten all about it, chatting about his school and his teachers.

Over the following couple of weeks, Pete helped Coughlan with his shopping a number of times, and soon Coughlan found that he was timing his trips to the supermarket to coincide with Pete coming home from school. Sometimes Pete would accept the old man's offer of a drink, gulping it down, but more often than not he would decline, telling him that he had to get home.

And then one afternoon, an hour or so before Coughlan was due to leave for the supermarket, there was a knock at the door. When he opened it he was surprised to find Pete standing there with a couple of bulging shopping bags in his hands. "These weigh a ton," he gasped. "Are you going to let me in or what?"

Startled and amused, Coughlan stepped aside to let him across the threshold. "What've you got in there?" he said, trailing Pete down the hall and into the kitchen.

Pete left the question in the air as he hefted the bags onto the counter. He let out a great breath, and then turned and rested against the counter, smiling and shaking his head.

"I don't understand," said Coughlan, frowning.

"The teacher was sick, so we got let out of school . . . I thought I might as well pick up your shopping for you."

"But that lot must've cost you a small fortune," said Coughlan, stepping forward and peering into the bags. "You didn't pay for it yourself, did you?" He had no idea how much pocket money Pete got each week, or whether he had a paper round or some other job, but, whatever, he should have been spending it on himself, not on an old man. "You must let give you the money."

Coughlan moved into the front room, the fire turned down low, and returned with his wallet. He took out a ten-pound note and handed it to Pete. "Is that enough?" he asked, looking at the remaining note in his wallet, a fiver. He felt that he should give the boy more for his thoughtfulness, but the fiver was all he had until he claimed his pension at the end of the week.

"Ten's fine," replied Pete. He took the crumpled bill from the outstretched hand and folded it into his front pocket.

"It was very kind of you, anyway," said Coughlan. "Very thoughtful."

"Look, I was thinking," said Pete, hesitant. His cheeks were flushed pink, and there was a fine sheen of perspiration on his forehead. "Why don't you let me do this all the time, get your shopping for you on my way home from school. I know it must be difficult for you, what with your hands like that . . . It's no problem, honest, especially as you always eat the same things."

Coughlan felt tears prick the back of his lids. "That's a great idea," he said. "Thanks."

"And then you can pay me when I get here," Pete added.

"But what if I'm not in?" said Coughlan, sniffing.

"Well, I don't know . . ."

"I might want to go out. I don't want you getting my shopping for me and then not being here to let you in."

"I don't suppose you've got a mobile phone, have you?"

"Er, no. No, I haven't . . ."

"Well, I don't know, then," said Pete, his forehead crinkled in thought. "What about if you let me have a key or something? Or how about leaving it with one of the neighbours?"

Coughlan thought about his neighbours, the born fighters. "I'll go down and get you one cut in the morning," he replied.

"Sorted," said Pete.

The new arrangement suited them both fine. But then Coughlan found that he was just waiting in for Pete to arrive, and not getting out and about as much as he would have liked. He let this go on for some time, until one afternoon, as he was looking out the window, the clouds above the estate parted, the solid shapes of the buildings started to soften around the edges, and he realized that he was just being ridiculous and decided to go out for a walk. Pulling on his jacket, he left the estate and headed down Castle Road towards the centre of Camden Town, past the boarded-up pubs, the disused tube station, the shops that sold little more than international phone cards, and the cafés with names in languages that he did not even recognize let alone understand. As he walked, he saw a number of walls and bridges littered with both the castle and YBT graffiti, the castle artwork faded and peeling while the YBT letters shone with a brittle freshness. It did not cross his mind for one second that perhaps Pete had been one of the artists.

At the junction in front of the Camden Town tube station there was a traffic island, a triangular slice of concrete and paving stones that for as long as Coughlan could remember had been known as Penguin Island. In the street behind the tube station, there was a Catholic church that back in the '50s had been frequented in the main by the Irish families living in the immediate area since the turn of the century. After the regular Sunday morning Mass had finished at 11.30, the men would gather on the traffic island to wait for the pubs to open at noon, while the women would go home to prepare lunch. Standing there in their uniform black suits and white shirts, with their hands in their pockets, shuffling around on impatient feet, the men had resembled nothing so much as a squadron of penguins stranded in the middle of a sea of traffic.

Coughlan smiled at the remembrance, but then another more potent image appeared beside the first one: Coughlan himself walking back from the church with his wife at his side, wanting to be on the island but not having the courage to tell his wife what he wanted. It had been the tale of his life, and he wondered if he would ever now get to Penguin Island. He pushed his hands deeper into his pockets and walked on.

When he returned to the flat an hour later, Coughlan was surprised to hear voices coming from the living room. At first he thought that Pete had arrived and turned on the TV to amuse himself while he waited, something that he had done before, but when he stepped through into the living room, he found Pete and another boy standing in front of the mantelpiece.

At the sight of Coughlan, Pete cast a quick glance towards his friend and then turned to look at Coughlan again, his mouth open in a mask of timid shock. The friend caught the apprehension in Pete's face and pushed back his shoulders and looked over towards Coughlan with a slow grin on his face.

"Yeah, this is . . . this is Keith," stammered Pete. "It's all right for me to let him come in and watch TV with me?"

"Well, I suppose so," replied Coughlan, distracted.

Coughlan looked across at Keith, took in the knowing look and the stance that told him that he was just as comfortable, if not more so, in Coughlan's home than the old man himself.

"Hello, Keith," said Coughlan, nodding.

Keith said nothing, just kept up the grin in response.

"I've put the shopping away," said Pete. "And I got you another one of those pork-and-pickle pies you like."

"Thanks, Pete."

"It was reduced so you might have to eat it today."

"Yes, thanks, Pete," muttered Coughlan again, embarrassed at discussing the state of his finances in front of a stranger. "Anyway . . . look, Pete, I don't mind you bringing your friends round here. But in the future, can you ask me first?"

"I'm sorry, I thought you'd be in," replied Pete.

"That's all right, no harm done this time," said Coughlan.

Pete kept a low profile for a short time after that, but when Coughlan came home late one afternoon a week later – to appear less needful he had taken to being out sometimes when Pete was due to call with his shopping – he found that Pete had not one but several friends with him. When Coughlan poked his head through the door, curious at the noise, there was a group of four or five lads sitting around the living room. One of them looked to be about the same age as Pete, but the others appeared to be about two or three years older, tufts of soft hair colouring their chins and their long limbs barely under control. Pete was sitting in the middle of the sofa and looked to be more at ease than he had been the time before, staring at the TV. He did not seem to have noticed Coughlan, but then none of them appeared to have noticed him, and Coughlan felt a tumble of emotions pass through him. On one hand, he felt that he should pull Pete out of the room and ask him to ask the others to leave, but then he did not want to embarrass the lad in front of his friends again. Without waiting to see if he had been spotted, Coughlan made a gesture as if he had forgotten something, and then turned and left the flat.

He walked up to Parliament Hill, through the park past the athletics track, and back down to Camden Town, his mind adrift on children and the past. When he reached home again, Pete and his friends had gone, but the smell of cigarettes and something else still hung in the air. Coughlan opened the top windows to clear the room and then closed the door tight and headed for bed.

Later that night, stretched out on his bed, unable to sleep because of the noise coming through the wall from his neighbours, Coughlan felt himself returning to the thoughts that had been troubling him during his walk earlier. He and his wife had not been able to have children of their own, and so he was not sure how he should have handled the situation with Pete. Instinct told him that he had done the right thing, but he wished to God that he had more than instinct on which to base his reactions.

In 1945, a short time before Coughlan had started courting his wife – he had known her since junior school, and in their teens the pair had lived just three streets apart – she had had a brief but intense affair with a married American soldier stationed in London. When the American had broken off the affair to return to his wife and home in West Virginia, she had just shrugged it off as if he had meant no more to her than a pair of old shoes. But then two months later she had fallen into a deep depression and not ventured out of the house for another three weeks. When at last she came out again, she had been a different person, as quiet in her new skin as she had been the life and soul in her old skin. And she had also then had some time for Coughlan, too, the quiet and dependable kid in the corner of the neighbourhood. Of course, there had been rumours that it was not depression that had kept her in the house all that time, the strongest of which was that following the American's departure she had undergone a backstreet abortion that went wrong and left her barren. Coughlan had ignored all the rumours at the time, grateful for her attention, and had maintained a closed ear even when she had failed to become pregnant throughout their long marriage. Even now, more than a decade after her death, he still refused to believe that the rumours were something other than malicious gossip, putting their childlessness down as something that was just meant to be.

The following afternoon there was a group of boys in his flat again, but this time Pete was not with them. There were just the three of them, smoking and watching *The Jerry Springer Show.*

"What are you doing here?" asked Coughlan, doing his best to sound indignant but finding a touch of fear holding him back.

The boys ignored him, grinning as the TV pumped out a hard rattle of cheers and applause.

"How did you get in?" said Coughlan, stepping further into the room.

The boys continued to grin and ignore him.

"I said, how did you get in?" repeated Coughlan, stepping in front of the TV.

"Your boy gave us his key, man," replied one of the guys at last, scowling, his pale face shrouded in the hood of his sweatshirt, arching to look around Coughlan at the TV.

"You mean Pete gave you his key?"

"If that's what his name is," sniggered the guys.

"Well, he shouldn't have done that," said Coughlan, reaching down to turn off the TV. "So I'd like you all to leave."

"I was watching that," complained one of the other boys.

"Yo, he gave us his key, man," said the first boy. "Gave us his key and told us to wait here for him. Said he had to do some shopping for you or something. You can't ask us to leave."

"Yeah, what's he going to say when he gets back here and finds us gone?" said the second boy. "What's he going to say when he gets back here and finds you kicked us out?"

"Well . . . that's different, then," said Coughlan, taken aback. "You should have said." And all at once he felt shrunken, as if he had betrayed Pete. He felt all the boys looking at him, judging him, making him out to be the villain of the piece. He did not know what to do, feeling like even his breathing was further condemnation, and after a few moments of just staring into space, he turned and walked through into the kitchen to look out across the estate, a terrible weight hanging in his chest.

Pete at last turned up half an hour later, but the next time that Coughlan came home to find a group of his friends watching TV in his living room, Pete was again not with them. There was still no sign of him an hour later, either, and so Coughlan climbed down from his stool in the kitchen, shuffled through into the living room and asked them to leave. This time the boys did so without much bother, clucking tongues and dragging feet, but it left the old man feeling confused and hurt.

The time after that the lads had the TV up loud and, despite Coughlan asking them a couple of times to turn it down, the noise remained constant. Coughlan did not have the strength to argue with them and kept to himself in the kitchen. After waiting for Pete for over an hour, he could take it no longer. He slipped on his jacket and headed out into the night.

He sat on a bench in the centre of the estate, watching people come and go. It was a warm evening and he felt comfortable out there, more comfortable than he did in the light, the twilight hiding the geographical sins and scars of the estate.

He sat for another few minutes and then decided to go for a walk. When he got home again about half past ten, the gang was gone but had left a mosaic of trash behind in his front room: crushed beer and Coke cans, fried chicken boxes, cigarette butts, neon bottles with chewed straws poking out of their lips. He tidied up as best he could and then went to bed, determined to confront Pete and ask him to give him his key back.

But Pete did not appear the following afternoon, or the one after that, and when he had still not turned up on the third afternoon, Coughlan felt his fragile resolve start to waver. Then one lunchtime, as he was looking for some tinfoil to wrap a half-eaten sandwich in, the ongoing tension made him lose his appetite, and he found something that fired him up again.

Standing on a chair in the kitchen, he was reaching into the top cupboard where he was sure there was some tinfoil, when he felt a cool plastic bag there. He could not see into the cupboard so he shifted his arthritic fingers around, attempting to make out what it was. An old carrier bag, stuffed with some linen napkins, perhaps. He tried to find purchase on the bag but his fingers kept slipping off. After a few failed attempts, he managed to catch hold of a corner of the bag and started to ease it out of the cupboard. Moving it a couple of inches at a time, he pulled it towards the edge of the shelf. And then there was a shift and a tumble, and a cascade of small plastic bags and little foil envelopes fell out onto the floor in a solid splash. A black bin liner followed like a winded kite. Coughlan looked at the mess in astonishment. There must have been at least two or three hundred little bags and envelopes spread across the kitchen floor.

It took him a minute to get there, but Coughlan had seen enough police shows on TV to know that he was looking at drugs. Hundreds, perhaps thousands of pounds' worth of drugs. He climbed down from the chair and sat for a moment looking at the hellish pile on the floor, wondering what to do with it all. He checked his watch and saw that it was almost five o'clock, Pete's usual time for coming around. Sighing at the situation, he levered himself down onto the floor, scooped all the small packets back into the bin liner, and hefted it up onto the table.

Fifteen minutes later he heard Pete's voice out in the hall, and then another voice behind the first. Coughlan held his breath, his heart beating loud in his chest, as he waited for them to walk along the hall and into the front room. He heard the TV being switched on, a quick pulse of canned laughter, and then seconds later a kid with black hair stepped into the kitchen. He saw Coughlan sitting at the table with the full bin liner in front of him and his pupils went dark and wide in anger.

"What the fuck d'you think you're doing with that?"

"I might ask you the same question," replied Coughlan.

"It's none of your fuckin' business."

"It's my flat," said Coughlan. "It's my home."

At that moment Pete walked into the room, lured in by the raised voices.

"Did you know anything about this?" asked Coughlan, pointing at the bin liner.

Pete glanced at the other boy, looking for the right words.

And then without warning, the other boy stepped up to Coughlan and punched him hard in the face.

Coughlan felt a great bolt of pain shake his spine and nail him to the chair. Tears sprang across his face and diluted the blood that bubbled from his nose. His head spun for a second, and then he fell unconscious face-first across the bag of drugs.

"You've killed him," squealed Pete. "You've killed him."

"He's not dead," said the other kid, poking Coughlan hard in the shoulder so that his head lolled back and forth. "Look, he's still bleeding. Dead people don't bleed like that."

"But he might be dead soon," said Pete, his face turning white and his tongue sticking in his throat.

"Don't be fuckin' stupid," said the other kid, stepping forward and giving Coughlan a hard shove. The old man slid off the table and dragged the bag of drugs onto the floor with him, spilling its contents across the battered linoleum.

Pete just stared at the old man, the spread of drugs.

"Well, go on, then, pick 'em up," said the other kid.

Pete hesitated for a second, his limbs telling him to run, but then did as he was told. He gathered the drugs together and tried to see if Coughlan was breathing all right.

"Come on, come on," snapped the other kid, tapping Pete in the side with the toe of his trainer.

Pete hurried to scrape up the remainder of the packets and stuff them back into the bin liner. He gathered the neck of the bag together and then tried to hand it to the other kid. But the other kid just told him to put it back in the cupboard.

"But what about Mr. Coughlan . . . ?"

"He's not goin' to be telling no one," came the response.

Coughlan came round moments later, more shocked than hurt. Drifting back into the here and now, he remained on the kitchen floor for a short time, listening for signs of other people in the flat. It all appeared to be quiet, and he was sure that it had been the slamming of the door that had stirred him. He ran a hand across his upper lip, wiping at the blood there. It had started to harden and it felt like his nose had stopped bleeding. He climbed to his feet and shuffled across to the sink. He turned on the tap and let it run until it got as cold as it was going to get. Cupping his hands together, he filled them with water, and then held his nose in the water until it had all leaked through his hardened fingers. He repeated the action. As the centre of his face started to numb, the numbness spreading out from his nose, he felt his strength returning and his mind clearing. He knew that he should go to the police, but he also knew that would be a mistake. He had seen what had happened to people who stood up for themselves, and he did not want to go through that himself. Rather than bringing an end to their torment, it had more often than not meant an escalation.

He shuffled through into his bedroom and changed into a fresh shirt, throwing the bloodstained one into the waste bin behind the door. There were a few splashes of blood on his trousers, but as he had just bought them a few weeks earlier, he was reluctant to throw them out too, and decided to keep them on. Once he had finished dressing, he walked into the bathroom to inspect his injuries in the mirror. He used a flannel to wipe the dried blood from his skin and then leaned in to the mirror to get a closer look. There was a small scratch on the side of his nose, and the beginnings of a bruise, but apart from that the damage appeared to be minimal, at least on the outside.

He went back into the bedroom and put on a thick sweater. Despite the warmth of the evening, the assault had left him feeling cold and he had goosepimples on his arms. Then he went back into the kitchen and looked at the blood on the floor, the bloodied handprints from the floor to the sink like the footprints of some great lost beast. The sight of it made him feel a little sick, and he told himself he would clean it up later. He turned and left the flat, closing the door behind him.

He walked through Camden Town, through the streets he had walked since childhood, feeling that he no longer knew them. His mind was all over the place, dislocated and lost within the familiar maps of his life. Earlier he had been quite prepared to confront Pete about letting his friends use the flat, but now he felt like he just wanted to forget that he had ever met the boy.

He tried to eat an omelette at a café on Chalk Farm Road, pushing it around his plate until it got lodged in the cooling grease, and then walked up to Parliament Hill Fields. There, he sat on a bench overlooking the athletics track, watching a group of girls messing about in the long jump pit. At one point, one of the girls ran across to the steeplechase water jump. There was no water in it, but she still jumped in and pretended to be drowning, waving her arms around and screaming. Her friends just ignored her and at last she returned to the sand pit.

The girls left when it started to get dark, but Coughlan felt too tired to walk home just then and stretched out on the bench to rest for a few minutes before setting off. The brittle summer stars spreading across the darkening ceiling of the world reminded him of a time during the war when he had dragged his mattress onto the roof of the outhouse to listen to the bombs dropping on the East End. Despite the noise and the threat of the bombs getting closer, he remembered it as being a time of calm for him, a time before he had met his wife, a time before the neighbour's house had been crushed. He let his lids fall, so tired and with a persistent headache, and when at last he opened them again it had started to get light. Surprised, he rubbed hard at his face to wake himself up and then climbed to his feet. His back ached but the pain eased up as he started walking towards the gate. When he checked the clock outside the jeweller's store on Kentish Town Road he was surprised to see that it was five o'clock in the morning.

He let himself into the flat and stood for few moments in the hall, just holding his breath and listening. Minutes passed but all he could hear was the regular sounds of the flat creaking. He appeared to be alone, but to make sure he went round each of the rooms, checking in cupboards and behind doors, before going back to the front door and locking it. Then he went back into his bedroom and climbed into bed, still in his clothes.

When he woke again it was after four in the afternoon, a dull rectangle of orange light spread across the bed beside him. For a moment he did not know where he was, and then he remembered falling asleep on the bench and it all came back to him. But in that fleeting moment of not knowing, he had felt at peace with the world. And now the knot was back in his stomach. He looked at his watch again to check the time. Pete or some of his friends would be around soon and he did not want to be here for that. He went into the bathroom to check on the wound, and then back into the bedroom to dress in a set of thicker and more comfortable clothes. In the kitchen he took his pension book from the drawer, slipped it into the back pocket of his trousers, and headed back outside. He took a quick glance at the drug dealers sitting near the phone booths, then turned and headed back up towards Parliament Hill Fields, calling in at a corner shop to purchase a couple of small pies and a carton of milk.

There were a few pensioners out on the bowling green, and a middle-aged couple were struggling to hit the ball over the net on one of the tennis courts. Coughlan stopped for a moment to watch them, aching inside at their casual grasp of the ordinariness of their lives, and then continued on to the bench where he had slept the night before. As he turned from the fence bordering the court, he started to panic at the thought that someone else might be sitting there. But when he reached the top of the rise and saw that there was no one else there, the feeling of relief that flooded his senses was just as great as if he had returned to his flat and found that Pete and his friends had decided to leave. He stepped up his pace until he reached the bench, took his seat, and then looked around, blinking in the high afternoon sun. There was no one on the athletics track, no one messing around in the long jump pit, nothing for him to watch and help pass the time. But on the main path there was a woman out walking her dog, and when Coughlan offered her a cheerful hello he was rewarded with a brief smile. It was the greatest reaction he'd had in a long time, the greatest acceptance.

Through the birch trees on the far side of the track and the cranes that seemed to be forever stalking the streets of London, Coughlan watched the sun go down until he became shrouded in darkness. The shroud felt a little colder than it had the night before, so he pulled his coat tight around his chest. A slight wind had also started to blow across the hill, and he thought that perhaps he might be too cold on the bench. He tried to think of somewhere else he might be able to sleep. There was a small café near the tennis courts, and he thought that perhaps he might be warm snuggled up there at the back of the kitchen. But then he remembered the bandstand further back. Not the usual kind of bandstand with a wrought-iron railing circling the stage, but one with a solid wall facing the path. Whenever the bandstand was in use, the audience would sit on the hill to watch. If he crept in there he would be sheltered from both the wind and people passing on the path. Taking one last look across the track towards the failing light, Coughlan bundled himself up inside his coat and headed for the bandstand.

Within an hour he was asleep. He dreamed of black-and-white creatures diving from a concrete island and swimming free, at ease with both themselves and their surroundings. From the opposite bank he stood and watched them for a long time before summoning up the courage to dive in and join them. His arms and legs felt awkward at first, stiff and making little progress, but soon he too was swimming free. At first the other creatures kept their distance, but after a few minutes he was accepted into their fold, and when the swim was over the creatures let him climb out onto their concrete island. When he looked back at the place from where he had dived into the water, it had disappeared.

The following morning he awoke feeling like he had just had the best night's sleep of his life, and he set off back to the flat with something approaching a spring in his step.

Walking across the estate, he saw that the door to his flat was wide open. Fearing that he had been burgled, he picked up his pace and hurried up the stairs. But as he approached the door, the fear was replaced with something else: relief at the fact that he no longer felt responsible for his own flat. On reaching the door, he stopped and listened for a moment, and then pulled it closed and carried on walking.

PART IV

LONDON CALLING

PART IV

SHE'LL RIDE A WHITE HORSE

BY MARK PILKINGTON

Dalston

A hundred wary eyes watched his approach through the yellow-stained sodium twilight. The cats were all around him, frozen as if ready to pounce, though whether towards him or away from him, he couldn't tell. Heldon considered himself a cat lover, but their stares forced a shiver of unease.

The pinpoints of light punctured the night – under trolleys and cars, on corrugated roofs, though most of them, attached to near-identical scrawny brown bodies, surrounded an overturned plastic barrel that had spilled a neat chevron of part-frozen meat and bone onto a torn newspaper headline: *Iran: Allied Generals Are Ready.*

By day, Ridley Road Market is the heart of Dalston. A heaving babel of traders and shoppers – East End English, West African, Indian, Russian, Turkish – squeeze past each other in a permanent bottleneck. The stalls – Snow White Children's Clothes, Chicken Shop, Alpha & Omega Variety Store – offer exotically coloured fabrics and cheap electrical goods alongside barrels of unidentifiable animal parts, unfamiliar vegetables and unlocked mobile phones.

But at night the market belongs to the cats. They are everywhere. They don't need to fight, there's always plenty of food to go round; they just wait their turns in the shadows.

At least they keep the rats away, thought Heldon, in a

transparent attempt to console himself. A foot-long rodent scuttled behind a wheelie bin. The cats' eyes remained fixed on the larger intruder. "Don't mind me," he said out loud, "just keep eating your dinner."

"Ignore the cats, they're just keeping an eye out for troublemakers."

The deep, careful African voice came from a closed stall within a concrete shell on the other side of the road; a tired-looking sign above a closed wooden door read *Bouna Fabrics Afr*, before trailing off into decay.

The cats returned to their business. Heldon crossed the road and opened the door.

"Hello, Ani. You've got yourself a few more cats since I was last here."

"Yes, my friend. At least they keep the rats away, eh?"

Aniweta smiled and the men shook hands. A Nigerian barrel of a man with a gold-ringed grasp to match, his strong dark hand engulfed Heldon's puffy pink-white flesh. He claimed to be in his forties. But his watery eyes and leather-tan skin made Heldon think he was older than that.

"It's good of you to see me," said Heldon.

"Well, it's not as if I have a choice, eh? Come, let's go out back, this place gives me a headache." Aniweta turned, pushed his way through the lurid yellow and green fabrics hanging from the ceiling, and disappeared.

A thick black curtain veiled a door leading into a small, dimly lit room. Lined shelves held rows of unlabelled glass jars containing dried plants, powders and things too deformed to be identified as animal, mineral or vegetable. A heavy wooden desk, its surface covered with what could just as easily be scientific or magical debris – scales, tongs, a pestle and mortar, stains, scorch marks and candle wax – stood near the wall facing the entrance.

Aniweta sat down on a sturdy wooden chair and looked expectantly at Heldon.

The sickly aroma of faded incense, overripe vegetables and old meat reminded Heldon of the first time he'd been down here. That was almost five years ago. Then he had been a little afraid, though he would never have admitted it at the time. Now he was just angry.

"There's been another one, Ani. But I suppose you know that already."

"Yes, I know. A girl this time. No doubt you will call her Eve."

Heldon knew the market well. You had to, working in this neighbourhood. Mostly it looked after itself, a closed system, and it was best not to get involved. The force had their own people in there, and the market presumably had its own people in the force. Recycled mobiles and other stolen goods were one thing. They could be dealt with quietly. But there were other things that could not be ignored. As the trade in guns and drugs got a little too casual, like it did every year, a few stalls were inevitably raided, as was the old pub on the corner of St. Mark's Rise, which was now less popular, though more peaceful, as a beautician's.

But all this was regular police work, and so no longer Heldon's business.

At first, bush meat was his business. Chimps mostly, but also the odd gorilla, brought in from the Congo and Gabon. An Italian punk girl had almost fainted on seeing a huge, dark, five-fingered hand fall out of brown paper wrapping as it was passed to a customer at the Sunny Day Meats stall.

The raids found no whole animals, only parts – heads,

feet, genitals, hands – most too precious for food and sold only for *muti* or *juju*. Medicine. Magic. They turned up something else too. The squad at first thought the bag contained parts of a baby chimp: fingers stripped of skin, a dark and shrivelled penis and scrotum, teeth. But forensics found otherwise. They were human.

The stallholder was arrested.

Heldon's team had kept the details from the press, but Aniweta had known. As a *sangoma*, a witch, he knew many things. Heldon knew very little about him, however, except that he had emigrated to London from Nigeria in the 1970s, had a UK passport and no criminal record. He had always proved a reliable source of local and traditional knowledge, and his calm manner, coupled with a dark sense of humour, had commanded Heldon's respect and, on occasion, fear.

At first Heldon had assumed the parts were imported. That was until September 21, 2001, the autumn equinox, when a boy was fished from the Thames outside the Globe Theatre. The five-year-old's body was naked, apart from a pair of orange shorts, put on him, it turned out, after he had been bled to death. Then his head and limbs had been severed by someone who knew precisely what they were doing.

They named him Adam. It was sickening to keep referring to him as "the corpse" or "the torso". They initially thought he was South African, but an autopsy revealed otherwise – inside the boy's stomach was a stew of clay, bone, gold and the remains of a single kidney-shaped calabar bean. The calabar bean was like a neon sign to the investigation. The plant grows in West Africa, where it's known as the "doomsday plant" because of the number of accidental deaths it causes. It's also used to draw out witches and negate their power – once a bean is eaten, only the innocent survive. The shorts were another clue. Bought in a German Woolworths, they were coral orange for the *orisha* spirit Ochun, the river queen of the Yoruba religion: the great diviner who knows the future and the mysteries of women.

The calabar would have caused his blood pressure to rise painfully, followed by convulsions and conscious paralysis; his screams imbuing the magic with a rare and terrible strength. Then his throat was slit and his torment ended by a final blow to the back of the head. Once dead, the butchery began. The blood was drained from his body and preserved; his head and limbs removed, along with what is known in *muti* as the atlas bone: the vertebra connecting his neck to his spine, where the nerves and blood vessels meet.

The boy's genitals, still intact, suggested that it wasn't his body parts the killer was after. It was his blood, drained slowly and carefully from his hanging corpse. Adam died to bring somebody money, power or luck. Perhaps the slave traffickers who brought him to London. His journey probably began when he was snatched or sold in Benin, and continued through Germany before reaching these shores, his final destination.

Somebody had cared for Adam before he died – there were traces of cough medicine in his system. Who knows whether he was brought here with sacrifice in mind, but had he not been marked for death, he might have ended up working as a slave, or as a prostitute. At least then he'd have had a chance.

Despite arrests in London, Glasgow and Dublin, and prosecutions for human trafficking, nobody was convicted of the boy's murder. Heldon had burned with frustration for months, but he had managed to keep it together, unlike others in the team. The three-year investigation had taken its toll on O'Brien, the detective in charge. He'd quit the force a nervous wreck at what should have been the peak of his career. Heldon had been his deputy on the Adam case; he'd seen the strain, the shards of paranoia puncture O'Brien's hard-man armour.

And now there was another corpse.

Aniweta was right. They had called her Eve.

The girl had been mutilated like Adam, her torso wrapped in a child's cotton dress; white with red edging. Dustmen had tipped her out of a wheelie bin on December 5, four days ago, outside a dry cleaner's on White Horse Street, near St. James's. She was probably six years old.

"What can you tell me, Ani?" Heldon asked the *sangoma*.

"I can tell you that this one is different."

"So far, forensics suggest that she was killed the same way as Adam."

"Yes, but she is different. Powerful." Ani nodded his head, impressed. "The red and the white on the dress are for Ayaguna. He is a young *orisha*, a fighter. You know him as St. James, and when he comes, he rides a white horse. Now she rides with him. He likes the girls, you see, he likes them young like this. Their blood is clean. This is strong *juju*. You'll find things inside her: clay, gunpowder, silver, maybe copper."

"Anything else?"

Ani, who had been staring at the stains on his tabletop, turned to look directly at Heldon.

"Yes, my friend, I can tell that you're not sleeping well."

Heldon was caught off guard. "Well, you might say I'm taking my work home with me."

"Like O'Brien?"

"No. And I don't intend to end up like him. But yes, this

has shaken me up. I didn't expect another one so soon. And then I suppose there's the war."

"There is always war, that is Ayaguna's business. But there will be no war where this girl came from. She is one of their own. A peace offering."

"I was talking about Iran, but yes, we think the girl was another Nigerian."

"No, she is not one of ours. She is from the Congo," replied Ani, with a certainty that Heldon could not question. "That's where the trouble is. But for now there will be no war. She died to end the fighting. She will keep Ayaguna happy for a while. How long depends how well the *sangomas* know him. If they know him well, she will have died with six fingers and six toes. Her skin cut six times with a blade and burned six times with a flame."

"If she died to prevent a war, why was she killed here and not in her home country?"

"The *sangomas* don't like war. It upsets the balance. So much death creates problems for everybody. Now the smart ones are over here."

"Makes sense. I don't like war either. Okay, thanks, Ani. We'll be in touch."

Heldon returned to the night. The cats were gone.

Forensics showed that Ani was right. Mineral analysis of her bones revealed that she was indeed Congolese. The girl had swallowed, or been forced to swallow, a mix of gunpowder, silver, copper and clay. She had been bound and stabbed several times, then scorched with a burning twig from the iroko tree. They had not found her limbs, so they couldn't count her fingers and toes; but Heldon suspected that if they ever found them, there would be six of each.

African newspapers revealed that the Congo had been on the brink of another bout of bloodshed, but in the past few days an agreement was reached between the warring factions. With over three million already dead, you would think they were tired of killing.

The story hardly made the UK nationals; the situation in Iran was worsening, despite the fact that things in Iraq had hardly improved since the Allied pull-out eighteen months earlier. And now they were regrouping, preparing to flex their muscle against a defiantly hostile Iranian leadership. The mid-term government disingenuously declaring that the opportunity for peace lay in the hands of the Iranians, not the combined forces amassing at the nation's borders.

More dead children.

Rather than desensitizing him to death, Heldon's work had revealed to him its full horror. He knew what a bullet meant: the torn, seared flesh; the shattered bone; the screaming; the smell of blood. He had no children of his own, but he knew that the statistics of war weren't just numbers. They were a thousand Adams, a thousand Eves. Blasted, mutilated, lying in rivers, in puddles, in the arms of their parents; caught in the camera's lens, denied over breakfast, ignored on the train.

As an inevitable war loomed once again, the anti-war protests had grown incandescent, seething with fury and frustration. Heldon took part as often as he could. He didn't tell his colleagues, just as he didn't tell them everything that Ani had told him. It was easier that way.

He didn't tell them about his other research either. There was no need. And he hadn't told Ani. Again, why bother? He probably already knew all about the killings anyway. They had occurred throughout Europe and Africa over the years.

Many, like Adam, were for power. Terrible as they were, they no longer interested Heldon. He was only interested in the others; the others like Eve. They were different. And they had worked. The evidence was there on the record – brief respites in long histories of warfare. Powerful *juju*.

She is one of their own . . . different . . . powerful.

Ani's words drove Heldon onward as he strode through the car park behind Kingsland Shopping Centre. Smooth, smothered by concrete, a no-man's-land between road and rail. Few people entered the mall through this back way. Once past the main entrance to Sainsbury's, the shops tail off into a mirror of what's available outside on Kingsland High Street.

A grey mid-morning on a school day. Any kids around now are avoiding something.

Now she rides with him.

He found her under the outdoor metal stairwell. Hood up. Not doing anything.

She was one of our own.

He had thought about this moment over and over again. Can a death ever be justified? Is one unpromising life worth ten thousand others? If it works, then yes, it is. Suddenly, Heldon knew exactly what he was doing.

"Hi. Shouldn't you be in school?"

"What's it to you? You a teacher?"

A flash of his card. "No, I'm a policeman. And I think you should come with me. Don't worry, you're not in trouble. I have a very important job to do, and I need your help. How would you like to ride a white horse?"

Without protest, the girl left with him.

SOUTH

BY JOE McNALLY

Elephant & Castle

As an incomer to London, I have – almost inevitably – found myself enchanted with the city, in more than one sense of the word. I have enthusiastically thrown my hat in with those who purport to read the city; I have picked and hunted for the obscure volumes which I hope will allow me to enter their hallowed halls through recitation of the *Sacred Names of the Lost Rivers*, and gestured endlessly towards the notions which underpin their fictions.

For the most part, my own experiments in drift have been confined to the northern shores and, owing to a specific confluence of geographical happenstance and the practicalities of car-engine maintenance, to the mysterious islets of the dead between Maida Vale and Ladbroke Grove; ghost country, the lands of the west. Too dead even for Ballard.

Think of London as *Mappa Mundi*: wealth and comfort in the west, wealth and sterility in the far north, squalor and industry in the east (less of the latter these days – heritage docks, churches turned Starbucks), and in the south, a cliché *Heart of Darkness*. Incongruous strips of pristine brickwork along the river, a seething, churning mess we'd rather not think about.

It's uncharted territory, our own little Third World, just a little too feral for the tame psychogeographer. Not the heritage poverty of the East End, this is the real thing, waving a shattered bottle in your face and ranting a cloud of whisky fumes before smacking you down and stripping you to your frame. There's a reason sorcerers don't cross running water; down here, they'd be trading your scrying glass for rocks within the hour.

But then it hits me, walking from tube to Thameslink at the Elephant, the peak of the delta – Old Kent Road another Nile, tarmac khem, its length vanishing off towards an unknown source in the mythic lands supposed to exist outside the M25. And here at the peak of the delta are the tunnels.

This could have been built for us, the self-styled cultists of the city still reeling from our frantic initiations of acid-fuelled underground trips, coke-blasted long marches across the city trailed by gibbering crackheads waiting to fire up the crystal snot on our cast-off tissues, graduation only by turning up some new obscurity to which the metropolisomancers can nail a thousand mad-eyed theses. Here, a series of far-sighted planners, true inheritors of the Dionysiac mantle, conspired or were somehow moved by unseen forces to create a playground for those unable to travel through an underpass without pausing to attempt to decode the hidden patterns brought to half-life by every patch of crumbling concrete and piss stain.

It starts as soon as you vanish back underground after emerging from the tube. (No, it starts with the name: Elephant & Castle. Gnomic, at first quaint, then taking on sinister overtones. The Guild of Cutlers, ivory and steel. Bone and knife blade, a union still celebrated here more nights than not.) The subterranean walkways, with their vandalized or opaque signs, are an immediate hook, an obvious nod to Crete – passages which seem carefully planned to evoke the dread that some bellowing theriomorph might lurk behind each blind turn, pure *panic*.

At some point, in a misguided attempt to defuse these chthonic terrors, murals have been added showing imagined scenes from some non-history of South London, jungle scenes, subaquatic fantasies. Sharks patrol these walls. But the *genius loci* won't be denied. It rots the cheer, warps it over time into mania. Each grin now takes on a sinister aspect, the jolly street traders and their well-fed horses projecting an air of vague unease, like nursery drawings on the walls of a burned-out house. Crumbling and fading, they have become a desperate illustration of something that can only be hinted at in the most oblique symbolism, a private, autistic blend of Hoffman and Ryder-Waite.

Between the two stations, I stop to talk to a homeless woman sitting cross-legged with her back to one of the walls. She could be five or six years younger than me, but looks ten older. She has an immense paperback open in front of her, and I ask what she's reading, steeling myself to be polite about Tolkien or worse. Instead, it's an anthology of classic detective stories – Chandler, Willeford, Himes – with the words *Pulp Fiction* blazing across the cover. She explains that she bought it because she thought it was something to do with the film. She's about halfway through it now. I give her a pound and tell her to put it towards another book.

A pound's the least I can do; she's already shading into fiction, working her way into the web of metaphor, a fate not to be wished on any human or bestowed on them without recompense. It's a kind of death, after all. There was a real woman sitting in the underpass, reading a real book, I did stop, I did speak to her, I did give her the money, but by reducing her to this incident I triumphantly deny her the rest

of her life, all the while patting myself on the back for my
razor-sharp literary instincts and dreaming of Mayhew.

She was drawn into the book – her anthology, not this
fiction, I'm the only one on this particular voyage just now –
expecting something other than what she got, but now real-
izes that she's better off with what she did get. Enter the
labyrinth and confront . . . The pat answer is usually some
reassuringly bleak psychobabble borrowed from half-heard,
never-read Freud or, worse, George Lucas – yourself, your
parents, your dark side. The truth is that you're confronting
the labyrinth itself, the ultimate manifestation of the journey
that becomes its own destination. Anything you may find is
a function of the maze.

An information bauble surfaces from the *Fortean Times*
days. A piece by Paul Devereux on a South American temple
which was designed as a shaman machine. The initiate would
be fed hallucinogenic cactus, then sent into the temple. Each
part was set up to accentuate some aspect of the psychedelic
experience – walls that went from echoing to acoustically
dead, water channels designed to create apparently source-
less sounds, weird lights.

The cactus they used, San Pedro, is now widely available
in Camden and Portobello Road. But bang a couple of slices
of that and venture in here, and I don't like to think what
you'd get. Certainly not the sort of mantic howler in the
outer darkness who lands regular spots in the LRB. Any signs
one could read here would sear the brain with revelation, a
freebase hit of pure kabbalah, rebridging the divisions
between left and right cerebral hemispheres and turning the
reader into an ambulatory conduit for the voice of the
labyrinth.

It continues. I stride edgily through the shopping centre

to the Thameslink. The whitewashed concrete hallway feels like an abandoned bunker somewhere deep in Eastern Europe. The floor is inches deep in rainwater, with helpful yellow signs to point out this fact. Nobody is there. The nearest thing to human contact comes from the monitors, relaying information keyed in hours ago in some other location, a cathode ray phantom, news from nowhere. I have an hour to wait for the next train. I've missed its predecessor by seconds as a consequence of my chat with the homeless woman. (See: she doesn't even get a name, but the entire narrative really hangs on her; without her, you would not be reading this, or at least not in this form.)

I make for the bus stop, where the bus I need appears within seconds of my discovering that I need it. Another omen, another metaphor. This is a fertile zone; tiny possibility bombs detonating and sending ripples through the various levels of my mind. The people milling around the shopping centre (the pink shopping centre, a Little England nightmare made of concrete – dusky colonials and the taint of lavender) become a personal message to me from something beyond.

Once on board, I set my eyes on a mysteriously empty seat, one of three unoccupied places around a dozing bulk. It's a long haul into *terra australis incognita*, and I'll be needing my strength later. The instant I sit, I realize why the seats have not been taken up by any of my travelling companions. The man at the centre of the exclusion zone smells. No, this barely does him justice. A truly heroic stench hangs around him, displaced each time he moves, sweeping out in almost visible curls before and behind him with every disturbance in his dream.

I deal with it for as long as I can, but eventually change seats (being a good middle-class boy, I wait until I am absolutely sure he is asleep; there is, I reason, no possibility that he is unaware of his miasma, and I have no desire to remind him of it again). From my new vantage point, I see that, in fact, the earlier journey through the tunnels was just a decoy, a warm-up. This, though, is the real deal. There are no signs to help me here, no friendly guides clutching books full of familiar names to ground me. I took my eye off the road and left it without even noticing.

I look briefly at each of the other passengers. Eventually, there is no one left to look at and I am compelled to turn my attention to the man in front of me.

He is sitting back yet leaning forward at the same time. A great buffalo hump squats on his back, forcing his head towards the space between his knees. A woolly brown suit of indiscernible vintage helps add to the air of something bovine. Sagging expanses of flesh the colours of corned beef – complete with waxy marbled patches of fat – droop from an acromegalic frame and turn his face into a system of soft caves. His eyes are almost buried beneath overhanging folds of puffed skin, which threaten to fuse with his cheeks: a wax-work Auden rescued, too late, from a conflagration. Messy spikes of hair protrude from his scalp like a crown of feathers. He is between sleep and waking, and the bus's occasional stops and starts make him jerk, sending a shudder through his body, which is echoed and enlarged by corresponding movements in the mephitic cloud that clings to him like a swarm of locusts. The breath flaps out of him from behind crimson jowls.

He seems not to belong here, a refugee from a Grosz painting suppressed as too terrible for public consumption. There would be something comical about him were it not for his awesome vastness and the animal reek around him. It's an *ur*-stench, building from base notes of piss, shit and sweat to encompass subtle undertones of days-old baby vomit and rank meat that linger in the brain much longer than in the nostrils.

I find myself rapt with wonder at him, barely able to contain my authorial glee. I am working heavy *juju* here; I set out telling myself that something worth putting down on the page would happen tonight, and it seems that I have managed to conjure this flesh golem out of pure narrative requirement – a notional space hitherto marked LOCAL COLOUR HERE fills out with something truly strange, an authentic and unfakeable encounter that a better author would have the sense to condense to a paragraph or even a phrase.

But I can't leave well enough alone, and my mind races to find some way I can steal this creature and tame him for my own purposes. The fact that he is clearly dreaming, his physical appearance, his foulness, these are all good. I wonder for a moment if there is some way he can be shoe-horned into some sort of fiction, some easy way I can turn this to my own advantage.

As I wonder on all this, he stirs and begins to gather his belongings to leave the bus at the next stop. Assaulted by the inevitable accompanying spread of his insulating cloud, I turn back to the book I've been concealing myself behind (Maurice Leitch, *The Smoke King*) and desperately try to avoid attracting his attention. He is, after all, my creation and I do not want to be held responsible for the consequences should such a perfect beast gaze by accident into the eyes of his creator.

The bus stops, and as the doors open he shudders towards them, white plastic bags flapping from each wrist, stirring up tornadoes which disperse his spoor to the four corners of the vehicle. I steal a sideways glance at him when he blusters out onto the pavement. As he steadies himself from a sideways lurch, one of the bags swings and hits the glass beside me with a noise I do not like. A pattern of darkness within momentarily resolves itself into what I pray is not a face, and the minotaur is gone.

WHO DO YOU KNOW IN HEAVEN?

BY PATRICK McCABE

Aldgate

R ight," I said, and phoned the cops.

"May I ask who's calling?" she says.

"Edgar Lustgarten," I said. "You might remember me from *Scales of Justice*. Then again, you mightn't."

"No, as a matter of fact, I don't," she says.

Not that it mattered, for I was gone.

The next thing you know, there's Feane on the *Daily Mirror* with an anorak over his head. But it was him all right – the two-tone shoes.

The worst thing about Mickey Feane was his relentless bragging. "Look at me – *I'm super-volunteer.*"

Never liked them Belfast bastards. Too cocksure.

He'd have all the time he wanted to brag now – any amount in Brixton prison.

Poor old Feane – yet another in a long line of slope-shouldered Irish felons in Albion, detained at Her Majesty's pleasure.

In the beginning it had been good – there can't be any denying that.

I think I'll go to London, I thought. Off I'll go and I won't come back.

"Goodbye, cows, " I said, "and streets – farewell."

Up your arse may they happily go and the rest of this miserable country as well.

After all, it was 1973. The whole fucking place was an outhouse, deserted.

"Goodbye, Daddy, Mammy. Goodbye, other kiddies. I hope you die," I said as I skipped.

I had met some very good friends indeed. They really were quite jolly good fellows. They wore zigzag tops and half-mast jeans.

The very first day I arrived in off the boat, Harrods blew up. Two cops stopped me and said, "Hello, hello." Believe it or believe it not, it's absolutely true. I gave them an envelope with the old man's name on it. They weren't too happy with that, they declared.

"You could get into a lot of trouble over here," they went on. "These are odd and hair-raising times, my wide-eyed little Irish friend."

I was tripped out of my skull for most of the journey. I drank a few pints with an old chap sporting a face like a ripe tomato.

"Do you know what the English did?" he said to me. "Hung decent fellows outside their own doors."

I had never in my life quite seen such a face. *The Incredible Melting Man from Tipperary,* that was the only name I could think of which might suit.

"I'll tell you something about London," he says, but I never heard what it was, for the next thing, *slurp,* down he goes right into the ashtray with a sprig of red hair sticking up like a flower.

As soon as I was sure there was no one looking, I reached into his inside pocket and effortlessly removed his bulging wallet. Inside there's a bunch of *in memoriam* cards with a small square picture of this big farmer smiling. That, I assumed, was the recently deceased brother.

There was a good fat roll of money in there – all tied up with an elastic band. Consummate cattle-dealer style.

Away I went in the direction of Piccadilly. I turned a corner and there it flashed – *CINZANO*, on-off.

I stood there looking at it – truly mesmerized. The reason for that was, it was on our mantelpiece at home. As a matter of fact, it was the last thing I had laid eyes on before departing.

"You're a bad boy, Emmet," Daddy had said.

I had expected the entire town to turn out to bear witness to my leave-taking. They didn't. It was, I'm afraid, a damp squib of an event.

I just pulled the door after me, and who comes flying right off the fanlight but his holiness – the Infant of Prague.

For the benefit of English people who never go to Mass, the Infant of Prague is a holy young boy who stands guard over doors with a gleaming golden crown and a sceptre in his hand. Sadly, on this occasion, his head had got broken. Which upset Mammy because she loved him so.

"Don't come back!" I heard her shouting.

Then I saw Daddy glaring from the shadows.

"Don't worry," I told him. "You'll be able to give her a proper kicking now."

He had always been very fond of football – especially whenever the ball was Mammy.

He always liked a game at the weekend. And maybe, if he'd the money, after the pub on Mondays, Wednesdays, Thursdays, Fridays – and Tuesdays.

* * *

I went into the great big neon-lit shop. A rubber girl, Rita, who'll never say no. A woman in a mask belting the lard out of a crawling-around city gent clad in a bowler.

"I'll teach you some manners," she says, and she means it.

"Oh no," he says, "please don't do it, but do it."

That would keep me warm, I thought, a good skelp like that, as I retired to my chambers along the banks of the Thames.

I thought of them all the way back there at home – all my turf-moulded fellow country-compatriots. By now they would have realized my feather bed had not been slept in. And great consternation would take hold in the midlands.

Little would those gormless fools know just what the true nature of my visit to London was to be. I shivered gleefully as I thought: *The London Assignment. A British cabinet minister is gunned down by an IRA assassin. It's a race against the clock and one false move will be enough to leave him dead before he reaches his target.*

I lovingly stroked the butt of my Smith & Wesson .686 – four inches, with Hogue grips – which lay nestled deep in the pocket of my jacket. My shiny jacket of soft black leather – standard-issue terrorist fare, perhaps, but comfortable and stylish nonetheless. What the well-dressed volunteer is wearing this autumn in the mid-1970s.

"Get out of the car," I heard myself say, "I'm requisitioning this vehicle on behalf of the Irish Republican Army. *One-Shot Emmet*, they call me, friend – for one shot is all it takes."

There was a big fat moon swelling above the gasworks, looking like the loveliest floaty balloon. The old man knew a song about that moon. I remembered it well. It went: *When the harvest moon is shining, Molly dear.*

Once I had heard him singing it to the old lady. One night in the kitchen not long after Christmas. Long ago. Or at least I thought I had. Then I fell asleep with my hotshot volunteer's jacket pulled good and tight around me.

So off I went – puff-puff on the train. All the way to Epsom in Surrey. What a spot that turned out to be – a hotel, a kind of club for dilapidated colonels. How many Jimmy Edwards moustaches would you say there were there to be seen?

At least, I would estimate, seventeen examples.

Big potted plants and women like vampires, Epsom Association Dawn of the Dead.

Sitting there yakking about gout and begonias.

"You're not very fond of work, are you?" says the boss. He had apprehended me sleeping under boxes.

I took in everything in the office. The barometer on the wall reading *mild,* the bird creature on the mantelpiece dipping its beak in a jar. Lovely shiny polished-leather furniture – with buttons.

"It seems quite extraordinary but you don't appear ashamed in any way."

I was going to tell him nothing. Mahoney – my officer-in-command – had always said if arrested to focus your attention on a spot on the wall.

He fired me. "Get out," he says. Well, fuck that for a game of cowboys.

By the time I got back to London I was edgy and tired.

Outside a Wimpy, I saw a woman with blood streaming down her face being led away by a man in a raincoat. For no reason at all I stood there for a minute looking in the window of a telly rental shop, and there on the screen is this fellow saying: "I was just coming out of my office when I heard the most frightful bang." The policemen were still shouting: "Will you please clear the area!" All of the pubs were closing their doors. I heard someone running past, shouting: "Murdering bastards!" I hid my face and found a hostel. *The London Assignment* was the name of my book. The book I'd invented to get me to sleep. I was on the cover in a parka – looking dark and mean. Behind me, a mystical pair of old-country hills. The old-timer next to me said: "What time is it now?"

It's the time of Gog and Magog, my friend, when the cloud covers the sun and the moon no longer gives forth any light.

I'd read that in a Gideon's Bible some other old tramp had left on my locker. He must have been unhappy for I could hear him crying.

I don't know why his whimperings should have done it but they got me thinking about Ma and Da. I got up to try and stop their faces coming. Then I saw the two of them – him just standing there with his hand held in hers.

"Ma," I gasped, "Da."

They were dressed in the clothes of all the old-time photographs. There was a picture on the hostel wall of a dance-hall in London and somehow it all got mixed up with that. It wasn't a modern dance-hall – one from the '40s or perhaps the early '50s. It was called THE PALAIS – with its string of lights waltzing above the heads of the fresh-faced queue. You'd think to see them that they'd all won the pools. I've never seen people look as happy as that. I could see the inside in my mind – palm trees painted over a tropical ocean and the two of them waltzing. Him with his hair oiled and her with a great big brooch pinned onto her lapel.

"I love you," I heard her say.

It was in those couple of years just before I was born. In the time of the famous detective Lustgarten, when all the cars were fat and black and nobody said *fuck* or visited dirty neon-lit shops. When everyone was happy because at last the war was over. We hadn't been in the war. Eamon de Valera kept us out of it. The old man revered de Valera. Talked about him all the time. He was probably talking about him now – to her. But she wouldn't want to hear about history. She'd simply want to be kissed by him. The history of that kiss would do her just fine. She needed no more than that to look back on.

The doors of the dance-hall were swinging open now and assorted couples were drifting out into the night in the loveliest of white dresses and old-style grey suits with big lapels.

Ma was lying back on the bonnet of a car. She put her arms around him and said she wasn't worried about a single thing in the whole world. Her laughter sailed away and I heard her saying that history was a cod, that the only thing that mattered was two people loving one another. He asked her would she love an Englishman, and she said yes she would just so long as it was him. Which was the greatest laugh of the whole of all time – the idea of her husband, Tom Spicer, being an Englishman.

"London," she whispered then, and whatever way she said it, it made the whole place just spread out before me like some truly fabulous palace of stars. Songs that I had only half remembered seemed to fill themselves out now and take on an entirely new life as they threaded themselves in and out of the most magnificent white buildings of solid Portland stone.

A nightingale, I thought, sang in Berkeley Square and it made me feel good for I knew that Da had liked it once upon a time. No, still did.

"Don't I?" he said as he tilted her pale chin upwards.

"*Stardust.*" She smiled, and I knew she meant Nat King Cole.

With the shimmering sky over London reflected in her eyes.

When I looked again, they were standing in some anonymous part of the city and it wasn't pleasant – there was this aura of threat or unease hanging around them. I wanted it to go away but it wouldn't. Ma was more surprised than anyone when he drew back his cuff and punched her in the face.

A spot of blood went sailing across the Thames. Far away I saw *CINZANO*, just winking away there, on and off. On and off. On and off. On and –

I heard a scream. I woke up.

I didn't manage to get back to sleep.

Noon, I went into Joe's Café. There was only one thing and it prevailed in my mind. That was the dance-hall whose name was THE PALAIS, with its coloured lights strung above the door. That was my *London Assignment*. To, once and for all, locate that building. I swore I'd do it – or die in the process.

I smiled as I thought of Mahoney and his reaction. He was standing by the window back at HQ, with both arms folded as he unflinchingly gazed out into the street.

"You were sent over there for one express purpose!" he snapped. "And it's got nothing to do with fucking dance-halls!"

I took out my revolver and placed it on the table.

"So be it," I said. "Then I'm out."

"You're out when I say you're out," replied Mahoney.

I could see a nerve throbbing in his neck. Mahoney had been over the previous summer with an active service unit that had caused mayhem. He was a legend in the movement. His London exploits had passed into history. He would have had no problem coming over himself and filling me in. Taping my confession and leaving me there in some dingy Kilburn flat, with a black plastic bag pulled down over my head.

"The Organisation is bigger than any one man," he said. "Or any," he sneered, "fucking dance-hall."

I finished my tea and got up from my chair, swinging from Joe's out into the street.

Not this one, Mahoney. Not this one.

I sat down for a bit in Soho Square gardens. There was a paper lying beside me on the bench. Looking out from the front page was a photofit picture of an IRA bomber in long hair and sideburns.

I shook the paper and sighed, kind of tired. You could hear the Pandas blaring nearby. I slid into a cinema and tried not to hear what I was hearing. Almost inevitably, there was Edgar – smiling down at me from the screen. How could he possibly have known I was in the city? I thought ruefully. Could my cover possibly have been blown?

It couldn't be, I concluded. Not even the great *Scales of Justice* detective could have managed to pull off a coup like that. I began to relax as I watched him bestride the screen. I dwelt on all his famous cases: *The Mystery of the Burnt-Out Candle; Investigation at Honeydew Farm; The Willow Tree Murders*.

"I know all about the dance-hall," he said. "That's my job – I'm here to help."

I was grateful to him for saying that, for I knew if anyone was able to help it was Edgar Lustgarten – having lived through the days when the streets of the great city had been the same as they were in the photograph, shiny and wet and full of grey overcoats, with great big double-deckers bombing around and Big Ben regally resounding across the world.

"Would you like to know what was playing that night?" he asked me. "It was 'Who Do You Know in Heaven?' by the Ink Spots."

"'Who do you know in Heaven?'" I repeated, as the coloured lights flickered above the door of THE PALAIS.

There can be little doubt that *The London Assignment* will go down in the annals as one of the most magnificent operations ever undertaken by the Organisation. Mahoney, I knew, would be especially proud.

I couldn't believe it when I arrived in Rayners Lane. I couldn't even remember how I got there. There was a dance-hall, but it wasn't the one I was after. It hadn't even been built until 1960. Anyhow, it was boarded up and left to go to rack.

I went into another café and had a cup of tea. My hands were blue and I was shivering.

I didn't want to hear it but they fell from the lips of a man sitting opposite. In my father's voice. The words: "We're rubbish, us Irish, and all our children – they'll be rubbish. We don't even know how to love or kiss or dance. All we can do is dress in rags. If we were in London now, that would be different. We'd deck ourselves in the finest of silks and we'd stroll down Pall Mall with our proud heads held high. Then do you know what we'd do? We'd go off to dinner in some swanky hotel, and after we'd called a toast to ourselves, we'd take a cab off to a dance-hall – we wouldn't really care where it was, just so long as the Ink Spots were playing – and what we'd do then is we'd foxtrot and waltz until our feet were sore and bruised."

He was leaning over to kiss her when I knocked over the teacup, its contents dribbling onto my feet.

I think one of the most beautiful days I can ever remember was Boxing Day three years ago. It had been snowing constantly and the city looked like something out of a fairy tale – as though it had been evacuated especially for me. On Trafalgar Square, the Landseer lions appeared even more august than usual, with their Mandarin moustaches of dusty white ice.

Starched and blue, Soho did my heart good. In the gutters, hardened wrappers possessed a special kind of poetry. It was like being a child all over again, when I'd walk the roads of the little country town which I haven't, sadly, been back to for many years now.

I'm looked after here – I've accepted this country as my home. I have a flat the council gave me – it's not far from Fenchurch Street, in the suburb of Aldgate.

There's a café which I go to, near Leadenhall Market. I sit at the back. The owner is an Italian – he fancies himself an intellectual. He thought I was writing a West End play. "No," I told him, "I'm writing a novel. A little thriller I've titled *The London Assignment*."

He took up my notebook and read – with superiority: "*Once upon a time there was a young boy who lived in a squat. He had to leave it for reasons best left unreported. The city in those days was as though a place under siege. Emmanuelle was playing at the Odeon. A Clockwork Orange was showing some-*

where else. On April 26, an old tramp, who happened to be from Ballyfuckways in the Irish county of Mayo, was stumbling good-humouredly through an underpass, throatily declaiming an old ballad, when he was confronted by three youths – each of them sporting a bowler hat and with a single eye mascaraed. They beat him with their walking canes and left him for dead. A bomb blew out the windows of a restaurant that night – on Frith Street, in Soho. Thirteen people were injured. Carrolls Number Six cigarettes cost fifteen pence for ten."

He handed me back the notebook and smiled – in that unfortunately unappealing, superior way.

"Did you ever hear of Griffith's theory of consistent memory?" he asked me. He then explained it, in even and measured tones, clearly anticipating my difficulties with its complexity.

"It's like this," he continued, "consciousness prompts you to hypothesize that the story you're creating from a given set of memories is a *consistent history*, justified by a consistent narrative voice . . ."

I half-expected Edgar Lustgarten to appear out of the throng outside, airily drift up to the window and press his gaunt face to the grimy glass. After a minute or two of this unsolicited advice, I no longer heard a word he said.

What must Sinclair Vane – complete stranger, retired physiotherapist and formerly of 7th (Queen's Own) Hussars – and indeed his wife, have thought when he returned to Frognal Walk, Hampstead, one night in 1973 to find his parlour window broken open and me, right there in his sitting room, talking to myself and clutching what I had decided was a lethal weapon – in reality a wholly amateur attempt at an imitation firearm, fashioned from a branch I'd found outside?

I can only surmise he received the shock of his life. My black bomber jacket was draped across my shoulders as I shivered and menacingly narrowed my eyes. I think I might have giggled a little, in what I thought was a sinister fashion.

"I'm the most feared terrorist in Ireland," I said. "You're going to pay for the sins of your country. I'm sorry to have to tell you but that's the way it is. I'm a soldier, you're a soldier. You're going to die, Mr. Vane."

If I wanted to describe him, I would say he was a young version of Edgar Lustgarten – still retaining most of his hair, complete with touches of distinguished grey.

I encountered him once – a number of years after my discharge from Brixton. The snow had passed and the gutters of Soho had been recently rinsed clean by a deluge of rain, twists of steam all about me rising up into the easeful autumn sky.

He was sitting by the window of a new European-style coffee bar, surrounded by chatting white-T-shirted youths and looking so out of place. It was hard for me to do it but I was glad afterwards that I had made the effort. At first he didn't recognize me when I said his name: *Sinclair Vane*.

As might have been expected, he formally stood to attention and extended his hand to shake mine.

We didn't talk much about that night. His soul was still saddened by the recent passing of his wife.

"She was an angel, you know. She really was."

I thought of her, his angel, as she'd encountered me that ridiculous night – weeping hysterically in the doorway by the stairs. Before Sinclair had expertly calmed her down. I recalled him in that photo on their mantelpiece – battalion commander S. Vane, in complete battledress, authoritatively squinting in the Egreb sun.

* * *

I don't know why I thought it, but it was as clear as day as I sat in the Sir Richard Steele one still and uneventful afternoon – this image of myself and Sinclair sitting so comfortably in a London black cab, gliding along before coming to a halt just outside a dance-hall whose entrance was lit by a string of warm and inviting multicoloured light bulbs.

"It was in Brighton all along," I heard him say, as the door swung open and he reached in his pocket for the fare.

Which I knew, of course, it wasn't – and, all of a sudden, hands of accusation seemed to reach out to grab me as I sat there in the corner of the Sir Richard Steele gloom.

I hadn't been allowed out of Brixton for the funeral of my mother, but after my father went into the home, his papers and effects were all passed to me. You can imagine my reaction when I discovered the old photograph – creased and faded but instantly recognisable. I didn't know what to think when I smoothed it out and, having examined it quite exhaustively, came to accept that the image I was looking at – and had been obsessed by – was that of two complete strangers, the inscription on the back reading: *Dublin 1953*. Neither of my parents had been to Dublin in their lives.

It was hard not to weep as I looked at it again, slowly beginning to accept that it definitely was THE PALAIS, and that the two lovers in it, well, they could have been almost anyone. For in those box-pleated suits and stiff-collared shirts, not to mention those fearful faces and averted eyes which seemed so grateful for even the tiniest morsel of hope, they could have been any pair of thrown-together souls, adrift in the black and washed-out grey of the lightless, shrinking sad Irish '50s.

* * *

The London Assignment had been an extremely effective operation – from the British establishment's point of view, not from mine. Or from Sinclair's, I hasten to add. I don't think he wanted me charged at all. My demise and subsequent incarceration hastened owing to the fact that the day before the trial had been due to begin, three cleaning ladies, a hotel porter and two foreign tourists had been blown to pieces in a restaurant in Piccadilly.

In these, the latter days of the '90s, I largely subsist by means of the dole and a couple of hours a night gathering glasses in a pub. I suppose you could say I'm well known around Aldgate. No one is aware of my murky past. I live in a tower block, not far from the station, which gets lonely sometimes and sees me perhaps in the Hoop & Grapes, nursing a tepid lager, or back in Trinity Square Gardens again, feeding the pigeons and surrounded by clamorous, insatiable, supremacist youth. Whose faith in the future I need to be near. Walkman stereos were just coming in '74. I was bundled into a van, not to see the light of day until mid-'95. I still derive a childish innocence from wearing mine, fancying myself a lone knight of the streets, immersed in shaky '30s-style strings and mellow muted jazz trumpets as I drift, a shadow figure, along the golden streets of Soho.

Among the personal effects forwarded to me after my father's death was a letter to her, written in 1949. I know it so well I can quote it verbatim.

Dear Maggie,
I hope this finds you as well as it leaves me. Well, since we last met things have not been so bad as you can imag-

ine things are busy here on the farm. I hope to be back up your way in about three or four months time. DV and I was wondering would you make an appointment with me I would be very grateful. My mother is a bit under the weather these times but Daddy is good thank God for that. I am doing a lot of reading at nighttime mostly because it is so busy. I like the Reader's Digest you will find a lot of articles about London in there it looks like a beautiful city although we shouldn't say it maybe but I would dearly love maybe to go there one day even if just for a little while. Anyhow Maggie I will sign off now and as I say I hope you are in the best of health since I seen you.

Yours truly, your fond friend,
Tommy Spicer, Annakilly

One of the chapters in my forthcoming book is called *The Hampstead Conclusion*. With a walk-on part by Edgar Lustgarten.

I'd wrecked the house that night, of course. And made a speech for the benefit of the Vanes. So that they might clearly comprehend my motivation – the reasons which led to *The London Assignment*.

"Then and only then let my epitaph be written!" – a segment from my Republican firebrand namesake Robert Emmet's famous courtroom speech – I remember bawling as I tipped a small glass table over. "Do you hear me, Vane, you imperious, self-regarding, cold-blooded Englishman?" I'd snapped, before delivering a lengthy soliloquy regarding the inadvisability of antagonizing a "nation who were educating Europe when others were painting themselves with woad", along with any number of references to a certain "Mahoney" whose

underground army was by now primed and about to launch a full-scale assault on "Her Majesty's government of despots and butchers, as well as . . ."

As well as nothing, as a matter of fact, for before I knew it, Sinclair Vane had somehow pinned my two arms behind my back and knocked me out with a well-aimed blow, something which I would have anticipated had I examined the mantelpiece a little bit more comprehensively – there were at least four photos of him attired in military fatigues – or applied myself with more diligence to my researches, particularly those pertaining to ex-servicemen who had distinguished themselves repeatedly in the field of combat, unarmed and otherwise. Particularly, it appeared, with the 7th Armoured Division with Monty at El Alamein.

The notice of his death I happened to come upon in *The Times*. I don't know why I went there – to the funeral in Willesden Cemetery – some unformed notion, a vague desire for closure, maybe. All I remember is shaking his sister, Miss Vane's, hand. She was so distressed I don't think she even saw me.

When I got home I explained to Vonya – or tried to. But in the end gave up about halfway through. I could see it wasn't making any sense. She was a lovely girl, whom I happened to meet quite by chance one day on my bench in Trinity Square Gardens.

She stayed with me but we didn't have sex. As I poured out the coffee, a young Muslim man was arguing with two policemen, employing body language I knew so well.

"But I lie to you," she said, a little choked.

Her mother was long dead, she'd told me. Her father had habitually abused her since childhood. That was the reason she had come to London, the very minute, practically, that she'd come of age. Except that none of it, it turned out, was true.

It was the morning the IRA bombed the Baltic Exchange. I heard the explosion – it's not that far away from my flat – and wondered had Mickey Feane, my old friend, been involved. But then I remembered – Mickey Feane was long dead, sprayed in an ambush on a back road in Tyrone.

I turned to say something and saw she wasn't there.

That was the last I saw of Vonya Prapotnik.

I'd sit there in the gardens opposite the Lutyens monument commemorating the Merchant Navy dead, and think of Mr. Lustgarten arriving – the fat black Panda pulling up outside the building as a burly officer opened the door, clearing a path for the internationally renowned sleuth as he made his way up bare concrete stairs, pushing the door open to reveal the dank interior. Where he'd find me lying prostrate on the bed. I don't know what title might occur to him as he observed me – rigor mortis having already set in, most likely – An Unfortunate Case, perhaps, or Felo-De-Se: A Volunteer's Farewell, or, perhaps, best of all, The Aldgate Assignment.

Yes, I think I like the sound of that.

I made the tape last night and it's good, I think – by which I mean that it's clear and unequivocal. Precise as any good confession ought to be, with or without a black plastic hood. I left it on the table where anyone will be able to see it – you won't need the skills of Edgar Lustgarten. I bought a jiffy bag and a packet of stickers, and in neat felt marker printed on the front: Who Do You Know in Heaven?

What I couldn't believe most of all was how wonderfully bright it was. THE PALAIS in red and yellow strung-up lights. When I went in, the band were already in the middle of their set, performing their dance steps in front of their music stands, with all their silver instruments gleaming. They were wearing little white jackets and neatly pressed greystripe trousers. The Ink Spots, in black, was printed on a drum.

When I heard her call out to me, initially I couldn't make out who it was. Then, to my astonishment, I heard my mother say: "Emmet, will you do something for me? Will you make sure the Infant of Prague is in his proper place on the fanlight and has his little face turned towards the church? We're getting married tomorrow morning at ten, son, you see."

I wasn't sure quite what to say – her taffeta dress looked so nice – and had to think for a minute to decide on an answer. But before I got the chance, the band had started up again, and as he placed his arm around her waist I saw her lean in towards him and smile.

But that was the last I saw of them because in the one or two seconds I'd turned to give my attention to the band, as effortlessly as though they'd grown wings, they'd sailed like moths out far beyond the stars, in search of the heaven they'd been dreaming of for so long.

BETAMAX

BY KEN HOLLINGS

Canary Wharf

1.

It starts with an accelerating whine that becomes a roaring through darkness and space. You'll find yourself hurtling into emptiness. Lights travel past your eyes at ever increasing speed. The flooring moves beneath your feet. You'll feel the rush, pulling you forward. The roaring continues. Everything lies straight ahead. The expressions around you seem dazed, eyes unfocused and distant.

The sound slows to a stop. A woman's voice speaks to you from out of nowhere. *This station is Canary Wharf. Change here for the Docklands Light Railway.*

Then another woman's voice: *This train terminates at Stratford.*

Everyone around you looks stunned. Lost.

A gun is a dream that fits into your hand.

"So I get out here?"

They used to sleep below ground in places like this. While bombs fell from up above. The steel and glass barrier will slide apart, separating you from nothing. A vast space of columns and moving stairways, designed for handling thousands of people in transit, opens up around you, but it will be almost empty at this hour of the day. On the platform, a young skateboarder drums with his bare hands on a metal guardrail. A little Muslim girl in a glistening pink dress crouches at the edge of the concourse, sniffing at an open pack of Juicy Fruit chewing gum. She holds it up to her face, avidly inhaling the smell. Her father wears black combat boots, the toecaps carefully polished. Behind them, the empty silent track.

You watch the barrier as it closes again, a yellow and black stripe running the length of it at waist height. Two sets of three isosceles triangles pointing away from each other move slowly together until they are almost touching once more.

Standing on the escalator, coming up towards the third level on the concourse, just beneath the surface of the world, you get your first glimpse of towers and tall buildings. Shining high-rise blocks of steel and reflective glass, housing a working population of over 65,000. You only have to kill one of them. But anything over that will also be acceptable.

A scratchy subtitle flickers before your eyes: *It is the acts of men who survive the centuries that gradually and logically destroy them.*

Buildings are machines: electrical systems that listen and see and respond. People are just a planet's biomass redistributing itself in time and space.

"You have a room reserved for me? Under the name Betamax?"

The girl at the reception desk will look up at you and smile brightly. "Yes, we do. Thanks for asking."

You'll be vaguely aware of the colour scheme in the hotel lobby: a deep rose pink with polished wood surfaces. Beyond them an empty concrete plaza and a fountain swept by the wind.

You're just product, denied a place in this world. Something played out on an old system, dated and worn. Set aside.

Step out of the elevator when it reaches the twenty-third floor.

"Room 2307?" you'll say. "It's along here?"

The maid will turn from her cleaning cart and smile brightly. "Fifth door to your right, thanks for asking."

Anything over that will also be acceptable.

Your name will appear on the TV screen in your room, incorporated into a message of greeting. You ignore it. You remember a blind operative you once knew who stayed at Holiday Inns all the time because the rooms were always laid out in exactly the same way. It made finding his way around a lot easier.

You will incapacitate your first attacker by crushing his windpipe. The second you will see reflected in the white tiles of the bathroom. That will give you enough time to turn and shoot him in the chest. Twice.

He will fall towards you, fingers trailing blood across the walls and floor.

You will call down to room service to have someone come and clean out the human grease.

"This better not show up on my bill," you'll say on your way out.

"I'll be sure to note that," the girl at the reception desk will reply and smile brightly. "Thanks for asking."

Things dazzle here, but they don't shine. Everything has a hard reflective surface to it. The dominant colour is a stormy green. You walk to the end of the block. There must be people in these buildings, but the interiors seem empty and devoid of life, despite the glass and the open structures. The sight of clouds in a vast blue sky moving across the straight edge of a building will give you a slow sense of falling.

You pause for a moment. Motorway. Distant sirens beyond the towers, the strange silence of cars passing, cold ragged wind generated by the close proximity of tall structures to each other, planes passing overhead.

Some of the buildings have names. *HSBC, Citigroup, Bank of America.*

Have your pass ready for inspection.

You feel like you're in transit.

A woman appears around the windswept corner of an office building. Long black hair, a swing to her hips. She must be an office worker: trim black skirt, black sweater, black patent-leather high heels. You wonder how she can walk in shoes like those. She carries a file of documents. The stiff breeze disturbs the hem of her skirt as she walks.

She will stop and nod towards the ambulance pulled up at the back entrance to your hotel. Two bodies strapped to gurneys are being wheeled out, their faces covered.

"What happened over there?" she will ask.

"Got in the way," you'll reply.

She watches the paramedics load up the ambulance, her file of documents held up to shade the side of her face.

"Wrong place at the wrong time?" she will ask.

"Not really," you will reply, then after a long pause: "Some people don't know it's over till they see the inside of a mortuary drawer."

"You sound like a trailer for a movie no one wants to see," she will say.

"I'm told I have that effect."

"And would it kill you to smile?"

"Why don't we find out?"

The faintest of smiles will appear on her face instead. "Okay," she'll say.

2.

Once you get outside the neat arrangement of precincts around Canada Square, things come apart very quickly. You can see how thin, how artificial and transparent, this shining cluster of buildings really is. You sit at a café table and think about ordering something. Someone has written *Public Enemy No. One* on a nearby wall in spray paint. Beyond that is the river: rusting cranes, empty sheds and disused landings. Worn concrete, green with age.

You will look across at her long black hair and wonder why she came with you so readily. Even so, you made it look like she didn't have any choice. CCTV cameras are everywhere, turning the entire area into a series of flickering electromagnetic shadows.

"They never tell me who I have to kill," you'll remark. "Usually I'm left to figure it out for myself."

"Is that what you meant by those people getting in the way?" she'll ask.

You slide a blurred black-and-white photograph across the table: a snapshot of a man with greying hair, smiling enigmatically, eyes black and closely focused.

"Look at the picture," you'll say. "He had a different name then."

* * *

A waitress in a green coverall will then come over. She'll be wearing a white plastic badge with her name on it and the message, *I'm going to help you*, printed underneath. She will look more like the kind of woman who'd have her first name spelled out in ancient Egyptian hieroglyphs on a gold charm around her neck. You order coffee.

"How do you take it?" the waitress will ask.

"Straight out the jug," you'll reply. "Like my mother's milk."

A silent pause accompanied by a blank stare. Last time you saw a face like that, the word *before* was printed below it.

"Black, no sugar," you'll reply. "Thanks for asking."

She will later hand you a cardboard cup covered with a plastic lid. You stare at it. A newspaper lies on the next table. You notice the headlines out of the corner of your eye. *Mars Robot Goes Insane. Weapons of Mass Destruction Found in New York.*

"You're not from around here, are you?" she'll observe as the waitress walks slowly away.

"Is anybody?"

The blurred black-and-white photograph still lies on the table between you.

"It's not what you've done that poses the biggest threat these days," you'll say. "It's what you owe. We want to extract our money before war breaks out in the ghost galaxies."

"And for that you have to find this guy, this . . . ?" She'll pause, waiting for a name.

"John Frederson."

She'll frown.

"I don't think I know him," she'll say. "Where's he from?"

"Standard Oil New York," you reply. "The Ryberg

Electronics Corporation of Los Angeles, Phoenix-Durango, Islam Incorporated, the Russian petroleum industry . . ."

"He gets around."

"Beijing, Moscow, Tokyo, London . . . It's amazing how much damage the system can take while still sending out signals."

"So it's up to you to track him down and . . ."

"Make him see reason."

"All you're missing is a raincoat and a gun," she'll say, a smile playing on her lips. Then she'll take another look at you.

"Well, maybe just the raincoat," she'll add.

"Is that a problem?" you ask before peeling the tight-fitting plastic lid off your cardboard cup and taking a sip.

"I don't like guns," she'll reply. "Guns kill people."

"Isn't that what they're supposed to do?" you'll say, pulling a face. The coffee tastes like weed-killer. "Come on," you'll say. "Let's get out of here."

Total Information Awareness and the Policy Analysis Market focus upon high-level aggregate behaviour in order to predict political assassinations or possible terrorist attacks.

"Where are we going now?" she'll ask, taking a pack of cigarettes from her black patent-leather purse.

"Do you have to?" you'll ask. "Cigarettes kill people."

Another scratchy subtitle appears before your eyes: *Ordinary men are unworthy of the position they occupy in this world. An analysis of their past draws you automatically to this conclusion. Therefore they must be destroyed, which is to say, transformed.*

"Isn't that what they're supposed to do?" she'll reply.

* * *

Welcome to the Royal Lounge of the Baghdad Hilton, the sign says. *No caps, no hoods or tracksuits after 7 p.m.*

You stand together inside the entrance of a cheap hotel, watching tired-looking girls appear and disappear behind a threadbare red-velvet curtain. Their movements are subdued and discreet: all shadows and cellulite.

A door in a dark side passage will open briefly onto a scene of Al Qaeda suspects kneeling manacled in their own private darkness, eyes, ears and mouths covered, held captive behind a chain-link fence that runs down the centre of the "Gitmo Room".

Prostitute phone cards in reception show high-contrast pictures of female GIs in camouflage fatigues leading naked men around on leather leashes. Each one of them reads: *Call Lynndie for discipline and correction. All services. Open late. Thanks for asking.*

"Well, you certainly know how to show a girl a good time," she'll remark.

"Keep quiet and follow me," you'll say.

You push your way through the velvet curtain, but a man in a dark suit puts an arm out to stop you.

"Hey, you can't do that," the man will say.

"I just did," you'll reply. "Get used to it."

Then you snap his forearm just below the elbow joint, breaking both bones instantly. You watch the blood leaking out from his sleeve.

On the second floor you stop outside one of the rooms.

"What are you doing?" she'll hiss at you. "*Trying* to start trouble?"

"Another operative was sent here a few months ago," you'll reply, tapping gently on the door. "He was supposed to contact me when I first arrived. He didn't show."

"Maybe he forgot."

"Impossible."

"Maybe you forgot."

"I know when I can't remember something." You sound dismissive. Impatient. Almost brutal.

"Okay. I have two things to tell you," she'll say after a pause.

"Yes?"

"One: I don't really appreciate you talking to me in that tone of voice, especially if you're still expecting me to help you."

"And two?"

"And two: there's some guy behind you pointing a gun at the back of your head."

You always know what you're doing.

You'll turn around and grab him by the throat. There will be a blind spasming of the flesh, and in another second there will be just you and the girl in the corridor again.

"See if he's got a pass key on him," you'll say.

"As dumps go," she'll remark, looking around at the room, "this is a dump. Who do you suppose did the decorating? The Three Stooges?"

But you're already staring at the body on the bed.

"Is that your contact?" she'll say.

You'll nod.

"What happened?"

"Electrocuted."

"You can tell just by looking?"

The closets and drawers are filled with the worn smell of clothes long unworn. There's dried shaving cream on the bathroom mirror.

"It stinks in here," she'll say, a flat statement delivered in a flat tone. "Should I open a window?"

It can be a small event: like a window opening in a nearby apartment block or blood sluicing onto the dock from a rusty outlet in a harbour wall.

"No, leave it."

She'll pick up a plastic entry pass from off the floor, its chain swinging gently from her long slim fingers. She'll point at the photograph on it.

"Looks like John Frederson's got a new face and name," you'll say, staring closely at the man in the picture.

She'll turn the entry pass over, examining it carefully on both sides. "This will get you into his private suite of offices at One Canada Square," she'll say. "I can take you there, if you want."

Outside the contact's hotel you'll be approached by a young Thai kid wearing a T-shirt with *Listen to Dr. Hook* printed on it. He's selling DVDs out of a black Samsonite case. *Homo Abduction: Series Red*, *Teenage Revolutionary Martyrs*. *Handcuff Party*. *Necktie Strangler Meets the Teenage Crushers*. *Baby Cream Pimp IV*.

No one's around: just the late afternoon glare.

"Anything I can't get anywhere else?" you'll ask.

The kid opens a back compartment in the case. These DVDs show people doing things that seem meaningless to you.

"Interested?" the kid will ask hopefully.

But you will just walk away.

3.

The tower at One Canada Square is not open to the general

public. It has 3,960 windows and 4,388 steps, divided into four fire stairways linking all fifty floors. It is 800 feet high. Seen through glass, the sun leaves long white streaks across the sky.

You wander through crowds of people in the underground mall directly beneath Canary Wharf, checking entrances and exits, noting the location of cameras, sensors and security points. Cities have scenes of their own destruction programmed into them. The world is in hock to itself.

You hear voices all around you, children playing, the rattling of cups on saucers, heels on tiled walkways. You notice frosted glass tables outside cafés, bars and restaurants. Curved metal and plastic chairs. Music playing. Laughter. Everyone has a sleepy tranquillized look. As if they've been caught too far from daylight. The only things that seem familiar to you down here are the names on the brightly lit storefronts: *Starbucks, Krispy Kreme, The Gap, Mont Blanc.*

People have become slaves to probability. You'll assume you've been on CCTV since you first arrived. A woman takes your photograph with her cell phone. She will have blonde highlights in her feather-cut hair and wear a gold plastic leather jacket, bleach-washed blue jeans and black Cuban-heel boots. You will have come to expect this kind of thing by now.

Chemical tests indicate that Prozac is now seeping into the main water supply.

The woman leans forward unobtrusively to get another shot, revealing a portion of flesh so suntanned that it looks almost grey when exposed to the strip lighting in the mall's main concourse.

You'll also notice that she has a tattoo at the base of her

spine. They all have tattoos at the base of their spine. Or on their ankles. It's a form of protection.

"Against what?" you'll ask.

At one minute past seven on the evening of Friday, February 9, 1996, a bomb concealed inside a flatbed truck wrecked an office complex at Canary Warf, killing two and injuring over a hundred. The device was detonated in an underground garage near Canada Square. It tore the front off the building next door, damaging the roof and shattering the glass atrium. Windows were sucked out of buildings a quarter-mile away. Bystanders were thrown to the floor and showered with flying glass. Things just kept on falling.

You search up and down the concourse again, checking the benches, the artificial displays of greenery, the rest areas and waste bins. You look at faces, gestures: arrangements of groups and individuals. Families are a bland nightmare when seen out in public: a series of aimless and incessant demands. The entire underground mall is designed to keep them moving. They look well fed and cared for and pink from the sun. As if they are all brand new.

You will think you can stay and rest for a moment, but you can't. You remain on the outside of everything that's happening down here, watching and waiting. But that's never really been a problem for you, has it?

You see people with laptops, people with wires trailing from their ears.

You wonder where she's got to: what can be keeping her.

Suddenly she's there again. Walking towards you from across the mall. You recognize the long black hair, the swing of her hips, the clicking of her high heels on the tile floor. At first she doesn't appear to be with anyone, but you quickly realize that she is not alone. Two security guards in dark suits will be following at a discreet distance. They're almost invisible, but they never move too far from her side.

A third subtitle flickers before your eyes: *It would not be logical to prevent superior beings from attacking the other parts of the galaxies.*

The tower at One Canada Square consists of nearly 16,000 pieces of steel that provide both the structural frame and the exterior cladding. It is designed to sway thirteen inches in the strongest winds, which are estimated to occur once every hundred years.

She will now be standing before you, the security guards taking up position on either side of her.

"Search him," she'll say. "He's got a gun." She'll smile as they pat you down. "I told you I didn't like them," she'll say.

You call her a name. She won't like that either.

The guards step in a little closer. "Another word out of you and we'll slice your heart in half."

They find the gun. You'll let them take it away from you.

"You're coming with us," one of them will say.

Crowds of shoppers move past you in a dream.

"Or what?"

"Or a bullet's going right through your head, so which will it be?"

They won't try anything here: you're fairly certain of that. All the same, you will go along with them.

Fujitsu high-definition screens read out Bloomberg averages

on the ground floor at One Canada Square. A market ana-
lyst sits back and talks on camera against a weightless array
of numbers. "The shares as you can see here are just digest-
ing reactions to that conference call, although their profits
next year, he said, are set to grow by as much as fifteen . . ."

The lobby contains over 90,000 square feet of Italian and
Guatemalan marble. It's the colour of spilled blood and grey
veins.

Percentages flash by on-screen: *Omni Consumer Products,
LuthorCorp, Heartland Play Systems, Wayland Yutani*. Nothing
arouses pity and terror in us like an unsuccessful franchise.
It's the same as watching the commercials in the middle of a
murder documentary on television: showing you things that
the dead can never see and will never know about.

You keep walking, trying to look casual, feeling the gun
that's been pushed into the small of your back ever since you
were first escorted up the stairs and into the lobby.

The tower at One Canada Square has thirty-two elevators
divided into four banks, each serving a different section of
the building. They form a central column just beyond the
main reception area. A heavy security cordon is in operation
around them at all times. Access to any of the upper floors is
impossible without a valid entry pass.

You're in a world made up of names and numbers now.
Reception, thirty-first floor: Bank of New York, Tyrell
Corporation; reception, forty-ninth floor: Cyberdyne Systems
Corporation, Computech, Stevenson Biochemical,
Instantron.

A nearby sign reads: *For your safety and security, twenty-
four-hour CCTV surveillance is in operation.*

Outside the wide lobby windows, a deep red sunset

shines through empty buildings and sheets of mirror glass, high-rise floors glowing scarlet in the far distance.

You will go where they take you in the sure and certain knowledge that you aren't the first and you certainly won't be the last. There will be a brief shadowy movement behind you just before the elevator doors open. Then the gun will come down hard on the back of your neck, catching you unawares.

"Okay, you're done," you'll hear one of the guards remark as you fall heavily towards the elevator floor. "Thanks for asking."

4.

Except, of course, you never get there.

You're already spinning round before the elevator doors have even closed properly. By the twenty-third floor, both security guards are down.

By the thirtieth floor, you will have stamped on one guard's head until his nose, mouth and ears are bleeding.

By the fortieth floor, you will have your own gun back and the other guard will be kneeling before you, begging for his life.

He will tell you he's afraid. That he doesn't want this. You shoot him once. Right through the left eye.

It's only then that you will notice there's Muzak playing in the elevator.

"Was that absolutely necessary?" she will ask, looking down at the bodies on the elevator floor and frowning. "The only reason I agreed to help you get up here in the first place was to avoid anything like this."

"Made me feel better," you'll reply with a shrug.

* * *

The building's floors have a compact-steel core surrounded by an outer perimeter constructed from closely spaced columns. It is capped by a pyramid 130 feet high and weighing eleven tons.

The exterior is clad in approximately 370,000 square feet of Patten Hyclad Cambric finish stainless steel.

She will throw her arms around you just as the elevator reaches the fiftieth floor. You embrace. Your hungry mouths will find each other.

An aircraft warning light at the apex of the pyramid flashes forty times a minute, 57,600 times a day.

"Coming with me?" you'll ask.

"No."

"Don't you want to see this through, now that we're both here?"

"I got you to his office," she'll reply. "That's what you want, isn't it?"

"That's what I want."

You exchange one last look. One last kiss.

"The pass we found in the hotel will get you through to his office," she'll say. "But you'd better get rid of the gun. It'll trip the metal detectors."

"Fine," you'll say. "I don't need it any more."

You toss the gun into a nearby waste bin.

"You're sure he'll be there?" you'll ask.

"He never leaves," she'll reply.

You are now entering the main reception area at Virex International, an uninflected machine voice will announce as soon as the main office doors slide open. *Thank you for not stopping.*

All the rooms but the last one will be empty.

You'll find him sitting at his desk, a wadded-up piece of human gum, drained and useless, gazing out at the sunset.

"John Frederson?"

His head moves slowly, painfully, away from the deep crimson light still spreading over London.

"No one's called me that in years," he'll say.

"Then you'll know who sent me."

And still he'll sit before you, empty and staring soberly at the sun: a baffling configuration of success and failure that has confounded history.

"A little far from home, aren't you?" he'll finally remark.

"We've had some . . . local difficulties."

John Frederson will nod.

"And the ghost galaxies hired you?" he'll reply. "I'm almost insulted. I'd have thought I rated better than a mere . . ." He'll pause, peer at you. "Do you even have a name?" he'll ask, looking like the man who just patented cancer.

You know why you're here and why we sent you. You're clean, filed down, all biometrics erased so they can no longer be read. The best false identity is no identity at all.

"Betamax," you reply.

John Frederson will nod again. You notice a moth skeleton still clinging to one of the net curtains over his office windows.

She'll be taking the maintenance elevator up to the pyramid by now. She'll remove her cell phone from the side pocket of her black patent-leather handbag and carefully slide off the back. Then she'll start removing the SIM card. The machinery around her moves with a smooth patience.

"You owe billions to the wrong people," you'll say.

John Frederson will shake his head and smile.

"No," he'll say. "They entrusted billions to the wrong person . . . They made an unwise investment."

"You overdrew your credit."

"Credit is a matter of confidence, of one party having trust in another," he'll say. "We can get that back in a second."

"You no longer have the time."

"Fifteen years ago there was nothing here but rusting sheds, dirty water and oil slicks," he'll say, and then wave a stiffening arm towards his office windows. "Everything you see out there took less than a decade and a half to accomplish. In ancient Egypt they couldn't even get a pharaoh buried in that time."

You can't argue with history, especially when it hasn't been written yet.

You stare at the moth skeleton instead.

Your name is Betamax, and you know what you're doing.

Banks of fluorescent lights flicker into life somewhere high above you, while the clicking of her high heels on the polished metal flooring continues to reverberate around the inside of the stainless steel pyramid.

She works as she walks, quickly and efficiently taking apart her cell phone, sliding a new card into the back.

You always know what you're doing.

You grip your left wrist in your right hand and twist. A liquid splintering sound comes from deep within your arm as bone, cartilage and gristle slide over each other. You'll watch the hand retract, your fingers folding themselves back into the hard geometry of a gun barrel.

* * *

John Frederson is still talking, but you're not listening anymore.

"It's no longer a matter of generating money but of determining how it's used, creating behaviour patterns, displacing populations, altering demographics, shifting perceptions . . ."

The gun starts to assemble itself from inside your flesh, pieces snapping into place by their own intelligence. Their movement trips a switch inside your throat. You swallow hard. There's a brief gagging sensation, followed by a mild electrical popping. You reach in and pull out the firing pin.

A pale sliver of movement flashes across a security monitor. She has finished replacing the chip in her cell phone and is preparing it to operate as a weapon. She will enter a numerical code using the phone's keypad. The device will automatically arm itself.

"Immortality . . . free-market commodities like reality and fame," John Frederson continues. "We're just the universe returning to itself. Humanity is simply another system, a wave of development that expands and dissipates, reaching out who knows how far into space."

You hold your breath and aim for the head.

He catches a glimpse of her on the monitor, standing at the centre of the steel pyramid, clutching the cell phone in a tight white fist.

He'll point at the monitor. "Who's she?" he'll ask.

One last scratchy subtitle appears before your eyes: *Those who are not born . . . do not weep . . . and do not regret . . . Thus it is logical to condemn you to death.*

"I thought she worked for you," is all you'll say.

* * *

Last-minute shifts on the international money markets indicate that an all-out strike against the London business sector is due to take place.

John Frederson will shake his head for the last time.

The framework of One Canada Square contains 500,000 bolts. Lifts travel from the fiftieth floor to the lobby in just forty seconds.

All over the planet, people will be switching on their television sets to watch the dust cloud rising darkly over London.

End transmission.

ACKNOWLEDGMENTS

Daniel Bennett would like to thank Catty May.

Joolz Denby would like to thank Justin Sullivan & New Model Army, Michael Davis & New York Alcoholic Anxiety Attack, Dr. Christine Alvin, Nina Baptiste, Spotti-Alexander & Miss Dragon Pearl, and Kate Gordon.

Cathi Unsworth would like to thank everyone who wrote a piece for this book. Also for help, support and inspiration: Michael Meekin, Caroline Montgomery, Ann Scanlon, Lynn Taylor, Mr. & Mrs. Murphy, Paul Duane and Michael Dillon.

ABOUT THE CONTRIBUTORS

Steve Gullick

BARRY ADAMSON (www.barryadamson.com) was born and bred in Moss Side, Manchester, before heading for the west side of London, where he has written and produced six or so of his own musical albums, including the Mercury Music Prize–nominated *Soul Murder*. Adamson has also scored several movies, TV shows and commercials, and he now writes stories and screenplays.

Diego Vidart

DESMOND BARRY is a rootless vagabond and the author of three novels, *The Chivalry of Crime, A Bloody Good Friday* and *Cressida's Bed*. He's been published in the *New Yorker* and *Granta*. He grew up in Merthyr Tydfil and moved to London, where he lived from 1972 to 1982. He currently teaches creative writing at the University of Glamorgan.

Catty May

DANIEL BENNETT was born in Shropshire in 1974, and has lived and worked around London for the past eight years. He recently finished his first novel.

Dieter Auner

KEN BRUEN is the the author of many novels, including *The Guards*, winner of the 2004 Shamus Award. His books have been published in many languages around the world. He is the editor of *Dublin Noir* and currently lives in Galway, Ireland.

Mark Rubenstien

MAX DÉCHARNÉ is the author of *Hardboiled Hollywood, Straight from the Fridge, Dad,* and three collections of short stories. His latest book is called *King's Road*. A regular contributor to *MOJO*, he was the drummer in Gallon Drunk and since 1994 has been the singer with the Flaming Stars.

JOOLZ DENBY was born in 1955. She has been an outlaw biker, a punk rocker, a Goth queen, and is an academic in the field of body modification. She is an internationally respected poet, spoken word artist, illustrator and author of the novels *Stone Baby*, *Corazon* and *Billie Morgan* (nominated for the 2005 Orange Prize). Check out www.joolz.net.

Glyn Roberts

KEN HOLLINGS is a writer living in London. His work has appeared in a wide range of journals and publications, including the anthologies *Digital Delirium*, *The Last Sex* and *Undercurrents*, as well as on BBC Radio Three, Radio Four, NPS in Holland, ABC in Australia, and London's Resonance FM. His mind-bending novel *Destroy All Monsters* is available from Marion Boyars Publishers.

Eugenie Dolberg

STEWART HOME was born in South London in 1962 and currently lives in East London. He is the author of twenty-one books, including the novels *Slow Death*, *Blow Job*, *Come Before Christ & Murder Love* and *Down & Out in Shoreditch and Hoxton*, all of which might be considered twisted love letters to his home town of London.

Marc Atkins

PATRICK MCCABE was born in 1955. His novels include *Carn*, *The Butcher Boy*, *The Dead School* and *Breakfast on Pluto*. He has written for stage and screen and has just finished a new novel, *Winterwood*. He lives in Sligo, Ireland.

JOE MCNALLY is a journalist and photographer who has lived in London for ten years. He has worked on publications as diverse as *Fortean Times* and *Take a Break*. This is his first published fiction.

Simon Crubellier

MARK PILKINGTON is the editor and publisher of *Strange Attractor Journal* and writes for the *Guardian, Fortean Times, Plan B* and *Arthur,* among others. He also performs with a number of experimental musical projects, including Disinformation, Stella Maris Drone Orchestra, Grok and Man from Uranus, and he broadcasts regularly on London's Resonance FM. He lives in north-east London. More info at www.strangeattractor.co.uk.

Alyssa Joye

SYLVIE SIMMONS, one the best-known names in rock writing, was born and raised in North London. She is the author of *Serge Gainsbourg: A Fistful of Gitanes,* the book J.G. Ballard declared his favourite of 2001. These days she writes for *MOJO* and the *Guardian.* Her latest book is the acclaimed short story collection *Too Weird for Ziggy,* and her latest address is San Francisco.

Neil Adams

JERRY SYKES has twice won the Crime Writers' Association's Short Story Dagger Award. His stories have appeared in various publications on both sides of the Atlantic, as well as in Italy and Japan, and a number have been included in "year's best" anthologies. He was born and raised in Yorkshire, but has lived in London for over twenty years.

Grant Wilkinson

CATHI UNSWORTH moved to Ladbroke Grove in 1987 and has stayed there ever since. She began a career in rock writing with *Sounds* and *Melody Maker,* before co-editing the arts journal *Purr* and then *Bizarre* magazine. Her first novel, *The Not Knowing,* was published by Serpent's Tail in August 2005.

Joe McNally

MARTYN WAITES was born and brought up in Newcastle upon Tyne in the north-east of England, but once he was able to make his own mind up about where he lived he moved to London. He now lives in East London, and his latest book is *The Mercy Seat.*

MICHAEL WARD was born in Vancouver in 1967 and grew up in Toronto before moving to Hull, East Yorkshire, when he was eleven. He briefly studied philosophy at Leicester University and moved to London in 1987, where he soon gave up a promising career sorting mail for the British Council to play in a band. A chance meeting in a pub led him into journalism, a field in which he has worked as a freelancer since 1997. He lives in Notting Hill.

JOHN WILLIAMS was born in Cardiff in 1961. He wrote a punk fanzine and played in bands before moving to London and becoming a journalist, writing for everyone from the *Face* to the *Financial Times*. He published his first book, *Into the Badlands*, in 1991, and his next, *Bloody Valentine*, in 1994. Following a subsequent libel action by the police, he turned to fiction and has now written five novels, including the London-set *Faithless*.

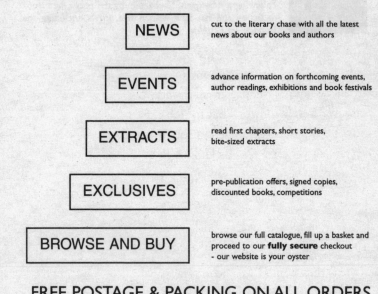

CONTENTS

GLOSSARY OF IRISH POLITICAL TERMS

Ard-Fheis	national convention (of political party, etc.)
Árd-Rí	High King (medieval)
Banba	Ireland (Irish-language newspaper)
An Claidheamh Soluis	the Sword of Light (Gaelic League newspaper)
coiste ceanntair	area council (Gaelic League)
Coiste Gnotha	executive committee
Conradh na Gaeilge	Gaelic League
craobh	branch, club
Cumann na mBan	women's auxiliary organisation for Irish Volunteers/Irish Republican Army (IRA)
Dáil Éireann (Dáil)	parliamentary assembly of Ireland
Fenian	member of IRB (Irish Republican Brotherhood) (colloquial; from Irish fian, soldier)
Fianna Fáil	Soldiers of Destiny (political party)
Fo-Ríocht	provincial kingdom (medieval)
gaeilgeoir	person dedicated to the revival of Irish-speaking, etc.
Gaeltacht	Irish-speaking area
muinteoir taistil	travelling teacher (Gaelic League)
Oireachtas	legislature; Annual General Assembly (Gaelic League); Irish Parliament since 1922
Sassenach	Englishman
Seoinín	England-lover, snob
Sinn Féin	Ourselves (name of a series of political parties)
Teachta Dála (TD)	Member of the Dáil

PREFACE

This book is the result of an awareness of the ideological shape-lessness of the separatist tradition that has dominated so much of Irish politics for better or worse for more than a hundred years. Because of this shapelessness, I have not ventured to write an intellectual history of Irish separatist political thought. Instead, I have focused on the period between the fall of Parnell in 1891 and the coming of independence in 1922 as the period in which separatism was most vocal and specific in its aims. This was also the period in which the young people who were to rule independent Ireland experienced their preparation for political life at home, in school and in the secret committees of little political organisations. I have attempted to reconstruct the mentality of this generation rather than its political thought, and to that purpose I have concentrated less on public manifestos, constitutional declarations or formal political treatises than on private letters and diaries and the often more revealing writings of casual journalism. Irish political culture is secretive, and the public and private faces of political actors are often very different. By looking at the social origins, activities and opinions of the revolutionary leaders I have attempted to divine their state of mind, in so far as this can be done.

The organisation of the book is quite simple, and thematic rather than chronological. However, I have permitted a chronological principle to organise the material within each theme.

My intellectual debts are many. A preliminary version of many of the principal arguments of this book was made possible by the generosity of the Woodrow Wilson International Center for Scholars, Smithsonian Institution, Washington, DC, which awarded me a fellowship during the year 1983/4. The Center gave me room, resources and encouragement at a rather trying phase of the project. I have benefited by the comments of colleagues at seminars held at the Wilson Center, at Colgate University, New York, at University College, Dublin and at the annual conferences of the Political Studies Association of Ireland at Magee College in 1985 and in Kilkenny in 1986. The students taking my third-year course in Irish Political Development at University College, Dublin over the past few years have also been of considerable assistance, more than they are perhaps aware.

My personal debts are also many. At the Wilson Center, James H. Billington encouraged me at the very beginning; without him, this book would certainly have been a lot longer getting off the ground. Ann C. Sheffield, Co-ordinator for History, Culture, and Society, gave administrative back-up and supplied the best cup of tea outside Dublin. I was also stimulated by conversations with Prosser Gifford, Samuel Huntington, Michael Lacy, Teodor Shanin and Robert Tucker at the Center. The Center also introduced me to the arcane art of wordprocessing. I am required by contract to say that none of the views expressed in this book in any way reflect those of the Wilson Center or its employees, and that they are my responsibility. In Dublin, I wish to thank the staff of the Department of Politics, University College, Dublin, and in particular Professor John Whyte, who has read my outpourings and overlooked my occasional AWOLs.

I would particularly like to thank my wife, Maire Garvin, who has endured the invasion of the family home by books, filing cabinets and electronic apparatus. I must also acknowledge the forbearance of my children Clíona, Anna and John, who now receive the reward of seeing their names in print.

T.G.

DUBLIN, DECEMBER 1986

NOTE ON IRISH-LANGUAGE TERMS

A work of this sort is bound to use many terms, as well as occasional long phrases, in the Irish language. To treat them all as foreign-language terms and to use italics consistently would be distracting. I have therefore adopted the contemporary Irish practice of treating some Irish words as being assimilated into Irish English: these are not italicised. Longer phrases and more unusual words have been accented and italicised. I have followed the same policy with French and German terms, e.g. bourgeoisie, but *Gemeinschaft*.

Ní h-é an bochtanas is measa dúinn,
Ná bheith síos go deo,
Ach an tarcuisne a leanann é,
Ní leighsfeadh na milliúin.

[It is not the poverty that is so terrible,
Nor being ground down for ever,
But the contempt that comes with it,
Could not be cured by leeches.]

—attrib. EOIN RUA Ó SÚILEABHÁIN (late eighteenth
century)

Do you not see, said Stephen, that they encourage the
study of Irish that their flocks may be more safely
protected from the wolves of disbelief; they consider it
is an opportunity to withdraw the people into a past of
literal, implicit faith?

—JAMES JOYCE, *Stephen Hero* (1904–6)

Out of Ireland have we come.
Great hatred, little room,
Maimed us at the start.

—W.B. YEATS, 'Remorse for Intemperate Speech' (1931)

You will find that every great conflict has been followed
by an era of materialism in which the ideals for which
the conflict ostensibly was waged were submerged.

—GEORGE RUSSELL (Æ), *The Interpreters* (1923)

The Western People had the most circulation. It was bad—during the Truce and it was a bad influence. Without the priests the Treaty would never have been put across. I was told by T.D.s that at Christmas the priests had got after them. During the Truce the priests dined them and wined them and made big fellows of them.

—TOM MAGUIRE, South Mayo IRA (1940s)

We lived in dreams always; we never enjoyed them. I dreamed of an Ireland that never existed and never could exist. I dreamt of the people of Ireland as a heroic people, a Gaelic people; I dreamt of Ireland as different from what I see now—not that I think I was wrong in this . . .

—DENIS McCULLOUGH, IRB

Brugha said that Document No 2 was not the Republic but Dev said it was. Well, he said, if you can say it is I can accept it. Liam Mellows said Tweedledum and Tweedledee. Séamus Robinson put his hand on his gun when I asked him.

—PATRICK McCARTAN, IRB (1922)

[By 1920] every mortal job was filled already, either by men who'd been a few years too old to fight, or by boys who'd been a few months too young. The poor bastards who'd happened to be born between 1890 and 1900 were left out in the cold.

—GEORGE ORWELL, *Coming Up for Air* (1939)

01 | IRISH REVOLUTIONARIES

REVOLUTION, IRISH NATIONALISTS AND MODERNISATION

The Irish revolution has been a long time dying. This is due in part to its artificial continuance in Northern Ireland and to the survival of its ideas as fossilised slogans guarded by vested interests in the official culture of the democratic regime in the Irish Republic. The generally unresolved nature of the political relationships between the two largest British Isles has contributed to the longevity of the tradition. The main phase of the movement is, however, long over and it has no political or intellectual heirs of any real significance.[1]

In an unpublished paper, J.G.A. Pocock has characterised Ireland's political experience since the Great Famine of the 1840s as one of revolutionary politics in the paradoxical context of a society which was becoming steadily more stable. The Irish revolutionary movement derived its energies from a series of grievances that were slowly being rectified.[2] The real enemy of the Irish rebel was not the British soldier or police but the reformer and the continuing steady adjustment of Irish society to commercialised, capitalist, modern civilisation. Emigration also acted as a safety valve to drain off the discontented and unemployed young. A further twist that can be added to this argument is that the rebels themselves sensed its validity and were tempted to preserve those evils in the society that generated discontent and helped their political project to survive.

Ireland has indeed been a modernising society since the Famine of 1845–7, although that modernisation has been slow and has been resisted by many elements. The tragedy of the Famine was itself the occasion of a great, even convulsive, modernising change.[3] In some ways, few European societies have travelled as far as Ireland has in the 'long century' since 1847. This is so despite a persistent popular and even academic stereotype of the country as unchanging. The highly disciplined and austere Tridentine Catholicism of modern Ireland dates from the mid-nineteenth century. Linguistically, the country was also transformed; the language of the masses changed from Irish to English, and literacy in English replaced the non-literate use of Irish. To change language entailed changing cultural worlds, and millions migrated mentally from the medieval Gaelic world to the modern world of the English language. Few countries have undergone so sudden and complete a linguistic shift; in parts of the island, the exchange of languages appears to have occurred in one generation. Again, the agrarian property system was revolutionised as a consequence of the Land War of the 1880s, as the land was transferred from a mainly Anglo-Irish and Protestant landlord class and became vested in the mainly Catholic and post-Gaelic tenantry. This tenantry in turn evolved into a newly dominant stratum of small- and medium-sized owner-occupier farmers.[4]

The economy was revolutionised. Whereas in 1830 agriculture was mainly subsistence and the island was encumbered with a huge landless rural proletariat, by 1890 commercial agriculture, based mainly on cattle exports to England, had become important. The rural proletariat had largely melted away and the owner-occupier farmer dominated the scene. An important turning point in the life of any underdeveloped country had been reached and passed; Ireland since the 1880s has had many serious problems, but they have been insignificant when compared with the appalling situation of much of the population prior to the Famine. By the end of the century the main outlines of the process were obvious;[5] one Anglo-Irish observer of that time saw it clearly as a huge social and cultural revolution, one which could not fail to be followed by a political revolution.

In those days the peasants were afraid to thatch their houses lest their rent should be raised . . . nor was there one peasant in our villages or in Tower Hill villages with a ten pound note . . . The landlords have had their day, their day is over. We are a disappearing class, our lands are being confiscated, and our houses are decaying or being pulled down to build cottages for the folk. Dialect, idiom, local customs, and character are disappearing, and in a great hurry . . . In another fifty years we will have lost all the civilisation of the eighteenth century; a swamp of peasants with a priest here and there, the exaltation of the rosary and whiskey her lot. A hundred legislators interested only in protecting monastries and nunneries from secular inquisition.[6]

Pre-Famine culture was ruthlessly dismantled by the people themselves in the decades after the Famine, almost as if there was a hatred for the heritage that had led them to such disaster. Diet, superstitious beliefs, sexual life, ideology, political life, dress and kinship systems were radically remodelled. The cultural revolution of Victorian Ireland prefigured much of what is happening in the underdeveloped world of the later twentieth century, where the efforts of peoples to cope with the invading culture and international economy of the West often bear an uncanny resemblance to the almost desperate attempts of the Victorian Catholic Irish to come to terms with the overwhelming culture and power of imperial England. The long political revolution of the period from the 1850s to the 1920s occurred in the midst of huge cultural changes, economic shifts and social reforms, and was both stimulated and threatened by their unsettling and pacifying effects. The successful conclusion of the Land War seriously weakened the revolutionary impulse.[7] Once the alliance of English Liberalism, Irish agrarianism and Irish constitutional nationalism had destroyed landlordism, the 'agrarian motor', which revolutionary separatists had hoped to use to move their own rather different cause along, slowly began to run out of fuel; it is arguable that had the 'accident' of the First World War not intervened, the Irish revolution would have died by the mid-twentieth century without realising its objective of complete separation of Ireland from

Britain. Since 1890 there has always been a curious revivalist quality to Irish separatism and republicanism deriving from their ambiguous attitude toward reform, cultural change, capitalist development and modernisation.

Republican separatist ideology was both modernising and nostalgic. Revolutionary imagery in many different societies has portrayed the desirable future in themes culled selectively from a real or imaginary past, combined with an equally selective set of images of the progressive future. The vision of the future depends on the vision of the past; this is obviously true of many of the classic nationalist movements and of various fascisms, but it is also true of revolutionary movements that have cloaked themselves in the rhetoric of socialism.[8] The sense of a significant past may be weaker in societies which have become thoroughly modernised than it is in those in which the modern and the traditional have been forced to live in uneasy juxtaposition for long periods, as happened in Ireland during the century after the Famine.

Change and reform as well as repression and reaction all came from England, and many nationalists identified capitalist modernisation with England, much as many contemporary radicals in underdeveloped countries see capitalism and Americanisation as identical. Opposition to English rule attracted different people for different reasons, and often for opposing sets of reasons. A reactionary might be attracted to such a stance as a means of defending the noble values of feudalism against English reformers; a pious Catholic would see it as a means of defending the religious convictions of the Irish people from English scepticism, anti-Catholicism and indifference; a nationalist of centrist inclinations might see it as a virtuous attempt to forestall state socialism, big business, trade unions and the malign effects the intrusion of English commerce had on the livelihood of the Irish shopkeeper, farmer or artisan; lastly, a radical might see separatism as an anti-imperialist campaign for a socialist Irish republic. Separatism's ideological proteanism reflected the wideness of its appeal.

Religion intensified both separatism and anti-separatism. The seventeenth-century conquest had imposed a settlement establishing a propertied Protestant minority over a mainly Catholic unpropertied majority. Religious differences had congealed and evolved into what were essentially ethnic or caste distinctions. The historical alliance between the Protestant cause and the British state continually threatened to delegitimise British rule in the eyes of the majority. This caste-like system still existed in the late nineteenth century, although it was increasingly coming under pressure from both Irish and British reformist forces. Caste-derived resentments, often coupled with religious fundamentalism, were to become important sources of separatist feeling; separatism could ally itself as easily with political primitivism as it could with ideological progressivism. In the wake of the Famine, a radicalised generation of young men, most of them Catholics and of modest social origins, put together an almost open, and certainly very widespread, conspiracy to eliminate British rule in Ireland. Much derided at the time, this conspiracy persisted for over sixty years; some would argue that it still exists. There was nothing spontaneous about the Irish revolution; it was created by the strenuous efforts of many activists over two generations.

In so far as such things can be dated, the Irish revolution started with the founding of the IRB in 1858. There is actually a good deal of vagueness about the original significance of the initials; it was held to signify either the Irish Revolutionary Brotherhood or the Irish Republican Brotherhood. The latter title earned a more general acceptance. The Brotherhood's alternative title, the Fenians, reflects the movement's intermittent historicist nostalgia; the name evokes a legendary warrior order of pre-Christian Ireland. The Fenians were, however, a rather determinedly modernising movement, despite the fact that much of their support was rooted in reaction against the consequences of social change.

Commercialisation was a major source of change. Commercialisation essentially meant a concentration on the few products in which Ireland had a comparative advantage. Chiefly, these were cattle and other primary products for the British market. Cattle farmers saw advantages in the British connection which others did not and became disliked by both separatist nationalists and their land-hungry neighbours. The artisanal and cottage economy declined in Ireland, much as it had done elsewhere in western Europe with the coming of the factory system and efficient long-distance transportation. A native Irish industrialisation, which might have compensated for the decline in the cottage economy, appeared impossible in the face of overwhelming English industrial superiority without the kinds of tariff barriers that were being experimented with in Germany and the United States.

Many analysts have noted the apparent connection between widespread social change, declining economic sectors and revolutionary fervour.[9] Such fervour is characterised by nostalgia for an older world, and in particular for an older social contract that is held to have been violated.[10] Calhoun has argued that many revolutionary movements have committed themselves to the defence of traditional cultural values and communal relations rather than to their replacement by new values and relations. They do this because such commitment is a condition of political success. Traditional social culture provides a ready-made framework for resistance to the spread of the market and its disruptive effects on the structure of local society. Thus, in nineteenth-century Europe, revolutionary sentiment was strongest among artisans and some peasantries, people with some status and property, however humble, to lose: the pre-industrial 'middle classes'.[11] Calhoun has proposed more boldly that these 'reactionary radicals' have been at the centre of most modern revolutionary movements. Artisans and property-owning peasants were in part tiny capitalists, their capital consisting of their skills, workshop, retail premises, membership of an organised and restrictive trade brotherhood or, in the case of peasants, the traditional and sometimes legally entrenched usufruct right to a piece of land. Traditional culture was not an inherited, unbroken 'cake of custom' but rather a praxis rooted in everyday experience and circumstance; whereas Marx emphasised that proletarian political unity arose out of new conditions of social existence, Calhoun suggests that older social bonds, threatened by capitalist change, are commonly the source of mass political solidarity. Cobbett, for example, appealed to traditional rights to justify radical political demands.[12]

Because these bonds are so important, radical political mass movements are typically more powerful at local than at national level, and a chronic tension exists between local and national leaderships. When extended beyond their area of origin, they tend to be taken over by special interests. The movements' images and ideas tend to echo the popular political culture's values of stability and fear of change, particularly change which is seen as coming from outside. The possession of this political culture makes this traditional 'micro-bourgeoisie' more effective revolutionary material than industrial workers, who are natural reformers rather than revolutionists. This proposition fits in well with the observed decline in the revolutionary *élan* of the crowd in European history since the end of the eighteenth century.[13]

These ideas also tie in well with Hroch's research into the geographical and sociological roots of European small-country nationalist movements in the nineteenth century. The zones in which the movements originated tended to be compact, unindustrialised and developmentally intermediate. Substantial small-scale production, geared to the local market, existed. These zones were commonly fertile, and agricultural production had gone well beyond subsistence level but had not yet developed into true large-scale capitalist farming. These core areas were affected by industrial civilisation but were not themselves true participants in it; capitalism had developed enough to generate problems, but not enough to offer solutions. Radical nationalism was a 'disease of development', reaching its peak at an intermediate stage of development in time and space. I shall argue that in Ireland the southern province of Munster, centred on the city of Cork, was a classic example of such a zone. This area, in the part of the island furthest from the industrialised province of Ulster, was developmentally intermediate and was the area where agrarian and separatist movements had their most sustained and ultimately most successful expression, culminating in the guerrilla warfare of 1919–23. A disproportionate number of nationalist leaders came from the province of Munster, and much of the ideological basis of the movement in its final phase was devised by Munster writers responding to the social conditions of the southern province.

In Ireland as elsewhere, nationalism's ideological nostalgia contrasted oddly with the modernity of its political means and of its ultimate goals. Irish nationalists, like Wolf's 'middle peasants' or Hroch's 'patriots', saw themselves as defenders of the community and its values against a process of transformation threatened by alien political, economic and cultural forces, usually perceived as emanating from the imperial government in London. They were, of course, themselves doomed to become agents of modernisation, and the nostalgic programmes which many of them held so dear had no long-term future.[14] What did survive was an image of the Irish as the moral, innocent and potentially corruptible People of God in an amoral, England-dominated world.

THE REVOLUTIONARIES AND THE REVOLUTION

The IRB certainly understood that there was a connection between its prospects of ultimate political success and the persistence of certain traditional attitudes of hostility toward the regime. Revolution in Ireland was seen as dependent on the discontent of certain social groups. Evidently the artisans and other urban middle sectors were important, but the prospects of general popular support for the separatist political project were bound up with the persistence of chronic agrarian discontent in rural society in the decades after the Famine and also with certain values associated with religion.[15] James Stephens, the Fenian leader of the 1860s, believed that by destroying so much of the cultural fabric of old Ireland, the Famine had also destroyed much of the prospect for an Irish separatist revolution. For similar reasons he regarded the emigration of young men to the United States with horror. The fact that post-Famine Ireland was a far more prosperous society and that the pre-Famine state of affairs could scarcely have persisted indefinitely signified little to this remarkably single-minded separatist.

Stephens saw that society was developing in a way that was inimical to the kind of insurrectionism which he favoured. It was therefore the true separatist's duty not to be discouraged by defeat or by lack of popular support but rather to bear witness to the heroic tradition of revolutionary separatism and to pass on the separatist ideal to the next generation in defiance of social trends: a few men faithful and a deathless dream. Stephens's implicit theory of political action was voluntarist and romantic rather than determinist. An elitism was also noticeable; since the people were at best only passively sympathetic, it was the Fenian leaders themselves, with their dedication to the attainment of the holy grail of an independent Ireland, who were the core of the Irish nation struggling to be reborn.[16]

Patrick Pearse, the leader of the 1916 Rising, echoed these sentiments in a more developed and quasi-mystical form a generation later when the process of capitalist modernisation and Anglicisation had gone much further. Pearse looked much more to the Irish language and the cultural tradition associated with it as the essential vehicle of Irish national consciousness. Were these to die, as seemed likely, the Irish nation would cease to exist. It should be recalled that by 1910 this language was unknown to the vast bulk of the population of the island. Pearse insisted that the student of Irish affairs who did not know 'Irish literature' (literature in the Irish or Gaelic language) was 'ignorant of the awful intensity of the Irish desire for Separation as he is ignorant of one of the chief forces which made Separation inevitable'.[17] Pearse, like Stephens, feared that the nation would die; in Pearse's case, this death was equated with the possible death of the Gaelic cultural tradition.[18] These ideas were commonplace in a cultural organisation with which Pearse was associated, the Gaelic League. The League's internal politics, examined later in Chapter 5, were crucial in the organising of the Irish revolution.

The League disseminated these ideas widely. Irish socialism came to be imbued with this ideological nostalgia as well. James Connolly saw the Irish bourgeoisie as usurpers, much as Pearse saw the English as usurpers. The great farmers had arrogated to themselves the land that, under the old Gaelic system, had belonged to the kin, or people, as a group; by means of an ideological conjuring trick, 'scientific socialism' was demonstrated to be akin to ancient Irish property systems, and the past could be evoked in the usual fashion to delegitimise the present-day state of affairs and to legitimise the promised post-revolutionary future. It is difficult to resist the speculation that something of Connolly's ancestral county Monaghan's Ribbon levelling tradition survived in his theory of property and in his synthesis of socialism and nationalism.[19] The capitalism that he opposed could easily be assimilated to English capitalism, and the workers whose cause he championed could similarly be conceptualised as the vanguard of the nation. The fact that Connolly was well aware that there were Irish national capitalists and regarded them as enemies could easily be elided by others, and duly was. Socialist ideas were assimilated to an ideological tradition that was non-socialist and separatist in the Fenian tradition.

As I will argue later, the clerics of the Catholic Church also became important carriers of the tradition of cultural nostalgia, particularly in the last years of the century and through the Gaelic League. Neo-medievalism was seen as a barrier against modernism and secularism, associated in their minds with the English-speaking world and, at times, with vaguely envisaged international conspiracies run by Freemasons and Jews. Priests and patriots were to forge an alliance of convenience around ideas of this sort.

Although the separatist leaders lived in towns, the cultural tradition to which they came to appeal was essentially rural. Its gradual weakening coincided in time with the decline of the classes most likely to be attracted to republican separatism. According to Stephens, the 1867 insurrection was supported by farmers' sons, mechanics, artisans, shopkeepers and labourers, whereas the wealthy and the professional men stayed aloof.[20] He could have added that the newly ascendant farmers denied the movement their support as well, with the significant exception of those in some parts of central Munster. Farmer support for separatism was very conditional and was subordinated to agrarian considerations; land reform threatened the revolution.[21] Land reform came about, and the revolutionaries were forced to take up the causes of cultural defence and religious fervour to breathe life into their political project; the war of 1914 was like a *deus ex machina*.

This superficially successful revival of republicanism has always had a curiously artificial character; republican separatism had to trick itself out in the garments of linguistic revivalism to appeal to the clergy and in the clothes of nationalist athleticism to appeal to the young men. In itself, the Republic had no great general appeal. A persistent atmosphere of make-believe has surrounded all variants of republican separatism ever since. After 1922 independent Ireland developed much as it had done before independence; independence made a huge difference, but not the kinds of differences hoped for by so many separatists. The Anglicisation of Ireland continued, and was to demonstrate itself to be independent of economics and politics. Long after independence, IRA veterans were often aware of this; their efforts had not resulted in a genuine cultural or spiritual revolution, never mind a social revolution. British rule was destroyed in most of the island, and eventually economic dependence on Britain was to be greatly reduced. But as countrymen, or as people who identified ideologically with a rural society, many of them thought of the real Ireland for which they had been fighting as the Ireland of farmland and village rather than the emerging Ireland of towns and cities with a modern Anglo-American popular culture; cities were less *Irish*. Daniel Corkery, a prominent Cork ideologue of the League and of the separatist movement, remembered the pronouncedly rural core of the separatist Irish Volunteers of 1913 who evolved into the IRA a few years later. In pre-independence Ireland, there was an extraordinarily strong cultural difference between city and country, a difference which was much greater than the normal differences between urban and rural ways of life and was ethnic and political as well: towns were English, and Dublin the centre of English colonial power, whereas the countryside was Irish, Catholic, resistant to city rule and even Gaelic. In 1958 Corkery wrote:

It is one of those inevitable deeply-based differences that not every historian takes notice of. In this long-enslaved country it is even still a very significant difference. It is more strident than the natural difference between rural and civic. It is a historical difference. After all it was not the Parliamentarians who in the nineteenth century dispossessed the English-minded landlords. It was the people on the land—the people themselves. And though the story of the struggle is usually told in parliamentary terms and phrases, it cannot but have been these almost unexamined deep-rooted traditions, so anti-English in sentiment, that were responsible for the extraordinary cohesion of it. And if that split between the parliamentarians and the separatists had not taken place [in 1915], we certainly should not today be living under a native government in Dublin.[22]

Many who thought like Corkery wished for a reversal of the Anglicisation of Ireland and the demotion of Dublin as the cultural centre of Ireland. In the long run, the city and city culture were to win. A classic contradiction between ideological nostalgia and the wish for modernity lay at the heart of Irish separatist sentiment.

02 | MEN IN THE MIDDLE

REVOLUTION AND THE PETTY BOURGEOISIE

The independent Irish state of the twentieth century was constructed by a revolutionary nationalist élite whose own formation took place during the 1890–1914 period. This élite was, in turn, the product of a secret separatist movement that even then was half a century old. This tradition was to take away the leadership of nationalist Ireland from the parliamentary nationalists during the 1913–21 period. The romantic and somewhat anti-parliamentary ideology of this élite has often been commented on, and has been commonly ascribed to the vacuum that existed in conventional politics after the fall of Parnell. The bitterness and disillusion which filled Irish political life and which had a profound conditioning effect on the minds of the young people who were to rule Ireland after 1922 are notorious, and are sometimes regarded as being peculiarly Irish; James Joyce is certainly partly responsible for perpetuating this view. It is rarely pointed out that the period after 1890 was a time of restlessness, disillusion, political romanticism and cults of violence everywhere in Europe. Both left and right developed new ideological strands that were hostile to constitutional styles of political action, voluntarist and, deep down, profoundly elitist; Leninism and fascism were long prefigured.

It was not simply the collapse of Parnell's uneasy blend of revolutionism and parliamentarianism that led to the retreat to ultra-romantic political modes in *fin de siècle* Ireland. The separatist movement of the new century, heavily informed by the political ideas of former decades, closely resembled other radical movements of the time, whether leftist, nationalist, palaeo-fascist or, as was common, some indeterminate mixture of all three.

A conspicuous feature of the politics of the period in many European countries at that time was the rise of political movements of an often extremely romantic and visionary character, dominated by relatively well-educated young men from the middle reaches of societies which were rigidly stratified into social classes. The Irish revolution came to be led by young men from the new Catholic middle class, and many of the most vocal and energetic of its activists came from the lower reaches of the middle class or from the upper strata of the peasantry or working class.[1] In Yeats's classic phrase, many of them indeed possessed great hatred and suffered from little room; little room was accorded them by Irish society or by the Anglo-Irish establishment, and great hatred was commonly the consequence.

The democratisation of political life in Europe at the end of the century entailed the evolution of a new kind of mass politics, involving large numbers of voters and activists organised together in great associations. Public organisations such as political parties and undercover secret societies alike were created by large numbers of individuals challenging the highly stratified politics of the period. There was an unprecedentedly heavy involvement in political life of individuals of modest social origins. Mass movements, whether working class or mixed in social composition, were characteristically led by men who either were or were becoming members of a new middle class. This development was new; only in the United States among major countries was this kind of politics usual and even traditional. Furthermore, many social theorists of the period did not grasp, or did not wish to grasp, that this kind of politics was the politics of the future. According to Marxist theorists, for example, the petty bourgeoisie was an obsolescent stratum in capitalist society, consisting of inefficient and outmoded producers on a small scale, retailers and petty functionaries such as government ministers, schoolteachers, middle-level army officers and most of the clergy. It was expected that these groups would be liquidated or reduced to insignificance by the further development of capitalism and the consequent increasing polarisation of society between big capital and big labour. Eventually these great forces would contend for mastery. This vision of the future spread far beyond Marxism; many Catholic analysts agreed with the prognosis, viewing it with horror rather than with hope. Many proposed various 'middle ways' between the two great heresies of the modern world, liberal individualist capitalism and radical socialist collectivism. Ideas and passions that were later to re-emerge as components of fascist, social-democratic or technocratic systems of political thought commenced their careers as defensive arguments of various middle-level groups which felt themselves to be threatened by the way in which society was developing at that time.

In the twentieth century it became evident that although large sections of the old middle class were indeed doomed, they were being replaced by newer middle groups with greater capacity to survive in modern society. In some cases individuals or families simply changed trades and survived, while in others they found themselves pushed aside by new people. The middle class came to be much larger and more indispensable than it had been. The older artisan, farmer and shopkeeper groups were joined and partially supplanted by new groups, most conspicuously an increasingly large stratum whose main capital consisted of training and education, which practised professional skills and which was often employed directly or indirectly by the state. Much of the skilled working class effectively became part of this new stratum. This political promotion was probably due as much to its increasing social indispensability as to the efforts of the trade unions or of leftist political parties. In the agrarian sector, there was a parallel long-term tendency to favour the middle-sized to large, modernising commercial farmer, this trend working against both the subsistence peasant and the latifundist.[2]

Old and new middle classes alike, however, shared one classic problem: that of succession. The children of the artisan, the civil servant, the factory manager, the junior army officer, the ecclesiastic or the clerk had no guarantee of inheriting their fathers' positions in society, unless the levels of organisational nepotism were very high. Even if one son did have such a guarantee, as in the case of property owners such as shopkeepers and farmers, the other sons, not to mention the daughters, were left without position. Economic growth often alleviated the situation by creating new positions commensurate with the ambitions of these young people, but could not always be counted on. Furthermore, the growth of well-organised and impersonal bureaucracies worked against nepotism and in favour of increasingly mechanical and 'meritocratic' forms of recruitment. Ascriptive recruitment in its traditional form of assessing people by their ancestry rather than by their personal ability tended to be replaced by prescriptive recruitment or hiring by assessed ability and educational attainment. Discrimination in favour of members of the aristocracy or of a more general upper caste increasingly came under pressure.

In the context of the often authoritarian family structures of late-nineteenth-century Europe, fathers and sons might conflict, but fathers would also usually be concerned for their sons' futures. The sons certainly would; loss of social status, a chronic problem in the middle classes in times of political and social instability, was perhaps most keenly felt during the period of young adulthood. Fear of failure could get converted explosively into political passion; in Tsarist Russia, 'the great-grandfathers failed in the 1820s and 1830s, the grandfathers failed in the fifties, and the fathers failed in the seventies. Each generation found itself unable to honour its father . . .'[3]

Geographically based traditional cultural, linguistic or even physical differences and caste discrimination commonly had the effect of aggravating class and generational differences. Areas within larger states which possessed cultural identities tended, in accordance with tolerably well-understood mechanisms, to develop distinct political identities and also to develop nascent political leaderships often derived from the lower middle class. The political culture of these groups tended to be a distilled and even exaggerated version of that of the petty bourgeoisie: nationalist, possessed of a work ethic, abstemious and hostile to both big capital and big labour.[4]

Education and training increasingly tended to become the main gateways to middle-class and skilled-worker positions in Western society, a fact that made the educational systems themselves a main target of political controversy. The nineteenth-century classic anti-privilege slogan *la carrière ouverte aux talents* has had many unforeseen implications. Among others, it came to suggest that personal failure in a career was no longer due to the will of God but to implied injustice in the organisation of society; a political system once seen as remote and about as explicable as the weather could increasingly be held responsible for one's personal misfortunes. The growth of educational institutions combined with uneven rates of economic development to produce large numbers of relatively well-educated and underemployed young men concentrated in the cities, which were inhabited by large and deprived proletarian populations as well. There was an ever-increasing supply of young men and women who were ideally suited to be the cadres of the mass movements of the twentieth century. Paris was the classic city of Bohemia, and possibly its birthplace, but every large European city had its Bohemia by 1890; even Dublin developed one of sorts. Marx was acerbic and Bakunin benign about the unemployed, educated young men who dominated Italian socialist politics as early as 1873. According to the former:

The [Socialist] Alliance in Italy is not a 'worker's union' . . . but rather a pack of déclassés, remains of the bourgeoisie. All the supposed sections of the Italian International are led by lawyers without clients, medical doctors without patients and without skill, students of billiards, by bagmen and other clerks and particularly by journalists of the small press of more or less dubious repute.

Bakunin, by contrast, thought them 'excellent poor youths', with plenty of generous intentions but politically ignorant.[5]

The classic Bohemia was in the city. However, it was commonly inhabited by young men from the country, and many European nationalist and socialist radicalisms had rural ancestries. Such syndromes are perhaps particularly common in underdeveloped countries, where not only do the towns and the country possess radically different cultures and often even different languages, but also the immigrants from the country to the towns retain the mental habits and social organisation of the peasant communities from which they came for a long time, along with direct personal and familial links with their native places. During the Russian revolution, for example, much of the new urban proletariat revealed its true nature by liquidating itself; it returned *en masse* to the ancestral villages so as to be able to eat in the disorganised Russia of the period. In Weimar Germany, residence in a rural community, combined with commuting to work in a larger town, reportedly encouraged a petty-bourgeois mentality among workers and has been held to have been associated with acceptance of National Socialist ideas among people whose 'objective' social class should have encouraged other political sentiments. Rural connections in many European societies commonly had the effect of both radicalising and conservatising politics; town ideas were transmitted to the country, and rural discontents found in the city a place where they could be openly expressed, away from the parish's system of social and intellectual control.[6] An Irish radical nationalist journalist ('Pat') wrote in 1906:

A remarkable thing happened the other night in Dublin, at the Dungannon Club. I gave a lecture on 'the Causes of Irish Decay,' dealing in particular with the terror of ideas in which we are brought up, and the lack of individual liberty in brains which cripples character and so makes progress impossible. The audience were mainly students and university people chiefly from our country towns, and I asked them how it was they could be so heroic in Dublin while they cowered in dumb fear in their own parishes at home, where heroism was so much more needed. At the end of my lecture I was much surprised to find my critics almost to a man charging it against the clergy! From beginning to last I had not said 'priest' once. Is it not far better to let the clergy know what the people are thinking?[7]

In Ireland the parish expressed itself through the priest; 'Pat' had a curious idea of the Irish people if he imagined his audience of middle-class and ex-peasant nationalist radicals reflected the sentiments of the general population; perhaps in a sense he was right, as their opinions were to become popular later. Furthermore, in the twentieth century, all political causes are pursued in the name of the people, and sometimes with the people's approval. The pronounced wavering between revolution and reaction characteristic of so many European radicalisms of the early twentieth century appears to be connected with this urban–rural dialectic in which Bohemia faces the Parish.

Ethnic and class distinctions, uneven development, chronic mismatch between education and opportunity, aristocratic resistance to democratisation and to the claims of the newly educated and the persistence of rural traditions all aggravated the tensions in most European countries. To a large extent, even western Europe was still ruled by what amounted to a pre-bourgeois order. An *ancien régime* of sorts prevailed in all the major states except France; only in France had the older order been decisively defeated, and even in France the old alliance of Throne and Altar was waging a very effective rearguard campaign. Nowhere had fully fledged liberal democracy based on universal suffrage emerged. In Ireland, government was also an affair monopolised by a small, remote and unpopular group, usually labelled 'Dublin Castle', and not all that much in sympathy with the Anglo-Irish, never mind the Catholic masses. Those commentators who in recent decades have pointed to the romantic and violent aspects of the 1916 tradition have commonly lost sight of the fact that pre-independence Ireland was undemocratic in the elementary sense of not being run by people answerable to the population which they ruled. Ireland was not unique; even the religious antagonisms of Ireland, so incomprehensible to certain kinds of English people, closely resembled those of central Europe, where clerical establishments competed against each other for souls and where religious distinctions were, in effect, caste and even ethnic distinctions as well. In semi-developed societies, ecclesiastics formed an important part of the middle class. Professional roles such as teaching, journalism and administration were commonly carried on by clergy and, in the absence of a large and well-educated middle class, priests had great political and cultural power. For the purposes of this analysis, the bulk of the clergy can best be thought of as part of this new lower middle class; most of the Catholic clergy came from the solid farming stratum and appear to have echoed their attitudes in many ways.[8]

The lower middle class has had rather a bad press; its very shapelessness has made it a useful scapegoat for the failure of many supposedly progressive political projects in the twentieth century. Most notably, this shadowy entity has commonly been held responsible for the rise of the fascist mass movements after 1918. Perhaps the most hysterical denunciations of the lower middle class have been Marxist. Erich Fromm, for example, generalises, as only Freudianised Marxists appear to be able, about the pre-1939 central European petty bourgeoisies, accusing them of 'love of the strong, hatred of the weak', of 'pettyness, hostility, thriftiness with feelings as well as with money' and of 'asceticism'. Their outlook on life was narrow, they suspected and feared the stranger and they were curious and envious of their acquaintances, rationalising their envy as moral indignation; their whole life was based on the principle of scarcity—economically as well as psychologically.[9]

Other writers have taken a more detached view. Michael Hroch has seen the petty bourgeoisie as the natural leader of nationalist movements. Such movements, while not initiated by the petty bourgeoisie in nineteenth-century Europe, typically tended to be taken over by it in their final, mass-movement phase; the new post-Versailles nation-states, among which Ireland can reasonably be reckoned, commonly acquired élites of petty-bourgeois backgrounds.[10] More generally it has been argued, as we have seen earlier, that lower middle-class elements have been far more responsible historically for the radicalism of many political movements than the workers or other classes, an argument that has been made with perhaps greater insistence in recent years.[11] For example, extreme nationalist, clerical and fascist mass movements in eastern Europe were commonly led by petty-bourgeois élites and enjoyed massive worker and poor-peasant support in the years after the First World War.[12]

Putnam has made the interesting general suggestion that elements of the middle classes turn to radical or revolutionary politics only when, because of discrimination, they find their political status in society noticeably lower than their political capabilities. They may be determined fighters for equality and freedom under certain circumstances but may, given different cultural traditions, espouse programmes of totalitarian levelling, with themselves in charge. The Old Bolsheviks, for instance, were an eminently middle-class, even near-aristocratic, Bohemian group before they came to power in wartime Russia. Putnam argues that potential revolutionary leaders are to be found neither in the mansions of the rich nor in the hovels of the poor, but among 'over-educated outgroups'.[13]

This admittedly wide-ranging discussion has made it tolerably clear that the terms 'petty bourgeoisie' or the even vaguer 'lower middle class' have often been used by different observers to refer to very different social groups. Commonly they are so vague as to conflate two very different categories with very different identities and interests, the rising new middle groups and the declining strata of pre-industrial society. Another group often lumped into the portmanteau term 'petty bourgeoisie' is that of the generally unsuccessful of all social backgrounds. De Felice's analysis of Italian fascism, for instance, describes it as having at its core the failures and *déclassés* of all classes, the lower middle class having some preponderance. The key desire that all had in common was that the state would rescue them from their plight.

> The bourgeoisie is represented, but it is the indebted bourgeoisie requiring support; the working class is represented, but it is the permanently unemployed who are unable to do battle and who are concentrated in poor neighbourhoods; the lower middle class comes flocking, but it is the ruined lower middle class; even property holders come running, but primarily those among them who have been dispossessed by inflation; there are officials and intellectuals, but they are officials without jobs and failed intellectuals. These constitute the nucleus of the movement, and it has all the hallmarks of a community of failures. It can expand ... into all the classes because it has social links with all of them.[14]

After the 1916 rebellion in Ireland the police were convinced that many of the local leaders were people who tried revolutionary politics in a society which offered them little opportunity. They rarely added that their failure, if actual, was often not their own fault, in the caste-ridden and machine-dominated society of the period. In an eerie anticipation of de Felice, a Wexford police officer described the rank-and-file of the rebels as 'all ne'er-do-wells, people who had failed in many things, and had tried Sinn Féin as a last resort . . .'[15]

It seems clear from the literature that the blanket term 'lower middle class' includes the following social categories: the artisanate, shopkeepers and smaller capitalists; professionals, in the broad sense, including teachers, lower civil servants, lower and middle management and clerks, and excluding only the higher professions, such as senior positions in law, medicine and accountancy; the highly skilled working class, or significant sections of its upper level; small and middle-sized farmers and peasantry; army NCOs; and intellectuals, again in the very broad sense, to include writers, artists, journalists and entertainers.[16] Another important category in the Irish case is the lower clergy, which should also be included. In many societies, including the present-day Irish Republic, junior army officers and similar grades elsewhere would also be included, but before 1914 the dividing line clearly ran below the rank of lieutenant and similar grades elsewhere.

When we turn to the politics of Irish separatism, the relevance of these European comparative perspectives becomes clear. Ireland suffered from the same chronic discontents of many other European societies that were outgrowing their political regimes. However, a major peculiarity of the Irish case was the general recognition which existed that some form of political autonomy or independence was going to occur. Thus all the actors had similar models of the political future and were, so to speak, playing the same game. The only questions were: when was it likely to occur, how generous a measure of Home Rule could be extracted, was total independence feasible, would Ulster be excluded and, most important for this discussion and perhaps to the leading political actors themselves, which set of local élites or would-be élites would inherit power once the Castle regime was finally dissolved?

Between 1890 and 1922 several competing sets of potential leaders of a new state jockeyed for the political leadership of the expected post-Union Ireland. Most of them were politically inexperienced; even the parliamentarians had no experience of government at the national level, and the new local councils had not been long in operation. There was a scarcity of educated and trained manpower. Much of the extravagance of Irish political argument at the time derived from political impotence and frustration; there was a chronic long-term uncertainty about British intentions and, of course, an inability of any Irish tendency, whether Home Ruler, unionist, separatist, Sinn Feiner or socialist, to do very much to affect those intentions; Britain was a super-power with worldwide concerns, and Ireland was not a high priority. Irish politics was the politics of unimportance.

The main groups competing for political leadership in pre-independence Ireland were, firstly, those among the Anglo-Irish who hoped to retain some shreds of their traditional social and political ascendancy under the coming new dispensation; secondly, the new Catholic middle class, internally divided, inexperienced and less than adequately educated; and lastly, the Catholic clergy, which wielded enormous power, mainly because of the weakness of the other two groups. A fourth group, the Ulster Unionists, in effect opted not to compete but to construct another arena. A small but intense socialist movement also existed, which in many ways was to trigger the violent phase of the revolution but which was not to profit from it. Big business was mainly unionist in politics; as I will argue later, one of the peculiarities of the Irish revolution is how small a role classic labour and bourgeois groups played in it.

Throughout the thirty years after Parnell's death, under the rhetoric of the Gaelic revival, the brilliant cultural last stand of the Anglo-Irish, and the increasingly hysterical and visionary nationalist rhetoric which echoed similar rhetorics elsewhere in Europe, there can be discerned a political debate between these groups, exacerbated by generational tensions within each section. In later discussion, I will concentrate mainly on the separatist leaders or patriots and on the priests with whom they eventually hammered out an alliance.

Like other radicalisms of the period, the Irish movement displayed a blend of romantic idealism and an exaggerated moralism. Real idealism existed, but it sometimes served as a cloak for personal frustrations, envy and social *ressentiment*. Most commonly, it was a psychological compensatory device for the abundant contempt which the powers-that-be entertained for the movement and its leaders, a contempt derived from traditional class distinctions, anti-Catholic ideology and a habit of underrating separatists. The patriots' attempts to compensate were reflected indirectly in many themes: the essential evil of English rule and civilisation, the virtues of Tridentine and Vatican I Catholicism, the ascription of a monopoly of evil to one's opponents, a contempt for compromise, ultimately a noisy retreat into asceticism and self-denial as a means of avoiding both ambition and envy. A moral elitism was also noticeable. In some cases a subterranean romantic dislike of rationalism, of Victorian science and of secularised or liberal perspectives on politics and society, reminiscent of German romanticism, existed. Xenophobia and anti-Semitism were sometimes present. In the minds of some Sinn Féiners, such as P.S. O'Hegarty, liberalism and individualism fought a battle with inherited deference to clerical authority. These ideological and psychological themes are examined below.[17]

CIVIL SERVANTS, TEACHERS AND OTHER SCRIBES

School was the way out of the parish. Education was the route to position for men of intelligence and no capital, and it was scarcely a reliable one.[18] Civil service posts in Dublin, Cork, London and the Empire attracted young men who had done well in public examinations, much as in other colonial and underdeveloped societies where only the state offered jobs of a recognisably modern kind. Status was often valued more than money in Irish Edwardian society, reflecting in part the school- and diploma-based, rather than monetarised, status system below the level of the gentry: shop assistants, often well-educated, might be patronised by those in the commanding heights of the system, but they were 'gentle', no matter how ill-paid, whereas carpenters, no matter how well-off, were not.[19]

Schoolteachers had traditionally held a similarly uncomfortable middle position in society, in that they possessed education and quite considerable social status in the parish while being formally and often actually denied any real security or independence. National Teachers (NTs) were the radical intellectuals of the parish and some of them were, through the Gaelic League, involved early in the project to revive the Irish language through the institutional vehicle of the national schools where the bulk of the population received its elementary education. Teachers were often IRA leaders a few years later and many other leaders had parents or other close relatives in the teaching profession. In the parish, the teacher possibly ranked second only to the priest in prestige and potential for political leadership. Teachers were in the curious position of being employed both by (usually) the Catholic Church and by the British state. Joyce may have been thinking of this symbiosis when he commented acidly in 'Gas for the Burner':

Ireland, my first and only love,
Where Christ and Caesar are hand in glove.

This arrangement afforded a major contrast with the French one, where village teacher and parish priest faced each other across a deep ideological divide; in Ireland the teacher was subordinated to the priest and could accept that subordination willingly or otherwise. If, however, the priest was at odds with the population politically and the teacher was not, the system of subordination broke down and a miniature political revolution took place. A teacher's salary was paid by the state directly to the parish priest, who had formal authority from the state to manage the state-financed school. In effect, the priest could, at his discretion, pass the salary on or withhold it in whole or in part. 'This distribution took many forms, depending on the personality—sometimes the idiosyncrasy, of the individual (clerical) manager . . . There were many complaints of carelessness and objectionable methods.'[20]

In 1894 the Catholic bishops conceded to teachers who had been fired by a clerical manager a right of appeal to themselves. A series of rancorous cases led to a rebellion in 1898 by the Irish National Teachers' Organisation (INTO) in the form of a protest to the Commissioners of National Education. The INTO described the NT as being in a position of 'practical slavery' and intimidated by the arbitrary authority being wielded over him. The teachers soon retreated from this 'advanced' position, but relationships between the teachers and the hierarchy remained uneasy, a relationship repeated in miniature in many villages across the country.[21]

The teacher experienced a curious mixture of power and power-lessness; he was appointed by the parish priest, who possibly selected for piety rather than intellectual originality, and who sometimes reportedly selected for kinship to himself. On the other hand, the priest's supervision was apparently typically rather lax. The teacher was occasionally visited by an inspector from the remote and politically stalemated administration in Dublin. He was usually of farming stock himself and tended to have an elaborated version of the local political culture; in particular he shared the farmers' attitudes to the land question in earlier decades. Like his pre-Famine predecessor, the hedge schoolmaster, he was often heavily involved in local political or agrarian agitation of a kind that was favoured so much by local opinion that the priest dared not stand against it. A stereotypical NT of the 1880s was described by a hostile observer as a 'doctrinaire' who drew his political opinions from the radical, nationalist provincial and Irish-American press. Although he was animated 'by a real love of his country', that love was 'fed by theories as insubstantial as soap bubbles, and these theories are but too likely to be for the present imbibed by the youth committed to his charge'.[22]

Thirty years later, in the middle of the Anglo-Irish War, another observer analysed the teacher's position in almost identical, if less patronising, terms. The teacher's financial and intellectual inse-curity made him the natural source of a vague radicalism which was commonly short of coherence or intellectual adventurous-ness. Teachers were discontented and were a natural source of opinion in the parish. They were spread across the country, as was the school system, and they inevitably had a pervasive influence on the young and, in the longer run, on the general political culture of the entire nation.

When men and women in such a position are underpaid, insecure and goaded into a position of profound discontent, they are likely to become active agents of revolution, none the less powerful because they cannot act openly. It is impossible to estimate, though it is interesting to guess, how far the present condition of Ireland is due to the influence of the National School Teachers.[23]

Intellectually inhibited discontent, total economic dependence on both Church and state combined with great local cultural influence to form an explosive mixture. Many IRA veterans ascribed their original indoctrination into extreme nationalism to their teachers. Others were teachers themselves, or had teachers as parents. Séamus Ó Maoileóin, for example, was an IRA leader and brother to another leader who actually was a schoolteacher. Their mother also had been a teacher. Séamus was later the author of one of the better memoirs of the Tan War, *B'Fhiú an Braon Fola*.[24] Dan Breen, a Tipperary guerrilla of some notoriety, fondly recalled the influence on him in youth of one Charlie Walsh (Cormac Breathnach), a rebel-minded schoolmaster of Donohill National School, county Tipperary.[25] Another NT, Humphrey Murphy, was a dominant figure in the Kerry IRA. Séamus Ó Maoileóin's brother Tomás ('Seán Forde') recalled their teacher mother's determined Gaelic revivalism, and in old age lamented the decline of the old language and culture which his mother had painfully pieced together from study and talking to old people in remote areas. Eventually she was to impart it to her two future guerrilla sons as small children. Their father was a farmer, a quiet man, and in a not uncommon pattern deferred to his wife's superior education. In another not uncommon pattern, the language revival issue became a means of expressing in Aesopian form the buried tension between priest and teacher; the Irish language issue was a stick which the subordinated layperson could legitimately use to belabour the sacred person of the priest. Ó Maoileóin recalled:

My parents, although religious in most respects, abhorred
ecclesiastical interference in cultural and national affairs. This
inevitably caused some difficulties, especially as my mother was
a schoolteacher. When I came to make my first confession, I had
to go to another parish, because my mother refused to teach me
the prayers in English . . . When I was about eight . . . she was
sacked by the Board, but that could not have happened without
the connivance of that priest.[26]

Tomás turned out a very aggressive IRA guerrilla, but he shot at
British forces, not at priests.

Schoolteachers appear to have inherited the role of the hedge
schoolmaster of the pre-Famine society. Before the 1830s, these
private-enterprise itinerant educationalists had earned their living
by teaching English, reading, mathematics and the classics; they
played a substantial part in the process by which Ireland became
English speaking. A century later, their successors turned their
energies to a Quixotic attempt to reverse this cultural revolution.
According to Cullen, the teacher also inherited an older tradition:
that of scribe, or guardian of lore and national literature, under
Gaelic or Old English patronage in pre-1690 times. The poet-
schoolmaster became the chief mourner for the dying Gaelic order
in the pre-Famine period. After the French Revolution, many hedge
schoolmasters imbibed a version of French republican radicalism.
Cullen claims that the teacher represented the fusing of two
traditions: the radical republican one of the 1790s and the older
aristocratic one of the seventeenth century. It is no coincidence
that Patrick Pearse, chief leader and martyr of the 1916 Rising, was
both a poet and a schoolmaster.

Schoolmasters have been conspicuous in revolutionary movements generally, and the role of teacher has been commonly
associated with that of revolutionary leader, both empirically and
in the rhetoric of post-revolutionary regimes; Mao was, after all,
the Great Teacher. In a sense, the schoolmaster is the ideal-type
of the displaced intellectual whose frustrations and articulacy
encourage noisy political radicalism, often of a rather abstract and
ambitious kind. Hoffer has suggested unsentimentally that most

modern revolutions reflect rather little of the wishes of the masses but much of the passions of the leaders themselves; the wishes of the 'scribes' in a newly literate society who feel themselves to be underemployed or unfairly subordinated. They are naturally attracted to the idea of a strong state run by scribes and to that of the political leader being teacher of the ruled and controller of the circulation of ideas. The concept of the leader being essentially the executive of the will of the ruled and chief persuader and organiser of that will is presumably less attractive. In view of the short-term outcome of the Irish revolution, it is difficult not to suspect that this stereotype fits the Irish revolutionary élite rather well.[27]

Teachers are noticeable people and bureaucrats often are not. Government employees of low and intermediate rank were noticeable figures in the Sinn Féin and IRA hierarchy after 1918. Because of their experience in running large command organisations and also because of their strategic location inside the state structure, they had key roles in the institutional takeover that was the central event of the 1914–23 period. Many of the revolutionary leaders had had experience of the British and Irish administrative machine, and had been recruited into it on the basis of examination results at the end of their school careers. In the case of a well-known Irish-language writer, things were once so arranged that he could offer Irish for his language proficiency test, set the paper himself, solemnly sit the examination and award himself full marks. Michael Collins, the organisational Trotsky of the Irish revolution and the envy of his less organisationally adept colleagues, had been an employee of the Post Office in London before he moved on to work for a stockbroker. The central Post Office at Mount Pleasant in London seems to have housed many Irish national radicals, particularly perhaps those from the Cork area, like P.S. O'Hegarty. Many of the young men who revitalised the IRB, the Gaelic Athletic Association (GAA) and the all-important Gaelic League were civil servants, and they felt more free to engage in this quasi-subversive form of activity after the advent of the Liberal government of 1906. The GAA and the League essentially masqueraded as non-political associations, much as did the widely resented Freemasons, and were therefore not subject to the usual rules prohibiting civil servants engaging in politics. The political energies of junior civil servants became channelled into putatively non-political but actually very politicised athletic and cultural organisations. Seán Ó Casey recalled that GAA hurlers, because of the social geography of the game inevitably of Munster origin by and large, acted as assault troops at political rallies in pre-1916 days. Even though they were not working class, O'Casey acknowledged that they were 'tough guys'. Some of them were civil servants, schoolteachers, customs officers and solicitors' clerks. Others were 'grocers' curates', while some others were farmers' sons, railways workers or dockers.[28]

It is striking that many of the radical nationalist ideologues had secure state employment as junior civil servants and, unusually in the Ireland of that period, were invulnerable to intimidation by their employers. As already argued, this proposition could not apply to teachers, but other state employment certainly gave one independence of a clerical establishment hostile to nationalist extremism. Ironically, another simple way of being independent of clerical controls was to be a Protestant or Jew; a large number of the older separatist leaders were Protestant or of 'mixed' background. Teachers' radicalism was often secretive, but so were the political sympathies of many Post Office employees, customs officers and policemen; the British administration in Ireland was ceasing to be trustworthy.

I will argue later that the split of 1922 was in large part between those who had had administrative experience and those, often younger, who had not.[29] Collins's penetration of the police, military and administrative establishments is legendary, and unsurprising when the extent to which that apparatus had become staffed by Irish Catholics is considered; his spies are reputed to have been everywhere. The unarmed Dublin Metropolitan Police appear to have been suborned by 1918. The spectacle of the British government being intimidated by Carson into partitioning Ireland demoralised parliamentary nationalism, but it is rarely noted that it badly damaged the morale of the Royal Irish Constabulary, the *gendarmerie* charged with the physical control of the country outside Dublin city; Seán T. O'Kelly observed that official connivance with the illegalities of unionism 'gave us

the Constabulary'.[30] IRA veterans often reminisced of their penetration of the London civil service as well, and of infiltration of
the Ireland–Britain shipping lines; Liverpool was a traditional
centre of Irish conspiracy going back to the Ribbon confederation
of the 1820s. One veteran of the Anglo-Irish War remembered:

> I went to Dublin with intelligence reports. We had men in
> Admiralty, Home Office and in the police, both men and
> women. We had one man in the Policeman's union who was an
> M.P., a junior minister, Assistant minister. There was a man in
> the Admiralty, a porter, who brought us out stuff to be copied.
> The Post Office was well organised.[31]

Bureaucratic skill came to be essential to the movement's
survival, and bureaucratic careerism a threat to revolutionary *élan*.
During the Truce, the coming split was already obvious to
observers within the IRA, Sinn Féin and Dáil government. The
Tipperary IRA began to lose faith in the movement's leaders long
before the Treaty. A distrust of administrators and of government,
originally aimed at the British regime, transferred itself to the
underground Dáil government as soon as it showed signs of
evolving into a real government. P.J. Matthews, a pro-Treaty Sinn
Féin administrator, explained the disaffection of the fighters in
exactly these terms of purist disgust with careerism: 'It is a historic
fact that most of those who voted for the Treaty were rewarded in
some material way and there was an unseemly rush of friends and
relatives for a share in the plums of office.'[32]

Another of the pro-Treatyite élite, on resigning abruptly from a
senior administrative position, was gently chided by the new
prime minister, W.T. Cosgrave, that be should get one of the 'plum
jobs' before they had all gone.[33]

A careerism–purism conflict split families in many cases. The
Irish Civil War became known in Irish as *Cogadh na gCarad* (War
of the Friends), and often came to be a war between brothers. In
many families, parents and children were ranged on opposite
sides, in others the elder siblings were pro-Treaty whereas the
younger ones opposed the compromise. The pro-Treatyite activists

naturally profited from their allegiance to the new state, whereas the anti-Treatyite losers suffered severe material deprivation. A common figure in the Irish political underworld after 1922 was the activist in illegal organisations who had close relatives in the governmental apparatus which he was presumably trying to subvert. Such links between the political underworld and the political overworld in post-revolution Ireland may have had a significant effect in overcoming the division; the Irish Civil War was in part an affair of class interest, but it was also in part quite literally a family affair.

Careerism was used determinedly to gain allegiance in 1922. Trainee schoolteachers in St Patrick's Training College in Dublin were conspicuous among Dublin IRA soldiers. J.J. O'Connell, an Irish-American pro-Treatyite, informed their company captain that he would guarantee that every member of the company who went pro-Treaty would 'be sure to pass his teacher's exam'. Reputedly no one took him up on this tempting offer. Perhaps the examination was not difficult.[34]

Men in the middle had characteristic dilemmas in European society on the eve of the First World War. Everywhere they were coming to an awareness of their growing importance and their indispensability to the running of modern societies; gentry, business and labour alike needed their skills. The coming of liberal democracy and the bureaucratised welfare state, already there in embryo before 1914, was to make them even more important. The Great War itself, of course, accelerated these trends. In Ireland the transition from a gentry-led to a middle-class society was abrupt and rather painful; it also had its comic moments. Much of the humour of the post-revolutionary period concerned itself with confronting the romantic and aristocratic dreams of the revolutionaries with the quotidian and rather grubby realities of life in independent Ireland. This contrast was itself an echo of the transfer of power from the Anglo-Irish gentry to lower middle-class Catholics. In popular memory, the coming of independence was often remembered in the terms offered by a cartoon in a Dublin humorous journal. Entitled 'The Night the Treaty was Signed', it depicted a horde of office-seekers thronging the road from Cork to Dublin.[35] There was, of course, more to it than that.

03 | THE FORMATION OF THE REVOLUTIONARY ÉLITE

INTRODUCTION

Revolutions are commonly thought of as short and dramatic events, the main occurrences being over in a few years, perhaps followed by a long aftermath. However, revolutions often have long gestations and do not run their courses even in the timespan of a generation. Many European revolutions have taken two generations to run their course from beginning to end.[1] The main course of the Irish revolution can be best conceived as running from 1858, the year in which the IRB was founded, to 1923, the year in which fundamentalist republicanism was defeated both politically and militarily by the moderate wing of the revolutionary movement. In this period of sixty-five years, the separatist movement went through three main phases. The first purist or 'Fenian' insurrectionist phase started in 1858, engineered an unsuccessful rising in 1867 and lasted until 1879. A second agrarian phase commenced with the agreement of the IRB to ally with Parnell's parliamentarians and Davitt's agrarians in the New Departure. The Fenians supplied manpower for the Land League and its successor, the National League, and showed signs of evolving a rather vigorous but fundamentally constitutional style. This phase ended in 1891 with the fall of Parnell. The final phase, one of romantic revolutionism, ran from 1891 to 1923. The movement was taken over by younger and rather different men, particularly after 1900.

THE REPUBLICAN ACTIVISTS, 1858–1900

The Irish Republican Brotherhood, or Fenians, was an extra-ordinary organisation. Despite years of failure and tragi-comic débâcles, it was its political project rather than that of the parliamentarians which was to prevail in Ireland, a project that still haunts the minds of the democratic leaders of the Irish Republic of the present day. Early Fenianism was to a great extent the creation of the Irish diaspora in the United States. It was dominated by strong, often fanatical personalities, liable to internal division and riven by factional division. It was created by a small group of people and in its first generation of existence it depended on that group's initiatives and on American money. In Ireland and Britain, it attracted not only the settled artisanate but also the floating Irish proletariat of the great British industrial cities. It also penetrated the Irish regiments of the British Army. In the combination of lower middle-class and still ruralised working-class support, it closely resembled Ribbon-Hibernianism, with which it was in competition. In Ireland its strongest areas were the towns of the east and the south, the peripheral and poor west being only weakly organised, as was the Ribbon and Orange north. As mentioned previously, the only rural areas to make a strong response to Irish-American Fenianism in the 1860s were the heartland counties of the south, where much of the support appears to have come from the rural labourers and the smalltown workers. Like other such organisations, it seems to have benefited greatly by kinship ties which supplied a ready-made principle of co-operation and trust. Fenianism's social base was reminiscent of Chartism's, the artisans in particular being common to both movements; some would say that the Irish were common to both movements as well. Both Irish and British artisanates were hit by the growth of the factory system, but in the case of the ruined Irish artisan or even more destitute superfluous farm labourer, a nationalist and anti-regime diagnosis made sense in a way that it could not in the case of their English equivalents: the English could blame the establishment, the upper class; the Irish could blame the English. Many of the Irish artisans, heirs to a tradition of ethno-religious revanchism, would be attracted to such an analysis anyway; the traditional strengthened the new. The official ideology of the IRB was nationalist and separatist, mildly modernising and radical in the nineteenth-century, non-socialist sense. It also had a strong streak of militarism. By and large it was hostile to ideas of revolutionising the property system, although many individual Fenians dreamed of dividing the land. It was also non-sectarian, which did not prevent some of its members thinking in sectarian terms. It was somewhat anticlerical, as the Catholic Church opposed the violence of Fenian methods. The movement was modernising despite the streak of nostalgia in its rhetoric, and it was democratic and egalitarian by the standards of the period. Ideologically it was extremist only in its uncompromising separatism.[2] Fenianism despised British parliamentarianism, seeing it as only very partially democratic and corrupt. Furthermore, it was a British, not an Irish, parliamentarianism. The Fenians skirted the agrarian issue gingerly; they were townsmen, and some of them had property.

Their political ideas were heavily influenced by the American political tradition, by Second Empire France and by their own experiences as a secret society under central, Jacobin-style discipline. The Fenian model constitution for an independent Irish Republic, disseminated during the mid-1860s, prescribed universal suffrage, a Bonapartist, indirectly elected president-for-life, a two-chamber legislature, a separation of powers à *l'Américaine* and almost complete Church–state separation. Although Fenianism usually favoured non-denominational education, the draft provided for considerable ecclesiastical say in educational matters. Its essential modernism is demonstrated by its proposed abolition of the traditional provinces and their replacement by a new set under geographical designations. Hatred of Dublin, the traditional seat of British power, was exemplified by the proposed reseating of the capital in Athlone and Limerick. The draft included detailed proposals for a considerable military and naval establishment.[3]

The leaders were classic examples of *émigré* national radicalism. Of thirty-nine Fenian leaders listed in the American, British and Irish biographical dictionaries, nineteen had emigrated at least temporarily to the United States, many of them in the aftermath of the Famine and at a very young age. Quite a few appear to have lost a parent or other close relative in Famine-related circumstances. An emotional and quasi-mythical account of the Famine as a London-engineered attempt at genocide had its roots in the experience of emigration of many young people in the 1840s. Certainly the young Fenian leaders of the 1860s came of this cohort; typically they were journalists, soldiers, small businessmen, often heavily involved in Irish-American politics in New York and elsewhere, not extraordinarily well-educated, but apparently intelligent and resourceful men. They came disproportionately from the Munster counties of Cork and Tipperary.[4]

Their military efforts failed predictably. Consciously or otherwise, their real purpose appears to have been propaganda of the deed; the making of a grand gesture that would mobilise the population and, perhaps, tempt France or the United States to help them. The Fenians perpetuated, and in part invented, a traditional rhetoric of revivalist and mythopoeic aggression, using folklore, journalism and popular song, that is still alive and did a great deal to prevent the legitimising of British rule in Ireland. One Fenian, writing in the immediate aftermath of the crushing of the 1867 rising, saw the separatist struggle as distinct from, and even at odds with, any striving for social or material well-being, a theme which was to become visible in more developed form in later versions of republican ideology. This particular Fenian valued the rising as a means of strengthening the traditional ill will between Britain and Ireland. He also felt that if Irish insurgents were to hold one large Irish town for a week against British forces, the United States or some other foreign power would be sure to intervene. The growing gentleness of British government in Ireland worried him because it threatened to succeed in legitimising itself in the eyes of the people.[5] This programme of seizing a town and holding out in expectation of foreign help echoed the ideas of eighteenth-century revolutionaries. It was to be carried out to the letter almost exactly sixty years later by a group belonging to the same organisation that had organised the 1867 rising. Fenianism did indeed get some response from some of the population. The movement's propagandists used newspapers and also distributed copies of the usual old prophecies which forecast, in millennial fashion, the fall of British and Protestant power in Ireland. These were of mixed Gaelic and English Catholic provenance and were scarcely needed to convince some of the people of the iniquity of British rule; a passive sympathy with Fenianism was widespread.[6] In west Cork, a core rural area for the movement, one well-placed observer commented in a private memorandum a year before the 1867 rising:

> ... I find by my intercourse with the peasantry that although very few of them are enrolled Fenians, yet they generally have a sort of vague sympathy with the movement, of which they know only that it is designed to free Ireland from the clutches of England. Their ignorance of the relative strength of the English government and of the Fenian army is so dense that they look on the chance of the conquest of Ireland by the Fenians as being quite on the cards. They arrive at this belief by a mixture of fact and imagination. They regard England as a country of preeminent wickedness and they believe that God only waits to overthrow her power, 'till,' as Carroll the slater said to me, 'the cup of her iniquity shall be full ...'[7]

This encounter between a cosmopolitan, or at least unparochial, political movement from outside the parish and the political mythology of the Irish countryside's 'little tradition' had happened before and would happen again.

The defeat of 1867 did not destroy Fenianism, but rather had the effect of gradually nudging it on to quasi-legal, if still conspiratorial, paths. The underground army evolved into a secret political party, similar to those of Poland and Russia described by Gross.[8] The IRB became an 'entryist' party which infiltrated nationalist movements of all kinds and attempted to bend them to its own purposes. It provided sinew for the Land League, took over the Gaelic Athletic Association in the 1880s and even influenced the literary movement of the 1890s. The network constructed in the 1860s reached a peak of sorts during the Parnell period of 1879–91, the years of the agrarian struggle. We happen to know quite a lot about this phase of the IRB. The Land League/National League was supported by farmers with the usufruct of at least some land, as distinct from the landless, and could fairly be described as a movement dominated by a nascent rural petty bourgeoisie. It was led, however, by townsmen of non-agricultural occupation who were drawn disproportionately from the commercial and manufacturing trades of town and village society.[9] The IRB net formed a large part of this cadre, and many of the non-IRB leaders appear to have been Fenians in their youth, or at least claimed to have been.

Of eighty-one IRB organisers, leaders and activists under police surveillance between 1880 and 1902, one-fifth were shopkeepers, usually in a rather small line of business, most of them publicans or combining a bar trade with general groceries or other goods. Another fifth were travelling salesmen, often in the liquor trade, commercial agents or middlemen. A further sixth were small businessmen, with builders and auctioneers predominating.[10] Another tenth consisted of journalists, provincial newspaper editors and proprietors of papers. Agrarian bourgeoisie (cattle dealers and large farmers) accounted for another tenth. The usual agglomeration of artisans, technicians, mechanics, clerks and shop assistants accounted for only one-sixth of the total; the Land League had taken over the Fenians as much as the latter had taken over the former. There were few labourers, small farmers or, unlike in later phases of the movement, teachers or state employees; local and central civil service posts were not yet open to Catholics in large numbers at senior or even intermediate level. Teachers were politically subordinated to the clerical school managers and were only beginning, rather timidly, to unionise.

The previous careers of twenty-five of the eighty-one could be traced, and it is immediately clear that the Fenian leaders were upwardly mobile; nearly one-third of the twenty-five had started off as shop assistants or clerks, eventually setting up in business on their own. Many were of small-farm background and appear to have improved their circumstances considerably. The classic Irish Victorian pattern of upward and outward mobility from the farm and, eventually, out of the parish and into retail trade serving the farming community was clearly visible. The trades and professions that these young men went into seem to have been typical of those available to young Catholics of that time. Careers outside the liquor business, construction, journalism and medicine were blocked to them, partly because of discrimination and partly because of the inadequacy of the education available to Catholics.

Other facts of social life conspired to narrow the career chances of these young men. There had been no industrial revolution in Ireland outside eastern Ulster, and the artisanate was under siege and by and large a closed shop. Emigration to the countries of the English-speaking industrial world, Britain and the United States, was the obvious and often inevitable option. If you were educated, well-connected and lucky, a job in Ireland meant medicine or the Bar. For many, it meant the priesthood; for more, it meant a clerkship in a Catholic-owned small retail business. With luck, ability, hard work and some cunning, a shop assistant might eventually set up on his own account in business, perhaps with the aid of a farmer's daughter's dowry, or perhaps with dollars earned in an American sojourn or remitted by emigrant relatives. Even as a successful trader or builder, he would find himself refused business by the establishment; he would be inclined to retaliate in kind. Eventually railway clerkships and posts in the lower levels of the police and administration became available in greater numbers as reform made an impact on the system; eventually both constabulary and bureaucracy were to be faced with the stark choice of defending the regime or throwing in their lot with rebels. Medicine had a peculiar importance, as it was one of the earliest of the higher professions to be opened to Catholics because of the different ethical systems of the Churches. Doctors in Catholic medical establishments were not in direct competition with their Protestant counterparts, unlike, for example, Catholic lawyers, who had to put up with considerable subordination. Doctors were noticeably radical and natural leaders of the emergent Catholic middle class.[11] Yeats described London Fenians with whom he consorted in London in the last two decades of the century as being 'almost all doctors, peasant or half-peasant in origins, and none had any genuine culture. In Ireland it was just such men, although of a younger generation, who had understood our ideas.'[12]

However, doctors and other professionals were not among the eighty-one organisers in any numbers; in the parish, doctors and other professional men were few in number and politically very vulnerable. Of the eighty-one, almost one-third were resident in Dublin, and appear to have been first-generation Dubliners. Disregarding Dublin, the now familiar pattern of over-representation of the south reasserts itself: over one-third of the non-Dublin leaders lived in Munster.

EDUCATION AND STATUS RESENTMENT

Vilfredo Pareto conceived of all human societies as being divided into the powerful and the non-powerful, élites and non-élites. This very simple idea has been held by many people, but it perhaps became particularly popular in the years around the First World War with the dashing of the hopes of romantic revolutionists as new élites replaced old ones all over Europe and the new democracies everywhere appeared to be a passing phase. Pareto and other thinkers evolved theories of élite replacement, Pareto dubbing the central idea of his argument the 'circulation of élites'. Sooner or later, élites will be displaced by 'new men' coming up from below. However, this process is rarely smooth and frictionless; because of structural rigidities of various kinds, possession of natural ability does not automatically entitle one to membership of the élite. Certainly, in a totally 'meritocratic' society, élite status and intelligence, energy, ability and, perhaps, ruthlessness or cunning would coincide, whereas in a society where the channels of social mobility had silted up, or had never been without silt, no such correlation could be expected. Such silting up occurs because of inertia and because of the wish of the incumbent élites to avoid competition and to pass on élite status to their children.

Mechanisms involving 'markers' which legitimate discrimination are commonly used to defend the status quo; kinship, caste, race, religion or even language, dress or manners are examples of such cultural markers. Markers vary in their permeability; kinship and race can scarcely be changed, and caste status can give almost as much difficulty. Religion can, of course, usually be changed, but often only at the expense of deserting one's native community and deeply held beliefs. However, accent, dress and speech are essentially learned behaviours that can be relearned; much education has had the obvious if unadmitted function of relearning social deportment for purposes of social mobility.[13]

Circulation of élites must take place, according to this theory. It will either occur in a delayed and perhaps explosive fashion or it will occur piecemeal, through the admission of able non-élite individuals to élite status and the concomitant exit from the élite group of less able individuals. However, the established élites frequently refuse to accept the *arrivistes*, or do so only slowly and reluctantly; commonly generations must pass before *arrivisme* is forgiven and forgotten. Resistance to *arrivisme* results in the 'new men' attempting to force their way in, commonly in the name of the non-élites ('the people') in general. In extreme cases, the old élite is ousted completely and no merger of old and new occurs.

The growth of a Catholic would-be élite stratum in late-nineteenth-century Ireland was steady and can, in outline at least, be traced adequately. Because of the 'accident' of the British political crisis of 1910–14 and the Great War, elements of this stratum were precipitated into power 'prematurely', being given a chance to grasp political power much earlier and more completely than they would have had in times of peace. The coming to power under one circumstance or other of a Catholic democratic leadership was long foreseen. Some dreaded it, others awaited it impatiently. It was obvious that Anglo-Irish leadership was not practicable under democratic conditions, and even the Catholic clergy accepted the need for a lay, popular élite of a kind that scarcely existed prior to 1914. Thomas O'Dwyer, Catholic bishop of Limerick, warned the Commissioners on University Education for Ireland in 1902 of the dangers of conceding political power to Catholics without first providing them with adequate opportunities for higher education; few Catholics received such education. He sketched a vivid picture of the intellectual inadequacies of the more politically ambitious Catholic young men. Limerick corporation was typical of the new democratic local authorities so abruptly conceded by the government in 1898; it consisted of a body of 'uneducated, unenlightened working men'.[14] He generalised this observation; the people of Ireland had 'no natural lay leaders' and no 'educated laymen who are in sympathy with them, and at the same time will control them and keep them within limits'.[15]

A rather narrow Catholic middle class had arisen under the Union, sandwiched uneasily between the aloof Ascendancy and the restless general population. Essentially it filled the professions, which were rather overstocked, and tended to be neither prosperous nor particularly self-assured, one witness to the Commission felt.[16] Another witness felt that these Catholic Irishmen were intimidated into silence by their priests and rarely expressed their real views on public affairs.[17] He could possibly have added that this reticence extended not only to issues on which the clergy had strong opinions but also to matters of concern to employers, politicians and even the leaders of secret societies; a highly authoritarian and parochial society had a less than fully institutionalised notion of free speech. As a Waterford farmer put it in the 1890s *à propos* of a local land agitation, 'we're all for it collectively, but we're all against it individually'.[18] Many commentators have given us a picture of a society which had very few truly independent leaders outside the Ascendancy and in which priests, schoolteachers and bureaucrats exercised abnormal influence because of this power vacuum. It could be argued (and was) that Catholic Ireland was less than fully prepared for self-government.

However, a political leadership was being created, as hindsight wisdom tells us. It was not to come from the older Catholic middle class but from a much broader and younger stratum, mainly of farming and peasant origin. As this cohort grew in numbers and became politically awakened during the last decades of the nineteenth century, it became deeply sensitive to its own political subordination, to the inadequacies of its own culture and education and to the aloofness of the Ascendancy. Furthermore, this emergent political class was to show a considerable amount of native ability, exemplifying perfectly the 'over-educated, under-regarded' element which élite theorists warned about. It was also watched uneasily by the power-holders in Irish society, both lay and clerical, nationalist and unionist. The unease was to be thoroughly justified by events.

THE EDUCATIONAL CUL-DE-SAC

The Irish educational system had many defects; Pearse termed it the 'Murder Machine', and was himself a product of it. He referred to the killing off of creativity and initiative by its mechanical emphasis on rote learning, its authoritarianism and its role in accelerating the decline of Gaelic culture. However, the system was not without its defenders; Pearse had rather advanced educational ideas, contrasting oddly with his cult of heroic archaism. From the 1870s to the end of the century, it was dominated by an incentive system based on 'results'. In essence, a proportion of each teacher's salary was dependent on the marks the children in his charge received at the public examinations run by the central education authorities.[19]

Whatever the shortcomings of the system, it is apparent that it had a pervasive effect on the learning habits of large numbers of people who passed through the schools in this period, and possibly an equally pervasive impact on their adult personalities. The numbers attending school grew enormously during a period of net overall population decline.[20] The system encouraged memorisation and 'grinding'; it was also held to encourage an unthinking, authoritarian conformism. A heavily literary, classical and mathematical curriculum was favoured, at the expense of the modern languages, the sciences or commerce. The Irish language, Irish history and Gaelic culture were ignored, even in Irish-speaking areas, much to the annoyance of the patriots but apparently often with the approval of the parents. Whatever the faults of the system, it does appear to have imparted a competent, if very narrow, education to a large number of potentially able young people with little tradition of formal education behind them; it represented to them a way of ceasing to be peasantry and of becoming citizens. A spokesman for the Christian Brothers, while echoing the complaints of other witnesses to the 1898 Commission on Higher Education, commended the system for instilling persistence, character and fixity of purpose into a population perhaps somewhat deficient in these qualities. It should be borne in mind that the Christian Brothers' schools, increasingly coming to dominate secondary education for poorer Catholic boys, scored very well in the examinations held under the 'results' system.[21]

Few Catholics received third-level education, and those who did commonly received it part-time or even by correspondence. This was because the undenominational Queen's Colleges were anathema to the Catholic bishops, as was Trinity College, while the Jesuit-run University College in Dublin was understaffed and ill equipped; fear of proselytism and secularism lay behind the bishop's prohibition on non-Catholic higher education. It is difficult not to suspect, however, that many clerics feared the emergence of a Catholic lay class which was intellectually equal to them; cultural power was a jealously guarded resource. Later, when the political ideas of Canon Sheehan and other politicised clerics of the period are examined, it will be argued that a fear of independent lay thinking was uppermost in some of their minds. On the other hand, some senior ecclesiastics, like Bishop O'Dwyer, may have been uneasy about the long-term consequences of the effective denial of higher education to young Catholics.

Higher education of a narrow, applied, but highly disciplined kind was, of course, enjoyed by candidates for the priesthood at Maynooth and the other seminaries, thus incidentally ensuring a continued intellectual ascendancy of priest over layman. O'Dwyer, with admirable powers of self-analysis, lamented his own lack of true higher education as a typical case.[22] Secondary education for Catholic boys was dominated, he said, by young priests whose educational background resembled his own. Clever men of 'great natural ability', they had received excellent philosophical and logical training at Maynooth, but were 'absolutely deficient' in all classical, scientific or mathematical education, as well as in 'culture', an attribute which included a 'sense of honour, and a right judgement with regard to the affairs of life'.[23]

The young men educated mainly by these priests and brothers under the 1878 Intermediate Education Act achieved literacy and a relatively high educational level. They were to form the nucleus of the mass nationalist movements of the next century.[24] The numbers of Catholics receiving post-primary or 'further' education more than doubled between 1861 and 1911, at a time when the figures for the other denominations were static. (See Table 3.1.)

Table 3.1 Religion and Further Education, 1861–1911: Numbers of Catholics and of Other Denominations Receiving Instructions in 'Superior Establishments'*

	1861	1871	1881	1891	1901	1911
Catholics	11,939	12,274	12,064	15,430	25,647	31,742
Anglicans	7,897	7,628	7,854	7,280	7,335	6,220
Others	3,549	4,268	4,775	5,059	5,583	5,175
Total	23,385	24,170	24,693	27,769	38,565	43,137
Catholics as % of total	51.1	50.8	48.9	55.6	66.5	73.6

*'Superior establishments' was the administrative phrase used to refer to secondary and tertiary educational institutions.
Sources: Census of Ireland 1891, 162; Census of Ireland 1911, 60.

Table 3. 1 makes it clear that the effect of the 1878 Act permitting substantial grants to further education for Catholics was obvious by 1891 and dramatic ten years later. Long before 1914, Catholics were knocking on the doors of the system in large numbers. In 1913 the London *Times* noted that the young men whom the Catholic schools were turning out were no longer satisfied to spend their lives working on the land. 'They desert the country for the town; they prefer to be clerks, civil servants, schoolmasters, journalists, rather than farmers or curates . . . The class thus created inherits the traditional feelings of the Irish peasant; it shares in his profound racial consciousness and his antipathy to the British intruder.'[25]

Catholic boys also did well academically at second level, this contrasting with their under-representation at third level prior to the founding of the National University of Ireland in 1908.[26] To some extent, the filling of senior positions in government, the professions and business with non-Catholics was due to the relative dearth of suitably qualified Catholics, an explanation that was accepted by some Catholic spokesmen, although not by very many.[27] However, organised discrimination by each 'side' in favour of its 'own people' was a folk tradition, one which penalised Catholics because of the relative weakness of the Catholic presence in positions of influence.

The existence of what was in effect a bar to progress to third-level education was reportedly producing a half-educated and intellectually under-equipped future political leadership. Many witnesses at the 1902 Commission reported a deep frustration and resentment in these young men, mobilised by the educational system and then left stranded half-way up the ladder, near enough to see the glittering prizes but not near enough to win one. One witness cited as typical a young Belfastman who would have been 'better off for higher education' had he been permitted by his religion and by his bishop to attend the Queen's College. The son of an organist, he ended up as a national schoolteacher and 'rather discontented'. Money was not a problem, but the prohibition of his bishop was.[28]

Many of these young men reportedly became teachers or jour-nalists, thereby achieving an opportunity of spreading their discontent by projecting their personal quandaries onto the social system in general, typically in the form of a noisy and romantic anti-British nationalism constructed from a mixture of traditional elements and new radical ideologies coming in from outside Ireland. At the 1902 Commission, Starkie noted that only a tiny percentage of Senior Exhibitioners went on to university education and that this fact had 'filled the country' with 'half-educated boys' who were unfit for farming or manual labour and who could look forward only to the entrance examination for the lower grades of the civil service; 'I do not think you could create a more dangerous class in the country', he remarked prophetically.[29]

In 1905 a clerical-nationalist paper, the *Leader*, echoed this assessment from a rather different point of view. Catholic edu-cation, it averred, had reached the stage at which Catholic students were getting more awards than other denominations. However, they had no chance of 'getting a start' in the banks or railway administrations because of religious discrimination.[30] Some years later it ran a series of convincing exposes of discrimination against Catholics in the public sector, apparently heavily penetrated by Freemasonry.[31]

Another reason for the passion with which clerkships were regarded by Catholic school-leavers was the fact that non-manual, indoor 'educated' work carried enormous prestige in the status system. The manual–non-manual distinction was, as suggested earlier, often psychologically more crucial than all but the most gross financial differentials. George A. Birmingham, writing in 1912, noted the extraordinary hunger for respectability among upwardly mobile young Catholics and their terror of slipping down; shop assistants could at least fantasise themselves as gentlemen, whereas workmen, however prosperous, could not. The new Catholic middle classes, bereft of traditional caste, and usually of capital as well, valued social status almost as much as money.[32] Many of the patriotic leaders noted this syndrome and commonly condemned it, even when they suffered from it themselves. The *Leader*, from its own standpoint of muscular rejection of the prevailing status system in favour of a new system based on neo-Gaelic and Catholic values, complained about it often. Typically, it alleged that Catholic young men had acquired this contempt for manual labour from their old masters, the Anglo-Irish landlords; actually they probably got it from the educational system and from their own personal experiences in attempting to distance themselves from the grinding toil of the farmer or the labourer.

> The prejudice is set deep in such middle class as we have. A man working with his hands for two pounds a week is John Smith; if he received fifteen shillings a week as a warehouse clerk he would be promoted to the social rank of Mr. John Smith; and if he earned twenty five shillings a week doing 'brain' work as a bank clerk, he would blossom out into John Xavier Aloysius Smith, Esquire.[33]

The hunger for respectability was to take some strange forms. The patriotic press was obsessed with 'snobbery', commonly associated with the Anglo-Irish and their Catholic hangers-on, as they were regarded. It was difficult for a Catholic to be fully respectable, but it was very possible for a Catholic to be *spiritual*; Patrick Pearse and Terence MacSwiney, with their exaggerated postures of self-sacrifice, were being respectable in a way possible only for Catholics. Puritanism, an exaggerated perception of English civilisation as being secular, depraved and, above all, vulgar, and a romanticised vision of Ireland as being as yet sufficiently unspoiled morally to be worth rescuing was eventually to be translated into self-righteous militarism in 1916.

THE REVOLUTIONARY ÉLITE, 1900–1923

In the 1890s the old Irish Republican Brotherhood was ageing, had divided internally and had less access to American dollars than of old. The movement was effectively moribund. The fall of Parnell and the resolution of the agrarian struggle took the heart out of the movement; it had taken agrarianism belatedly to its heart and then found itself with no other ideas. The new socialism of the trade unions did not attract the old Fenians, possibly because of their own non-proletarian social background, but also because Catholicism acted as a cultural vaccine against such ideas; despite its differences with the clergy, the IRB remained by and large Catholic. The Boer War and the general European crisis which followed galvanised the IRB and its ancillary nationalist, social and cultural organisations rather artificially, much as similar causes were galvanised elsewhere. Young men were channelled into the movement through the Gaelic Athletic Association and the Gaelic League. A Home Rule Bill was introduced in 1912, and it appeared evident that it would be passed over the heads of the House of Lords before 1915. With Tory, Army and German support, Ulster prepared to resist it in arms. Protestant paramilitarism begot Catholic imitation, and in 1913 the Irish Volunteers arose to face the Ulster Volunteers. The coming of the First World War left the IRB in control of a hard core of perhaps 5,000 essentially separatist and anti-war Volunteers; these were to become the IRA.

The conspiracy had its own private army, but inside its own cabals lurked yet another conspiracy, one which wanted a symbolic insurrection. In 1916, much to the horror of many IRB members, this insurrection was staged, in traditional eighteenth-century style, in Dublin. The leaders were executed and the British lost whatever political legitimacy they had ever had in Catholic Ireland. The hostility was made active in 1918 by the decision to conscript Irishmen, and Sinn Féin, now under the control of insurrectionists, won virtually all seats outside eastern Ulster in the British general election of December 1918. British Ireland had finally come apart.

Sinn Féin refused to take its seats at Westminster, but instead constituted itself a separate parliament for Ireland, Dáil Éireann, which met in Dublin in January 1919 and declared a Republic.

Guerrilla war followed, and in 1921–2 the British conceded effective independence to twenty-six of Ireland's thirty-two counties under the title of the Irish Free State. This split the movement irrevocably, as earlier explained, and the movement came to an abrupt and painful end in civil war. During the following thirty years the bulk of the die-hards reconciled themselves to constitutionalism.

In the remainder of this chapter, I will present a social analysis of the IRB/Sinn Féin/IRA élite at the height of its development between 1913 and 1922.[34] The élite is defined as all Sinn Féin or Republican Labour MPs (entitled *Teachtaí Dála*, abbreviated TD, in Irish) elected in 1918 and 1921, in republican reckoning the members of the first and second Dáils; all IRA leaders of the guerrilla war deemed significant enough to be included in the standard *Who's Who* of the War of Independence; all officers of Cumann na mBan, the women's auxiliary to the IRA, similarly included; all members of the Supreme Council of the IRB, 1920;and all sixteen leaders executed after the 1916 Rising. These categories overlap considerably, as many of the leaders held several positions, frequently simultaneously; for example, many IRA commanders were elected unopposed and, in effect, ex officio, to the second Dáil. The élite as defined came to 304 individuals, and included all the well-known Sinn Féin, IRB and IRA leaders while also including many less well-known local figures and central administrators within the separatist hierarchy.

Like revolutionary leaderships elsewhere, the Sinn Féin élite, as I shall term the general leadership of the movement somewhat inaccurately but in accordance with colloquial tradition, was young.[35] The dates of birth of most of its members were ascertained, and it is fairly clear that unreported dates of birth were disproportionately of the younger and less well-known members. Most were born in the 1880s and 1890s, with some bias in favour of the latter decade. They were nearly all male and nearly all Catholic. This élite, which claimed the right to govern all Ireland, was far more Catholic than the island itself. The élite was clearly non-northern; the six counties which came to form Northern Ireland were dramatically under-represented, and this would be so even if account were to be taken only of the Catholic population of those counties. The noisily anti-partitionist Sinn Féin élite was itself partitionist in make-up, and the pronouncedly southern origins of the élite were the cause of the incurious attitude towards the north displayed by most TDs during the Treaty debates of 1921–2. Taking account only of the twenty-six counties that were to become the Free State, the élite favoured the south and rural areas generally in its origins. The Dublin area was the birthplace, or place of early rearing, of only one-sixth of the leaders; the rest of Leinster was the province of origin of about one-third, a slight over-representation in relation to population, and Munster, with 113 out of 304 leaders, was over-represented. Connacht had few leaders, and few were born outside Ireland. Cork was the most over-represented county, west Cork being the most conspicuous area of origin. Cork, Tipperary, Limerick, Kerry and Waterford were represented in that descending order of importance. Rural Limerick was far more conspicuous than was the city. This pattern of rural and southern over-representation combined with under-representation of the cities and the north echoes that of the IRA campaign and of earlier Irish movements.

Leaders tended to come from the two extremes of the urban–rural spectrum. Whereas 30 per cent did come from big towns such as Dublin, Cork, Limerick, Belfast or Waterford, only 24 per cent came from the small towns that dominated the countryside commercially and, at times, militarily as many of them were garrison towns and Royal Irish Constabulary (RIC) centres. In fact, Sinn Féin's top urban leaders, many of them only first-generation urbanites and with strong kinship connections with the countryside, appear to have joined hands with rural activists against the towns: a massive 42 per cent of the activists came from completely rural places. Ernie O'Malley noticed this: 'in the country the small farmers and labourers were our main support, and in cities the workers with a middle-class sprinkling; towns we could not rely on.'[36] Towns were often dominated by the garrisons, giving employment to young men, and by shopkeepers; the separatists had always hated the garrisons, as being rivals for the hegemony over the young men which the separatists coveted. Even where local opinion was sympathetic to the rebels, police super-vision of society was probably more effective in the small towns than in either the cities or the countryside. Sinn Féin's charac-teristic social signature reflected the joining together of the worker and petty-bourgeois radicalism of the cities with the agrarian radicalism of the countryside, dying but not yet dead in the early twentieth century. Irish republicanism's studied avoidance of any elaborated ideology other than that of separatism and cultural renewal reflected in part the disparate sources of its support.

Irish political organisation had been historically most effectively developed in rural areas, being weaker in towns and cities. Sinn Féin leaders tended to have local power bases in country areas where they had many relatives and were regarded as part of the local community. If they left their native areas, it was not to go to neighbouring counties where they would be resented, but to Dublin or even London. Country-born men in Dublin had the advantage relative to native-born Dubliners of being 'county men', attached to a particular area by links of blood, school and neighbourhood which amounted to informal freemasonries. The exceptional conspicuousness of county Cork is an extreme example of this effect: one-sixth of the entire élite came from the city or county of Cork and was widely seen as a distinct entity within the movement.

Munster was in many ways the most self-sufficient, insulated, and self-assured part of nationalist Ireland. The political, as distinct from social or economic, defeat of Protestantism had occurred early there; Victorian Munster was not quite as blanketed by English culture as was the east or the north. It was the province of origin of the Christian Brothers and of the Gaelic Athletic Association. It had generated a formidable opposition inside the Gaelic League, as will be seen later, and in many ways it resembled the core areas of other European nationalisms, as was argued earlier. The area was one of dairy rather than beef-cattle farming, reliant less on British and more on local markets; land distribution was relatively egalitarian, thereby enhancing local solidarity and softening status distinctions with the owner-occupier farming community. Much of the wealth of the province remained in

Protestant hands; Protestant status and wealth was combined with political weakness and therefore maximised irritation and political self-confidence.

The idea of a stabilised, conservative, egalitarian Irish Republic dominated by the yeoman farmer made direct sense in Munster, as that province had virtually achieved the elements of such a polity in the late nineteenth century. Popular nationalist nostalgia was more commonly directed at the familial, rural, English-speaking and petty-bourgeois society of post-Famine Victorian Munster than at the wilder, more romantic, Irish-speaking subsistence peasantry and fisherfolk of the western fringes of the island. Later the novels of Charles Kickham and Canon Sheehan will be discussed, both of whom sentimentalised rural Munster society; Kickham, author of melodramatic and sentimental sub-Dickensian novels set in Tipperary in the generation after the Famine, was the Gorky of the Irish revolution, and not the cosmopolitan and esoteric W.B. Yeats, possibly to the latter's chagrin. Both Kickham and Yeats were, in their respective days, members of the IRB. Far from Ulster physically and psychologically, the southern counties of Ireland were as insensitive to Protestant fears as they were immune to Orange threats. In some ways, Sinn Féin became dominated by Munster elements; it was also in Munster that the split that finally wrecked the movement was most intense in 1922–3, and it was in western Munster that the die-hard republicans made their last stand in the civil war in 1923. Later, with the development of democratic electoral politics, Munster was to be rivalled by political forces based on the western peripheries, partly because Munster had become so thoroughly divided.

Occupationally, the leaders were middle class, as is usual among revolutionary leaders everywhere. Many were so young at the time that their reported occupation deflates their actual social status. Of 248 whose occupations at the time could be ascertained, eighty-eight were members of the professions, divided more or less equally between the higher professions (medicine, law, academia, accountancy) and the lower professions (teaching, journalism). The retail trade, so conspicuous in Irish politics both before and after independence, was fairly well represented, at least thirty-nine being involved in it. Civil servants and 'clerks' amounted to thirty-six. The proportion engaged in farming was probably no greater than one-fifth, in view of the fact that although eighty-six of 212 were born in rural places, most of these had non-farming occupations. It should be recalled that over 50 per cent of Irish Catholics earned their living in agriculture at that time. Reported occupation appears, incidentally, to belie the extent to which these young men were actually businessmen or at least had ambitions in that direction. The occupations of their parents certainly suggest this, as does the subsequent composition of Irish parliaments in the 1920s and 1930s. The occupations of the parents of 157 leaders were ascertained; extraordinarily, half of these 157 leaders had parents of agrarian background, most of them 'comfortable', if not large, farmers. A further quarter had parents in business of some kind, very often in connection with rural produce. Three-quarters of the 157 came of rural bourgeois background. It should be remembered, however, that unascertained occupations of parents are likely to have been humble.

In sum, the élite was non-agrarian and middle class, highly educated and socially mobile, but with very recent rural social origins. Nearly half had achieved some third-level education. Many IRA leaders, propagandists and technical instructors were students at or recent alumni of the teacher-training colleges or the new university colleges where Catholics were at last being given the chance to receive a third-level education of a kind acceptable to their religious susceptibilities. In their first academic generation, these colleges were heavily dominated by nationalist and clerical political forces.

Social and cultural marginality have often been offered as explanations of revolutionary extremism.[37] De Valera, Erskine Childers, Maud Gonne, James Connolly and other separatists were either born outside Ireland or were not ethnically Irish and would be examples of such marginality. However, such marginality was not very visible in the leadership; the vast bulk were Irish born, and only twenty-eight could be ascertained to be marginal in the sense of being non-Catholic or having at least one non-Irish parent. If these are regarded as culturally marginal to Catholic and nationalist Ireland, marginality has little relationship to extremism or fundamentalism on the Treaty issue. In fact, marginality was associated with seniority in the movement, a seniority deriving from the pre-war phase of the movement, when it was itself, as shall be argued later, somewhat marginal and eccentric by the standards of Irish society; the upheaval of 1916–18 brought many decidedly non-marginal people into the élite. The overall lack of relationship between marginality and extremism is obscured by the fact that of ten marginal deputies in the Dáil, eight opposed the Treaty, much to the xenophobic rage of Griffith and Collins.[38] Most members of the élite outside the Dáil with marginal characteristics appear to have supported the Treaty. Sinn Féin was, then, a fairly centrally situated group sociologically, other than being well above average in social status. This tallies well with recent research which indicates the ethnic typicality of nationalist and socialist revolutionaries. This is not to deny the proposition that a sense of foreignness might have encouraged overcompensation; the exaggerated postures of de Valera, Childers or Gonne virtually dictate such a conclusion.[39]

However, foreign experience was very important in the development of the leaders. Well over 40 per cent, possibly over 50 per cent, had lived outside Ireland for considerable periods, usually in Britain or the United States. The 'returned emigrant' syndrome, so noticeable in Fenianism, was conspicuous in the revolutionary élite. There appears to have been no particular relationship, however, between foreign experience and extremism as indicated by position on the Treaty issue. In some cases, residence outside Ireland certainly transmuted a traditional *ressentiment* into a full-blown ethnocentrism, and experience abroad as a member of an often despised, alien ethnic group aggravated existing sensitivities. Michael Collins reminisced bitterly during the Treaty debates of the contempt in which the English workers held the Irish, contrasting it with the sympathy British upper-class people had extended to him, probably unexpectedly, during the Truce.

I know very well that the people of England had very little regard for the people of Ireland, and that when you lived among them you had to be defending yourself constantly from insults. Every Irishman here who has lived amongst them knows that the plain people of England are more objectionable towards us than the upper classes. Every man that has lived amongst them knows that they are always making jokes about Paddy and the pig, and that sort of thing.[40]

Supersensitivity deriving from their unpleasant experiences of social subordination in Ireland combined with social marginality in England or elsewhere was often a significant feature of the leaders' emotional make-up.[41] The fact that returned emigrants were as likely to support as to oppose the Treaty should caution us not to make too much of this effect. Foreign experience could work the other way; P.S. O'Hegarty, like Collins a Corkman and a one-time employee of the Post Office in London, appears to have been secularised by his experiences, and repeatedly rebuked his stay-at-home school friend Terence MacSwiney for his sub-servience to political Catholicism. In true Fenian tradition, O'Hegarty advocated separation between Church and state, between ethics and politics, while admitting that he had not been fully aware of the virtues of this arrangement until he got out of Ireland and the mental atmosphere of Irish Catholicism.[42]

In many cases, the effect of foreign experience was to moderate rather than aggravate Anglophobia, sectarianism and *ressentiment*. A classic love–hate complex toward the metropolitan country and its cultural heritage was common among the returned emigrants turned revolutionaries; on the other hand, the stay-at-homes would have had less of a problem, their Anglophobia being derived directly from a traditional refusal to recognise the legitimacy of any authority external to their community.

Although it is difficult to prove, social marginality of a different type may have been important in conditioning political attitudes. There is strong comparative evidence for the importance of certain characteristic lower middle-class quandaries in the development of political radicalism. Many of the leaders had invested much psychic capital and personal energy in the Gaelic League's forlorn attempt to bring about a spiritual and cultural revolution through the campaign to revive the Irish language. As suggested later, many of them knew at least subconsciously by 1914 that this campaign was running into impassable social obstacles and may have felt impelled to resort to insurrectionary political activity in part as a compensatory device. Anecdotal evidence also suggests the significance of unsuccessful business careers in the case of some of the leaders or of their immediate families. Pearse, for instance, had chronic financial difficulties; Terence MacSwiney's father was a failed businessman and the family was very impoverished, while still being 'respectable', that is, non-proletarian; and Diarmuid Lynch abandoned an American business career to return to Ireland and get involved in the IRB. Many others experienced discrimination and felt slighted by the establishment in Ireland or Britain. The social marginality of Irish Catholics in the English-speaking world as a whole created feelings of being unfairly snubbed and patronised.

The separatists were far more bourgeois, in the strict sense, than their Redmondite predecessors. They were often not related to the Irish Party leadership and were far less likely to be members of the higher professions. Comparison is difficult, as the revolutionary leaders came into politics at a period when their own careers had not yet become clearly defined. A comparison of the Irish Party MPs with the Dáil deputies of 1918 does not reveal an enormous gap in status, but a comparison of the nationalist MPs of 1910 with the separatist élite in middle age is quite revealing; by 1948 Dáil deputies were only half as likely to be members of the higher professions as the 1910 group had been, and were far more likely to be businessmen, farmers or trade union officials.[43] Patrick Hogan, a prominent pro-Treatyite TD, described the second Dáil in March 1922 as containing 'about one hundred businessmen'.[44]

04 | PRIESTS AND PATRIOTS

INTRODUCTION

The young men and women of 1900 who were to become the leaders of the revolution were children of their time. Like their contemporaries elsewhere in Europe, they sensed that the twentieth century was going to bring great changes; they anticipated with dread or longing the great wars that so many writers predicted; they frequently tended to rebel against their elders, often in the name of ideals inculcated by those elders; and they tended toward a romantic and messianic nationalism.[1] The cultural atmosphere of the period was suffused with an often anti-modern romanticism, a sense that a civilisation was perhaps dying and a scepticism about the possibility or even desirability of mass democracy. In this chapter, some of the leading themes in the thought of clerical and clericalised ideologues in Edwardian Ireland are looked at.

The emergent leadership often organised its thought moralistically rather than scientifically, and its social thought derived from ethics or even theology rather than from economics or politics. The culture from which it came was dominated by a Christian or specifically Catholic world view, and its real intellectual mentors were the priests of the Catholic Church. The great majority of the leaders had been educated either directly by the clergy or by lay teachers under clerical control. Many had seriously considered the religious life and, after the end of the fighting, a considerable number did exchange politics and guerrilla warfare for the priesthood or the convent. Despite the existence of liberal and socialist themes in their thought, by far the greatest influence was the Catholicism of the period. During this period international Catholicism was endeavouring to come to terms with the emerging secular world, with the 'isms' of the twentieth century and, in particular, with the claims of the secular state, whether couched in conservative, nationalist or socialist terms. These claims challenged the Church's traditional role in the education of the young, the regulation of sexual relations, social welfare and popular culture. Inevitably, the Irish leaders were to be infused with many ideas echoing these concerns. All revolutions need ideologues, and the Irish one was no exception. Irish nationalist politics was to take a permanent impress from the ideas and passions of these young people; much of their mentality was to become institutionalised in the cultural revolution of sorts that accompanied the political upheaval. Their ideas were to become fossilised in the political culture, parties, public shibboleths and policies of independent Ireland.[2]

PRIESTS AND THE FEAR OF THE MODERN
Outside the industrial enclave of eastern Ulster and Anglo-Irish, middle-class Dublin, by 1900 the island was dominated by a rural and village society that was piously Catholic. The Anglo-Irish aristocracy had been broken by Parnellism, although the completeness of that ruin was not always fully understood. Other defeats were also occurring. The Irish-language culture of pre-Famine Ireland was disintegrating even in its last western redoubts. The rural landless proletariat, much shrunken by the Famine, was menaced by the coming of farm mechanisation. Emigration had become a way of life for many. Many agricultural workers earned their living by periodic migration to England or Scotland while maintaining a home in Ireland. Rural society as stabilised after the Famine appeared to owe much of its stability to emigration. To some, that stability appeared akin to death, and emigration to the draining away of the nation's lifeblood. The young men and women of the countryside and of the villages were enormously

attracted to the great American cities, particularly in view of the fact that Irish society produced far more people than it was capable of employing.

The tenant farmers, now becoming owner-occupiers of farms ranging in size from a few acres to several hundreds, were the new dominant stratum in Irish society. They were, of course, over-whelmingly Catholic in faith and mentality; their priests, though they had no monopoly of political or even intellectual leadership, had enormous influence. This clerical leadership was being gradually supplemented and, perhaps, challenged by the growth of a lay Catholic educated stratum.[3] The priests who educated these young men were disproportionately of agrarian origin, tending to come from the middle reaches of agrarian and small-town society.[4] They tended to echo not only doctrinal and ideological trends of international Catholicism but also the values and interests of the farm society, obsessed with the stability of family property and inheritance. In turn, they tended to give form to those values. In a stimulating essay, Maurice Goldring has suggested what the structure of that value system was by an analysis of Father Peter O'Leary's *Mo Scéal Féin (My Story)*, a highly influential Irish-language text used extensively by the Gaelic League and by the school system.[5] O'Leary, of west Cork farm stock himself, offered a simple-minded, evil-city-versus-virtuous-village polarity, tied up, of course, with an iden-tification of England and English modes with the former and Ireland and Irish-language traditions with the latter.

This ideological polarity certainly dominated the minds of many priests. An Irish Catholic version of London as the Great Wen dominates the writing of Canon P.A. Sheehan, for example. Sheehan was a fluent and enormously popular novelist and essayist, combining Catholic and nationalist themes in ways that were very satisfying to his mass Irish and Irish-American readership. A guru of sorts, he lectured extensively on ethical, social and cultural themes to Gaelic League and clerical audiences; in particular, he concentrated on young audiences of seminarians and schoolchildren. He was born in Mallow, County Cork at mid-century, not far from O'Leary's birthplace and near the home place of Charles Kickham. Sheehan was educated locally and at

Maynooth; he was influenced intellectually by the famous nationalist archbishop of Tuam, John McHale. He ended his career as parish priest of Doneraile, County Cork. He died in 1913.[6]

Like many other priests and patriots, Sheehan was appalled at the character of both the popular and the intellectual literature that was pouring out of England into Ireland in late Victorian times. Unlike extreme cultural nationalists, he did not propose the banishing of all literature in English from Ireland, as did, for example, O'Leary. His real complaint was aimed at modern trends in that literature. In 1896 he denounced the 'pagan realism' of the 'squalid and nauseous literature of the past few years'. He proposed that 'Christian idealism' be tried in literature instead, and that this cultural experiment be tried in Ireland as a means of counteracting English post-Christian thought.[7] He was not too optimistic, however, as he felt that Ireland had suffered a great moral and cultural degradation due to English cultural influence and the coming of popular and democratic modes of thought, styles, songs, and reading.

> The literary instinct has died out in Ireland since '48. Our colleges and universities, with one or two exceptions, are dumb. The art of conversation is as dead as the art of embalming. And a certain unspeakable vulgarism has taken the place of all the grace and courtesy, all the dignity and elegance of the last century.[8]

Sheehan, much influenced by German Catholic writing, linked this decay in culture and manners with the general European tendency to desert Christianity, a trend which he saw as stemming from the French Revolution and, ultimately, from the Reformation. Materialism was the motive power behind this process of 'retreat towards Paganism'. However, he was willing to see even in the reformed versions of Christianity a potential core of resistance to the encroachments of the modern world.

> The intense devotion, the sweetness, the delicacy, the elevation of thought, that belong to Catholicity are beginning to pall on a world that is every day becoming more egotistic, more selfish,

more sensual. But to all pure and lofty minds ... in every one of the dissolving creeds that spring from the fatal Reformation, the divine and holy spirit which breathes through the testaments of Christianity, will still appeal ...[9]

Toward the end of his life, possibly under the influence of the young insurrectionists of the Gaelic League, Sheehan began to see a connection between the ideology of anti-materialism and a cult of violence, a connection which other 'men in the middle' were making all over Europe. In his last novel, *The Graves at Kilmorna*, set in Tipperary and Cork in the generation after the Fenian rising of 1867, Halpin, a Fenian village schoolmaster, sees that the growing materialism of modern Ireland can only be countered by self-sacrifice and violence. The country is becoming indifferent to everything but 'bread and cheese'. Ireland needs 'blood-letting a little'. The Fenian rebels are not soldiers but rather 'preachers, prophets and martyrs'. Their message is to be not principally in words but rather in the form of heroic acts.[10] The hero, Myles Cogan, dreams of an Ireland preserved from the materialism of other nations. An honest man, he cannot be a successful business-man in this degenerate modern world; his rivals outstrip him by means which the author gives us to understand are dishonest. Cogan sees that democracy is bringing cultural and moral decay; democracy in turn will inevitably lead to socialism, uniformity and cosmopolitanism. He is comforted by a visionary monk who prophecies that Ireland will become industrialised and prosperous in the future, and will inevitably undergo moral degeneracy in the process. Eventually, however, the country will become disgusted with itself and will revert to the ancient Irish anti-materialist and monastic ideal.[11]

Sheehan saw the priests as the main line of defence against neo-paganism. However, he also counted heavily on the women; he tells with evident approval and hope an anecdote of a lady and her two daughters who visit the National Gallery in Dublin, evidently for the first time, 'with that eager look which people assume when they expect something delightful'. When they see the classical nude statuary, however, they seem 'transfixed into marble themselves, so tense [are] their surprise and horror'. The three rush out of the gallery 'into the open air'.[12]

In December 1903 Sheehan gave a public lecture to an audience of Maynooth seminarians. The world, he argued, had experienced an intellectual death in the nineteenth century; there were no more true intellectual ideas, merely clever applications of the great ideas of fifty years previously. Poetry was dying. The great intellectual ideas of the century had been Rousseau's humanism and scientific empiricism. Both were now bankrupt.[13] With hindsight wisdom, there is something deeply ironic in this vision of intellectual death being experienced at a time when Einstein was commencing his intellectual career; Sheehan, with his provincial and moralistic obsessions, was utterly unaware of the potential of the new century.

Turning to Ireland, he saw a menace inside the gates. This was the growth of a new breed of educated or semi-educated laymen who, in Ireland as elsewhere, were seeking a place for themselves in the scheme of things and were suffering from certain characteristic frustrations. Many of these would become the 'educated unemployed' of the future, he warned, and would chafe under the traditional clerical constraints which their fathers had willingly accepted. He suggested that their inevitable tendency to complain should be countered by further education and by the 'judicious employment' of the best of them. They would no longer listen to their priests and were showing signs of being attracted to fashionable anti-Catholic writers such as George Moore. Sheehan urged the student priests to ensure that they retained the intellectual leadership of Ireland which they still enjoyed. In view of the inevitable anti-clericalism of the newly educated laity, the priests would have to retain that intellectual lead for half a century.[14] The same fear of education, and of consequent cultural intellectual leadership, of Catholic laymen that was visible among clerical educators was clearly articulated by Sheehan. Eventually this was to result in the establishment of a clerical monopoly of the social and moral sciences in the new national university that was set up for Catholics in 1908. The poverty of so much lay Catholic social and political thought in Ireland during the subsequent half-century was a direct result of this ecclesiastical intellectual monopoly; professors in the social sciences and philosophy at the new University College in Dublin came to be appointed directly by the Catholic Archbishop of Dublin, and the diocese had a major input into the internal affairs of the college.

However, clerical and clericalist political forces were not concerned just with controlling lay intellectual life. At the level of popular culture, there was a concerted effort to build up a Catholic popular literature which would act as an antidote to the secularism of the age. In particular, the last decades of the century saw concerted efforts to produce popular magazines and newspapers of a specifically Irish Catholic character to compete with English and non-Catholic publications. The *Irish Messenger of the Sacred Heart*, the *Irish Catholic* and the *Irish Rosary* all commenced publication between 1885 and 1900. The *Irish Rosary*, under Dominican auspices, commenced in 1897. In its first number, the editor asked rhetorically: 'how many are kept out of the Church simply because they see her only through the distorted medium of the old, lying, Protestant traditions?'[15] A major series written in 1898 concerned itself with atrocities committed against Catholic priests by the British during the great uprising of a century earlier.[16] The clerical subculture had a long memory; this was no isolated example of retrospective clerical outrage. O'Leary, in an article published in 1901 on the monastery of St Feichin, informed his readers that the foundation would still be doing its good work were it not for the 'murderous robbers that came to us over here from England three hundred years ago'.[17]

Nationalist priests wrote for the lay press as well, in particular for D.P. Moran's influential clerical-nationalist *Leader* from 1900 on. In 1903 Sheehan complained in its columns about English writing from Darwin to *Tit-Bits*, while lamenting that the average sale of an important book about Ireland was about twenty copies.[18] The mixing of the sexes in schools as practised in England and America was denounced by a priest in its columns in 1905 as being a Protestant idea which led to immorality and immodesty.[19] O'Leary, in an almost deranged piece published in 1908, demanded of the paper's readers whether the English language was not actually poisonous to faith and patriotism:

... although Irish speakers of English may still retain some dim, faint rudimentary relics of the old Gaelic tradition of faith and patriotism, they also have that in the very fibres of their mental and moral nature, which is essentially destructive of those remains; and growth in the understanding of English speech, being a more complete assimilation of the English tradition concerning God and Ireland, means only a more complete obliteration of the historic Faith and Patrotism of Ireland.[20]

Before 1916 the support of the general body of the clergy for the Irish-Ireland and separatist movement was probably not great, although younger priests in particular, having been indoctrinated by the Gaelic League, looked on it with some sympathy. Sheehan, O'Leary and others had considerable influence on the minds of the future élites, both lay and ecclesiastical. Lay ideologues like D.P. Moran and Eoin MacNeill understood well that the support of the priests was required if it was intended to organise mass support for a neo-Gaelic nationalist project. The *Leader* consistently sought clerical support and condemned the anti-clericalism of some of the young firebrands. The Irish language came to be used as an ideological device to cement an alliance, essentially of convenience, between priests and patriots while excluding all those who, whether Catholic or Protestant, aspired to English or Anglo-Irish cultural standards. In the next chapter, the role of the Gaelic League in making this alliance possible will be analysed.

At this time the Irish Catholic clergy were probably at the height of their influence in the English-speaking world. Maynooth seminary, near Dublin, was at the centre of this international network.[21] Although the largest Catholic seminary in the English-speaking world, it was scarcely an intellectual centre, a proposition admitted by many priests. Both Sheehan and Walter MacDonald were scathing about the intellectual deficiencies of Maynooth alumni. MacDonald felt that the narrowness of the training which was given in Maynooth and the other Irish seminaries had combined with the incentive system of the Irish Church to encourage hard pastoral work and silence.[22] Because of the severe discipline and the emphasis on memory work, free spirits did not prosper.[23]

A *vox populi* expression of a common perception of the character of the training received by priests was supplied by the Edwardian Dubliner who, when passing a novitiate, remarked, 'that's where they *dhrill* them for the priesthood'.[24]

The Church's basic building block was the parish, and the bishops were the Church's joint rulers. The dioceses recruited young men locally, commonly from particular families that had traditions of producing young men for the priesthood, and sent them forward to the seminaries for training. On completion of their course of studies, the young priests generally returned to their dioceses of origin. Even at Maynooth, the essentially cellular structure of the Church was maintained; intermingling of the students from the various dioceses was discouraged. Each student was assigned to a group consisting of the students from his own diocese for purposes of companionship: 'each diocesan batch was a family circle'. The effect of this was to preserve the localism of the system while building up a sense of camaraderie and solidarity among the group of young men who would in the future work together in running the diocese back home. Significantly, the introduction of a special non-geographical 'batch' of Irish speakers at the end of the century had the effect of setting up an Ireland-wide solidarity based on language and, most likely, on political ideology as well, a solidarity that was not limited to particular dioceses. The Irish-language movement in the Church cut across its localist and cellular structure and became, by a curious twist, a means of escape from the localist pressures of the diocese; the system was to find *Gaeilgeoir* priests difficult to handle.[25] Intellectually unadventurous, highly disciplined, reverential of authority to an almost Stalinist or military degree and personally extremely disciplined, with his attention fixed on local rather than on national or general concerns, the type of priest the system produced was admirably geared to the needs of the similarly localist society which most of Ireland was. The price paid for this was a constitutional inability to separate intellectual opposition and evil intent, an inability to see non-Catholic or non-clerical viewpoints and, perhaps, a deep-set difficulty in thinking about the future of the apparatus as a whole because of excessive preoccupation with the practical details of day-to-day administration at local level. The Church resembled a civil service operating according to prescribed and detailed sets of rules rather than a government geared to initiating policy changes; its characteristic reaction to outside challenge was defensiveness and an attempt to consolidate its position further. A 'what-we-have-we-hold' response was built into its whole structure; its traditional self-image of being under siege in a Protestant and secularising world blended with the fashionable *fin de siècle* fear of the modern world so evident in the writings of the nationalist priests.

ÉLITES IN A SIEGE CULTURE

Catholic Ireland's sense of being under siege was not new. The absence of overt persecution in recent decades had not totally reassured the priests. Memories of past persecutions were kept alive in the capacious collective memory of the clergy. Keenan has argued that an element of millenarianism existed in the Church's self-image; it habitually saw itself as a righteous and persecuted group. The fusion of Catholic and ethnic identity which had occurred in the seventeenth century was reinforced in the late nineteenth by means of an elaborate exercise in the revival of older conceptions and a mingling of those ideas with newer romantic visions of the People of God led by their good shepherds and with the corporatist and anti-capitalist as well as anti-socialist notions of late Victorian Catholic political thought.

The image of the Church as leader of the people of Ireland through the valley of evil that the English- and Protestant-dominated modern secular world appeared to be attracted many. It clearly came to obsess the minds of at least some of the young, usually Catholic, men and women who were attracted to the Gaelic League and other popular organisations. These organisations, tolerated by an imperial British complacency, were to become vehicles for radical nationalism in the last years of the nineteenth century and the first years of the twentieth.

England, big capitalism and socialism came to be seen as sources of spiritual contamination by respectively the nationalist, the socialist and the bourgeois ideological tendencies in the separatist movement. A vivid vision of the Church as the cultural defender of the Irish Catholic nation as the People of God was clearly dominant in many clerical minds. The entire complex of ideas tended to be simplified for popular consumption as the image of Ireland as a female figure, persecuted and bullied by an emphatically male John Bull. The image of the bullying husband and father appears to have had a particular resonance for young Irishmen of the period; the role of the priest as defender of the women against the men was already well developed, and it took little creativity to extend this to the political arena. Another reason for this ideological fusion of Catholicism and Irish identity was the interdependence of priests and patriots; politically each needed the other as a prop.[26]

Passion influences political behaviour at least as much as does rational calculation of one's interests. Certainly, emotion rather than rationality appears to have dominated the behaviour of many political actors at that time. Why this was so is not clear, but it does appear to be linked with the rising tide of political emotionalism all over Europe. After all, this was the time when Gustave le Bon in France and Graham Wallas in England were writing their pioneering studies of the non-rational nature of collective political behaviour. The suffocating and repressive nature of Irish society may also have made political action become an emotional outlet in a society where opportunities for emotional self-expression were rather few. Perhaps the kind and extent of education available to Irish Catholics had something to do with it also. Memorising rather than rational argument was encouraged, so that debate in Ireland resembled rhetorical warfare rather than a reasoned exchange of views; a strong element of rant is noticeable in the political literature of the period. Frank O'Connor commented subsequently on the style of thought of the young men who became the leaders of the people. Michael Collins, whom O'Connor admired, had, like nearly all his colleagues, 'no power of abstract thought', and what most of the others had was 'emotion disguising itself as abstract thought'. This was a general cultural characteristic of the generation: 'When an Irishman talks of "principle" he is a menace to everybody, because he has been brought up in an atmosphere in which the free play of thought is not encouraged.'[27]

Cultural fear was a key 'emotion in disguise' and the disguises it took were many, some of them bizarre. Catholic self-assertiveness and the obsession with the Irish language were two such expressions. However, there were other rather revealing manifestations of the fear of cultural change coming from outside and destabilising the rather fragile entity of Catholic Ireland, built up so painfully in the decades since the Famine. One such manifestation was a general obsession, shared by clerical and lay leaders alike, with the moral fibre of the population, which was supposedly under threat. This was expressed most typically in the form of denunciations of the real and fancied ill-effects of alcohol. Prohibitionism tends to prosper when a rural society is challenged by industrialisation and Ireland was no exception, even though the industrialisation to which the Irish were reacting was situated mainly outside Ireland. There was a strong prohibitionist undercurrent in the Gaelic League and Sinn Féin; Catholic bishops ceaselessly deplored the evils of drink during the last decade of the nineteenth century.[28] Irish Catholicism is the only branch of the international Catholic Church to have a strong, almost evangelical, tradition of total abstinence, originally imported from America.

The lay leaders echoed this concern; the *Leader* ran rather witty attacks on 'Mr. Bung' and his 'drunkeries'. The licensed trade and its grip on the Irish Party were satirised. The dislike of drink was sometimes expressed in terms of nationalist ideology; there was a common interpretation of the failure of earlier Irish insurrections which laid the blame on drink. Teetotalism was commonly allied with a general puritanism, partly derived from a resentment of the relaxed manners of the Edwardian establishment. C.S. Andrews has given us a fine description of his own group of young nationalists in the post-Treaty years, products of this turn-of-the-century cultural revolution and its Irish version of moral rearmament:

We held strongly to the social ethos of Republicanism in that ... we were puritanical in outlook and behaviour. We didn't drink.

We respected women and ... knew nothing about them. We disap-
proved of the wearing of formal clothes ... of horse racing ... of
any form of gambling ... of golf and tennis ... of anyone who took
an interest in food ... of women 'making up' or wearing jewellery.[29]

Liam O'Flaherty took a more jaundiced, but fundamentally
similar, view of these Gaelic Cromwellians. In *The Assassin*, he
contrasts the easy-going and corrupt ethos of the pre-1914 older
generation with the new puritanism of the post-war generation. A
politician of pre-war vintage is sketched as a good-natured, corrupt vicar of Bray who has survived the upheaval and has wormed
his way into favour again in the new Free State: In spite of that, he
was very popular. 'He had all the genial qualities of the older
generation, that is now being swallowed up by the dour puritanism
of the young generation, arisen since the revolution.'[30]

Drink was only one of many targets; as we have seen, literature
of all intellectual levels was another. One contributor to the *Leader*
let that particular cat out of the bag rather completely in 1905,
when his plea for the creation of an authentic Irish literature was
revealed to be motivated mainly by a hatred for English literature:

The Irishman who studies the history of his country, and who
sees the national character being gradually sapped, undermined
and washed out by English influence, will hear with pleasure of
this exclusive devotion to so needed a work [as the creation of
an Irish national literature]. He will hear with a certain savage
satisfaction that even a small body of his countrymen have
pronounced a comprehensive curse on all English literature. It
may be going too far, but your true Irishman will have a
sympathetic understanding of such an attitude.[31]

The Dublin stage and popular music hall, mainly showing
imported plays and shows from London, horrified both priests
and patriots. In the case of the clergy, this horror appears to have
been magnified by the fact that they were forbidden to see the
offending shows and had to rely on their own imaginations or
second-hand information; empiricism was not their forte. The

Leader was shocked in 1904 by the fact that the Viceroy's wife could attend a 'dirty play' and see it merely as a 'charming musical comedy'.[32] A 1906 play at Dublin's Gaiety Theatre was described as 'putrid filth'.[33] The famous *Playboy* riots of 1907, when the patriots protested against Irish peasantry being portrayed as possessing less than totally pure minds and habits, were merely a highlight in a long campaign.

The fears and frustrations of Irish Catholics also expressed themselves sometimes in fear and dislike of Freemasons and Jews, often imagined to be in alliance in an international conspiracy. The Dreyfus case had immediate echoes in Ireland, and the clergy were commonly noisily anti-Dreyfusard. Significantly, the lay, more bourgeois and more republican sections of the movement, as distinct from the clerical and clericalist sections, were not anti-Dreyfusard and avoided priestly anti-Semitism; in particular, Griffith's Sinn Féin and the IRB seem to have avoided this particular ideological cul-de-sac most of the time. In 1896 the *Irish Catholic* accused French Freemasons of engaging in devil worship.[34] Karl Lueger, the notorious anti-Semitic mayor of Vienna who came to be one of Hitler's early inspirations, was fulsomely praised in its leader columns in the same year.[35] It soon turned its attention to the tiny Irish Jewish community. The number of Jews in Ireland had always been small, but there had been a noticeable immigration of Jews in the last years of the century. The fear of the outside soon expressed itself in the classic form of anti-Semitism. Clerical and lay anti-Semitism expressed itself in different ways. A Dundalk Dominican, in a sermon prominently reported in the *Irish Catholic* in 1902, denounced Jews as having a 'deep-seated hatred, daughter of unbelief, for the person of Christ'. In modern times, 'Jews, heathens and heretics' had organised their hatred of the Church by means of Freemasonry.[36] Echoes of the conflict between Church and state in France were evident. Irish lay nationalists seem to have been level headed enough to discount the more extravagant forms of conspiracy theory; most opinion-formers seem to have understood that Freemasonry was essentially a means by which Protestants discriminated in favour of 'their own' and against Catholics. After all, Protestants were at least as anti-

Semitic as Catholics, and possibly more so. Interestingly, the *Leader* expressed a fear rather than a hatred of the Jews, a fear which was derived from a clear and well-organised perception of the incompetence and vulnerability of Irish Catholics. In 1904 Ireland's only pogrom ever occurred in Limerick at the instigation of a Redemptorist preacher, who apparently denounced their trading practices among the poor of the city. Many Jews were driven out; the bishop of Limerick showed scant concern for the victims of the rioters. The *Leader*, predictably, defended the Redemptorist and the rioters. However, it defended them in a rather revealing way: Jews were dangerous not because of some sinister conspiracy with which they were associated, but rather because they were hard working and sober, unlike so many Irish Catholics. It was inevitable, the paper argued, that the demoralised, slum-dwelling Catholics of the Irish cities should become easy prey for the Jews because of their own 'liquoring, improvident, thriftless habits', but the real danger was that the farmers, the backbone of the nation, might also come under the financial control of the Jews. Irish Catholics, the paper suggested, should imitate the Jews rather than attack them or complain about them, thus giving them a backhanded compliment. Again, the source of the anti-Semitism was the fear of the modern, the fear of change and the belief that the Catholic Irish were not well equipped to survive and compete in the modern world.[37]

The patriots were far more interested in the Freemasons than they were in the Jews, the ravings of Dominicans notwithstanding. As early as 1901, the *Irish Rosary* suggested that a committee 'of prominent Catholic businessmen be set up to organise Catholic business interests and counteract the general discrimination there was against Catholics in the commercial world.' A correspondent agreed, observing that Protestants were organised, so why weren't Catholics?[38] The *Irish Catholic* complained, for instance, that nearly all senior posts in the Irish administration were held by Protestants.[39] However, the *Leader*, as usual, was the most determined campaigner in favour of the interests of the burgeoning Catholic middle class. Over the years, it documented, in rather impressive detail, the hiring practices of various Irish institutions.

In 1905 it reported cases of alleged discrimination against Catholic RIC men.[40] In the same year it aggressively claimed that Catholic children were winning more examination qualifications than Protestant children, but had no chance of 'getting a start' in many banks, railways or other private concerns.[41] The public sector was a favourite target; the Post Office in particular was accused of not hiring and not promoting Catholics in appropriate numbers.[42]

Another general worry was 'race-death'. There was an essentially historicist notion around that the Catholic population of Ireland was going to continue to decline as it had done since the Famine. In fact, the rate of relative decline had slowed and was about to reverse itself. The *Leader* solemnly offered the cure of the Irish language for the disease of emigration, arguing that emigration was essentially a psychological rather than an economic phenomenon. Emigration was psychologically easier if one had a command of at least elementary English, and contact with the English-speaking world outside encouraged a cultural syndrome which a later generation was to label the 'revolution of rising expectations'. The paper's first issue, in 1900, argued this proposition energetically.[43] Essentially, emigrants were demanding that Ireland give them a standard of living not wildly different from standards widely available in Britain and America. However, Irish Catholic business, with its puny resources, could make no such offer; eventually, what it did was to argue noisily for the moral superiority of lower standards of living if combined with egalitarianism and good moral standards. In its issue of 5 September 1903 the *Leader* warned that nearly half a million had emigrated in the ten years ending in 1902 and calculated in historicist fashion that if this trend were to continue the island would be uninhabited by 2002.

Emigration was seen as being due to psychological, or at base moral, causes. Emigrants were occasionally accused of desertion, although other correspondents demurred from this harsh assessment of the wish of the young people for a better life than they could get at home. The *Leader*, however, generally averred that emigration was due to 'lack of self-reliance' and also to the 'snobbery, stagnation and ignorance' of the Irish Catholic (upper) middle classes, caused by snobbish college and convent secondary education.[44] At the time of the Limerick pogrom, a correspondent, in terms worthy of the *Völkischer Beobachter*, painted a picture of Ireland being drained of its Irish Catholic population to make room for Jews: 'Ireland is, at present, being drained of its Gaelic population by emigration, and Jewish colonists are trooping in to fill up the places of the emigrants, and to turn Ireland into a filthy Ghetto.'[45]

Priests were particularly worried about 'race-death', and discussions cropped up occasionally in the *Irish Ecclesiastical Record*, particularly at census time. A climax of kinds was reached in 1921.[46] Again, fear of imported ideas of family limitation lay behind uneasiness about the willingness of Irish Catholics, once offered alternatives, to reproduce at the traditionally high rate.

A minor theme was uneasiness at the possible politicisation of women.[47] In Edwardian times it was not yet a major issue, but it was beginning to be seen as yet another baneful influence coming from England. As late as 1913, John Dillon felt able to tell Redmond that, on the issue of women in politics, Ireland was fifty years behind England. In Ireland, women took no part in elections as they did in England and, though Catholicism did not forbid the enfranchisement of women, 'the whole attitude of mind' inculcated by Catholicism in women was one of 'reserve, retirement, modesty' and therefore militated against their politicisation.[48] Issues such as women's suffrage did have some impact on Irishwomen even before 1900, but mainly on those who were middle class and Protestant. Educated women were few and were complacent; in 1908 the *Leader* complained that the women who dominated in high society had no intellectual interest in politics. The paper was careful to distinguish between such an interest, which it felt would be appropriate to patriotic Irish ladies, and the kind of activist politicisation to be associated with 'the hoydenish pursuits of the new woman or the English suffragette'. The ladies could solve their difficulties by also learning about Irish history, culture and language; for them, language school was also recommended.[49] However, in 1911 an unmarried female correspondent declared that women did not need the vote, as they had the very important power of 'rearing chivalrous sons for Ireland'.[50] In 1912–13 suffragettes were represented in *Leader* cartoons as ageing English spinsters whose real interest was in getting husbands.[51]

The fact that printed matter was now available to a wide reading public was a source of upset to many, and the sensationalism of the new popular English press was held to be a major source of the labour unrest that was growing in both islands in the first decade of the century. A contributor to the *Catholic Bulletin* complained in 1913 about the false picture of the world given by the newspapers: 'It is largely an age of falsities. Almost everything about it seems to be more or less false. It has false hair, false teeth, sometimes false cheeks and false eyebrows. It is practically all cunningly artificial and designed to deceive.'[52] The press was commonly taken to be under the control of capitalists, Freemasons or Jews.

Fear of the modern external world was derived in part from a rather realistic perception of the frailty of the public ideology which priests and patriotic publicists had built up over a generation. It was felt that it might not survive a massive encounter with English or American modern civilisation intact. The vulnerability of the ethical system which the priests had built up and the equally delicate nature of the patriotic ideology which the nationalists had built up was intuitively grasped. Fear was aimed not only at outside popular culture but also at intellectual critiques of favoured clerical or nationalist intellectual positions. An overriding concern was the perceived lack of self-assurance of the Irish people, seen as lacking civic courage. In Kickham's *Knocknagow*, that enormously popular novel that became a kind of nationalist scripture from the Parnell period on, an old 'Croppy', or veteran of the 1798 rebellion, supports security of tenure for the farmers because it will give them a courage which they have previously lacked.[53] It is clear that what is meant is a quality akin to civic virtue, and the later nationalists echoed this idea; the priests wanted pious and obedient faith, but the lay patriots wanted citizens and soldiers.

Priests and patriots differed in motivation. Priests saw the preservation of the people's moral integrity, which was under threat from outside, as the first priority, whereas the patriots, while echoing these concerns, had other preoccupations as well. Obvious objectives were *la carrière ouverte aux talents*, and the detachment of Ireland from England if possible and necessary. Culture, sport and traditional hatred were all valued, not for themselves but for their potential use toward political objectives. As will be argued later, the lay separatists, unlike the priests, were developmentalists. There is a curious myth, essentially derived from one or two of de Valera's speeches, that the separatists wanted an agrarian, non-industrialised society. It would be truer to say that the future Ireland of which they dreamed was industrialised, modern and at the same time culturally authentic in the sense of being a lineal descendant of Gaelic culture. Rural Ireland was to coexist with the cities of the new Ireland as a modernised rural Ireland which retained all its traditional values; Denmark was to come to Knocknagow. The new Ireland was also to be teetotal, Irish speaking and an international cultural beacon. Like many ideologues, the separatists wished to have their cake and eat it; their visions of the future were wild mixtures of modernising practicality, romantic anti-modernism and a vision of society in which the classical political virtues would be realised. In this, they resembled not only the romantic right-wing radicalisms of the period but also the many nationalisms of the twentieth century, of which they were the forerunners. Only the clerical ideologues were clearly anti-modernist and dreamed of a society that was rural, pious, static and retained all the values of the *Gemeinschaft*. It is likely that it was this clerical version of the ideology that de Valera echoed a generation later.

None of the themes we have looked at was unique to Ireland. In fact, the Irish were exhibiting a local variation on general European themes of the period. The local mix was odd, however, in that the Irish version of the general European recoil from the modern world took place in an intellectual context where English liberalism faced not only the demand for democracy but also elaborate non-democratic ideologies coming in from Europe through the cultural conduit of Catholicism. Many of the priests' and patriots' ideas are strongly reminiscent of the pre-fascist sets of ideological attitudes labelled 'cultural despair' by Stern.[54] Canon Sheehan's vision of London as the modern Babylon echoes German themes of the time, for example. Cultural despair in the Germany of the time involved a hatred of liberalism, of 'Manchesterism', of materialism, of the loss of true spirituality in the modern world, of democracy and of the lack of true political leadership in modern mass society.[55] In Germany, much of this mood's anti-Christianism essentially had the same sources as Sheehan's terror of secularism; Christianity in the German case and secularism in the Irish Catholic case were associated with spiritual decay, intellectual and artistic mediocrity and scientific specialisation at the expense of general ideas about the relationship between man and the universe. Christianity in Germany and secularism in Ireland came to be hated by certain people because they were associated with the spread of democracy and individualism.[56]

Pathological themes surfaced in times of crisis, and the general hysteria of the war appears to have had a direct effect on the Irish national radicals. In January 1914 the usually quite calm and analytical *Irish Review* carried an extraordinary piece by one Ita O'Shea, entitled 'The Messiah—A Vision'. The redeemer of Ireland was already born, and would soon lead the nation out of darkness into light. Although born in Ireland, he had spent most of his life outside the island. He was still under 30 and combined in his person the authentic glorious heritage of the Gaelic past and the capability of transforming Ireland into a modern society: 'He is intensely Irish in every fibre of his being, and not less intensely modern. He is the Incarnation of the Spirit of Ireland—the heir par excellence of her Past—destined to be the dominating figure of the spacious days of her not so remote future.'

He would be a military genius in the coming war, and would defeat both of the foreign powers (presumably Britain and Rome) that occupied Ireland.[57] Pearse, incidentally, while awaiting execution in 1916, wrote to his mother in terms that indicate clearly who he thought *he* was: 'People will say hard things of us now, but we shall be remembered by posterity and blessed by unborn generations. You too will be blessed because you were my mother.'[58]

Messianism and the sense of external menacing evil, which seem to be elements in the psychology of fascism, emerged clearly in the *Catholic Bulletin* after 1916. The *Bulletin* was quick to generate a cult of the martyrs, despite the fact that Pearse heartily disliked its editor, J.J. O'Kelly, and with good reason; O'Kelly had opposed Pearse politically in his Gaelic League days, sometimes venomously. Photographs and biographies of the executed leaders were published in a series of issues after the rising, hagiographical themes being conspicuous. In the same series of issues there appeared a detailed pseudo-scientific exposé of the alleged tradition of ritual murder of Christian children by Jews, based mainly on a Tsarist *cause celèbre* of some years earlier. These articles, by a Father Thomas A. Burbage, were followed the next year by an analysis of the relationship between Freemasonry and the Antichrist by the same author. Among other claims made was the assertion that both the French Revolution and the world war had been caused by this international conspiracy. During the middle of the First World War, nationalist messianism and clerical proto-fascism briefly joined hands in Ireland.[59] However, in Ireland the twin forces of English-style liberal democracy and a strong integralist Catholicism came to an uneasy but lasting understanding with each other; Daniel O'Connell came to terms with St Augustine, so to speak, at the expense of Cuchulain and Sorel. This alliance eventually contained and tempered the forces of Irish revolution. In Germany, of course, there was to be another outcome.

05 | THE POLITICS OF LANGUAGES AND LITERATURES

THE GAELIC LEAGUE

The Gaelic League was in many ways the central institution in the development of the Irish revolutionary élite. Most of the 1916 leaders and most of the leading figures in the Free State, whether pro-Treaty or anti-Treaty, had been members of the League in their youth and had imbibed versions of its ideology of cultural revitalisation. Although formally non-political and even anti-political, the League had profoundly political purposes and offers a prime example of how culture can be bent to purposes that are very non-cultural. It could be argued that in the long run the true loser was general Irish culture and intellectual life, whether expressed in the English or the Irish language. The politicisation of culture effected by the League in the early years of the century was to create an official cultural ideology which was arguably hostile to much of the real culture of the community; 'Gaelic Unrealism' might be a just term for it. This official ideology was to dominate much of Irish cultural life for a generation after independence.

The Irish or Gaelic language had been dying in Ireland for a considerable time. The medieval social order which had been associated with it had been finally defeated in the seventeenth century; it had not even survived that century as the first language of Irish Catholicism. Protestantism and Catholicism were at one on at least one issue; in the long run, English was to be the administrative and commercial language of Ireland. By the early nineteenth century Irish was already a minority language, spoken outside the towns and in areas far away from commercial penetration. It was associated with poverty, backwardness and failure to adapt to the modern commercialising world. The considerable cultural achievements of the Gaelic tradition were forgotten, and the fact that it had been one of the first vernacular literary languages in post-Roman Europe, for example, was unknown. The Anglicised culture of the post-Cromwellian regime dismissed it as barbarous, in part out of a subconscious defensiveness. Edward Gibbon wrote it off as a degenerate form of Scottish culture rather than acknowledging it as the parent of Scots Gaelic culture.

The Famine of the 1840s, of course, further weakened the language, and by the end of the century it was in full retreat even in its last western redoubts.[1] Unlike Scottish Gaelic, it did not even have the advantage of being the normal language of worship, as Catholicism's support of the English language, even in Irish-speaking, or Gaeltacht, areas, was consistent.

The League came out of a tradition of antiquarian research into Gaelic civilisation and was fundamentally similar to other nationalist movements in Europe dedicated to the rediscovery and perhaps revival of national pasts. Anglo-Irish liberal interest in Celtic remains and nationalist political purpose joined hands. Gaelic was apparently particularly popular among the Irish emigrants in London and New York, and many of the ideas of the League appear to have been derived from *émigré* political feeling.

The League was inaugurated in 1893 and was formally dedicated to the preservation and revival of the language and the celebration of, and if possible the resuscitation of, traditional dress, dances and customs, in so far as these could be reconciled with the canons of late Victorian respectability. Its mixture of scholarly research and unintellectual recreation appealed enormously to a wide variety of people, in particular, perhaps, the newly educated young of the villages and towns. Twenty years after its foundation, it had become a mass movement, with 100,000 members and 1,000 branches.[2] Much of this mass membership was young.

Originally, however, the League was a coterie rather than a mass movement, and its character changed significantly when it grew beyond its original membership. It had grown out of an impulse toward unionist–nationalist encounter in Trinity College, Dublin and in its first years it was dominated by a mainly Dublin-based group of middle-class scholars and dilettantes.[3] Douglas Hyde, the son of an Anglican clergyman from County Sligo, was its first president and served from 1893 to 1915. He consistently claimed that he had originally insisted on a non-political stance for pragmatic reasons, wishing to avoid the divisiveness of Irish politics, but had always expected that in the long run the League would evolve into a great political movement once its cultural purposes had been fulfilled. He also observed that even those members of the League who wished to use it for political purposes accepted the non-political pose for pragmatic reasons.[4]

According to Hyde, the reasons for the League's avoidance of politics were many. In the first place, it preserved the League from attack by the British government and from the attentions of the police; actually, the police took little interest in it and appear to have underrated its long-term political potential. Secondly, as most of the League's branches around the country were run by 'officers and secretaries who were largely either National Teachers or Customs and Excise officers', and as these men were forbidden by their terms of employment to engage in normal political activity, an openly political stance would have crippled the League at local level. These teachers and civil servants were 'full of national feeling of the best type but could find no outlet for it'. Essentially, the League gave an outlet for repressed political passion and 'let loose a lot of energy for the good of Ireland which would otherwise have been lost'.[5] Another reason was, of course, the attempt to keep unionists and nationalists, Protestants and Catholics and the various classes of society together in harmony in the League in so far as that was possible.

Ironically, in the light of subsequent events, the Irish language had quite an appeal to certain Protestants who saw in it a way of claiming an Irish identity without having to pay the heavy price of giving up their religion and conforming to the Catholic faith of most Irish people. After all, an Irish-speaking Protestant could logically claim to be more 'Irish' than a monoglot English-speaking Catholic;

he might also irritate him. The League had a strange political evolution between 1893 and 1915, eventually being turned not just to political purposes but to insurrection. It was colonised by people with different purposes from those of the founders. As already suggested, it was a perfect vehicle for those whose occupation forbade or discouraged political action of a conventional kind. Given the political vacuum that existed in the aftermath of the fall of Parnell, its appeal as a substitute for politics was all the greater; culture became a surrogate for politics.

In an examination of the biographies of thirty-two early Leaguers and 'Irish-Irelanders', Waters found that three were Protestants, seven were civil servants, two were teachers, four were journalists, three were priests, three were in business and four were 'gentlefolk writers'. Six were unclassifiable. Interestingly, at least seventeen had been emigrants and of these at least twelve had become involved in the League first while living outside Ireland. At least half were of 'peasant origin'. The biographies gave a general impression of 'energetic and moderately successful men whose careers provided inadequate scope for their talents and ambitions'.[6]

Elements in the League saw early on that it would need the support of certain powerful groups in Irish society if it were to prosper and become a mass movement. Eoin MacNeill, possibly the original inventor of the concept of the League, was a young law clerk in Dublin at the beginning of the 1890s. A Catholic from the glens of Antrim, he had the reputation, unlike many patriots, of being trusted by the Catholic clergy. As early as 1891, MacNeill urged in the pages of the *Irish Ecclesiastical Record* that the Catholic priesthood take up the cause of the language on the grounds that it would help preserve an Irish identity and would defend Irish Catholicism against the inroads of English culture.[7] It should be remembered that MacNeill was striking, rather cleverly, while the iron was hot; in 1891 the Church was at odds with advanced popular nationalism because of Parnell, and presumably would be receptive to any proposal by which the authenticity of its claims to be the leaders of the Catholic nation could be bolstered. Not for the last time, the language was to be used for purposes external to itself. MacNeill's appeal had some success. In 1898 a priest writing in the *Irish*

Ecclesiastical Record drew a specific parallel with the priest-led Flemish linguistic revival movement of the period, noting that the linguistic revival in Belgium had been supported by the priests because it offered a barrier against 'the inroad of corrupting French literature'. Irish, he argued, was well suited to performing a similar function in Ireland against English, as traditional pious Christian phrases were embedded in its everyday idioms.[8] Hyde himself used this kind of argument to sell the language to the clergy; like MacNeill, he realised very early on that they would have to be seduced if the Gaelic League's cultural project were to be truly successful politically. In 1902, for example, he urged an audience of Athlone schoolchildren to be like that marvellous people the Jews, who had their own language for family and community life and who relegated English to the menial role of language of commerce. He urged the children to study Irish language and literature and to read Irish-language weeklies rather than 'penny dreadfuls, shilling shockers, police intelligence, garbage and snippets . . .'[9]

The Catholic Church as an institution never accepted the language or the League wholeheartedly. The Church's historical commitment to English was well entrenched, and elements in the ideology of the Gaelic revival movement looked suspiciously pagan. However, many of the lower clergy did become neo-Gaelic ideologues, and the Christian Brothers accepted the language as a vehicle for building an ethos of self-respect and patriotism. Clericalist lay Catholics, as represented by the *Leader* or the *Catholic Bulletin*, used the language as a means of denigrating English culture. It was typically suggested that Irish was somehow a Catholic language and that English was therefore a Protestant, or, even worse, a pagan language. In 1905, for example, a *Leader* correspondent argued that the corpus of English literature since Shakespeare was essentially non-Catholic if not anti-Catholic.[10] Caution did prevail, partly because of a fear of ridicule; Shakespeare in particular was too beloved to be dismissed, and in *Stephen Hero*, Joyce presents us with a comic Jesuit professor of English desperately trying to prove that the Bard of Avon was a Catholic.[11]

The idea of the English language being a vehicle for corruption was quite widely held. For obvious reasons, an opinion that could easily be represented as barbaric or ridiculous tended to be expressed more widely in private than in public. However, the hatred, envy and contempt for English language and culture gained support from exotic and unexpected quarters; even international aesthetes with an anti-democratic and anti-bourgeois obsession such as George Moore regarded the English language as being irreversibly vulgarised by becoming an international lingua franca. In 1907 D.P. Moran was prepared to describe the public mind in English-speaking areas as 'enfeebled' by Anglicisation. *Seoinín* (England-loving) attitudes in the general public were causing the Gaelic League to run out of steam. Moran was, however, uncomfortably aware of the comic potential of the entire movement: 'the worst thing I can think of is to give the West Britons real cause for laughing at us'.[12] As we have seen, O'Leary argued that English threatened any remnant of piety or civic virtue that remained in the people.[13] Another clerical correspondent, in a piece that was later published as a pamphlet, declared the study of Irish and all things native to be a sovereign remedy for all kinds of social ills; it prevented 'snobbery' and also 'drunkenness, gambling, music halls, suggestive plays and immoral literature'.[14] In 1909 a Cork correspondent reported that a native speaker of Irish had advised him to desist from his efforts to learn the language as "twill lave you with a head fit for nothing else'. The correspondent appeared to believe that the language's apparent capacity to obsess the mind to the exclusion of all other, presumably alien, influences was a major merit.[15]

The League appealed to those who wished for cultural reform, but more, perhaps, to those who wanted to raise Irish political consciousness. In particular, the League attracted many whose objectives were political and to whom its cultural activities were of little interest. Many of these were clerics, but most were laymen; the IRB became involved in the League quite early on. In many areas, the Catholic clergy adopted it as a way of regulating the social life of the young, particularly the better-educated and more adventurous of the younger generation. In 1906, in Portarlington, County Kildare, a row between the local League branch and the parish priest erupted over precisely this issue; the League's local language classes were being used as an occasion for the young people of both sexes to meet unchaperoned. The League's impecuniosity, not its liberalism, was the reason for there not being two language classes, one for men and another for women. At Sunday mass, the parish priest acknowledged the respectability of the League's officers, but objected to 'young girls' attending mixed classes. He expressed doubt that it was 'nothing but Gaelic they wanted'. Noting that the seasons had not yet sufficiently advanced for the town to be lighted up, he suggested that 'perhaps if it was lighted they wouldn't want to go there at all', a remark which produced 'an indecent titter' in parts of the congregation.[16] In this case the priests got the worst of the argument, but usually the local League branches co-operated closely with the clergy, sometimes becoming their instruments.

In a penetrating and prophetic article published in 1904, the *Belfast Newsletter* saw the League's political potential. It noted the artificial character of the organisation. Its appeal to adults was limited, and it attracted children and adolescents rather more, often because of adult encouragement. The adult classes having lost momentum, the League had turned to the children and was attempting to use compulsion on them and on their teachers. In particular, the League had used political pressure through the clergy and the Commissioners of National Education to force the teachers to learn Irish. Furthermore, the branches of the League did not confine their discussions to cultural matters but were essentially centres of political indoctrination.

If the founders intended the organisation to be non-political and non-sectarian, then the local branches have travelled very far from the original design, for at present the great majority of the local branches are hotbeds of political and religious agitation. Their meetings are usually held after mass, or on a Sunday meeting, and generally the local curate is in the chair. The chief business is usually an address from the chairman, an address bristling with hatred of England and everything English, with exhortations to his hearers to hold fast to the religion and language of their fathers.[17]

The League grew rapidly in the first years of the new century, partly because of the impact of the Boer War on public opinion, dividing nationalists into pro- and anti-imperial camps. As the League became larger, it became more Catholic, less Dublin oriented and more clericalist. MacNeill and Hyde had invited this evolution, but sometimes appeared less than totally happy with its consequences. Hyde delphically remarked later on that the League had been very charming until it became powerful.[18] It was also claimed later that the clerical-nationalist campaign waged by the *Leader* had the effect of driving out the Protestants and bringing in the clergy.[19] Certainly the *Leader* disliked the pretensions of Protestants to the political leadership of advanced nationalism. In 1901 it asked bluntly: could a Protestant be Irish?

> The type of Non-Catholic Nationalist to whom we refer has been pampered in vanity. He could not be a mere Home Ruler, so he found it necessary to differentiate and be a Protestant Home Ruler; he thinks that Ireland practically never had a leader who was not a Protestant—that is one of the fruits of commencing Irish history at the year *1782*; he sometimes writes poetry which no Irishman understands or rather which no Irishman troubles his head to read; he thinks Catholics are superstitious and believes in spooks himself; he thinks they are priest-ridden and he would like to go back to Paganism; he is a bigot who thinks that he is broad-minded; a prig who thinks he is cultured; he does not understand Ireland—a fact which would not be of much import if he did not firmly believe that he is a philosopher. However, he means well.[20]

By March 1904 the *Church of Ireland Gazette* had denounced the Gaelic League, and in 1905 a Church of Ireland bishop seriously suggested a separate Gaelic League for Protestants. The famous Dublin branch Craobh na gCúig gCúigí (Five Provinces Branch) became known sarcastically as the 'Branch of the Five Protestants'.[21] By the middle of the first decade of the twentieth century, an organisation that had been started with inter-faith cultural intentions had been transformed into a mass organisation dominated by Catholics and increasingly subservient to political forces that were republican, separatist or clericalist. The Irish language was to become an ideological weapon in the armoury of nationalist and fundamentalist Catholic tendencies. For that reason, it became feared by Protestants and increasingly regarded as foreign and hostile.

It should be recalled that the League appealed to many, perhaps most, for essentially non-political, non-religious and even non-cultural reasons. Like most successful mass organisations, the League appealed to many for reasons of recreation and socialising. In particular, of course, if offered a legitimate occasion for the young of both sexes to meet; in the 'flat dullness of an Irish village or country town, the League class was an unexpected source of light and gaiety'. Most of the middle class fought shy of it, and those who aspired to rise further under the existing social and political regime avoided it for prudential reasons. It did, however, appeal to clerks, a minority of the doctors, solicitors and teachers in country towns. 'The lady members will be the more eager and serious-minded women of the town, with perhaps a few who like dancing or eager-minded men.'[22] In many cases these seem to have been those who were kept out of the charmed circle of Masonic and Hibernian circles and did not have powerful friends or relatives at court. Some of them were eventually to fight their way to power.

The League interacted oddly with the often labyrinthine snobberies of small-town life in Ireland. Moran, with the optimism of a cultural pioneer, had claimed in 1899 that both snobbery and anti-snobbery would be useful to the League in the new phase of expansion that was about to begin. In areas where the 'highly respectable people' took up the League, the general mass would follow along out of deference and snobbery. But where 'the honest people, who cannot wear their Sunday clothes on a week day' took up the movement first, things would be even better, and the League would 'become the vehicle of anti-snob sentiment'.[23] However, by 1907 he was complaining that the League could scarcely provide forty different branches for the forty different grades of society which inhabited the average Irish town. He cited an incident in Kerry in which a woman claimed social superiority over a 'small farmer from the mountains' who was an Irish speaker. In a tone of 'conscious superiority', she proudly announced that her husband was a railway linesman. One implication appears to have been that her husband, being English speaking, was an inhabitant of the modern world.[24] Irish was seen still as the language of lower prestige, of poverty and of backwardness, and the League found itself having to fight ingrained attitudes of all kinds.

MANY YOUNG MEN OF TWENTY GO TO LANGUAGE SCHOOL

The Gaelic League had an appeal which went far beyond culture, recreation or even politics in the ordinary sense. It appears to have offered a psychological escape from the rather extreme restrictions of society. It appealed to certain kinds of young men whose personal ideology and value system were conservative and who had imbibed in the austere and heavily disciplined schools of the Christian Brothers and the Holy Ghost Fathers a strong work ethic of a kind perhaps not traditional in Ireland. In part because of career frustration and discrimination against people of their creed and class, they were attracted by political agitation. As such agitation was ruled out because of the general alienation from conventional politics, the curiously abstract and romantic radicalism of the neo-Gaelic cult offered a substitute for it. Also, of course, the League denied the importance of class, offering the common name of Irishman as a substitute for class distinctions.

Hyde was well aware of the psychological comfort the cult gave young men and women of this kind. Hyde, Moran and the other leaders appear to have been quite clear in their minds that the true value of teaching the Irish language in schools was actually psychological rather than pedagogical; it built character as much as it did intellect. Hyde argued that Irish people from rural or small-town backgrounds, of post-Gaelic stock and lower-class cultural backgrounds were engaged in a hopeless and humiliating attempt to become accepted in the English-speaking world; they were socially 'impossible', to use that word in a Nancy Mitford sense, and could never become 'possible'. No matter how hard they tried, no matter how many examination triumphs they had, they would never become accepted. Even their organs of speech, he argued in Lamarckian fashion, were unfit for speaking English because the millennia during which their ancestors had been Irish speaking had caused them to evolve into different shapes, presumably, from those on the neighbouring island. Hyde's ideology was non-sectarian and non-racist; it could possibly be labelled 'linguism'. He further argued that Irish people should therefore learn Irish and abandon the humiliating attempt to become fully fledged citizens of the British system.[25]

Eleanor Hull was struck by the extraordinary appeal which the League had for young Irishmen and women living in London at the turn of the century. It typically was taken up by those in clerical jobs who had emigrated from small-town and rural Ireland. She was also impressed by the 'enthusiasm and earnestness' with which they had taken up the language and lore of rural Ireland. The exercise appeared to have 'both an intellectual and moral influence' on the students who were engaged in routine office work by day.

> Many of them are young men engaged all day in public offices, and young women, employed in the General Post Office. Yet, after a hard day's work, they meet together to study the language, with an energy and perseverance, which I have never seen applied to any other intellectual pursuit ... they [also] find a new and healthful field of recreation in gathering the folk-lore and songs and studying the antiquities of their own part of the country.

Some went further, and returned to Ireland like missionaries working in reverse to engage in quasi-political action, disseminating 'healthy Irish literature' to counteract the 'debasing influence' of the cheap 'English sensational fiction' that was circulating among 'the peasant classes in Ireland'.[26]

Self-respect and self-confidence were important fruits of participation in the Gaelic League in both Britain and Ireland. The *Leader* in 1902 argued in typical fashion that the psychological boost that the League gave to its members had the effect of dispelling the sense of paralysis, of absence of political will, so well described by James Joyce as being the dominant feature of Irish social culture in Edwardian times. The League was held to offer a psychological escape route from the enervating sense of self-contempt, inferiority and mediocrity which colonialism generated and which the prevailing status system copperfastened onto one.

> The Irish revival, the arriving at the conviction of its necessity by process of thought, the effort to follow where that conviction leads, the immediate effect on the self-respect of an Irishman once he is possessed of the Irish-Ireland conviction—all this at once tends to operate on our energies, to give us real ideals, and drag us out of the ruck of general mediocrity.[27]

Status resentment, leading to the attempt to devise a counter-culture, lay behind much of the enthusiasm which the League attracted. One's style of speaking English could be used to 'place' one very accurately by class, region and even religion; Irish, on the other hand, reflected regional dialects only and echoed no elaborated and oppressive class system. Ironically, conflicts between the various dialects at times became as obsessive as concern with accent in English. Resentment was aggravated by both deliberate and unconscious slighting of these thin-skinned people by a remote and insensitive establishment. Possibly an even more intense resentment was aimed at those Catholics who had made their peace with the regime and achieved some preferment. The 'Cawstle Cawtholics' aspired to ascent within the system by imitating English manners, accepting English ideological assumptions and sending their children to Catholic imitations of English grammar or public schools, or even to Protestant schools in England or Ireland. They were also willing to acquire higher education for their children, often in the face of episcopal disapproval. The *Leader* and other papers railed against the deracination which they imagined such education involved. In 1904 the *Leader* even blamed the general Irish propensity to emigrate on a national lack of self-confidence, which it blamed in turn on what it termed the 'middle classes', evidently meaning the Catholic middle classes. Their 'stagnation, snobbery and ignorance' were produced by 'College and Convent education', which was mainly a reach-me-down and slavish imitation of English prototypes. In particular, high-status Catholic colleges such as the Jesuit-run Belvedere College in Dublin were anti-national and snobbish. 'The colleges depend on the most irritating section of the country, generally known as the "highly respectable class". The Irish "highly respectable class" did not grow up in a night, it did not grow up of its own volition . . . it is now trying to be both English and Irish, with the more decided leaning towards the former.'[28]

Many of these resented people were actually immediately descended from well-known nationalist families, often with a violent past behind them. Even the students of the new University College in Dublin appeared excessively snobbish and Anglicised to the *Leader*. In 1912, four years before many of the students and some of their lecturers took part in an insurrection, it described University College students as 'poor white-livered lads' who had no understanding of Irish history, whose upbringing had been 'mean' and who were inclined 'to think it "smart" to despise [the] Irish [language]'.[29] Not only the Anglo-Irish establishment but also the rather insecure Catholic upper middle class were targets for the resentment of the newly educated upwardly mobile Catholic lower middle class and its working-class allies.

Status resentment, then, could be cured only at the high price of assimilation into the establishment, a cure available only to a few. The alternative status system offered by the League was cheaper; fluency in Irish, proficiency in rural dances, adherence to a strict Catholic morality, an exaggerated lower middle-class respectability and an informed, even obsessive, knowledge of the history and antiquities of Ireland together added up to a considerable challenge to the system, which valued non-Catholic religious affiliations and English upper-class manners far more than things Irish, commonly seen as quaint, provincial and backward. The sense of liberation was often very intense; a young London Irishman remarked, on discovering the Irish language, 'well, hang them for *Sassenachs*, we have at least one thing they can't lay claim to, anyway'.[30] Many other observers came to similar conclusions. W.P. Ryan saw the League as a symptom of what might nowadays be described as psychic political modernisation acting on the minds of the young laymen and priests: '[The younger priests] saw that we were passing out of a semi-patriarchal and also somewhat serf-like age, that much of the new generation had schemes and purposes of its own and would not endure the leading-strings of the old.'[31]

The American consul in Queenstown, County Cork, writing in the immediate aftermath of the 1916 Rising, was struck by the effect the Gaelic League had on young Catholic students. The League had tried to build up national character by inculcating an awareness of past cultural achievement. 'In fact, the movement was a character cult fully as much as a political manifestation ... Most Catholic students were politicised by Sinn Féin and it appeared to really inspire and improve them'.[32]

Status resentment had, then, a major influence on the formation of the ideology of the young men who were to become the founding fathers of independent Ireland. The emergent élite was obsessed by a sense of moral superiority and anger at the contempt in which is sensed it was held by the establishment. A curious inverted snobbery encouraged the embracing of a partly artificial counter-culture, constructed as a compensation for the discomfort generated by the existing status system. The neo-Gaelic counter-culture also acted as a convenient source of ideological stances, in particular an alliance between separatism and certain sections of the Catholic clergy.

THE PARTY POLITICS OF IRISH

The League was essentially a political party which denied that proposition. Its expansion after 1899 was spectacular, its membership expanding enormously and its revenues increasing also; its annual income increased from about £1,000 to about £7,000 between 1900 and 1904.[33] Before 1899 it scarcely had a formal constitution, as it was dominated by a small Dublin group who knew each other well. It staged its first Oireachtas, or general meeting, at which various cultural activities such as dancing and singing competitions were held, only in 1897.[34] The 1899 constitution provided for a regular representative structure, with an executive committee (Coiste Gnotha) elected annually by a delegate conference (Ard-Fheis) from the branches. The Ard-Fheis delegates were elected by the branches (craobhaca) in proportion to the certified memberships of the branches. There were periodic constitutional shake-ups every few years as the organisation grew larger and more impersonal. The basic structure remained intact, and appears to have been an important prototype for later nationalist political parties.[35] Two types of member of the Coiste Gnotha were stipulated by the 1899 and later constitutions: residential and country. The former were required to reside in the Dublin area, whereas the latter were to represent the provinces. Originally, half the members were residential; this proportion tended to decrease, under pressure from the new country branches. Because of the expense that country members necessarily incurred in travelling to Dublin, residential members of the Coiste Gnotha tended to have a natural advantage in influencing the League's internal affairs.

The early Ard-Fheiseanna had about 150 delegates, but later ones had swollen memberships of up to 400. The Coiste Gnotha originally had twenty members, but grew rapidly to forty-five in the mid-1900s in part at the insistence of the new, more rural membership.

As the League grew in popularity, it came to be looked upon with unease by many party politicians, who sensed that it somehow represented a threat to their quasi-monopoly of nationalist public opinion. It also became the target of entryist tactics on the part of the IRB, the Irish Party, clericalists and Sinn Féin. There were personality clashes, while regional and dialectical differences sometimes aggravated differences over policy and ideology. At times, the League's internal politics were spectacularly bad tempered; the tradition of the cabal soon dominated League politics.

A basic opposition, combining regional feeling and political ideology, existed in the League between those who wished to construct a standard version of the language which would be acceptable to speakers of the three main dialects (Ulster, Connacht and Munster) and those who claimed that the southern, Munster dialect, because it could claim a respectable literary tradition, should have primacy. The supporters of the Munster dialect, sometimes referred to as 'Provincialists', tended to despise the Connacht dialect in particular as being the language only of poor and unlettered peasants and fishermen. Hyde and Pearse, who spoke Connacht Irish, naturally defended dialectical pluralism, as did MacNeill. The Munster branches, together with some Leinster branches (there was no developed Leinster dialect), supported the southern dialect. In particular, the very active Keating branch in Dublin tended to represent the southern cause against the dialectical pluralism of the Central Branch and the League's Dublin-based establishment. The Keating branch, founded in 1901, consisted mainly of expatriate Munstermen living in the capital, in particular J.J. O'Kelly (Sceilg) and Father Patrick Dineen, SJ, compiler of a famous and entertaining dictionary. Cathal Brugha, a Dubliner of part-English descent and an extreme separatist, was also a member.[36] In the early 1900s, Sceilg published a little magazine, *Banba*, in opposition to the League establishment as personified by Pearse, Hyde and MacNeill, but also vitriolic in its criticism of many Cork Leaguers. Hyde referred to it as 'that narrowest, meanest, and most bitter of Irish publications'. The pugnacious Dr O'Hickey, professor of Irish at Maynooth, referred to the Keating group as 'footpads'.[37] The Munster opposition was particularly active in opposing the appointment of Pearse to the editorship of the League paper, *An Claidheamh Soluis* (the Sword of Light), in 1902.[38]

According to Hyde, it was Munster 'Provincialism' that instigated factional politics in the League, culminating in competitive elections to the Coiste Gnotha every year. Admittedly, the growth in size of the League probably encouraged the development of stable factions. 'The Keating branch, a Dublin branch to which most of the Dublin Munstermen belonged, including nearly all those who, to me at least, seemed to give the most trouble in the Gaelic League, ran a "Munster ticket" and the Connacht men once or twice ran an opposing one.'[39]

The increase in size of the Coiste Gnotha to forty-five members in 1904–05 turned what was originally an executive into a larger, less decisive and more discursive body. Hyde remembered that full meetings of the executive looked more like a little parliament than a cabinet meeting.

Munster had a strong Gaelic tradition, and the language had been the vehicle there for much verse of Jacobite, anti-English and agrarian sentiment. The province soon got a reputation for efficient and energetic organisation. Munster performers did particularly well at national competitions, the west Cork branches being very successful. An ex-civil servant from London, Fionan Mac Coluim, worked in Munster as League organiser and was reputed to be the League's most effective such organiser.[40]

The result of the League's expansion and of Munster's self-assertiveness was the decline of the dominance of Dublin and the Central Branch. The city's strength at the Ard-Fheis and the power of the resident members of the Coiste Gnotha waned. At the 1902 Ard-Fheis, Dublin still had fifty-six out of 187 delegates, or 30 per cent, whereas Munster had only twenty-nine, or 16 per cent. The following year, Dublin had declined to forty-three delegates out of 257, or a mere 17 per cent, whereas Munster had climbed to 20 per cent, and Connacht had also expanded considerably. By 1912, of 202 delegates from the four provinces, Munster was to boast a massive eighty-four, or 42 per cent. The League became ruralised and provincialised at the expense of Dublin and the original founding group.[41]

This pattern was not confined just to the level of branches of Ard-Fheiseanna. Forces based in non-Dublin areas, and in Munster in particular, penetrated the Coiste Gnotha decisively. In 1904 six of the fifteen non-resident members were from Munster, and in 1907 seven were. However, 'on the ground' Munster's superior organisational tradition showed itself. By the end of 1906 the League had established district committees (coisti ceanntair), mainly at Munster insistence, to fund and administer the travelling-teacher systems locally and to generally supervise the local areas' revival efforts. Of forty-nine such committees in Ireland, nine were in Leinster, ten in Ulster, twelve in Connacht and eighteen or 37 per cent, were in Munster. By early 1908 this Munster dominance had become even greater than two years previously; the figures were sixty-four district committees in Ireland, of which seventeen were in Leinster, twelve in Ulster, seven in Connacht and twenty-eight, or a massive 44 per cent, in Munster. In that year forty-six of 111 League teachers, or 41 per cent, were active in Munster.[42]

One consequence of this expansion was to increase the numbers of rural clergy serving as delegates and committee members. In the League, as in other Irish political and social organisations, clergy were particularly important activists in areas which were remote and poor and lacked educated laymen: the clergy 'stood in' for a middle class in these areas. Regional tensions became greater as Munster and even Connacht became more assertive. The League also became more vulnerable to penetration as it became less of a caucus and more genuinely a branch organisation. Arthur Griffith's group, named Sinn Féin (Ourselves) in 1905 but in existence since the late 1890s, was an early interested watcher of the League. Griffith's group was Dublin centred, and tried to evolve a policy that was intermediate between the constitutionalism of the Irish Party and the separatism of the IRB. Sinn Féin was noticeably weak in Cork.[43] Griffith believed in industrialisation as a cure for Irish ills, to an extent that made him hostile to labour, as it often pointed out, but also to the ruralism of the priests. He was rather hostile to the neo-Gaelic ideology of the more extreme Leaguers, and also to the clericalism of D.P. Moran's *Leader*. Griffith's little Sinn Féin, perhaps the most purely 'bourgeois moderniser' of the nationalist groups, impressed contemporary observers with its energy and detachment from the emotionalism of so much of the little world of nationalist politics. An English journalist in 1906 saw his party as consisting of

clear-eyed, forceful men, who mean business and have backbone. Except among the extremists of the Ascendancy Party I do not recall meeting any body of men who made Upon me an equal impression of tenacity; and the tenacity of the Sinn Féiners is the tenacity not of obstinacy but of a cool, far-seeing and inflexible purpose.[44]

Although Griffith was not particularly sympathetic to the League's ideology, his lieutenants were quick to exploit its political potential. They were 'nearly always among the more active members' of the League and they tended to push out the more lethargic committee members in the 1900–06 period. However, Sinn Féin remained a narrow cabal, and was apparently unable to compete with IRB entryism from about 1907 on.[45] While the Catholic hierarchy probably never seriously considered capturing the League, despite dark rumours to that effect, the League did become very clericalised. It could be argued that the League was penetrating the Church as much as the reverse; it had a strong ideological appeal to many of the younger clergy. They listened sympathetically to the League's exhortations to teach Irish in the schools and to imbue the young with a knowledge of Irish history and a pride in the remnants of its traditional culture. In the poorer districts of the north and west, the local priests appear to have been quite indispensable, as there were so few educated laymen of any means.[46]

The League's original posture of aloofness from parliamentarianism eventually crystallised into a settled distrust of it. This was eventually to make it more vulnerable to the anti-political politics of many of the radicals. Hyde believed that Patrick Ford and the *Gaelic-American* had controlled much of the flow of dollars from Irish America to nationalist organisations in Ireland. Because Ford's group of *emigré* nationalists approved of the Gaelic League, it had little trouble from the parliamentary nationalists or from the agrarians; they danced to Ford's tunes. However, the true separatists were apparently immune to financial pressure from that quarter. 'I never heard even a mention of evicted tenants. The trouble was to keep out politics of the Wolfe Tone or Fenian type. These growing stronger by degrees came on in a rush in 1914 and 1915 and ended by capturing the League, its officers its machinery and its money.'[47]

The hostility to the parliamentarians, descended from the old rancours surrounding the fall of Parnell, antedated the IRB coup, however, and helped to make it possible. In 1910 an Irish Party employee engaged in translation from English to Irish of party literature complained of this political bias, observing that many League members

—have a sort of 'strangeness' and narrow-minded distrust of politicians, no matter what their knowledge of Irish or how earnest their efforts towards its revival . . . in face of the supposed non-political shibboleth of the Gaelic League, the vast majority of its members and officials have up their sleeves a paltry prejudice against politicians of the Nationalist type, and, in fact, I myself have heard many of them freely preach that prejudice.[48]

The Sinn Féiners of Griffith's little party were in two minds about the League. A similar ideological ambivalence toward linguistic revival existed in the minds of the physical-force separatists, who colonised the League less out of neo-Gaelic enthusiasm than out of a clear view of its political potential. Hyde believed many of them cared little for the language, but the younger men whom they inducted into both the League and the IRB were inculcated with an explosive combination of linguistic and militaristic ideologies. Even socialists belatedly saw the League's significance, and Larkinites penetrated the Dublin regional council. Hyde complained that the leftist influence on the Coiste Gnotha drove away the rich and influential, he himself being forced to wear old clothes to meetings so as not to raise the ire of the new democracy.[49] A correspondent in the *Cork Constitution* indignantly asked in September 1911 whether the putatively non-political Gaelic League should not desist from consorting with 'alleged or real revolutionaries.'[50] The IRB was, of course, to be more successful than either the Sinn Féiners or the socialists. By 1910 the takeover of the League by the Brotherhood was well under way. A group described by the *Irish Independent* as a 'combination of socialist, anti-clericals, anti-teachers, extreme Sinn Féiners and Provincialists' came close to taking over the 1911 Ard-Fheis. Actually the IRB was racing other political groups and was winning. The *Independent* described the process:

This is how the game is worked. The country branches usually elect some prominent local workers as delegates to the Ard-Fheis. The cost of a journey to Dublin and of a week's stay there is considerable, and often, at the last moment, the local delegate finds himself unable to go. He, perhaps, has been canvassed in view of this eventuality. He signs his delegate's ticket and sends it to someone in Dublin with whose name he is familiar, asking him to procure a substitute. The opportunity is availed of to put in as delegate some Dublin adherent of the above combination.[51]

Certainly, the rural delegations appear to have been thoroughly worked by the conspirators.[52] Seán T. O'Kelly, business manager of

An Claidheamh Soluis and long-time Dublin IRB agent, confirms this general account in his Irish-language memoirs. IRB men were ordered to canvass for particular candidates who were regarded by 'the firm' as politically sound. O'Kelly piously claimed that he would certainly not have supported anyone who was not good at the League's own business, regardless of the orthodoxy of his separatism.[53] It may have been that political fervour and cultural revivalism often reinforced each other, but there is a fair amount of evidence to suggest that the older separatists knew rather little Irish themselves and came to regard it essentially as a device to capture the minds and imaginations of the younger men, who acquired a naive ideological mixture of revivalism and separatism; culture came to the aid of politics. Hyde remembered the final takeover of 1915 unsentimentally in 1917–18:

> Now I was told by several people that Sean O Muirthile had got 50 proxies which instead of distributing to various Irish speakers as he was meant to do, he handed over in one bunch to the Sinn Féin secretary in Dundalk, who handed them over to fifty Sinn Féiners, who did not speak Irish, did not care for the language, had never even joined a branch of the Gaelic League, but who now got their orders to walk in as delegates with passes in their hands and vote on a pre-arranged ticket for all the Sinn Féiners and politicians and followers of Arthur Griffith who were candidates for membership of the Coiste Gnotha.[54]

Poor Hyde was still confusing Sinn Féin with the IRB, much as the mass media and the British authorities did. Given the entangled character of Irish political organisations, such confusion was understandable. The 'Sinn Féin', i.e. IRB, tactics worked well. In 1912 O'Kelly had won the third-highest delegate vote for residential member and Thomas Ashe the seventh, out of fifteen seats.[55] The growing politicisation of the League reflected itself in various ways. Pearse, although not a member of the conspiracy, became increasingly 'political' and strident in his writings. The atmosphere of acrimony in the League's affairs deepened. In some ways the League became more energetic, efficient and aggressive. The

Coiste Gnotha was made smaller, and more an executive than a deliberative body. A reorganisation of the branch organisation was put in train.[56] However, the ousting of the League establishment was essentially a matter of aggressive committee politics. The Brotherhood had repeatedly used such tactics to take control of the Gaelic Athletic Association on at least two memorable occasions, once during the Parnell period and once in the late 1890s. Caucuses of the IRB based mainly on Dublin took advantage of the ruralised and decentralised character of the Gaelic League. Another tactic was to blame the establishment for the slowness of the linguistic revival campaign. The depressing linguistic statistics in the 1911 census, which documented the unrelenting expansion of the English language, were laid squarely at the establishment's door. Hyde described the older and less outgoing members of the leadership being driven from office and even out of the League by a simple campaign of personal abuse. 'When having got rid by this simple process of abuse first of O'Hickey and then of Mac Neill they proceeded to play the same game with me I turned on them furiously and appealed to the branches of the League all over Ireland to protect me, and succeeded in quenching them for the time . . .'[57]

In effect, the extremists confiscated the language, much as they had confiscated Gaelic games. By doing so they identified the language and the games with a particular political ideology and thereby ensured that anyone who did not share that ideology or who was not willing to at least pay lip-service to it would boycott them. Protestants naturally excluded themselves, but so did most of the Catholic middle class.

The IRB appears to have convinced itself in 1914 that there would be an early German victory in the war, and that out of that victory would come a dismemberment of the British Empire and, of course, an independent Ireland, presumably allied with the Reich.

Many older officers were driven out of the organisation by this simple means, but Hyde held on until 1915. By then, of course, the subversion of the League was complete and it became another front, like the Irish Volunteers, for the IRB and the insurrectionist wing of the League led by Pearse. Eventually the insurrectionist cabal was to deceive the IRB leaders themselves and stage the 1916

Rising. Pearse had, however, written the League's epitaph in his prophetic manifesto for the Irish revolution published in the League's own newspaper in November 1913:

> I have come to the conclusion that the Gaelic League, as the Gaelic League, is a spent force; and I am glad of it ... I mean that the vital work to be done in the new Ireland will be done not so much by the Gaelic League as by men and movements that have sprung from the Gaelic League or have received from the Gaelic League a new baptism and a new life of grace ... There will be in the Ireland of the next few years a multitudinous activity of Freedom Clubs, Young Republican Clubs, Labour Organisations, Socialist Groups, and what not; bewildering enterprises undertaken by sane persons and insane persons, many of them seemingly contradictory, some mutually destructive, yet all tending towards a common objective, and that objective: the Irish Revolution.[58]

The arming of the north and the counter-arming of the south was the accelerator of revolution in Ireland. The growth of European war fever also contributed. However, it also seems that a subconscious sense of the Quixotic hopelessness of the League's programme of linguistic revival prompted a retreat from cultural failure to the paradoxically easier task of staging a revolution; British power in Ireland was less impervious than was the wall of quiet but implacable resistance to Gaelicisation which the common people of Ireland erected against the League's teachers. Although political agitation had established Irish as a taught subject in many schools and had eventually forced the National University of Ireland to require it for matriculation, the revival remained essentially artificial and confined to certain middle sections of society. The census recorded the tide of English rising even in the Gaeltachtaí despite the Canute-like efforts of the muinteoirí taistil. As early as 1905 *An Claidheamh Soluis* had asked: 'Is the Language dying?'[59] A cold-eyed report from Waterford in the same year stated categorically that the language was dying in the Decies; fundamentally people did not want it, and the priests in the area were generally hostile.[60] This letter was by way of rebutting an optimistic report,

probably written by Pearse, claiming that people in the linguistic
borderlands of west Galway were actually resuming the speaking
of Irish because of the Gaelic League's teaching and propaganda.[61]
By 1908 Pearse himself was desperately fighting pessimism and
resorting to the imagery of warfare, although so far the war was
visualised as a cultural one: 'We are NOT losing; and even if we
were losing, it would be bad tactics, and worse—it would be
treachery,—to say so in the face of the enemy.'[62]

From 1906 on, contributions to the central language fund began
to fall off, and the League became more dependent on Irish-
American funding. *An Claidheamh Soluis* suggested the decrease
was due to increased local retention of money, but a certain
diminution of energy and interest was to be suspected.[63] In 1908 a
Mayo teacher contributed a depressing and convincing account of
the very limited impact the teaching of Irish had on the long-term
linguistic habits of pupils. The League at times appears to have
become uneasy and to have lost its sense of purpose; disagreements
such as that about dialects festered, and at one stage Sceilg launched
vicious personal attacks on the Coiste Gnotha. Dineen's sharp-
tongued and often funny attacks on the League's establishment
were derived from a shrewd assessment of the League's failure to
make swift progress toward its primary objective.[64] By 1910 sales
of the League's publications were falling off and financial bank-
ruptcy was seriously contemplated in public.[65] Some feared failure,
others used it as a stick with which to beat the leadership. A nasty
little pseudonymous letter in the *Irish Independent* in 1913 accused
Hyde of corruption, not brooking rivals and letting the League
wither away.[66]

Increasing bad-tempered desperation and authoritarianism was
the reaction of some Leaguers. *Irish Freedom*, the IRB paper, called
for Ireland to hold fast to her 'soul' in 1911; it was felt that eventually people would have to be forced to save their cultural and
political souls. The desperation of failure bred a truculence:
'Therefore we call for language bigots, for aggressive language propagandists, for people who are quite truculent and quite unrea-
sonable, to go out into the highways and byways and speak the
language and shove it down the throats of all and sundry, whether

they like it or not . . . the Irish nation depends on [the language] . . .'[67]

Desmond FitzGerald, an IRB activist in Kerry in the years before the Great War, saw the language even then as a dying one. It was becoming impoverished in vocabulary and syntax; older men spoke a richer version of it than did the younger. 'We were subconsciously aware that the continued decay of the Irish language was bringing ominously near a further great break with the past.'[68] A common theme later on was to blame politics and politicians for the decline of the revival movement and the continued retreat of the Gaeltachtai; in fact, since independence the Irish government has been berated for permitting the language decline to continue. Siobhan Lankford, a north Cork activist, recalled that in Mallow the League's classes went on amid great fervour throughout the Anglo-Irish War until the news came down from Dublin in 1922 that a compromise Treaty had been accepted.

Almost overnight the enthusiasm evaporated and the classes faded away. At first we couldn't believe the classes were not going to continue . . . one of the most intellectual of the students . . . said 'Well, the enthusiasm was great because we expected to have a Republic, and its dignity would demand the native language, but now we'll still be part of the British Empire, and have a divided country—not worth the effort of learning a language—English will be good enough for us.[69]

An alternative explanation would be that the essentially politically motivated interest in the language could not be a long-term substitute for a general and genuine public interest in language change, an interest that is historically very unusual in circumstances analogous to Ireland's. The end of the political revolution in 1922–23 exposed the hollowness of the cultural movement which the revolutionaries had hijacked. The IRB separatists were men of secret societies, authoritarian and obsessed by political goals to the near-exclusion of cultural, economic or social considerations. Some had a covert streak of religious bigotry; they read little. Essentially, the Irish language was valued not for itself but as a symbol of national distinctiveness. Beyond that, it was fit only for children and for others who needed protection against English civilisation.[70]

Behind the idealism of Pearse, the ruralism of clergy and the single-mindedness of IRB leaders, there sometimes lurked another emotion: status resentment and personal ambition cloaked in nationalism. In 1910 a letter to the League's paper complained about the unfairness of the public service examinations, which did not accept Irish as a subject, while accepting foreign modern languages such as French and German. Significantly, the Irish ethnic identity was seen by this writer to actually exclude not just the upper classes or Protestants but apparently anyone who had had the advantage of a Jesuit education in Ireland: 'It is a crying evil in every sense of the word. We want to have Gaelic Leaguers in every walk in life. As the matter at present stands, the Clongowes snob can walk into a position which is barred to an Irish lad on account of his fearless avowal of his nationality.'[71]

THE POLITICS OF ENGLISH POPULAR CULTURE

A major theme of Irish-Ireland and Catholic thought was, of course, the menacing growth of a large market in Ireland for English popular literature and popular culture generally. This was a by-product of the growth of mass literacy, ironically itself a result of the upgrading of national school education under clerical auspices. As already suggested, the Gaelic League itself was in part a reaction to this growth of an Anglicised popular culture and its consequent real or imagined demoralising and deracinating effects on the minds of the young and easily influenced. Countrymen noticed how much further this process had gone in the big towns and in Dublin; to a countryman, a Dubliner of the period seemed at least as English as he was Irish. As a schoolboy, Ernie O'Malley, later to be a well-known IRA guerrilla, had felt the Dubliners' disregard for things national and things rural when he and his family moved to the city from Mayo during his schooldays. He found himself regarded as a culchie (countryman, rustic) among jackeens (Dublin townies). O'Malley knew little of the Anglicised townsman's culture into which he had been thrown, and had

picked up from maidservants and from the Gaelic League a
version of Ireland's Gaelic past.

> Our accent was mimicked, and back to back my brother and I
> fought a ring of tormentors; in the end we were left alone, as we
> were both lithe and hardy. We told our school chums stories of
> Fionn and Cuchulain, but they laughed at us. They had read the
> latest Buff Bill, could talk of the Red varmints of Indians, colt-
> emptying frontier fighters, of split-up-the-back Eton suits and
> the rags of that other public school life of the Magnet and the
> Gem. Only to ourselves now did we talk about the older stories.

Privately, O'Malley was contemptuous of the Dublin IRA,
although its officers were good, in his opinion.[72] The officers appear
to have been disproportionately of non-Dublin background and
more 'Irish' than the Dubliners themselves.

An obsession with public morality and with the powers of the
popular press to corrupt the population was common among the
young patriots, as it was among the priests. Dublin was the symbol
not only of the arrogant and unforgivably brilliant achievements
of eighteenth-century Anglo-Ireland but also of the readiness of
the native Irish, in their debased urban and proletarian condition,
to accept Anglo-American vulgarity and corruption while ignoring
the cultural riches of the Irish past and of rural society. Naturally,
the idea of cultural protectionism became popular. It is striking
how much more popular cultural protectionism was than was
economic protectionism; after all, the latter divided, whereas the
former united, separatist supporters. Many businesspeople, while
sympathetic to nationalism, would have been uneasy about protectionism because of fears of British retaliation, and the issue of
tariffs was to be a major divisive force after independence. However,
everyone was against dirty books.

The limitations of the Gaelic League as a *cordon sanitaire culturel*
were evident to many, and some clericalists resorted to direct action
and experiments in censorship. Burning of papers and books
occurred sporadically in the years after 1910. The *Leader* regularly
denounced the 'Penny Dirties'. In 1908 it contrasted the moral

atmospheres of Ireland and industrial England in a revealing essay:

> Vice and immorality exist, and will always exist, in every country; but what astonishes one accustomed to Irish surroundings is the complete shamelessness with which indecency of every kind is paraded in public [in English cities]. In the shop windows, in the streets, in the railway stations, in every public place, one's sense of decency is continually offended. If the unwary Christian goes into a shop and asks for some 'comic' postcards he is likely to be surprised. The girl behind the counter invariably hands him a collection of invariably indecent and suggestive cards.

The following year a priest asked the nation in its columns, 'Irish or Infidelity, Which?', warning against the corruption of English industrial civilisation.[73] The Irish language was now identified not only with a glorious past but with the Victorian puritanism of Irish Catholicism and with its fear and hatred of modern industrial civilisation as represented by England. The Gaelic League, already blamed for the lack of progress of the linguistic revival movement, almost came to be held responsible for the continuing Anglicisation of Ireland. The argument also took a new tack; since it was evident that the Irish people were not going to throw away their English tastes and embrace those offered them by the Gaelic League, they would have to be approached through the medium of the English language. Tacitly, the clericalists were admitting that Ireland was going to remain an English-speaking country. Of course, they were never to admit it in public, and continued to blame politicians for the irreversibility of the linguistic shift of the nineteenth century.

The *Catholic Bulletin*, edited from 1911 on by Sceilg, questioned the efficacy of the League's efforts more directly, thereby reiterating the 'Munster' critique of Hyde and company.[74] It suggested that towns and villages be supplied with English-language books suitable for Catholics, and that an index of permitted books be drawn up under ecclesiastical auspices. Catholicism should not just attempt to keep out English vulgarity, it should compete with it in the English language. If there was no market for Tara, there might be one for Knocknagow. A distaste of the English 'gutter press' would ensue. Irish novelists should try to provide a wholesome popular literature somewhat, perhaps, on the lines of the novels of Charles Kickham and Canon Sheehan. These writers had achieved a genuine popularity and had put forward a view of Irish society which was sympathetic. Rural life should be glorified, and people should not be rendered dissatisfied with the perhaps humble station in life which fortune had allotted to them. In particular, the *Bulletin* objected to portrayals of glamorous, cosmopolitan lifestyles by English popular writers, the Edwardian equivalents of Mills & Boon: 'the spruce and dapper Edwin, stepping from his mansion to woo and win some soulless Angelina, a vision of furs and laces, should be replaced by the blithe and merry working man who sings at his plough, greeting the pure-souled, cheery milkmaid as she croons on her milking stool.'[75]

Pearse appeared to echo this theme rather oddly and in a characteristically different context in *An Claidheamh Soluis* in early 1913. He was preaching to the Irish the theme of the teacher as hero and as giver of example to his pupils. He urged the inculcation of 'manhood' and 'hardening', in strange contrast to the gentle themes he had hitherto used in discussing education: 'I would bring back some of the starkness of the antique world . . . '. Only sentimentalists believed that the era of force was past or that 'henceforward the duty of every man is to be dapper'.[76] 'Dapperness' was the mark of city slickness and the unheroic style of the cockneyfied urban dweller of the English world; locally he was the Dublin cockney or jackeen, proletarian cousin of the *seoinín* so hated by the Irish-Irelanders.

Fundamentalist Catholicism and the wish to create heroic patriots were two reasons to fear English popular culture. As usual, self- and class-interest sometimes hid behind general ideological considerations. In 1911 a lady contributor to the *Bulletin* bitterly complained about a 'crying evil'; ever since the maidservants had learned to read, they had become ill behaved. Their penny-dreadful love stories awakened 'longings only too frequently to be realised through sin', and rendered employees restless and unwilling to work in a disciplined and reliable fashion:

In the workrooms of mills and warehouses, the books are concealed, to be taken out at the dinner hour and devoured with even greater interest than the scanty meal of the worker. The little maid who pushes your baby's perambulator has her novelette concealed beneath the rug to be easily perused in the park or along the country road, while baby is left to his own devices. The errand boy sitting upon his basket's handle, forgets his errands and grows careless of his master's interests while he burns to emulate Dick Daring, the Gentleman Burglar, or Sappy Sam, the Champion Rider of the Plains.[77]

This fear of restlessness generated by the media was political as well as prurient; labour unrest was caused by the media, as was the unruliness of domestic servants. The Vigilance Committees set up to monitor the English press were commended by the *Leader* in 1912: 'They have crushed the wealthy Reptile Press, laughed at morbid "intellectuals", lovers of licence, and advocates of filth'.[78] A correspondent announced in the *Bulletin* in January 1913 that the newspapers were all lies, dictated by the greed of their shareholders, and that their sensationalism aggravated social unrest.[79] Even the IRB paper, *Irish Freedom*, sympathised with the general hostility to the English media. The ideological foundations of the censorship system of independent Ireland were well laid, and by a wide variety of political forces; clergy, clericalists, neo-Fenians and *Gaeilgeoiri* all supported it for slightly different reasons.

06 | IDEOLOGICAL THEMES OF SEPARATIST NATIONALISM

PAST, FUTURE, YOUTH AND AGE

In a famous quotation, Marx has pointed out that human beings make their own history, but they do not make it as they please but under circumstances 'directly encountered, given and transmitted from the past'.

> The tradition of the dead generations weighs like a nightmare on the brain of the living. And just when they seem engaged in revolutionising themselves and things, in creating something that has never yet existed, precisely in such periods of revolutionary crisis they anxiously conjure up the spirits of the past to their service and borrow from them names, battle-cries and costumes in order to present the new scene of world history in this time-honoured disguise and in this borrowed language . . . the heroes as well as the parties and the masses of the old French Revolution, performed the task of their time in Roman costume and with Roman phrases, the task of unchaining and setting up modern *bourgeois* society.[1]

This classic assessment of the mentality of revolutionaries has at least two tacit and Olympian assumptions behind it: that its author knew the real purpose of the revolution and that he knew the nature of the post-revolutionary future. Marx was good on the political nostalgia of other revolutionaries; what he missed, both in himself and in others, was the equally unreal political futurism of so many revolutionaries. It was easy, perhaps, in Victorian England for even a revolutionary to be as confident as a bourgeois that the future belonged to him and to people like him.

In reality, modern revolutionary ideologies mingle nostalgia and futurism in ways that are easily recognisable. The common theme is the deprecation of the present, and this deprecation is common to both the reactionary and the radical or 'progressive' revolutionary. This common dislike of what is explains why the line between proto-fascist and proto-communist is so difficult to draw when both are still at the stage of parlour or bar-room revolution rather than actually winning political power. Before the Great War, both types were still powerless to realise their fantasies, and it took the war to enable them to gain power and to prompt them to take sides. There is a difference, however. The reactionary, as Hoffer has pointed out, uses his own reconstruction of the past as a blueprint for his proposed ideal future. However, his reconstructed past is inevitably based less on what actually existed than on what the reactionary wants the future to be; 'he innovates more than he reconstructs'. The radical also rejects the present in favour of a better future, but by rejecting the present finds himself forced to link the world with 'some point in the past'. If violence comes to be used in achieving the new world, 'his view of man's nature darkens' and he tends to adopt an existential pessimism resembling that of the reactionary.[2] Pearse and Connolly are indeed partners.

Irish people were commonly described as being obsessed by history; they were possessed not by a love for it, nor often of a well-informed view of it, but of a habit of mind that referred all things present to things past for explanation or, at least, cultural mapping. Irish political radicals often had a fascination with the past, but this could often be analysed rather easily into a hatred for the 'long present', or immediate past of the previous two centuries, combined with a noisily announced nostalgia for the rural society from which so many of them had sprung and an artificial reverence for the remote Gaelic medieval and pre-medieval past that had preceded the hated Anglo-Irish past of the eighteenth and nineteenth centuries. History was indeed seen as a nightmare; whether, like Stephen Daedalus, the young Irishmen of the period really wanted to awake from it or merely wanted to substitute a Gaelic daydream for the nightmare is another question. The mood of many politicised young people was best expressed, I suspect, by the young man in Dublin who, at some occasion in the 1910–13 period, reacted to Bulmer Hobson's conventional evocation of Ireland's 'glorious past' at a meeting by jumping up and exclaiming that it was a 'rotten past' and that instead of talking about it they should found a rifle club.[3] The ideologues of the Gaelic League, Sinn Féin and the IRB knew far less about the Gaelic past than is now known, as the impressive scholarship of the twentieth century had yet to be done. Ironically, the picture of Gaelic Irish civilisation that emerges is very different from the one which the rebels had in their minds, and is also far more interesting. What is also clear is that the manners and customs of the ancient Irish were not such as would have been approved by Edwardian Catholic puritans. The utility of Gaelic Ireland to them was that they could ascribe any virtues to it that they fancied, as so little was actually known about it.

The Great War did not have the effect of separating radicals and reactionaries into opposed ideological camps in Ireland—or, indeed, even in Britain—to anything like the same extent that it did in much of the European mainland. Quite apart from a British Isles parochialism, there were local Irish reasons why the elaborated European ideologies of conservatism, liberalism and socialism were not suitable for the purposes of the separatists. Firstly and most obviously, a traditional solidarity built around a popular Catholicism dominated the minds of most, if not all, nationalists. Again, socialists, although in a minority, came to be seen by the non-socialist revolutionaries as useful allies to be placated and given some ideological concessions; nationalism and Catholicism were to swallow up socialism.

Further, conservatism had become a monopoly of the British and Irish unionists; no matter how objectively reactionary a Sinn Feiner might be, he could never admit, perhaps even to himself, to being a conservative. Conservatism was not so much the ideology as the label of his enemy. Furthermore, the nationalist's hatred of the recent past debarred him from taking up a Burkean incremental conservatism which treasured past ways while accepting gradual innovation. The separatist was commonly a restorationist of an extinct past rather than a preserver of continuity with the recent, genuine past. Similarly, liberalism was the ideology of individualism, commerce and international capital. It was the ideology of modern England. It exalted the individual above the community, it preferred the *Gesellschaft* to the *Gemeinschaft* and it legitimised British commercial penetration of Ireland and Ireland's reduction to a monocrop dependency. In the minds of Catholics, it was intellectually cognate with modernism while also encouraging an exploitative and neo-pagan society, and was therefore doubly anathema. Socialism was beyond the pale for similar reasons and also because it was a threat to the small-property owning society that had emerged in Ireland since the Land War. A curious blend of Catholicism, nationalism and authoritarian socialism did develop in the minds of some of the separatists. Nationalism of the integral kind espoused by so many of them demanded the subordination of the individual to the group and, perhaps, the sacrifice of the individual to the group. One of the reasons for the rabid anti-intellectualism of many separatists was the instinctive recognition that the natural individualism of the intellectual made him a threat to the collectivist and conformist ethos which nationalists wished to foster and, if necessary, impose. Ironically, the separatists were intellectuals themselves; anti-intellectualism is itself an intellectual posture, one perhaps associated sometimes with a traditional Catholic distrust of human reason because of a shrewd sense of its limitations.

Elaborated systems of political ideas were unattractive to the separatists for these structural reasons rather than for the often touted reasons of provincial isolation or ignorance; these sets of ideas appeared 'not to work', to be irrelevant or to be undesirable. The ideologies were available, but were rejected. Catholic social thought made inroads, but perhaps more important was a retreat to history that was often of startling intensity. History, often impersonated by pseudo-history, offered itself as a functional equivalent of political ideology; one might hate one's real or imaginary past, but real or imaginary it has its uses. The separatists therefore developed the habit of looking to historical precedent as a source of lessons for the present and also as a means of legitimising the courses of action that they had decided upon. As A.J.P. Taylor has remarked, the lesson of history is that there are no lessons of history; historicism therefore can be thought of as the ultimate ideology of the pragmatist.

Irish historical consciousness was in great part folklore: experienced rather than learned. In many cases it was derived from the collective memories of communities or extended families rooted in particular country areas. Family history and genealogy were vividly present in people's minds and often had an immediacy which is nowadays perhaps difficult to imagine. The MacSwineys, living in poverty in Cork, had a collective history or pseudo-history of their family; they believed the family to have been of medieval Norse origin and to have come to Muskerry, west Cork in the fourteenth century. Their land had been taken from them by a 'Cromwellian trooper named Swete. The MAC SWINEYS never travelled far from their ancestral home, preferring, like so many other Irish chieftains, to remain as tillers of their native soil than to leave it altogether.'[4]

Kathleen Keyes McDonnell, in an informative memoir describing the mentality of Catholic middle-class and farm society in the Bandon area in this period, recollected:

> It is essential to know the historic background of the Elizabethan settlement of Bandon in order to appreciate the impact of the Easter Rising of 1916 on an alien community [of Protestants], and so to understand why, after more than three centuries after the foundation of Bandon, the descendants of the settlers fled before Irish wrath or fell to rebel bullets.[5]

Family memories often spanned a century or more. The length of these memories may have been increased by the 'long generation' effect of the abnormally late age of marriage in the post-Famine era. Michael Collins's father, for instance, was seventy-five when Michael was born in 1890; presumably he was born in the year of Waterloo. Michael had vivid pseudo-memories of the Famine years, and probably very immediate folk memories of 1798. Collective memories of this kind were admittedly selective and often confused, but sometimes surprisingly detailed and accurate. The history of Ireland and its relationships with Britain was commonly thought of as an extension of these family histories, thereby creating a direct psychological link between the individual, his family and the history of the island as an entity. The American consul at Queenstown, County Cork, reporting Irish public opinion in the south of Ireland in the wake of the 1916 Rising, was struck by this intense cultural historicism. He believed the taste for Irish history was inculcated by the priests and the schoolmasters, and was retained into adult life. The educated Catholic Irishman was 'steeped in the history of his country', and his intellectual life was centred on the contemplation of the 'distressful annals'. There was something almost religious about the Irishman's fascination with history. Furthermore, it provided a vocabulary and cultural map with which political issues could be handled without references to political theory.

The taste for Irish history which is implanted by priests and teachers in the minds of Irish children is carried forward into mature years with painstaking refinements; and hardly an intelligent Irishman is to be found, in any walk of modern Irish life, who is not steeped in the history of his country. The assimilation of the voluminous literature on ancient and medieval Ireland is almost the cardinal point in the culture [of] the better class of Irishman; and a common way for men of this type to seal a mental friendship with their fellows is by the exchange of esoteric volumes dilating upon some phase of the distressful annals.

The Irishman's daily conversance with his history affects his daily acts, just as the daily use of devotional literature affects the conduct of a religious enthusiast. The current events in Ireland can only be understood by keeping firmly in mind that the actors in these events are haunted and counselled from hour to hour by the really shocking facts of Irish history.[6]

Dreams of the future Ireland that would evolve once British rule was over commonly displayed clear evidence of a ransacking of the real and imaginary past, often combined rather comically with present-day spite. 'We lived in dreams always,' a Belfast IRB veteran remembered. They scarcely enjoyed these obsessional dreams of an Ireland 'that never existed and never could exist', of an heroic, Gaelic people utterly remote from the actual Irish people of the twentieth century.[7] Like the German anti-modernist ideologue Paul Lagarde, some of the young Irish romantic nationalists became accustomed to 'hate concretely' while attaching their love 'to an ideal object that was dead and beyond recovery'.[8]

Irish history became an ideological football and two competing accounts of the island's past evolved, one Protestant and unionist, the other Catholic and nationalist. The former tended to emphasise continuities, for example, between the medieval Celtic Church, with its remoteness from Rome, and the modern reformed versions of Christianity; the latter similarly asserted a continuity between the suffering Gaelic and Christian people of Norman Ireland and the equally down-trodden Catholic population of post-Reformation Ireland. At times, the illusion was given that each community lived in different Irelands, with very dissimilar histories.

The vivid visions of the glorious past also served as models of a future Ireland; a kind of folk-Platonism gripped the minds of many of the separatists; Protestant history was denied, as was much of modern thought. However, the separatists were divided about this, and some were irritated by the anti-modernism and impractical daydreams of their comrades. Griffith's people, with their self-conscious modernism, particularly disliked this habit of mind. After all, Griffith himself was scarcely typical of the separatists. He was not very taken by linguistic revivalism and was certainly sceptical about the idea of basing the new Ireland on rural society. He wanted an industrialised Ireland, built up behind tariff barriers; he even contemplated Ireland getting her place in the sun, in the form of African colonies. A common and perhaps accurate criticism of Griffith was that what he really wanted was not a resurgent Gaelic Ireland, but *Sacsa nua dara' ainm Éire* (a new England called Ireland) or a Gaelic Manchester. In 1903 Griffith's paper, the *United Irishman*, complained about the widespread habit of disparaging modern thought and of keeping one's eyes firmly fixed on the Middle Ages.

Furthermore, this practice of praising the past and running down modernity was carried on by clever young men who knew quite well that it was nonsense. Although the paper did not say so, it seems likely that it was speaking of the young nationalists who were trying to curry favour with the priests by aping their ideology. The paper insisted that Ireland should look out at the modern world and try to learn from it. Nationalist political thought was deeply divided on the question of modernisation, the priests by and large disliking it while the laymen were rather attracted to it.

The *United Irishman* remarked:

This cocky disparagement of the work of modern thinkers is characteristic of the shoddy side of the Irish revival. According to this gospel we are to keep our eyes fixed on the Middle Ages—and then wonder we are decaying . . . The world outside has been thinking and growing, Ireland preserves her picturesque ignorance —which her smart young men, who know better themselves, tell her is more sacred than the wisdom of an infidel world—and Ireland emigrates. We require the breath of free thought in Ireland.[9]

The dreamed future was sometimes represented with heroic unselfconsciousness as just a dream. The Gaelic League's annual jamborees were seen rather pathetically as parliaments of an emergent Gaelic Ireland. The neo-Gaelic fantasy was often quite elaborate. In 1906, for example, one *Gaeilgeoir* dreamed fluently of a League Ard-Fheis of the year 2006. By then, Ireland would have been long rid of British tyranny and English culture. It would have been both re-gaelicised and modernised. The bogs would have been drained and the reforestation of the island would have had the incidental effect of raising the general temperature several degrees, thus improving the climate mightily. Dublin was visualised as having been transformed into a Gaelic Paris: open-air cafés, tree-lined boulevards and no public houses. A neo-Gaelic kingship, with *Árd-Rí* and *Fo-Ríochta*, was going strong, and an august assembly known as Dáil Éireann solemnly governed the growing multitudes of Irish speakers in the new Ireland. Because of the conquest of England by Russia during the Great War, English had become reduced to being the vernacular of a few Somerset peasants. In Ireland, of course, Irish was the main language, and the Dáil was seriously debating the introduction of Japanese as a second language in port areas for commercial reasons.[10] As late as 1919, proposals for a neo-feudal Gaelic polity were offered, usually by clerics. More commonly, the fantasy of an Irish-speaking Ireland which was also modern, mechanised and internationally revered was offered, English being a little-known foreign language while the Gaelic-speaking young were amused by the rather foreign-sounding Gaelic of their parents, raised under the English regime or soon afterward.

A more common theme was a fairly practical blending of tradition and modernity. The *Leader*, for example, was quite willing to contemplate a partitioning of the island into Protestant and Catholic sectors on the basis of not being prepared to coerce the unwilling or the culturally and ideologically indigestible Protestant inhabitants of eastern Ulster. The paper was also prepared to be associated with rather untraditionalist proposals for the urbanisation and industrialisation of Ireland, which were combined, however, with a stabilised rural society that had a modernised agriculture. Sinn Féin similarly came out with practical proposals for the modernisation of the civil service and the encouragement of business enterprise.[11] The grip of neo-medievalism was emotional rather than rational; neo-medievalism and Gaelic revivalism were essentially clerical, Gaelic League and schoolmaster in origin and were covertly regarded as well-meant nonsense. The rejection of the present and the concomitant retreat into nostalgic and futurist fantasies were related, as elsewhere in Europe, to inter-generational tensions. Father–son conflicts were a major literary theme everywhere in Europe during the last decade of the nineteenth century.[12] In novels and plays, the figure of the rebellious and vaguely ambitious son who sees possibilities beyond his father's imaginings were universal; the son rejects the orthodoxies of Victorian civilisation in favour of a romantic individualism, an imagined medievalism, a nationalism or a new Christianity. Certainly, this theme is very noticeable in the extraordinary Irish literature of this generation. The Playboy of the Western World,

Christie Mahon, proudly claims to have killed his Da; Stephen Daedalus will succeed where his father, the old Parnellite, failed; Yeats creatively reacts into mysticism against the scientism and rationalism of his father.

Nostalgia and futurism as ideological themes reflected a conflict of generations among political activists as well. The revolutionary generation had had to oust the older men to get control of the IRB after 1900. In Cork, 'the old men who had been in the Fenian organisation lived mostly in the past . . .' and resented the pushy young men with their activist and extremist demands. The generational tension was greatest among the ambitious young. The unambitious and the poor quietly accepted the provincial, Anglicising Ireland in which they lived. Liam de Roiste, a Cork schoolmaster and early separatist, remembered his own contempt for those of his own generation who were not of the ultra-nationalist set; 'to young men of the mind of Terence MacSwiney the Irish nation had sunk very low'.[13] Much incidental evidence indicates a strong element of generational tension during the entire period in which the revolutionary generation made their ascent to power; they achieved this power, after all, as very young men. By 1918 sons in rural areas were reportedly intimidating their fathers into voting for Sinn Féin by threatening not to work for them on their farms if they voted the wrong way.[14] In the run-up to the 'Pact' election of 1922, the local IRA appears at times to have been a collective tyranny of the young men over the old men: 'I can prove that the IRA are using the authority of their officers to compel the members to do against their will what they would not otherwise do . . . Responsible and highly placed officers of the IRA have informed me that they will not permit their fathers etc. to vote in the coming elections.'[15]

In a well-known description of Munster IRA leaders, Sir Henry Lawson characterised them as being mainly farmers' sons, some of them schoolmasters and fairly well educated by the standards of the place and the time. They were ignorant of the world, but extremely sincere, single minded, idealistic and religious. They possessed 'an almost mystical sense of duty to their country'.[16] Generational tensions were often very great in farm families, particularly as the rules of inheritance favoured the father and only one son as against other sons. The shutting down of the safety valve of American emigration after 1914 aggravated a tension that had always been there. One observer noted in 1916 that although it had been anticipated that the land settlement would make the farmers and their sons into 'contented slaves', in fact they were as good or better, from the separatist viewpoint, as ever they had been. It was 'the son of the well-to-do farmer' who was often the best nationalist, while 'the poor of any class are not self-respecting and often drunkards and hence are not good Nationalists'.[17]

The youth-versus-age phenomenon was not confined to the agrarian sector but was visible among some of the Anglo-Irish, was generally visible among middle-class Catholics and was conspicuous among the Catholic clergy. The temperamental differences between young and older clergy had been noted by many different observers in the decade before the war. In 1914 the same activist (Patrick McCartan) wrote: 'The young priests are as a rule all O.K. You would be surprised.'[18] The division in the clergy became greater during the war, however. By the time of the conscription crisis of 1918, the curates were 'everywhere out of control' and the students at Maynooth were openly Sinn Féin politically. The police described them as openly applauding or hissing the bishops according to their political views.[19] The Galway RIC described the priests in that area as having been let off the bishop's leash; they had been covertly sympathetic to Sinn Féin, but once the bishops came out against conscription, the young priests had 'thrown off all restraint and indulged in the most extreme Sinn Féin propaganda, utilising their position as priests to push their political positions'.[20]

This generational cleavage was related to the great social changes that were occurring in European society generally and divided the 'Generation of 1914' from its elders all over the Continent. The recent past was rejected, and sentimentalised versions of the past were constructed and proposed as blueprints for a better future than that offered by modern commercial civilisation. In Ireland, the future was perhaps rather more nakedly envisaged as a return to a mythical Golden Age of the past, but the same cultural syndrome of nostalgia and futurism operated. In a moment of genuine self-insight, the

Leader noted in 1904, before the nationalist hysteria had grown too strong for such calm observation, 'Perhaps the greatest of all difficulties which underlie the whole of what is known as the Irish Revival is the length of time we are obliged to go back before we arrive at any mode of life that may with truth be termed distinctively Irish.'[21]

In one European country after another, youth came to be seen as a superior state, in reaction to the crumbling ascendancy of age that had been traditional. Youth came to be associated with cultural renewal. In opposition to the older correlation of age with wisdom, age came to be associated with weakness and degeneration, and with a society stereotyped as materialistic and crass, war came to be seen as a cleansing thing; young intellectuals and upwardly mobile brain-workers sometimes noisily bewailed their fate of having been born into a selfish and hateful society and felt that with the Great War that was expected a new moral sense of common purpose would develop, and eventually a new, more ethical, social type, based on a sentimentalised version of themselves, would gain ascendancy at the expense of both the bourgeois and the proletarian, both seen as morally and culturally inferior.[22]

Hysteria was a common feature of this generational conflict. Women, escaping from the purdah-like seclusion enforced upon them by Victorian society, have commonly been described as being attracted to political hysteria; however, the counter-examples of hysteria among men like Pearse in the 1913–16 period, or de Valera and many others in 1922, offer impressive counter-factual evidence. Both sexes were prone to it. As noted earlier, hysterical messianism was often evident, in the form of visions of a heroic leader coming from the people to lead them into the promised land. It seems likely that many of the young men who took part in the insurrection had, at least in the backs of their minds, notions of being such a militarised saviour.

Some of this hysteria appears to have been related to a general retrogression into primitivism, again by no means confined to Ireland; similar phenomena was occurring in all the warring nations. In 1915, for example, the *Catholic Bulletin* actually seriously reexamined the prophecies of St Malachy, an early nineteenth-century forgery which prophesied the eventual defeat of British power in Ireland.[23] Incidentally, the Fenians had encouraged the spread of the prophecies in the hope that they would get the peasantry of the 1860s to join an insurrection.

POLITICS

The separatist tradition was carried by people who were excluded from political power. They therefore were never required to test their political ideas in the practical, everyday world, and a rather pathological divorce between political dreams and a low-grade, unambitious empiricism developed in the political sub-culture of separatism. Even pragmatic minds like those of Griffith and Collins tended to be infected by the impulse to retreat to political dream worlds. The political thought of those who were in the separatist tradition must therefore be assessed in the light of the fact that it was the political thought of people trying to overcome the handicaps of inadequate and narrow educations and their condition of political impotence. The fact that they were often energetic and intelligent sometimes merely had the unfortunate effect of rendering their political projects more extravagant than they might otherwise have been.

The Fenian tradition was republican, and separatists usually imagined an independent Ireland as having republican institutions. The neo-Gaelic and neo-medieval fantasies of Gaelic Leaguers and some clerics never quite dislodged the image of the Irish Republic, although some 'republicans' were, like Pearse, content to contemplate some sort of constitutional monarchy as long as the Irish state was genuinely independent. In 1862 John Pigot, a Fenian publicist, had written a constitution for an independent Irish Republic, and versions of his ideas remained current in the fantasy world of Irish underground separatism generations later. Pigot envisaged a modernised Ireland, with a strong army and navy; the Fenians were keen on sea power, and Irish-American Fenians were later to construct the first serious military submarine, the idea being to attack British commerce and military shipping on the high seas. The machine was later to generate far more interest in Germany than in either Britain and America; it could be argued that the

Fenians were the begetters of the U-boat. Pigot envisaged that the new independent Irish Republic would have an alliance with either France or the United States and would control the western approaches. He proposed a rather Bonapartist constitution, heavily influenced by French and American models. This involved a directly elected lower chamber and a president-for-life elected by the upper chamber. Presumably the presidency was tailored with James Stephens in mind. Executive and legislature were to be separate both legally and physically, the legislature to be located in Athlone, an undistinguished garrison town in the centre of the island, and the executive in Limerick, a decayed western port that looks out at the United States. Dublin, the eastern centre of British power in Ireland, was not considered suitable as the capital of a free Ireland. As we have seen, the theme of hatred of Dublin was to recur. The rather striking modernism and 'French' character of the document was exemplified in particular by its proposal of universal, secret manhood suffrage and the proposed abolition of the four traditional provinces of Ireland in favour of a larger number of administrative units with non-traditional geographical designations. There was considerable emphasis on a strong military and naval establishment. Control over education was almost casually conceded to the various churches.[24]

Versions of these ideas surfaced regularly in IRB literature. Among the separatists, the IRB men appear to have been the only ones to have given serious consideration to the kinds of political institutions an independent Ireland would require. That sort of thing was often left to Irish Party lawyers or even to British civil servants; the political institutions of the present-day Irish Republic owe as much to the series of Home Rule Bills produced between 1885 and 1920 as to Fenian political thought. In 1911 *Irish Freedom* ran an interesting series on the constitutional forms which an independent Ireland might adopt. The pseudonymous writer ('Lucan') remarked that his personal preference would be for twenty years of military dictatorship by an 'Irish Cromwell', a man with 'patriotism, fanaticism, single-mindedness and clear hard courage'. Failing a new Lord Protector, a democratic republic was to be preferred, with tolerance for religions, free compulsory education, democratic representative institutions and universal suffrage. However, university graduates, professional men, politicians, officers and businessmen would be entitled to extra votes. A national militia was to be preferred to a conscript standing army. Parliament would have two houses, the lower house sitting for six years and being elected by the population, the upper house being elected for three years by the possessors of multiple votes.[25] Military service was to be universal and obligatory, the coinage would be decimal and both English and Irish would be recognised languages.[26]

Other writers, most notably John. J. Horgan, a well-known Cork parliamentarian, contributed articles on this topic. Horgan proposed many institutions that actually materialised, in particular proportional representation, a modernist idea that appears to have had an immediate attraction. Horgan also made a plea for a second chamber which would have the special function of protecting minority rights, a proposal that was given concrete form in 1922.[27]

Electoral democracy, then, was generally accepted as the form which the politics of independent Ireland would take. However, there was a noticeable hankering after the cult of the leader. Such a hankering was natural in a country which had had much of its political development dominated by two charismatic leaders, O'Connell in the pre-Famine period and Parnell in the post-Famine period. Furthermore, the violence of the years between 1914 and 1923 encouraged a political authoritarianism among many separatists, which was sometimes to congeal later into a hostility to democracy. Certainly, the people's wishes as expressed at election times were not always taken as authentic expressions of Irish aspirations. The contempt for the Irish Party, the perception of the Irish people as corrupt and enslaved and the cult of militarised youth aggravated tendencies toward political and moral elitism among many separatists and IRA. Even the wave of popular support for Sinn Féin in 1918 did not eradicate this tendency among the revolutionaries. The more purist IRA leaders adopted a rather robust attitude toward the elections of 1918–23. One Limerick IRA leader (Jerry Ryan) recalled: 'There were no free elections. In the 1918 elections I was on the run and I organised the transport to vote. I told the Redmondites not to go to the polling booths and they did not go. The people did swing around [from Redmondism to separatism in 1918], but they swung back.'

Ernie O'Malley noted that Ryan had been long accustomed to impersonation and 'voting the dead' and supposed that no electoral figures for these years were really reliable; 'Mick [Leahy of Tipperary IRA] had no respect for elections as a test'. In 1922–23, the IRA attitude to elections was to become obvious.[28]

A noticeable theme in the writings of separatists and clerical ideologues was the desire to devise a 'middle way' between the political economies of capitalism and socialism. Ernest Blythe, writing in 1913, proposed a 'cooperative commonwealth', evidently inspired by Belloc's 'Servile State'. 'Anarchic' free enterprise capitalism would not be permitted; as agriculture was 'the mother of all industry', no stable economic system could endure that was not based on agriculture. No big industrial trusts and no big trade unions should be permitted. Rather, property rights and voting control over the productive process should be spread as widely as possible among the population. Instead of the adversarial relationship of labour and capital, a harmonious, democratised political economy would develop and soften the distinction between labour and capital by combining both principles in each citizen of the commonwealth.[29]

These ideas, inspired by Belloc's distributivism and by the papal encyclicals of the period, were further elaborated by clerical writers, most notably perhaps Father P. Coffey of Maynooth. In a well-written series of articles written for the *Catholic Bulletin* in 1920, he offered an elaborate critique of the now-martyred James Connolly's 'campaign against capitalism'. Coffey agreed with Connolly that capitalism was evil, but for rather different reasons than the exploitation emphasised by Marxists. Capitalism's real evil consisted in the fact that it had the effect of making the ownership of property impossible for the vast bulk of mankind. Capitalism had the effect of splitting society into haves and have-nots. This conventional Marxist analysis of the dynamics of capitalism was followed by the very un-Marxist proposition that state socialism was evil too, as it subordinated the individual to the state. Coffey suggested an attempt to spread ownership widely among the workers and bending of financial institutions to the purposes of a co-operative commonwealth.[30] These ideas, which were to remain current until the 1960s, were in part echoes of the Catholic social thought of the period, but they were also echoes of the success of the co-operative mechanism in Irish agriculture, particularly in Munster, in the previous two decades. More remotely, they seem to have fit in well with the communalist ethos of so much of Irish political culture of the time. In particular, fear of the disruptive impact of big capital and big labour united right and left in the ranks of nationalism. Both big capital and big labour, after all, appeared to be British inventions.

In sum, if the neo-Gaelic fantasies of some writers are disregarded, the independent Ireland envisaged was to be petty-bourgeois and democratic, with as many safeguards against the dual menaces of capital and labour as possible. The ideology was essentially centrist. In its extreme forms, it resembled fascism. Fascism was also a centrist ideology, appealing in particular to middle strata feeling threatened by the top and the bottom of capitalist society; unlike democratic centrist ideologies, of course, it rejected electoralism and substituted cults of heroism, elitism and scapegoatism. The extreme and fundamentalist wing of Irish separatism was reminiscent of fascism in that it contained moral elitism and also xenophobic and anti-Semitic themes. Maud Gonne was extremely anti-Semitic, as were J.J. O'Kelly and J.J. Walsh. Arthur Griffith was mildly anti-Semitic, but pro-Zionist. Anti-Semitism does not seem to have been a predictor of nationalist fundamentalism; Gonne and Kelly were anti-Treaty in 1922, whereas Griffith and Walsh supported it. Walsh lived to be pro-Axis in 1939–45, and was sufficiently ill informed as to anticipate a partial Japanese victory as late as the end of 1943.[31] Gonne had been the mistress of a well-known extreme-right wing French nationalist leader in her youth. Her perception of England as a plutocratic, Jewish-dominated empire of oppression was combined with a noisy Irish nationalism and with the fervent Catholicism of the convert. She became a member of the Third Order of St Francis. She later sympathised with Italian fascism and German Nazism, but did object to the Nazis' male chauvinism. She also believed in witchcraft.[32] Her main hatred was of England, and much of her Anglophobia was originally shaped by the ideas of her French right-wing comrades. The rulers of England were imagined by her to be very evil and gifted with an almost supernatural cunning; England's cunning diplomats and 'Jewish allies' were responsible for Ireland's ills in 1899. John MacBride's notorious drinking habits were the result of the machinations of English secret agents.[33] England's unforgivable sin, however, was to be urban and modern and to have increasingly little place for a traditional aristocracy or gentry. London and the other great cities were great wens.

England is in decadence. The men who formerly made her greatness, the men from the country districts, have disappeared, they have been swallowed up by the great black manufacturing cities; they have been flung into the crucible where gold is made. Today the giants of England are the giants of finance and the Stock Exchange, who have risen to power on the backs of a struggling mass of pale, exhausted slaves.[34]

To be fair, Gonne was not a representative figure; she was one of those curious English or half-English radical figures who feel impelled to adopt Ireland. She was, however, conspicuous at an early stage in the movement and helped to set a certain tone of proto-fascist rant. The native pragmatism and unintellectualism of the bulk of Sinn Féin were adequate to sufficiently damp down themes of this kind to make the movement palatable enough for some Irish Jews. It remains true to say that an ascetic and pseudo-aristocratic revulsion from commercialised and vulgar modern society, of a kind commonly seen in fascism, was common among nationalists. Significantly, these themes do not correlate with attitudes to the Treaty of 1921 or with attitudes to democracy; the Treaty issue split rightists from rightists, leftists from leftists, democrats from democrats and élitists from élitists.

None of this was peculiar to Ireland. Once again, Irish radicals were exhibiting ideological syndromes similar to those elsewhere. Discussing Georges Sorel, Isaiah Berlin has remarked:

There is an anti-intellectual and anti-Enlightenment stream in the European radical tradition, at times allied with populism, nationalism or neo-mediaevalism, that goes back to Rousseau, Herder and Fichte, and enters agrarian, anarchist, anti-Semitic and other anti-liberal movements, creating anomalous combinations, sometimes in open opposition to, sometimes in an uneasy alliance with, the various currents of socialist and revolutionary thought.[35]

The incoherence of Irish ideological positions can be related to the fact that their holders had only two political languages which they could use and which they were familiar with. These were British democratic liberalism and international Catholicism. All Irish radicals had to enter into an 'uneasy alliance' with one or the other, or even devise a synthesis of both, as one of the cleverer, Eamon de Valera, eventually did. Liberalism and Catholicism made it difficult for people to articulate fascist or Marxist ideas, as these were not on the culture's 'agenda'. In this the Irish were very British.

The enduring difficulty Irish political analysts have had in trying to distinguish Irish leftism from Irish rightism has its roots in this situation. As all groups, with the exception of Griffith's little cabal, had a horror of English society in common, whether that horror was derived from romantic anti-commercialism, clerical moral puritanism or Marxist anti-imperialism, the normal stereotypes of left and right became apparently irrelevant. Many who started on the far left ended up rather far to the right. All they had in common was radicalism. Their discontent hid the fact that ideologically they covered the entire spectrum.

The Irish-American leftist, J.T. Farrell, visiting Ireland in the late 1930s, met many of the IRA veterans, particularly from its diehard wing. He was startled to note the way in which nationalist, Catholic, fascist and socialist ideas could run together in their minds. Their politics, he felt, was a class-derived emotionalism rather than an organised set of political ideas.

The Old IRA men explained that they did not want Farrell to get the impression that the Abbey crowd was Ireland. They told him that the only Irish writer they liked at all was James Joyce, even though Joyce had repudiated everything they stood for. They saw in Joyce a man of lower middle-class origins like themselves, whose feelings and responses to all sorts of things were like theirs. In this sense he was their writer. Farrell was again keenly interested in the politics of these soldiers. He found them, like many Irishmen he had met, curiously insular and eccentric in their political attitudes, with good words for Mussolini as well as for Stalin, paradoxically favouring totalitarianisms of the right and the left.

Similar mixtures existed on the left; James Larkin was a Catholic communist, believing in a familialist ideology and refusing to appear on the same platform as an American socialist leader on the grounds that he was divorced.[36] Admittedly, this was a politic decision to take in the Ireland of the time.

CLERICALISM, ANTI-CLERICALISM AND INHIBITED SECULARISM

Many of these ideological syndromes we have been looking at derived, of course, from the fact that in Ireland modern democracy and modern political ideas had to come to terms with a uniquely popular Catholicism. To find parallels, one might perhaps have to go to eastern Europe or even to the Muslim world. In the metropolitan, west European Catholic countries, anti-Catholicism or anti-clericalism were almost inevitable concomitants of radical or revolutionary ideology, given the rigid anti-radical stance adopted by the Church since the mid-nineteenth century. Even the great influence of the Catholic liberal democratic tradition represented by Daniel O'Connell failed to quiet the unease of the clergy when faced with the spread of ideas among the population which were not controlled by them and which were sometimes hostile to their beliefs or interests. However, the Catholic population of Ireland appears to have internalised a version of the Church's distrust of radicalism early on. Those who wonder at the poor showing of labourism and socialism in the democratic politics of post–1922 Ireland should contemplate the fate of the English romantic figure William Morris, who visited Dublin in the mid-1880s and gave a lecture at a vaguely Fenian workmen's club in Dublin's north side. He told them of the damage unbridled capitalism was doing to the artisanal culture in both islands, and mourned the death of artistic and craft traditions.

> When Morris had finished, a local orator rose up—an artisan also, but there are exceptions everywhere—and began to declaim the most commonplace theories of militant socialism. Instantly he was hooted . . . Another working man rose up . . . Socialism meant Atheism, and Atheism meant blasphemy; and if the English people took up Socialism, so much the worse for them; but he wished to God Mr. Morris . . . would keep these revolutionary ideas for his own side of the Channel and not come here to disturb a decent quiet country with them.[37]

James Connolly and other socialists found that they had to drastically tailor their ideas to placate the Catholic tradition, and even then had little success in penetrating the minds of many people. Instead, odd syntheses of Catholicism and socialism emerged, sometimes combined, as in the case of Peadar O'Donnell, with a set of attitudes best described as a fusion of liberalism, Stalinism, Irish nationalism and populism.

All nationalists had to come to terms with the Church, and they did so in an interesting variety of ways, from complete clericalism, sometimes combined with a more-Catholic-than-the-Pope psychology on the one hand to a covertly anti-clerical secularism on the other. J.J. O'Kelly announced in 1917 his complete acceptance of Catholic teaching, even in defiance of his own understanding, a common enough position.[38] In a correspondence with a liberal Protestant clergyman in the 1920s, Mary MacSwiney displayed an incapacity to imagine a secular political world beyond the sacred world ruled by the Pope. When asked by a Church of Ireland clergyman of liberal opinion about the proposed prohibition on divorce legislation, she replied:

> With reference to the frank statement that, since Ireland is a predominantly Catholic country no anti-Catholic legislation can be provided for, you ask 'who is to judge what is Anti-Catholic?' Surely the answer is obvious:—anything that is

inconsistent with the laws and teaching of the One, Holy, Catholic and Apostolic Church, of which the divinely appointed Visible Head is the Pope of Rome.[39]

Because of the peculiar half-ally, half-competitor relationship between priests and patriots, a full-blown nationalist anti-clericalism was scarcely possible, although a supine clericalism was. What did develop was a deep and often unadmitted dividedness as to the role of the clergy in political life and a tendency to handle such issues secretively. The typical Catholic separatist had to decide for himself the limits beyond which he would not tolerate clerical intervention in political life, and choose between medieval and modern answers to that question. Mary MacSwiney and Terence MacSwiney seem to have accepted the finality of clerical judge-ments. On the other hand, P.S. O'Hegarty, in a 1904 letter cited earlier, rebuked Terence for failing to draw a line between ethics and politics. Pointing out to Terence that the Gaelic League was more respectable than they, the IRB, were and therefore more attractive to the clergy, he continued:

I don't hold that the priests are our natural enemies but I do think strongly that they have acquired the habit and that nothing but strong determined actions will break them of it. They ruined every movement—directly or indirectly—since the passing of the Maynooth Grant in *1795* and we have to put them in their places if we are going to do anything ... Most of the fellows here [in the London IRB] are anti-cleric to a greater or lesser degree ... It is only when a man leaves Ireland that he begins to see straight on some things, this among them.[40]

In another letter in the same year, O'Hegarty expanded his atti-tude to the priest in politics, in response to some pieties transmitted to him by Terence from Cork.

You appear to assume that anti-clericalism is atheism, which it is not. Anti-clericalism, as I look at it and as most fellows I know look at it, is simply anti-political-priest-ism ... If you say a word against the political priest, against any political action or dogma of his, you are an atheist, a damned soul, you are anathema, and you know that as well as I. You may do the magnanimous and try to distinguish between the priest and the Church but he won't let you, he deliberately and immorally utilises his priestly influence to supplement the want of reason in his attitude.[41]

A current of mild anti-clericalism ran through much of the separatist movement. This anti-clericalism was not the systematic, secularist anti-clericalism of continental ideologues but rather a belief that the priests were failing in their duty by not supporting purist republicanism wholeheartedly. Many separatists appear to have regarded themselves as more Catholic than the Pope, or certainly more Catholic than many of his local representatives. Republican hostility became aimed at the secular clergy and, in particular, at the bishops after the split of 1922, when the episcopacy strongly supported the moderates and opposed republican fundamentalism. Many dissident priests, and in particular many Capuchins and Franciscans, continued to support republicanism covertly, in line with the radical traditions of these orders everywhere in Europe.

Even the anti-secularist piety of Mary MacSwiney, for example, did not prevent her from having a ferocious public row with the bishop of Cork in the 1920s. Between the priests and the clericalist wing of the laity there existed a curious egalitarian relationship, almost as though the priests and the lay clericalists were rivals rather than allies. The tension between nationalist extremism, whether nominally clericalist or anti-clericalist, and the institutionalised Catholic Church in Ireland was very great, a tension that extended through the structures of the Church itself; after all, many priests shared separatist sentiments, while many lay separatists, while often disliking clerical interference in politics, shared much of their anti-capitalist and almost anti-modernist ideology.

It should be remembered that even to make the usual analytical distinction between laity and clergy and apply it to Catholic culture of the period in Ireland is to run the risk of making a distinction that is only partly valid. Priests were held in very high regard, and probably most Catholics were closely related to clergy; certainly, many of the leaders had intimate friendships with priests, and it was very common for political activists to take ethical or political advice from the clergy. Even W.P. Ryan's *Irish Peasant*, later renamed *Irish Nation*, which peddled a mixture of socialism, agrarianism, neo-Gaelicism and secularism and which had attracted the aggressive and effective hostility of Cardinal Logue and other clerics, appears often to have expressed views with which many clerical ideologues agreed. Father Coffey's espousal of democracy was cited approvingly by it in 1906, for example. Its main complaint was directed less at the priests than at the bishops; the Church's 'obscurantism' appears to have consisted mainly of its secret hostility to the revival of Irish.[42] The *Irish Peasant/Irish Nation* represented a kind of peasant-centred radicalism hostile to big property, combined with Gaelic revivalism and a hatred of modern English society. This ideology was fairly summarised in a piece written by 'Eoin' on 26 June 1909, in an issue which denounced episcopal hostility to the revival. In essence, the bishops were being indirectly accused of not being sufficiently sensitive to the immorality of capitalist and Anglicised society.

> I should like to see Ireland peopled with a really national and cultured race. It cannot become so while present-day civilisation endures. That civilisation is simply refined barbarism. It contains nothing bright or noble, nothing artistic or divine—for the overwhelming bulk of the people. It is unjust, vicious, immoral and unnatural ... cultured or not, a vein of animalism runs through the Englishman—from the highest to the lowest—that borders on savagery. Capitalism has begotten this state of affairs.[43]

This analysis could be Canon Sheehan's, but it could also be Herbert Marcuse's. Differences between lay separatists and clergy tended to be derived from political competition with each other, the laymen claiming a larger share of local political power than many of the local clergy, kings in their little parishes, were willing to concede. McCartan wrote from Tyrone in 1912:

> The greatest obstacle to the progress of [extreme] nationalism is undoubtedly the Catholic Church or more correctly the Bishops and priests of Ireland. Now I'm not an anti-cleric but probably on the way to becoming one so don't imagine I see phantoms. It is bitter reality. You may be a better Catholic than the Pope but if you differ from your P[arish] P[riest] who neither thinks nor reads but boasts that he will not read you become a subject for a 'sermon'.[44]

Only the more recent graduates of Maynooth had taken up the ideology of the Gaelic League and Canon Sheehan, he reported. He thought that the older ones had a deep distrust of political radicals and even of ideas. However, the general population was becoming restless and available for great political endeavour. There was some hostility to the clergy in the public mood, he felt. His complaints against the clergy could have been the classic covert grumbles of a frustrated village schoolmaster complaining in the back snug about the arbitrary habits of his clerical manager; he was actually a country doctor.

> The people are naturally rebelling and there is a rumbling murmur all over the country. One objects to [the clergy] pitching their relations into positions with a religious fork; another because they openly or secretly oppose the Irish language and Irish games; another because they build churches and never give accounts of receipts and expenditures; another because they suddenly become enthusiastic U[nited] I[rish] Leaguers in order to stay the progress of Sinn Féin.[45]

The Catholic bishops were in a tricky position. Separatism threatened the not uncomfortable arrangements that the Church and the British government had worked out over the years. John Redmond felt that the Catholic bishops actually feared a Dominion settlement because a native Irish government would never tolerate the enormous patronage enjoyed by the Church under the Westminster government, thereby echoing an old judgement of George Bernard Shaw.[46] Eventually, Sinn Féin, led by inexperienced, young

and very Catholic men, made enormous concessions to the Church
in the educational field in particular so as to get its support.[47] It could
perhaps be argued that once the conscription crisis had pushed the
bishops into the Sinn Féin camp, such concessions were unnecessary.
However, the concessions were probably given out of conscientious
conviction rather than out of political opportunism.

ECONOMICS

The stereotype of English capitalism distorting Irish economic
development dominated the nationalists' thoughts on political
economy, a stereotype with very good foundations in the experience
of the Irish economy in the nineteenth century and in the historically
often expressed English wish to convert Ireland into a monocrop
cattle ranch for metropolitan England. The fact that most of Ireland
had no comparative advantage in the United Kingdom economy,
except in the sphere of growing cattle on grassland, sinisterly echoed
the seventeenth-century recommendation of Petty that Ireland
become populated by 200,000 ranch hands; a large version of the
Falkland Islands. Griffith, of course, was fascinated by Listian
economics and proposed that an independent Ireland would be
able to erect tariff barriers against goods from outside and engage
in what might now be described as import substitution, creating
a balanced and diversified economy, with both agricultural and
industrial sectors, behind the tariff walls. Opinions among the
nationalists as to whether an independent Ireland should concentrate on agriculture or industry differed; Griffith was an almost
Stalinist industrialist, while Blythe, as we have seen, was almost a
physiocrat in his belief that only agriculture-based industry created
real wealth. Underlying much of what passed for economic
theorising appears to have been the exaggerated faith of the
politically powerless in the efficacy of state action, a belief that is
noticeable among many different types of political radical because
of a lack of real political experience. Soviet statism, for example,
derives in part from the fact that the Soviet Union was founded by
men who had lusted after state power from afar all their lives and
had been excluded from it completely. Similarly, American
coolness toward the merits of the strong and unified state was in

part caused by the long experience of quasi-democratic self-government which the American colonies had had before independence in 1776. The Irish rebels were good at agitational politics and conspiracy, but knew nothing about real government. They fondly imagined that the independent Irish state that was to be born would solve problems of culture, and even problems of human nature; economic problems would be easy. Unfortunately, they had a subconscious assumption that an independent Irish state would have the kinds of capabilities which they witnessed in the British imperial state; the full implications of Irish independence did not impinge upon them, and they did not understand that the weaknesses of Irish society and economy would be reflected in the structure and performance of any state that emerged in Ireland.

A second determinant of their economic thinking was an essentially moralistic cast of mind, derived from a religious formation that denigrated individualism and the 'cash nexus' in favour of a rather strenuous ethic of self-sacrifice for the community, often conceptualised as a large family. Even Griffith's paper denounced the evils of the English-style factory system and dreamed in Wellsian terms of technological revolutions that would make such developments unnecessary in Ireland. In 1899 it prophesied that technology would permit the 'domestic system' to compete with the factory system, that it would be possible to reconcile production with village life, that there could be many little industries scattered across the country rather than having the satanic mills all concentrated in one overpopulated industrial slum. Motor transport and the road would break the monopoly of the railway barons.[48]

However, Griffith was deeply sensitive to the importance of economic thought and aware of its absence in any organised form among the separatists. In 1909 *Sinn Féin* insisted that the new Irish university system should have, above all, three faculties: Irish Studies, Economics and Commerce, and Agriculture. It also remarked that snobbery would endanger the creation of these evidently essential centres of study. In the same year, it published a cartoon depicting Ireland armed with a sword entitled 'Irish Language' and a shield in the form of the *Déanta in Éirinn* (Made in Ireland) stamp which could be affixed to Irish-made products;

moral rearmament, Gaelic League-style, and economic progress were seen as going together.[49] Griffith's paper, although often seen as the organ of the emergent Irish bourgeoisie, was quite capable of the usual ferocious denunciations of capitalism, occasionally seen as a Jewish creation.[50]

Socialism was disliked and occasionally feared, but there was a general confidence that the people would be unlikely to be attracted to socialist nostrums. In 1901 the *Leader* pointed out the evident foolishness of socialist theories and deftly connected them with England; Irish people were too shrewd about human nature to believe that socialist theories could ever work. They would never be impressed by 'any of the socialist dreams that attract so many minds on the Continent, in England and America. We doubt if there is a native Socialist born in Ireland; and the few third-rate hangers-on to the skirts of some cheap school of Socialism that may exist here and there are, at bottom, only victims of Anglicisation.'[51]

Horace Plunkett noticed the near-hostility of many priests to economic priorities, and it appears that it was this cast of mind, transmitted to laymen, that encouraged an economic thought that was really a branch of ethics rather than a social science.[52] The nearest they came to economic thought was to preach the virtues of co-operation in rural areas, on the lines pioneered by Plunkett. As we have seen, the idea of a distributivist and co-operativist commonwealth had considerable appeal to the clerics, schoolmasters and minor civil servants who dominated the movement intellectually.

Another obsession was reforestation. Ireland had been denuded of her trees in the eighteenth century and by 1900 had one of the lowest proportions of tree-covered land in Europe. Much of the tree-felling occurred in the eighteenth century to provide grazing land, fuel, pit-props for English mines and timber for the Royal Navy. Again, the real desire for reforestation was rooted in aesthetics and restorationism rather than in economic calculation. Gaelic poets in the eighteenth century had eloquently lamented the cutting down of the forests as symbolising the end of the Gaelic and Catholic order in Ireland. To grow forests would be a very impressive physical symbol of the undoing of the conquest and an effective answer to the eighteenth-century poet who had asked so plaintively, '*Cad a dhéanfaimid feasta gan adhmaid?*' ('What will we do henceforth without timber?').

The *Catholic Bulletin* commonly saw economics as essentially a means of stabilising rural society. It proposed the abolition of public houses, in part so as to foster a work ethic and to prevent people wasting money on drink, the stabilising of the labourer population by granting each labourer three acres and a cow and the introduction of pensions for farmers so as to increase the attractions of rural life and encourage early retirement.[53] Economic effort was culturally determined and popular literature was destroying what work ethic there was in Irish culture.[54] Catholics had little experience of business and even had a snobbish distaste for it, preferring the professions or public service.[55] Later, the *Bulletin* evolved a critique of both capitalism and socialism, coming down in favour of a 'middle way'.

Most of the nationalists saw economic progress as a psychological problem. They agreed, in effect, with thinkers in the Max Weber tradition who saw economic endeavour as connected less with market opportunities than with ethical formation as performed by the great world religions. Irish Catholics would have to learn a version of the Protestant work ethic, which would involve their learning self-respect and throwing off slavish and derivative habits.

It was also widely believed that Ireland had far too many parasitical elements and far too few truly productive workers, on whose backs the former rode. In 1899, the *United Irishman* clearly announced on whom it counted for support: the Plain People of Ireland, who were to have a very long innings in Irish politics in the twentieth century as a political concept, particularly when democracy became established after 1922.

We have for too long submitted to have matters Irish elbowed out of their rightful place. From the English element and their hangers-on we look for nothing. They could not give it, for they haven't sufficient confidence in their own brains to risk offending their masters; but we do look to the shopkeepers and workers of all grades, skilled and unskilled, who are the real people of Ireland, to see that their sympathies are at least considered, and that as much as possible of their money shall be spent in Ireland on subjects that we can take an interest in, because they are our own.[56]

In 1901, the *Leader* published a self-portrait of a true Irish worker of the new era; he lived in a provincial town in the south of Ireland on £1 a week. He had five children, a wife and two parents to support. His rent was 3s. 8d. a week, and insurance and charities cost a further 1s. 6d. Thus he has 12s. to 14s. a week to live on, had no entertainments and had never been in Dublin. He was a Catholic, a confraternity member and a proud Gaelic Leaguer.[57]

Usury in country areas was a common target, particularly of the more radical elements among the patriots. The local gombeen-man, or usurer, was a stock figure of social criticism; he was also easy to associate with the local Irish Party or Hibernian machine against which Sinn Féin and its allies were pitted. Again, the critique was a moral rather than an economic one in the formal sense; gombeenism was just one more facet of the parasitical character of those who possessed political and social power in Ireland. In 1911 George Russell portrayed the politics of the western areas as being dominated by publicans and usurers:

. . . swollen gombeenmen straddling across whole parishes, sucking up like a sponge all the wealth in the district, ruling everything, presiding over county councils, rural councils, boards of guardians, and placing their relatives in every position which their public functions allow them to interfere with . . . They are publicans, and their friends are all strong drinkers . . . All the local appointments are in their gift, and hence you get drunken doctors, drunken rate collectors, drunken J.P.s, drunken inspectors—in fact around the gombeen system reels the whole drunken congested world, and underneath this revelry and jobbery the unfortunate peasant labours and gets no return for his labour.[58]

A puritan, prohibitionist, neo-Gaelic, popular cultural revolution was the first essential development; economic progress would scarcely be possible without it, but would be inevitable once it had succeeded. Self-sufficiency, buying only Irish goods and hard work would solve economic problems eventually. Unless men's characters were improved, Ireland would remain in the state of spiritual paralysis which both Sinn Féin and James Joyce believed she was in. The cultural revolution had to come first, political and economic transformation would follow; this was the doctrine the Gaelic League transmitted to the new generation of political leaders. A new, self-disciplined and altogether more serious type of personality would have to evolve in Ireland to replace both the stage-Irishman and the easy-going, inefficient and sometimes hard-drinking peasant or worker of Victorian times. Ireland was going to modernise, and psychic modernisation came before economic modernisation; it also came before political modernisation.

EQUALITY

James Connolly, a somewhat isolated and unrepresentative figure among the revolutionaries, has had the effect of making the ideologies of the revolution appear retrospectively more egalitarian than they actually were. The fluency and occasional brilliance of Connolly's writings, combined with the new fashion for socialist ideas that emerged in the 1960s, have intensified this effect, as has the refraction of his ideas in Pearse's later writings.[59] Because both men became martyrs, they have been held to be representative; in fact, both were to the left of the movement, and it would be difficult to say which was the further away from its centre of gravity, although in very different directions. Their prestige was so great that a mildly socialist flavour was given to the Democratic Programme of the first Dáil in 1919.

The concept of equality was usually subordinated to the concept of the people, formed into a nation. The nation, of course, was conceived as having a continuity with the Gaelic past; in Pearse's version, it was the suffering Irish nation that had endured great privations but had not succumbed. Again, in Pearse's eyes, the nation was seen as a collective Christ; it should be remembered

that Pearse's version was idiosyncratic.[60] Other adherents of the
theory of continuity entertained a less pseudo-religious version of
it. Even then, however, an unconscious historicism gripped their
minds. Eoin MacNeill, a fine scholar with a genuinely scientific
mind, never seems to have questioned the Gaelic League view that
the true Ireland was the Gaelic Ireland. J.T. Farrell noticed that by
the late 1930s a 'wall of silence' had arisen around the more
egalitarian writings of the revolutionary tradition, in particular the
writings of Connolly, Lalor and Davitt. Catholicism and neo-
Gaelicism had drowned egalitarianism.[61] In large part, this is an
example of the optical illusion I have referred to; the egalitarian
thread in the revolutionaries' thought was not socialist, but was
anti-aristocratic and favoured equality of opportunity rather than
a general levelling. Society in British Ireland was unequal in part
because of the large disparities of wealth between rich and poor
but also because the routes from rags to riches were few and often
blocked. Upward mobility rather than redistribution of wealth
dominated the minds of the revolutionaries, who thought in terms
of establishing the rule of a new Catholic middle and skilled
working class, which would then, no doubt, rule the poor in a benign
and moral fashion. Some seem to have been scarcely democrats;
there is a Whiggish flavour in *Irish Freedom's* constitutional proposals, for instance.

The obsession with Anglo-Irish and English disdain is a symptom
of this status resentment that was discussed earlier. Some years
after the event, on the subject of the spread of Gaelic football into the
towns in the 1880s, the *United Irishman* reminisced that many
drapers' assistants had attempted to join rugby clubs and found
themselves slighted; the Cork Drapers' affiliation cheque was
returned by the Irish Rugby Union. Hence the attraction of Gaelic
football. 'The drapers of Cork resented the insult; they sternly resent
it to the present day . . .'[62] The paper recounted the alleged reaction of
an English rugby team brought over to Dublin to play Trinity College
in 1904, when asked by the president of Blackrock College to play a
game: 'Haw! Haw! you dahn't know, dahn't you that we only play
Varsity men?' Blackrock was advised to take up the unsnobbish and
national Gaelic game of hurling. The college, incidentally, did not

take this advice, and has always had an excellent rugby tradition. Eamon de Valera played rugby there as a schoolboy.[63]

This thin-skinned fear of being disdained was sometimes justified in reality. Disdain did not always come from the Anglo-Irish or English upper classes but sometimes even from upper-crust Irish-Americans, not always completely impressed by their transatlantic cousins. John Quinn, the New York art collector and sympathiser with Irish nationalist causes, grew increasingly disillusioned with the separatists. His disillusion started with his perception of Dublin as a cultural desert, despite the literary revival supported only by a dedicated minority. In 1908 he noted: 'The Dublin people are mainly Whigs and Tories without any appreciation of arts and with unlimited conceit.'[64] Some months later he remarked:

> Unsuccessful people, it seems to me, seem to need and require soft cushions to repose gently upon and at the same time keep their self-esteem. Too many of our Irish friends are too fond of quoting the great achievements of the Irish in the past—the Book of Kells, the Missionaries, St. Patrick, and so on—as a sort of implied excuse for inefficiency in the present.[65]

By 1912 he was complaining to Yeats that visitors from Ireland appeared to have in common a loutish propensity to kick his furniture.[66]

Egalitarianism was meritocratic rather than socialistic, and *la carrière ouverte aux talents* the ideal. A certain hostility to the idea of a truly democratic polity existed in many quarters. *Irish Freedom* proposed in 1913 that the principles of nationality and democracy were actually opposed; rebuking Seán O'Casey and other socialists who supported a free Ireland only if it were to be materially better off, its contributor announced himself not to be a democrat, and trusted that a free Ireland would not be 'ruled and dominated by a Triumvirate composed of the artisan, the mechanic, and the peasant'. He trusted that a generalised aristocracy would survive the transition to independence.[67]

The state that emerged in the 1922–37 period reflected many of these values. Paradoxically, it has been held to betray the values of the Irish revolution because it failed to fully reflect the ideology of Pearse, let alone of Connolly. As I have suggested, these two conspicuous thinkers have mistakenly been assumed to express views shared by the bulk of the revolutionary leadership. In fact, it was more conservative than either, and that is perhaps why Pearse's progressivism in so many matters appeared strangely contemporary even in the 1980s. As Joseph Lee has argued, Pearse was a moderniser, particularly in his professional field of education, and was so despite the archaism of his nationalism. However, he was far too advanced even for the majority of the separatists, and his educational theories were remote from the beliefs and ambitions of most Irish people. Education was not a means of intellectual or even spiritual self-realisation. Rather, it was a means of 'getting on', particularly if you were a young man of some ability, energy and little capital. That was the real Irish idea of equality.[68]

07 | THE IDEOLOGY OF DEFEAT: THE MIND OF REPUBLICANISM AFTER 1922

THE DELEGITIMISING OF BRITISH RULE

The Irish revolution had its climax in the years after 1912. The illegal arming of Ulster Protestants with considerable establishment connivance to resist Home Rule made it clear to many that the regime itself was not bound by its own laws. The perception that the government was not acting even-handedly was very widespread and delivered much of the population, at least temporarily, into the hands of militant separatism. People who were lukewarm about the project of independence and cared rather little about cultural revival increasingly came to see the government as remote, unfeeling and bullying. They came to share the views of the extreme nationalists to some extent at least, views that would have been regarded as somewhat eccentric a few years earlier. The 1916 Rising had mobilising effects on the population; it was a very successful example of the propaganda of the deed, but the Home Rule crisis of 1912 had started the process. The decision to impose conscription in 1918 was merely the final straw that impelled a naturally conservative society into revolution. The American consul in Cork prophesied guerrilla warfare as early as 10 May 1918:

I cannot give you a short account of the feeling in this county [Kerry] over the conscription proposals, except that we are on the verge of an insurrection. Nine-tenths of the people say our guns are taken from us, and house-searches are made for these, while in Lord Londonderry's home there are stacks of Orange rifles, and other Ulster Orangemen are allowed to keep their guns and ammunition. We have fought constitutionally for a generation for Home Rule and won it only to find that a small minority, less than 17% of the manhood of Ireland, were able, because of their religion, to veto an Act of Parliament. As far as Irish Catholics are concerned, they must still be ruled by the ascendancy and have their rights denied them. Pearse and the other Dublin 'Rebels' are shot, Carson and other Orange rebels are made ministers of the Crown . . .[1]

The British authorities agreed that, despite intimidation, the wave of support for Sinn Féin and even the IRA in 1918–19 was genuine and quite broadly based. Somewhat later, a reluctantly respectful British military intelligence estimated that 90 per cent of the population were Sinn Féin and supporters of 'murder'.

Judged by English standards the Irish are a difficult and unsatis-factory people. Their civilisation is different and in many ways lower than that of the English. They are entirely lacking in the Englishman's distinctive respect for the truth and their answers are usually coloured by a desire to say what their questioner wishes. Many were of a degenerate type and their methods of making war were in most cases barbarous, influenced by hatred and devoid of courage.[2]

However, it was admitted that the IRA could scarcely have sur-vived by fighting conventionally, and the curious admission was made that the leadership was idealistic and consisted of 'serious young men' who had undigested political ideas. They were sober, incorruptible, humourless and 'quite determined not to accept any facts which do not square with their preconceived ideas and theories'.[3] This mixture of contempt and admiration is visible in the reactions of many British observers to the separatist movement.

These were, of course, years of war and revolution all over Europe. Pre–1914 Europe was in many ways an *ancien régime*, which the war finally brought down, in the west as surely as in the east. France was the only major European state to have achieved stable representative democratic government, and even there the forces of throne and altar, ensconced in the Church and the army, were fighting an effective rearguard action against secularisation and the expansion of the state into fields such as education. Imperial Germany was run by an entrenched oligarchy based on land, the army, the bureaucracy and co-opted elements of big business; the Kaiser habitually referred to the Reichstag as the 'Chatterbox'. Even in the United Kingdom, the franchise was still property based up to 1918 and quite restrictive. The oligarchic distribution of power in society was only beginning to be challenged seriously. Ireland, at the periphery of the Kingdom, was internally non-democratic, despite the existence of electoral institutions.[4] Everywhere in the Kingdom, class distinctions had an intensity which is now inconceivable, and it was possible to minutely 'place' most people in the British Isles by accent and dress. Religious prejudices were not just Irish survivals; they retained much of their old power in Britain also. Ireland suffered from extreme versions of these class and caste tensions: 'Ireland to me is a sad, wet, empty country—a country of frustrated natives and detached, patronising, smart, unsympathetic English people'.[5]

The compromise settlement of 1922 was doomed to be seen as a defeat by some; even a thirty-two-county republic would have been a disappointment to those who imagined a culturally authentic, neo-Gaelic commonwealth. A twenty-six-county British Dominion looked intolerably mean and anti-climactic; Ireland was doomed to go through a post-revolutionary ideological hangover, a hangover that was abnormally prolonged by the extraordinary political longevity of the revolutionary élite, many of whom still dominated the democratic politics of the Irish Republic as late as the early 1960s.

THE SPLIT OF 1922

The British offer of a cease fire and negotiation came in mid-1921; coercion by police and military had turned Ireland into a battleground and a major political embarrassment. The unity of the separatist movement, made up of such a variety of tendencies, had always been rather fragile and, ironically, dependent on British pressure. The Truce immediately threatened the solidarity of the movement. The proposed Treaty underwrote the partition of the island, disestablished the underground Republic of 1919 and substituted for it a Dominion-status Irish Free State within the British Commonwealth and Empire that appeared to be far less independent that it really was. Most galling of all to the purists, sensitive to questions of personal honour, the Free State constitution was to require an oath of fidelity to the British monarch in his capacity as head of the Commonwealth. The oath was meaningless, but not obviously so; as a symbol, it repelled many in a culture where symbols meant much. The split in the movement that gradually developed in the year after the cease fire was between those who accepted, for whatever motives, that a messy and not very noble compromise was inevitable and those who felt that they were bound by their oaths to the 1919 Republic. This concern with personal honour and with one's word being sacred once given had several sources. Ironically, one of them appears to have been an aping of English gentlemanly ethics; another was the concern of many Irish Catholic priests with words, a concern which was that of a canon lawyer. Words were weapons to be used against the strong, but could also be turned against oneself, and to break one's sworn word was not only dishonourable, it was to throw away the only weapon the weak had against the strong.

The fact that the Treaty was a political revolution and that it marked the final political defeat of Anglo-Ireland was scarcely understood by some. The electorate repeatedly gave the settlement huge majorities in 1922 and 1923 in the general elections. There was some correlation between social class and support for the Treaty, with employers, big farmers and many urban middle- and working-class people supporting it, while other workers, small farmers and inhabitants of more remote areas opposed it. At the level of the élite itself, however, there was little obvious correspondence between class origin and position on the issue of the Treaty.

The split that destroyed the movement took place slowly and reluctantly; the memory of the Parnell split was vivid, and many of the leaders feared the bitterness of a new one. They did not have the constraint of having to calculate electoral advantage as yet because they did not yet understand that electoral competition for the votes of the general population was the process by which political power was going to be allocated; mentally, they were still pre-democratic. Splits were dreaded, but disloyalty was a cardinal political sin in the secret societies of the nineteenth century, and fundamentally it was disloyalty which each side imputed to the other. The pragmatist who supported the Treaty accused the fundamentalists who opposed it of 'holier-than-thou' attitudinising, of a lack of realism, of hysteria and irresponsibility. Underneath these accusations lay a belief that the fundamentalists were indulging their emotions at the expense of the community, a subtle form of disloyalty. The purists, of course, accused the pragmatists of disloyalty to the Republic of 1919, but also, interestingly, revealed something of their own social uncertainties by accusing them of careerism, power-mania and snobbery.

The personal hatreds and distrusts that surfaced among the leaders in 1921–22 cast a revealing light on the tensions which had been inside the separatist movement and had lain buried for four years. Sir Neville Macready cynically observed that he was not at all surprised that the Treaty was disliked by many in the Dáil, as it promised peace. Many TDs were IRA leaders to whom the prospect of peace was distinctly unwelcome, as it meant that they would have to work for a living for a change.[6] A senior Anglo-Irish civil servant (Mark Sturgis), who had been an observer of the movement from the not altogether suitable vantage point of Dublin Castle, felt that the division was between the 'ruffians' and the 'decent part of the party'.[7] He acutely noted that the real problem that Sinn Féin faced was not their natural distrust of the British but their intense distrust of each other.[8] The American political scientist Warner Moss, writing in the 1930s, argued that those whose experience had been on the administrative side of the movement had developed an awareness of, and perhaps an appetite for, government and 'running things', while the younger people, the women and the guerrillas 'on the ground' had increasingly come to define the struggle as a war with little political aspect.[9]

The purists developed a conspiracy theory about the split, one that still survives in republic folklore. It was essentially believed that Collins had been seduced by the bright lights of London and the flattery of the British aristocracy; absurdly, offers of marriage to a royal were alleged. In turn, Collins and his lieutenants had used the secret network of the IRB to cajole, bribe and bully TDs and IRA leaders to support the Treaty. Almost certainly, Collins signed the Treaty in good faith, but the purists needed an equivalent of the Nazi *Dolchstosslegende*, a myth of the victorious IRA foully betrayed in mid-fight by internal betrayal and the preternatural cunning and corruption of the British establishment. A *Dolchstosslegende* was reassuring to the purists, as they could at least feel morally superior to their venal, if victorious, opponents.[10] O'Malley felt that Collins and his allies were intellectually and morally inferior to the more 'spiritual' martyrs of 1916. Certainly, it is clear that Collins sent O'Duffy and other lieutenants around the country to 'turn' local key men in the IRA by argument and by offering them jobs in the new state's army, police and administration.[11] Local priests were pressed into service as advocates of the settlement, and the press was generally noisily in favour. A figure we have already seen fixing committees, Seán Ó Muirthile (John Hurley from west Cork), went around the south persuading people to accept something less than a republic. A Tipperary veteran recalled: 'Probably O Muirthile was doing the buying then offering jobs and paving the way to get men around to his point of view. I suppose that must have been his job. Always he got hold of the money: a soft kind of a man he was, like Joe MacGrath.'[12]

However, serious argument rather than simple bribery was also used. Jerry Ryan, from Horse and Jockey in Tipperary, remembered Collins and Gearóid O'Sullivan pleading with IRA leaders at Beggar's Bush barracks in Dublin during the Truce: '"Do you think I'm not as good a Republican as Liam Lynch or Liam Deasy. My idea is that if we can get our own army we can tell the British to go to hell," shaking his lock of hair.'[13]

Collins was desperate not to end up in Arthur Griffith's pocket and to bring the IRA leaders with him into the Free State. He argued on prudential grounds as well, telling the IRA leaders: 'If ye drive me into that oul' bollocks's hands ye'll pay for it.'[14] They did; it is clear that there was a general acceptance of the Anglo-Irish Treaty of December 1921 among the population, and that many local IRA commanders were swayed one way or the other by genuine political conviction. In some cases, the old Fenian idea of handing on the flame of separatism to another generation by going down in glorious defeat operated on their minds. The public accepted the Free State with relief and without enthusiasm.

A statistical analysis of the vote in the Dáil strongly suggests that the division was indeed one between administrators, who were pro-Treaty, and local guerrilla leaders, who were against. It should be recalled, and often it is not, that the second Dáil was not a normal, democratically elected assembly. The second Dáil, regarded by purists such as the spokesmen of the Provisional IRA as the second and last rightful democratic parliament in modern Ireland and only legitimate successor to the first Dáil of 1919, was not a body that had been elected by the population, and was remote from that population in various ways. Furthermore, it knew it. The second Dáil was elected *en bloc* in 1921, and nearly all of its members had been elected unopposed in conditions of guerrilla war. The TDs were actually selected by a small caucus centred on Collins and consisting of Diarmuid O'Hegarty, a fellow west Corkman, and Harry Boland, member of a well-known Dublin Fenian family. The selection was tantamount to nomination, which was, in the circumstances, tantamount in turn to election; the selection itself was made from lists of proposed candidates sent up from the constituencies by local Sinn Féin branches, often controlled by the local IRA; the nomination was commonly in gift of the local IRA leader.[15]

Of 124 TDs, eighty-four were born or reared outside of a large city or town, and of that eighty-four about half were of small-town origin and half were rural. While perhaps not wildly cosmopolitan, the deputies were more so than the general Sinn Féin élite analysed earlier, and far more so than the general population of Ireland. They were also somewhat older, and only six of them were women. A quarter had reported occupations in the higher professions and a further fifth in the lower professions. A further fifth were small businessmen and very few were farmers. However, of sixty-five sets of parents traced, just over half had been engaged in farming and a further quarter in business, usually small scale, or shop-keeping. The same picture emerges of a rising political class of rural and small-town petty-bourgeois origin, itself becoming more urban and educated.

Many of the TDs had lived for some considerable time outside Ireland; two-thirds had been 'out' in 1916, an experience that was to become almost an essential qualification for high political office in post-independence Ireland. Three-quarters had had some elementary political experience, usually in local government or in the tribunals and land courts of the underground Republic. One-quarter appear to have had only guerrilla experience: the 'gunmen'. The deputies were 94 per cent Catholic. Seventeen were from Cork, a number almost equal to Dublin's contribution. One-third had at least some third-level education, while an unknown, but considerable, proportion had left school very early, a fact that was often concealed; many local IRA leaders were very poorly educated. The Dáil was, in fact, characterised by a very wide *range* of educational levels, much like other revolutionary assemblies. The deputies were, like the rest of the élite, typically both horizontally and vertically mobile, being of better social status and more urbanised than their parents.

This was the assembly that was to ratify the Anglo-Irish Treaty and which was, by that vote, to split nationalist Ireland from top to bottom with a decisiveness which dwarfed the split after the fall of Parnell. The bitterness of that split is scarcely dead two generations later, and it was the foundation of independent Ireland's party system. The best predictor of the vote, statistically speaking, was sex: all six women voted against the Treaty. Several of the women had little political existence of their own, being connections of male figures in the movement or the relicts of martyrs. One of them made a very clear statement of her ideology in the debate in the Dáil on the Treaty. Her view of women in politics appeared to be that their significance was that they could mother or espouse male martyrs. An appropriate term for the ideology would be madonnaism, a role for women modelled on the role of the Virgin Mary and her relationships with Christ, as taught to girls in Catholic schools of the period.

When it was found that the women Deputies of An Dáil were not open to canvass, the matter was dismissed with the remark: 'Oh, naturally, the women are very bitter.' Well now, I protest against that. No woman in this Dáil is going to give her vote because she is warped by a deep personal loss. The women of Ireland so far have not appeared much on the political stage. That does not mean that they have no deep convictions about Ireland's status and freedom. It was the mother of the Pearses who made them what they were. The sister of Terence Mac Swiney influenced her brother and is now carrying on his life's work. Deputy Mrs. Clarke, the widow of Tom Clarke, was bred in the Fenian household of her uncle, John Daly of Limerick.[16]

Religion also correlated with the vote, as did birth outside Ireland; in classical marginal style, Protestants and the foreign-born were more inclined to fundamentalism. The mechanism is easily visualisable; people marginal to the ethnic group chose to join it, rather than merely finding themselves part of it by the process of being born into it, and tended to take collective values more literally. Age was not a strong predictor, but there was a slight tendency for older leaders to favour the settlement. Education was a strong predictor, but its effect was only visible at third level; graduates were far more likely to be pro-Treaty, but those with completed second-level education were no more likely to be pro-Treaty than those with only primary education. Higher professionals were slightly more likely to favour the settlement than were lower professionals, as were shopkeepers and farmers. In true aristocratic radical style, those few leaders who were of opulent family background were more likely to oppose the settlement; perhaps if one is rich in Ireland one is socially marginal. Those deputies who had lived outside Ireland tended rather to favour the Treaty.

Intriguing as the effects of these socio-economic variables are, they are inconsequential compared with the apparent effects of those variables which measure political experience. Veterans of the 1916 Rising were more likely to favour the Treaty than were non-veterans, and this effect was strong and independent of age. In part this was an effect of Cork's 'missing the bus' in 1916, which encouraged the Cork IRA to overcompensate in 1922.[17] It also echoes the old senior IRB's support of the Treaty. Region was important, Munster and the western IRA being more hostile to the settlement. Those whose experience had been administrative rather than military were, as already suggested, more likely to see merit in the Treaty, and the guerrilla–administrator dichotomy overlapped with the Munster-versus-the-rest opposition. Many 'gunmen'—nearly half—were actually pro-Treaty; length, rather than exact character, of an individual's experience in the move-ment appears to have been the crucial variable, and 'insiders' rather than late-comers were more likely to favour compromise with the British.

The small group of pre-1914 republicans who had survived politically tended disproportionately to favour the Treaty; the extremists of 1912 supported the Thermidor of 1922. Of known IRB men in the Dáil, two-thirds supported the Treaty. It should be recalled that one-third opposed, and that many intensely uncom-promising leaders had left the secret society previously, thereby abandoning the organisation to Collins and the compromisers. It should also be recalled that there was a strong anti-insurrectionist tradition in the IRB; the 1916 Rising had been engineered by a secret cabal inside the secret society against the general wishes of that society. The IRB's ideology contained a doctrine of popular consultation that Pearse and company had rejected, mainly on the grounds that the population was too corrupt or sunk in apathy to heed the message of national destiny which the cabal had for it.

Generally, those with technical skill in law, finance, business or 'running things' were far more likely to refuse to accept the funda-mentalist argument, as were those who held key administrative positions in the movement. Of twenty-six TDs who held key administrative positions in the Dáil government or the movement outside the cabinet, two-thirds were pro-Treaty (the Treaty was ratified by a bare majority). It is unknown whether many TDs were secret agents of the British, and this information has either been destroyed or will be locked up in the London Public Record Office for a century or more after the event. It was claimed in British military circles that one TD who had been an agent at some stage voted against the Treaty. Presumably we will discover who he was (if he existed) in 2062. Even at that late date, the news may be controversial.[18] In general the anti-Treaty vote reflected a back-bench revolt or, to use a possibly more appropriate military image, a mutiny of army middle ranks against the general staff and civilian authorities, abetted by a minority among those authorities.

The split spread rapidly down through the movement and out into the country from Dublin. Munster and north Connacht IRA leaders opposed the settlement, but a key set of leaders in north-west Munster and south Connacht, centring on the strategic fulcrum of Limerick, were 'turned' for the Treaty by Collins, O'Duffy and Ó Muirthile, with the assistance of local rivalries. The Dublin IRA split and Ulster tried to stay aloof, but tended to favour the settlement. The anti-Treatyites tended to be younger, and it was the southern and western sections of the old IRA which were to become the main heirs to the republican tradition outside Catholic Ulster. Defeated decisively in 1923, within ten years they were to come to power democratically under de Valera and were to dominate Irish politics for the following half-century. They were, in turn, to be challenged by a newer and even more uncompromising IRA tradition which disagreed with them more on matters of means than of ends. The mentality of this defeated group has in many ways dominated most radical nationalist politics in Ireland and even Irish-America ever since.

REPUBLICANISM IN DEFEAT

It is naturally impossible to reconstruct the mental state of an entire movement sixty years after the event. In this section it is intended to document certain aspects of republican mentality after the split and the civil war which appear to have had permanent effects on the belief systems of many republicans in both the majority, or constitutionalist, tradition and the minority, or physical force, tradition.

The *Dolchstosslegende* dominated republican folklore. However, a noticeable ideological theme of republicanism was a covert but persistent perception of the political unworthiness of the Irish people. By 1923 the original movement was quite dead, its purist wing defeated and its pragmatic wing ensconced in power over most of Ireland as the government of the new Irish Free State. The Free Staters won the 1923 election handily and proceeded to demobilise their huge army and to release IRA prisoners into a cold and unwelcoming world. The anti-Treatyites were badly split themselves; many IRA soldiers, though disliking the Treaty, had had little stomach for civil war and had opted out, often expressing their sentiment practically by emigrating to the United States. The bulk came tacitly to accept Free State democracy under de Valera's leadership in the late 1920s, without ever admitting aloud that this was what they were doing. As Fianna Fáil, they formed a government in 1932 and developed an uneasy, but enduring, middle position between fundamentalists and Free Staters. In the mid-1920s, the purists themselves split into the new IRA on the one hand and a small and shrinking group of second Dáil anti-Treaty TDs on the other who continued to regard themselves as the rightful government of all of Ireland.

All republicans, including those Free State republicans who had accepted the Treaty in the hope that it would eventually lead to a republic, were caught in a philosophical dilemma, which they attempted to resolve in different ways. The separatist movement was democratic in theory and was also dedicated to a programme of national cultural renewal. It was evident that most people were at best only mildly sympathetic to purist republicanism's nostrums. People regarded the purists rather as they regarded the Gaelic League: with bemusement and with the belief that they probably meant well. These perceptions were also sometimes accompanied by the fear which the non-fanatic has of the fanatic. It could be argued that only one-quarter of the population of the island was actually separatist, one-quarter being unionist. The remaining half were mildly nationalist, but not emotionally caught up in nationalism. Few wanted social revolution, and few were interested in the Irish language. One could say that this non-moral majority were the true Sinn Féiners; they wished to be left alone by both British and Irish political forces. Anti-Treatyite leaders commonly coped intellectually with the extreme moderation of the Irish electorate by portraying the population as intimidated and brainwashed by the British, the newspapers, the Free State and the clergy. However, it soon became evident that militant republicanism was still, as it always had been, the creed of a minority, although a large and intense minority in a population which had a vague and lukewarm sympathy with republicanism but was far more interested in a quiet life.[19] One of the many ironic effects of partition was to render this minority a larger proportion of the population, and far more important politically, than it would have been in an all-Ireland state.

A common response of extreme republicans to this faithlessness of the majority was an almost Nietzschean contempt for that majority, typically concealed under an aggressively nationalist majoritarian rhetoric. During the Anglo-Irish War, this attitude was common among local IRA leaders and among their British opposite numbers as well. Both military forces came to see the population as an inert and unorganised mass with little real will of its own, to be pushed about and moulded by organised political forces external to itself. In the view of General Macready, commander of the British forces, the rebels had grabbed the levers of local social power and, in a country like Ireland with little civic spirit, the people would submit themselves to those who controlled those levers. Ireland could only be governed by secrecy, intimidation and intrigue, because the Irish were not fit for democratic government. The government of Ireland would inevitably have to be an affair of spying and intimidation being used to counter intimidation and spying. The Sinn Féin police had usurped the RIC as enforcers of local order in most of small-town and rural Ireland by taking over the RIC's network of local informers.

> Sinn Féin, in my opinion has gained ground from the point of view of obtaining more adherents throughout the country, either from fear or conviction. Nearly every day one sees in the papers that the S[inn] F[ein] Police are able to round up malefactors where the RIC are powerless, and that of course is merely because the S[inn] F[ein] have now at their disposal the very men who formerly were used by the RIC to get their information, that is, the loafers and hangers-about in the various towns and villages.

Long before this business broke out, I heard that the main sources of police information in this country since the Secret Service was abolished in 1906 were the corner boys and loafers and such like, who gave information to the police, and indeed acted as their jackals. This class have now [1920] placed themselves entirely at the disposal of S[inn] F[ein].[20]

IRA leaders had similarly unsentimental pictures of the dynamics of Irish 'public opinion'. After all, like their British opponents, they aspired to soldierly status and shared the usual soldiers' contempt for civilians, slackers and pacifists. The British and IRA pictures of the population coincided. After the Truce, British and Irish soldiers were to meet and often be surprised by finding a mutual respect and liking. Neither had much time for civilian politicians, whether it were Griffith or Lloyd George.

A Tipperary IRA leader privately recalled that the real effect of the 'shooting war' that was sparked off by the ambush at Solohead Beg, County Tipperary in 1919 had been the intimidation of informers and of civilians generally, rather than the breaking of British power.

The RIC were at sea when they pimped and pried yet could not gather scraps of news through their ordinary sources in pubs or fairs, or by talking to men who had met men who came in from the country; or by talking to pub owners. The once prolific sources of talk-supply were drying up. In Tipp due to Solohead the people were warned and afraid of talking and so they kept their minds to themselves and their neighbours. As a result the South Tipp people did not talk much.[21]

Local IRA chieftains had come to view the population long before the Treaty as less than totally committed to the separatist cause, and assessed their political potential coldly. After the Treaty had been signed, they were to find that covert hostility or indifference were replaced in many cases by overt opposition to them and refusal to assist as so many had done during the fight against the British. Irish fighting Irish for a point of almost theological principle interested few. One Sligo IRA leader recalled that he had relied on old men in the locality to assess the people's mettle for him. In the close-knit rural society of the period, the characters not only of individuals but also of collectivities such as families, townlands and villages were subjected to continual and shrewd assessment by the neighbours.

> Our local informants in Sligo were 100% correct also about people whom he and Duffy's father considered were no good. . . . [Máirtín Ó Braonáin] thought they were all right, but they who had the memory of the Fenian days were able to sum up the people around us. Perhaps the descendants of people whom they knew in their time to be faithless, wavering, spies detractors or no bloody good for king or country. And in the Civil War especially we found that these old men were right.[22]

The proposition that a majority of the entire population were 'no bloody good' seemed to follow naturally from the electorate's massive rejection of republicanism in 1922–23. Most republicans rather shied away from this apparent corollary because it left them in an ideological and philosophical cul-de-sac. One Donegal republican, writing to Mary MacSwiney in the mid-1920s, was actually prepared to argue in private that the population of Ireland was essentially slavish in culture, a theme which is visible in much nationalist writing over the previous few decades.

> The situation as I see it is this: 25% of the Electors are Republicans, more or less sound; 75% are venal, cowardly and ignorant—the bread-and-butter people lauded by Mrs O'Driscoll. These are people who, under compulsion of the Conscription Scare, when Redmond was selling them as conscripts, gave us the Republican majority in 1918. The problem now is how to induce a sufficient number of these people to vote so as to return Republicans as a clear majority over all parties combined—say 80 TDs. The only appeal that can be made is to their greed and fear, and if backed by another conscription scare, which seems not unlikely, it might work. It ought to be put to these people that if they will give us

a clear majority over all parties (77 to 80 TDs) our Republicans will enter the Free State Parliament, taking the oath if demanded, and having secured control of the machinery of Government will make a drastic cut in salaries and other expenditure with a corresponding reduction in taxation.[23]

In a later letter, possibly trying to rationalise the emergence of Fianna Fáil and certainly espousing a philosophy consonant with support for de Valera, he proposed that the majority of the population were slavish, as the Gaelic aristocrats had left the country in the seventeenth century, leaving the unfree clans behind after the defeat of the aristocratic Catholic cause at the Boyne: 'The unfree, on the other hand, increased and multiplied from the breaking of the clans as gombeen men traders huck-sterers etc and some of their descendants are represented by the lawyers and other professional people of the larger towns . . . it seems clear that the great majority of the supposedly Gaels are descendants of the Mogs [serfs].'[24] This possibly racist, and certainly supercilious, account of the development of Irish social culture had the comforting Leninist corollary that republicans, even though a minority, were a moral élite who had, in principle at least, the right to use any manipulation to gain power. Bitter contempt for the people was frequently mixed with a comic arrogance. Words like 'noble' and 'spiritual' were favoured adjec-tives when discussing people approved of, whereas 'slavish' and 'materialist' were descriptions of people who did not go along energetically enough with the republicans' political project. Echoes of the arrogant clerical sub-culture of the period were present in much of their political discourse.

Mary MacSwiney's correspondent offered a particularly logical statement of a political position which justified a combination of purism and manipulation. Many republicans heartily despised electoral democracy but nevertheless set out to make it work for them; many of them were to prove very good at winning elections by making promises which they frequently had little intention of fulfilling. Contempt for the people legitimised the practice of telling them anything they wished to hear. Those republicans who rejected even this Machiavellian acceptance of 'Free State democracy' and its self-righteous cynicism also tended to share this view of the population as so much raw material. The suffering and sacrifice of the republicans (suffering and sacrifice which no one had asked them to undergo) and their fidelity to the cause of Ireland gave them a moral right to rule; republican ideology, apparently populist, contained a covert elitism based on a modest assessment of the moral worth of the average citizen. There was no populist ideology of the common man, although a populist rhetoric was faked for political purposes.

The Irish people were held to have a duty to history, and that duty consisted of sacrificing themselves, indefinitely if need be, so that the fight for independence and cultural authenticity could be won. Arthur Griffith railed against this characteristic republican attitude during the Treaty debates. He recalled that he had urged the underground Dáil cabinet to negotiate with the British during the fighting. 'I was told "No! This generation might go down, but the next generation might do something or other."' Griffith asked the Dáil if the assembly's real duty was to the living generation or to history: 'Is there to be no living Irish nation? Is the Irish nation to be the dead past or the prophetic future?'[25] Arthur Griffith, founder of Sinn Féin, was no Sinn Feiner, much as Karl Marx was no Marxist; he had little Irish and was sceptical about much of the general ideological package concocted by the Gaelic League and the clerics.

The putative unworthiness of the Irish was connected with materialism, a traditional Irish Catholic bugbear. The fundamentalists feared and despised materialism and dreaded its moral and political consequences: political agnosticism and weakening of revolutionary *élan*. Their radicalism, though fervent, was abstract and moralistic. While they opposed English capitalism, they were happy to contemplate a very frugal future for the population of their imagined independent Irish Republic, ruled over by republican saints. Cultural restoration, national honour, independence and moral living were worth the price of prosperity, and many believed that that price would have to be paid. One pro-Treatyite TD noticed this association of material prosperity with political backsliding in the minds of the purists. Claiming irritatedly that the sons of rich farmers had been as patriotic as anyone else during the Tan War, he indignantly exclaimed that the notion that virtue was a monopoly of the poor was nonsense: 'you may as well say it is essential to reduce one's body to poverty to save one's soul'.[26]

Liam Mellows, since apotheosised as the leading left-wing figure in the Dáil, feared the corrosive effects material wealth might have on people's civic morality. In the Treaty debates he insisted that the Irish people would prefer poverty outside the British Empire to prosperity inside it and enthusiastically offered the idea of a poor, frugal, egalitarian, but virtuous and proud, independent republic. The old Fenian idea that striving for that ideal was itself a virtuous activity which apparently could be justified independently of its prospects of success dominated his mind: 'the victory was not everything, but to me the winning of it was everything'.[27] Mary MacSwiney denounced the pragmatists with puritan fervour: 'You, who stand for expediency, you who stand for the fleshpots, for finance, for an army, you can give in. We cannot'.[28] Sceilg reminisced twenty years later on the occasion of Mary's death:

Maire [MacSwiney] remains most vividly in my memory as she was in the fervour of the masterpiece she contributed to the debate on the 'Treaty'. As she proceeded, she first removed her hat; then, as her ardour grew, she unconsciously shed articles of apparel from her neck and shoulders until ultimately she stood somewhat as on the mortuary card.[29]

A British judge who had interviewed nearly two thousand 'Sinn Féin' activists after the 1916 Rising noticed the same mixture of revolutionary puritan Catholicism and political radicalism: some were 'really dangerous men, some of whom I am content to label as fanatics, but others as really bad characters'. Some of the 'fanatics' had the idea, he thought, of 'running Ireland as a sort of Christian Communist state'.[30]

Even on the pragmatic, 'Free State' side, many feared materialism's power to sap political purpose.[31] Money was associated with England, and the fear of materialism and modernisation was expressed as a fear and hatred of English political and cultural influence, the rhetoric being derived from the Gaelic League, the clergy and the separatist press. England was practically a source of spiritual disease; de Valera wrote in late 1922 that when the draft Treaty was published in Ireland, he had felt 'as if a plague were being introduced into the country'.[32] For the rest of his career, one of the major themes of this political discourse was to be the virtues of the frugal and familial *Gemeinschaft* culture which he associated with rural Ireland and which had been an important theme in Gaelic League ideology. Another was the creation of a psychological atmosphere in Ireland of remoteness from British opinions and concerns.

Puritanism bred an expectation of greed in others. Mutual distrust and personal ambition threatened revolutionary solidarity in Sinn Féin long before the Treaty split the leadership. Self-denial, often righteous or self-righteous, was a common response to careerist temptations, whether one's own or other people's. Asceticism is a common characteristic of the modern revolutionary leader.[33] In Ireland, the revolutionaries saw politics as a dirty game, and a game at which the British were adept, whereas the virtuous Irish were likely to be ensnared by it. One British observer remarked in February 1921:

> The disappointing thing is Distrust. They profoundly distrust the [British] Government and they distrust Carson. They fear that they will be promised something and then have it whipped away. O'Flanagan talked of Security and I said their finest security would be to have Ulster at one with them. And above all they distrust themselves. I'm sure de Valera is afraid of going to Carson because he feels no match for him.[34]

A naïve cynicism about politics and a fear of its power to corrupt made the revolutionaries draw back when actually offered some real political power by the British in 1921. Liam Mellows struck the right ascetic note when he remarked during the period of the Truce: 'I don't know what is going to happen. I don't know what Mr. de Valera may do or what anyone may do, but all my life

I have been in the wilderness and if I spend the rest of my life in the wilderness it will not hurt my feelings a bit.'

Mary MacSwiney was more direct, and believed that the pro-Treatyites had accepted bribes.[35] In this belief, she was echoing a traditional perception of British practice, a perception which had its roots in the British habit of buying the political support of Irish politicians during the previous two centuries.

In the minds of many of the leaders, the combination of self-denying asceticism and a kind of moral arrogance was explosive. Hoffer has observed unkindly that 'the vanity of the selfless, even those who practise utmost humility, is boundless'.[36] One well-placed internal observer of the Treaty split noted in a private memoir that both sides became trapped by their own vanity, which they mistook for principle: 'The truth is that neither set of leaders was big enough to sacrifice their pride for the common good'.[37] Significantly, many of the activists appear to have been attracted by the religious life in the post-revolutionary period.

OBDURACY AND THE HISTORICIST DREAM

Dublin Castle administrators noted an intense seriousness and humourlessness about the Sinn Féin leaders, combined with an obduracy which they found enraging, a fact which suggests that the obduracy was effective, as indeed it was. Mark Sturgis, an Anglo-Irish official in the Castle, bitterly complained about the stiff-necked attitude of the rebel leaders at the height of the Anglo-Irish War. Interestingly, he distanced himself ethnically from them. When the first tentative diplomatic feelers were going out between the two contending sides, he noted irritatedly: 'These Irishmen are the most approved pattern of swine and will not stretch out their hands for what is offered, the Government must come cap in hand and fill their mouths and ask them to spit it out if it's not completely to their liking.'[38]

A triumph of the will of the weak over the physical power of the strong was exactly what the rebels were trying to achieve. They compensated for their lack of great military resources by clever political propaganda, guerrilla warfare, political assassination and, above all, obduracy. By portraying themselves as a collective David facing the imperial Goliath they impressed American and even British opinion. They came to impress themselves as well. Hypertrophy of the political will was eventually to lead some of them into impossible positions. Terence MacSwiney's celebrated formula stated that victory would come to him who could endure the most suffering rather than to him who could inflict the most suffering. However, the key assumption was that the inflicter was inhibited in the amount of punishment he was prepared to hand out. The strategy also counted on the world being aware of and impressed by the suffering. In the more cynical era of the 1980s, such tactics scarcely worked; in 1920, they had some power. The cult of obduracy as a tactic of the weak against the strong was best used by people who took themselves very seriously indeed; significantly, Michael Collins, perhaps the most politically canny of the physical force wing of the movement, was perceived by the British as the rebel with the greatest sense of humour and faculty of self-criticism. Collins was also the leader the British felt they could most easily negotiate with.[39] Furthermore, he was the pro-Treatyite leader most liked and trusted by the anti-Treatyites. Many Sinn Féiners took themselves very seriously indeed, and their personalities sometimes seem reminiscent of Catholic seminarians: capable of great self-sacrifice, obsessed with moral principle, often humourless and lacking in emotional outlets. The men were often puritan in their attitude to women, and often influenced by them politically. A stream of anecdotal evidence depicts many young men being urged into intransigence by their girlfriends in 1922–23. These women, products of a society which subordinated women to men intellectually, were even more politically inexperienced than their menfolk and often less compromising. Some of the women appear to have been driven by hysteria rather than by organised political conviction.

In the Four Courts, it appears to have been the girlfriends who urged the men into intransigence at a critical juncture.[40] The anti-Treatyites were occasionally jokingly referred to as the 'Women and Childers Party'. We have already noticed the anti-Treatyism of the women TDs. The ideology appears to have been a madonnaism rather than a genuine political radicalism, as already suggested; the women were deeply Catholic in culture and were very conservative. The image of a virtuous and female Ireland being attacked by a male and menacing Britain was common Sinn Féin propaganda. Desmond FitzGerald, in a little-known letter to Gavin Arthur in January 1923 at the height of the civil war, expressed a classic Sinn Féin disappointment with the people:

> I am forced to recognise that our country is going through an hysterical crisis. The only defence I can put up is that all countries do from time to time and if ours is not as superior to the others as we thought she was, at least she is not as bad as she is depicted. And please God, when the hysteria is gone, it will be soon forgotten.[41]

As we have seen, The Sinn Féiners were historicist in their thought. The Irish nation was preferably thought of as having a long and distinguished history, possibly older than those of Greece and Rome. An impractical ability to take an extraordinarily long view was well developed, and some had an almost Spenglerian or Toynbeean capacity to envisage political action as aimed at some goal far off in time. The image of an eternal war between native and foreigner, between Gael and Gall, was an old one, with its roots in medieval tradition. It was certainly in the minds of many of the leaders, their heads stuffed with Gaelic League renditions of the polemics of previous centuries. Irish history was seen not only as going a long way back but as going a long way forward, and the political action of the present must be performed while keeping the long past and the long future in mind. On Easter Saturday 1916, John MacBride indicated that he fully understood that the rising was militarily hopeless: 'All we can do is have a scrap and send it on to the next generation.'[42] Even the pragmatists of 1922 saw the settlement as temporary; Collins referred to it as a stepping-stone, the first instalment rather than a final settlement. Many anticipated further struggle, correctly as it has turned out. Desmond FitzGerald, on being upbraided by a woman colleague for supporting the Treaty, remarked: 'The way I look at it, for our generation, we have gone far enough. Let us leave it to the next to finish it.'[43] George Russell (Æ) published an allegorical play in 1922 which portrayed the rising being re-enacted in Dublin centuries in the future.[44] On the anti-Treatyite side, a similar mentality existed. After the civil war, a Kerry republican wrote:

> The all-important thing to keep in our minds is that the recent proclamations of our President's are in no sense of the word 'surrender.' The fight is not over—and never will be until—Yes! 'Until,' but I am afraid fighting on a large scale is over for this present generation. Oh! the unhappy generation next to come. They will have to repeat '1916' and the war of the last seven years all over again. How they will curse us for not having completed the job undertaken. And God Knows, it is as likely as not that those who curse us most will be the children of the present Free Staters. We are indeed a strange people.[45]

CONTAMINATION AND THE PRESENT

As argued earlier, the determined refusal to give priority to the needs of the present was connected with a hatred of that present, which was seen as degenerate and a creation of the Ascendancy. This hatred of the recent past of Ireland, essentially an Anglo-Irish past, was expressed in many ways. Denigration of Anglo-Irish cultural effort, for example, was a way of expressing this hatred, as was setting up a cultural standard more consonant with the restrictive and puritan social ethos most of the republican élite favoured. Daniel Corkery argued for a view of Irish literature which excluded from that canon the writings of Irish-born people who appealed to foreign rather than to Irish judgement. The problem with that argument was that it left very little over to be regarded as true Irish literature except, perhaps, the rather dim and now virtually forgotten literary works of Corkery himself. Hatred of the old Ascendancy and fear of its continued influence in the cultural arena was the real thrust of Corkery's argument.[46]

A wish to destroy physical reminders of the Anglo-Irish cultural achievement was noticeable. Extreme nationalism commonly evinced a hatred of Dublin as the seat of English power in Ireland. The Fenians had dreamed of moving the capital to the west. The *United Irishman* informed its readers in 1902 that the old Gaelic 'city' of Tara had had many of the latest American conveniences, and that Anglo-Irish Dublin was really very badly planned.[47] The *Leader* carried a contribution in 1914 in which the destruction of Georgian Dublin was recommended. The great town houses of the eighteenth century were unsuited to modern purposes, and eventually the remaining great squares would degenerate into reeking slums as so many others had already. Dublin should develop modern suburbs, linked with a new modernised centre by motor car. 'Dublin, then, as we know it, must be destroyed. *Delenda est Eblana*. It seems a harsh thing to say. It rather gives one pain to write.'[48] During the troubles of 1913–23, very little loss of life occurred by the standards of twentieth-century warfare. However, it is striking how much symbolic violence against conspicuous buildings occurred. Commonly this took the form of the destruction of buildings prominently associated with the regime. Many beautiful, or at least prominent, buildings were destroyed by both British and Irish forces, but the Irish appear to have had a particular preference for the destruction of spectacular examples of Georgian architectural genius, mementoes of the British colony in Ireland during its most successful century. Eventually the Four Courts complex in Dublin was destroyed in the course of a siege of its anti-Treatyite occupiers by the new army of the Free State in 1922. The destruction of this building also involved the burning of the Public Record Office and its contents, easily the greatest single cultural loss that Ireland suffered in the twentieth century. It was watched with satisfaction by Ernie O'Malley, who watched the ashes rain down around him while he read French poetry. He imagined the records consisted mainly of accounts of payments to informers. Actually they contained the social history of his own country.[49] Harry Boland, who joined the anti-Treatyites, ranted revealingly at the beginning of the civil war:

Read Ireland's history and you will find that in all time since England first polluted our shores, there has been 'the King's Irish' and the 'Irish.' We have the same today. Lloyd George has brought [sic] half of those who made the fight for the past six years. Men who would drag Ireland into the Empire . . . The world will yet honour Ireland for her devotion to freedom, even tho' 'this' be left a smouldering heap of ruins the world shall know that there is one land that preferred death to dishonour.[50]

In a famous passage already referred to, Marx described revolutionaries as people who, to make themselves equal to the task of ushering in a new society, constructed a make-believe political world to hide from themselves the reality of what they were doing. By 1922 a large part of the separatist movement was in the grip of just such a fantasy, derived from the reconstructed Irish history which the Gaelic League and the clerical ideologues had built up. The gap between their idealised and even imaginary Ireland and the actual country around them was not one which they could easily bridge intellectually or emotionally. Coming to intellectual terms with it meant repressing emotional commitment, while retaining the emotional commitment involved suppression of the critical faculty.[51]

Certainly many appear to have been unable to come to terms with reality because they had invested so much of themselves emotionally in the vision. While Pearse and Yeats are commonly credited with inventing this vision, it is clear that it had older cultural roots; comparative studies have shown that the ideologies of peasant and post-peasant revolutionary movements are commonly patchworks of images and ideas left over from agrarian society, the theme of the restoration of a past Golden Age being apparently universal.

The social reality of Ireland, a country slowly emerging from serfdom and pre-literate culture, in many ways underdeveloped, with clearly non-noble antecedents and mentally distant from the ideology of the Gaelic League, was subconsciously denied. The fact that the real Ireland could only be built up by gradual and long-term effort, that it was only partially in sympathy with the aims of the rebels and that it was not even potentially the heir to a Gaelic civilisation continually threatened to awaken the patriot dreamers during the revolutionary period. The Treaty woke some of them up; some of them coped with that awakening, commonly by retreat into an exaggerated pragmatism. Others became prisoners of their own rage and disappointment. Others again developed a contempt for the people. A few searched vengefully for the betrayers of their dream.

Recent years have seen greater attention being paid to the roles of lower middle-class groups in revolutionary movements. *Poujadisme* and similar movements are far more the legitimate successors of the great nineteenth-century upheavals than is commonly admitted. In the case of the Irish national revolution, the anti-materialism, the ethos of self-sacrifice and the fear of betrayal which are so evident in the minds of the leaders were related to a set of recognisable social attitudes characteristic of the Catholic lower middle and working classes that came to dominate Irish society in the late nineteenth century. Only recently emerged from agrarian feudalism, only partly affected by urban culture, denied political power by the colonial establishment, without any self-assured intelligentsia other than their priests and the young men whom the priests had educated and with the social and moral perspectives of an emergent free yeoman-farmer society, the romantic dreams of nationalist revolutionaries reflected their desire to achieve power and were ultimately valued as ideological devices which legitimised their coming to power.

'Sinn Féin' means 'ourselves', and the notion of the non-aristocratic, non-proletarian but virtuous Catholic Irishman as the rightful representative of the Irish people came naturally to this new middle class, far more than the futurist notion of constructing a completely new social type out of exotic Gaelic cultural materials. Séamus Robinson, a well-known IRA leader, wrote: 'I want to show that the insurgent Separatists of Ireland were the normal, natural, (common)-sensible people in Ireland. All others must be adjudged as in some degree abnormal, unnatural: that, because we youngsters were normal, that is, without a taint of heresy or near heresy, natural or theological, we were Irish separatists.'[52]

The notion of heresy or moral contamination was a common one. The separatists often displayed a wish to hold themselves apart from both the lower and the upper reaches of society. Religion segregated them from the upper classes, but it connected them with the lower classes. Contamination and, literally, heresy lurked above, as did sexual depravity, which was a threat to the purity of Irish Catholic girls; one of Mary MacSwiney's most impassioned denunciations of the Treaty was concerned with the prospect of young Catholic girls continuing to participate in imperial levees at the Viceregal Lodge in Dublin under the new Free State.[53]

Contamination could also come from below, however. Fear of social slippage was sometimes visible. The period before the First World War was a time in which the class structures of European countries were coming under pressure from processes of modernisation. Ireland was no exception to this, and a general unease about one's class and status and an extreme sensitivity to threats to one's social position existed there too. For example, it appears that much of the opposition to conscription in Ireland during the war was class derived; the greatest resistance to conscription reportedly came originally from the 'farming and commercial classes', because educated Catholics were likely to have to serve in the ranks. This was particularly so in the early months of the war, as commissions were usually reserved for public school alumni. Fear of proletarianisation, rather than either cowardice or nationalism, prompted resistance.[54] The image of the virtuous, honourable and clean-cut young Catholic man or woman making his or her way, like Christian, in a world of upper-class vice, snobbery and dissipation, and of lower-class slavishness and boorishness, ran through much of Sinn Féin. A military example of this pervasive self-image is provided by a Kerry IRA leader in the civil war, deriding his opponents in the Free State Army, of whom many would have been veterans of the Tan War and many others British Army veterans:

It is a strange fact that the Army these men instituted for the purpose of destroying the glorious work of a Pearse, a MacSwiney, Kevin Barry, Liam Mellows, Rory O'Connor and a countless army of brave and clean men, should have on it all the earmarks of the drunkard, the traitor, the wife beater, the tramp, the tinker and the brute. This I positively declare is the make-up of the National Army, so-called.[55]

Peadar O'Donnell, one of the few self-consciously Marxist-minded activists in the movement, remarked in old age and with magnificent insouciance that his side, the anti-Treatyites, were politically and intellectually bankrupt by 1922. The opposition of the leaders to the Treaty had been essentially moral and religious rather than derived from any radical or even coherent political programme. Had they won, the outcome would have been little different from the actual outcome.[56] David Neligan, who had been Collins's spy in Dublin Castle, often wondered if the entire struggle had been worth the price.[57]

A theme of this book has been the proposition that the real enemy of the Irish revolution has been the long-term transformation of the island from a rural society depending mainly on subsistence agriculture combined with monocrop commercialised agriculture into a fully fledged, if modest, member of the Western group of developed and liberal-democratic nation-states. This transition was given political legitimation by clerics and lay leaders combining nostalgic and futurist images, communalism and religion, in an ideological package that could be used in various ways. Its protean character has given the package some longevity, although intellectually it is moribund. Economic and social development, usually extolled by present-day Irish governments as something which the founding fathers would have unreservedly endorsed, actually poses a great threat to the blend of Catholic communalism and petty-bourgeois values which lies behind so much republican passion. Under de Valera, an attempt which could be described as both intellectually and psychologically uneasy was made to blend these communal and Catholic values with those of British-style liberal democracy. The contradictions have never gone away, and the most important, that between the transcendent values of Irish separatist nationalism and Irish Catholic puritanism and communalism on the one hand and the rather grubby everyday realities of Irish electoral democracy with its English-style liberal and individualistic implicit values on the other, has never been resolved.

Irish governments are elected by people, most of whom are descended from slaves, as is most of mankind, and the ideological package put together 100 years ago is gradually disintegrating. The political marriage between republican leaders cynical about the people and an electorate which appears to vote mainly for the immediate advantages offered it by cynics has resulted, two generations later, in a leaderless political system; each has found the other out, perhaps to the ruin of both. In a remarkable book, Robert J. Lifton has analysed Mao Tse-tung's long and hopeless obsession with preventing the death of the Chinese revolution.[58] De Valera certainly had a similar obsession. In the Irish case, the revolution has been dying for a long time, since the time of de Valera's birth rather than since his death, and de Valera certainly sensed it, while never admitting it. To have admitted it would have been to declare the Irish people unworthy of their great destiny. De Valera, a politician of genius, knew what many others knew in the backs of their minds: that Ireland was gradually ceasing to be a country of political purisms and of reigns of terror and virtue. The Irish revolution itself, even at the height of the 1913–23 crisis, was in large part a fight, using symbolic rather than real weapons, against revolutionary death rather than a real war. The Irish poet and scholar Arland Ussher, who lived through the revolution, remembered: 'The whole of the Irish "War of Independence" from 1916 to 1922, had to my sense a certain atmosphere of *playing* . . . when a revolution can be made without horrors it means, I think, that the need for any revolution at all has disappeared.'[59]

The Irish guerrillas fought against a political death which the long-term pattern of Irish social development promised to bring about; they confused the death of their revolution with the death of the nation. They created a political system which was democratic but with a bad conscience, and which was ideologically irresolute in the face of the modern world.

08 | EPILOGUE

AFTERMATH

Both pragmatic and fundamentalist wings of the Sinn Féin movement found themselves having to govern a country, the former in 1922 and the bulk of the latter in 1932. They were ill equipped in many ways to do so. Little real thought had been given to the actual practical problems of governing a country, as distinct from imaginings of the ideal conditions which the citizens of the country would eventually enjoy under the benign governance of patriots. The policies that were followed were only in part derived from the ideas of the Gaelic League, Sinn Féin or the Democratic Programme of the first Dáil. In the first place, the pressures of everyday reality tended to have their usual effect of postponing long-term policy planning in favour of sometimes hurried improvisation. This was perhaps particularly true of the early years of the Free State, as the new and inexperienced government had to fight a civil war, demobilise its army, deal with a serious economic recession and govern a country with a less than totally civic culture. The fact that it succeeded represents in itself a major achievement.

The reality principle presented itself in another way too. The new politicians found themselves dependent on the experience of civil servants who had been trained under the British government and who scarcely shared the values of the League or of Sinn Féin. It was not until the 1950s that generational change was to ensure senior civil servants who had values like those of the political class. The encounter between the rebel-in-office and the bureaucrat has not been well documented, but some anecdotal evidence has survived. The power of the civil service had grown great because of the impotence of politicians. George A. Birmingham, writing in 1913, ascribed this weakness of politicians in Ireland to the collapse of Irish party politics that had followed Parnell's fall and explained the huge power of bureaucrats as being a consequence of the political vacuum. The higher officials, he believed, had a secret contempt for elected politicians of all kinds, nationalist, unionist, British and Irish. The senior official had 'kept Ireland going, so to speak, during that peculiarly difficult period when almost all Irishmen combined to reduce her affairs to a deadlock'.[1] The political deadlock was resolved in 1922 by independence and partition, but many old habits and attitudes persisted.

Much of the old mentality of dependence on Whitehall survived, presumably much to the irritation of the new masters. As late as the 1950s, the senior officials of a putatively independent state were consulting their British opposite numbers about budgetary policy. A palace revolution in the 1950s put a stop to that, but it is surprising how slow old habits were to change.[2] A major modernising project, a scheme to supply hydro-electricity to the country by harnessing the Shannon River, was adopted by the Free State government in the 1920s. However, the project had to be smuggled into cabinet and hidden from the eyes of the senior officials in the Department of Finance.[3] This scheme, revolutionary at the time, horrified conservatives but had a major psychological impact on many dissident republicans. A clearly modern and modernist project, it appeared to show that the Free State government took the values of Arthur Griffith and others in the revolutionary movement seriously. The new police, a disarmed constabulary in contrast to the armed gendarmerie of the RIC, systematically participated in Gaelic games and Irish-Ireland activities, becoming quickly integrated with the central ideological institutions that had instigated the revolution.[4] The government showed itself to be as eager as its critics to further the cause of the learning of Irish. The primary-school system was bent to the purposes of linguistic nationalism with great determination, much to the detriment of the system; science, art and nature study were sacrificed. The new politicians and the civil servants established a *modus vivendi*.

This process was greatly helped by the narrowness of the original Gaelic League and Sinn Féin programmes, and also by their self-contradictoriness. Some of the founders had called for a ruralisation of society, others for industrialisation; some wanted rapid re-gaelicisation, others were privately sceptical about it; some were in favour of state enterprise, others had a dislike of it; some wanted centralised government, others wanted decentralisation. These differences divided even allies within the same party, as the original split, although it had some class basis, did not split the original movement into two ideologically opposed groups. Ideological incoherence forced a hyper-British pragmatism on both sets of leaders. De Valera's attempts to apply Sinn Féin-inspired protectionism in the 1930s came rather late to revive the enthusiasm of the rebels' youth, and eventually protectionism came to be seen less as a nostrum than as another policy to be assessed on its merits. George Russell opined in 1933, one year into de Valera's long reign: 'We have passed out of the romantic phase of Irish nationalism now and are concerned about dull matters like tariffs. I am glad I was born in romantic Ireland. It is a little dull today compared with twenty five years ago'.[5]

But then the rule of the saints is always dull, if one is lucky. De Valera was no Cromwell or Mao; rather, he attempted to blend together the communal, nostalgic and futurist themes in the ideology and use them as a rhetoric of democratic politics. By doing so, he helped to reconcile republican vision with bureaucratic realism, and both with the manifold petty desires of a democratic electorate. It is perhaps only appropriate that he should have been born in New York and had a Spanish name.

COMPARATIVE PERSPECTIVES
John Newsinger has suggested that Ireland's combination of revolutionary ideology and Catholicism is unique.[6] Each revolutionary movement is, of course, unique, but this does not prohibit the

drawing of analogies; if each historical event were truly unique, as extreme empiricists sometimes appear to argue, it would perhaps be logically impossible to think about them; incomparable events are necessarily supernatural.

Whatever the uniqueness of the combination of revolutionism and Catholicism in Ireland, there is no scarcity of examples of the combination of religion and revolution. It could be argued that the concept of revolution itself grew out of the Christian and Jewish religious traditions that dominate Western cultures. The Old Testament theme of the Chosen People has been echoed numberless times by nationalist and other mass movements, and the New Testament theme of the saviour who dies for his people or who otherwise sacrifices himself has been imitated by many revolutionary leaders besides Patrick Pearse. The Czech Hussite revolution of the fifteenth century, in so many ways the forerunner of modern revolution, combined a reformist Christianity with a nascent Czech nationalism; the People of God and the new nation came together as one blended concept. Again, the English revolution of the seventeenth century, the indirect and unacknowledged ancestor of the Irish nationalist revolution, used the vocabulary of religion throughout its course.[7] Ironically, the English revolution was the direct ancestor of the Orange counter-revolution in Ireland. It is only since 1789 that institutionalised religion and revolution have come to be seen as automatically opposed, mainly because of the overwhelming examples of secular and scientistic revolution offered by France, Russia and China in the last two centuries. Even in these cases, the role of religion in supplying general superordinate values is missed, and secular substitutes for it have been touted. Reason and socialism make unsatisfactory substitutes for religion, but they have been so used. The quasi-religious cults of Hitler, Lenin, Stalin and Mao are vivid demonstrations of the need that even anti-religious revolutionary movements have for the legitimation that religion traditionally gave. In Ireland, of course, pagan themes surfaced in the League, and Pearse's ideal was a strange mixture of modernism, Christ and Cuchulain. Pagan themes were sometimes resorted to when the message of Christianity seemed unsympathetic to the aims of the revolutionaries. At the turn of the twentieth century, when the younger seminarians were beginning to be seduced by the rhetoric of Sheehan and the cult of the League, one dissident Maynooth priest pointed out that, contrary to Peter O'Leary's opinion, Catholicism depended on no language, and that the entire neo-Gaelic cult reeked of paganism.[8] In Irish political culture, Rome distrusted the cult of Celtic heroism; however, the two had to get on with each other and Aquinas had to live with Cuchulain, much as John Stuart Mill had to live with Theobald Wolfe Tone. The recent outbreaks of revolutionary messianism in the Islamic world are further examples of the uneasy relationship that commonly exists between essentially secular or neo-pagan revolutionary movements and the outraged anti-secularism of traditional religious believers.

Revolutions are made by élites, not by masses, although they are commonly made in the name of masses. This is true of revolutions that are nominally communist, nationalist, democratic or fascist. Admittedly, élite–mass relationships differ; the Irish case offers us an example of revolutionary fervour both fed by religion and inhibited by it, and eventually tempered by the studied moderation of an electorate. Revolutionaries tend to come from the middle sectors of society, but because they are usually young, to be socially somewhat indeterminate. Comparative studies suggest that both leftist and 'bourgeois democratic' revolutionary leaders are noticeably likely to be of upper middle- or even upper-class origin and to be relatively well educated, whereas European fascist leaderships have tended to be of lower middle-class origin and to have lower levels of educational attainment.[9] The Irish élite displayed a mixture of both types, echoing its ideological irres-oluteness. Many other revolutionary élites, most notably the Russian, have displayed a dichotomy between urban-born, or at least urbane, humanistic intellectuals and rural-born organisers: a kind of yogi-versus-commissar contrast that supplies much of the inner dynamic of the entire movement.[10] To put it in Irish terms, Patrick Pearse encounters Seán Ó Muirthile.

Schoolmasters and priests have made enthusiastic revolutionaries in many cultures. Like other modern intellectuals, the revolutionary often appears to have a passion to teach and to preach. Castro and Gadaffi give speeches to captive audiences which last for hours and which are listened to by people who have developed a capacity to sleep with their eyes open. In the Soviet Union, at least until very recently, the entire population appears to have had this relationship to the official culture and doctrine as expounded through the media. Commonly, the revolutionised country, taken over by armed philosophers and quasi-philosophical gunmen, is turned into 'a vast schoolroom with a population of cowed, captive pupils cringing at [the revolutionary's] feet'.[11] In Ireland, the revolution went furthest in the schools, and the Irish-language and history curricula were systematically used to inculcate an uncompromising nationalism derived from Gaelic League ideas. The schools were used in an attempt to reverse the cultural history of the previous century and a half.[12] However, the cultural revolution stopped there; its net effect was to give a vague legitimation to the new regime and some career advantages to some students coming from poorer and rural backgrounds. By and large, the revival of Irish was not popular, and the Irish people used against it the same tactics of passive but massive resistance which had been used to such great effect against British governments in the previous century.[13]

Revolutionary nationalism in Ireland was, and is, radical in style and means, but not in ends. At times it has displayed a striking resemblance to Lipset's 'extremism of the centre'; Lipset identified this middle-class extremism as the core of fascism in the social system, but it is an extremism which can take other forms than those of classical fascism.[14] In Catholic Germany, middle-class voters showed more resistance to the appeals of Nazism than did their equivalents in Protestant Germany because of the encapsulating effects of Catholic political organisations such as the *Zentrum*. Instead, the Catholic Church itself showed signs of fascism, while not going over completely to fascist doctrines. Extremist Irish Catholic nationalism developed certain ideological and social characteristics reminiscent of classical fascism; fascist themes coexisted with Catholic, liberal-democratic and socialist themes in a movement that avoided achieving any doctrinaire ideological character and was steered, somewhat reluctantly, into the path of conservative democratic parliamentarianism. Hostility to big capital was balanced, as in classical fascism, with dislike of powerful unions; dislike of urban commercial civilisation and idealisation of rural and pseudo-medieval values was combined with a confused, but not contemptible, longing for a developed and modern, while culturally authentic, future; and a generous internationalist nationalism consorted with xenophobia, anti-Semitism and a paranoid perception of England as the home of all evil.

The tendency of Irish separatism to drift into fascism was inhibited by the general structure of Irish society, which had undergone little of the wholesale disruption that fed the fascisms of central Europe. Culturally, Ireland was Anglo-American and was too much part of that cultural area to be attracted by the exotic political apparatuses of fascism. Again, the organic character of Irish Catholicism acted as a substitute for the organic vision offered by many fascists.

Anti-clericalism, a feature of many European revolutionary movements, whether fascist or otherwise, was inhibited in Ireland for similar reasons. Essentially the clericalist wing of the movement had a natural advantage over the anti-clerical, as the near-identity of Irish nationality and Irish Catholicism had given the priest near-ethnarch status in the culture. Another perhaps more basic reason for the demise of the anti-clerical tradition and for the intellectual subservience that so many of the separatists displayed in their relationships with the Church was the absence of a true bourgeois element in the movement and a consequent absence of political and intellectual self-assurance. Essentially lower middle class and working class in origin, deprived, mainly by the actions of the bishops of their own Church, of a developed tradition of further education and deriving from small-town and rural society, many Sinn Féin leaders lacked a capacity for fully independent political thought or action. The natural bias in the electorate toward clericalism merely heightened a propensity that already existed in the élite.

As already suggested, within a generation of independence the bureaucracy had begun to resemble the élite itself. A similar selection of young men of relatively poor and rural origins, highly intelligent and the products of a rather narrow and authoritarian education, came to dominate the polity. As products of petty-bourgeois society, their instincts were to seek out security of tenure, avoid great changes, make whatever decisions were deemed necessary in secret and avoid public debate. The strength of the nationalist trade unions that had emerged during the revolutionary period ensured that the public sector remained large and, if not well paid, at least unsackable. The contrast between the revolutionaries' original romanticism and the political system which they built could scarcely have been more stark. Eventually there was to be no more room for the romantics; unlike in Russia, they were not purged. Rather, they were kept busy translating English-language popular books into Irish or unread legislation into an even less-read form, or else they were permitted to emigrate to London, from which vantage point they were able to denounce the polity they had done so much to create.

In his excellent Marxist study of Liam Mellows, Greaves argues that the Sinn Féin élite operated in a political context in which all the classes were split on the issue of independence and that there consequently emerged a leadership drawn from the petty bourgeoisie: 'small businessmen, younger professional people, rural schoolteachers and curates, journalists and artisans'.[15] Class hegemony was, he contends, temporarily suspended in favour of this leadership, but long-term domination of Irish society by the petty bourgeoisie was not possible; Marxian theory apparently can be held to prohibit such an outcome. Eventually one or other of the principal contending classes, the bourgeoisie proper or the proletariat, must assert itself. Greaves sees the Treaty as this assertion of the political hegemony of the bourgeoisie; 1922 is indeed the Irish Thermidor.[16]

This analysis leaves out a central feature of the Irish revolution, which is the relatively small part that was played in it by either the bourgeoisie or the proletariat. Large sections of both of these classes were located in Ulster and were Protestant. In effect they opted to defend their own patch and stay on the sidelines; they had little to do with the outcome in most of Ireland. The independence movement had very widespread support, in large part because of the alienation many people felt from the British government. It started as a petty-bourgeois movement but became a mass movement in 1918, with substantial cross-class support. Another notable feature which Greaves elides is the extent to which the revolution focused on changing the government; it had as its theme the struggle to take over the Irish state, either from outside by agitation and force or from inside by infiltration and co-optation. In effect, popularly supported separatists laid siege to Dublin Castle, and in 1922 the Castle fell. The form the Treaty split took reflects this proposition; it divided those who wanted to run a country from those who feared such power. The state which emerged in Ireland was bourgeois in some extended sense of that very flexible term, but was scarcely run in the best interests of the *grande bourgeoisie*. It was democratic, with a conservative electorate dominated by petty-bourgeois and Catholic ideas. Rather than being run by a committee of the bourgeoisie, it came to be dominated by an alliance of bourgeois, petty-bourgeois, farmer, clerical and labour forces which imparted stability to a markedly centralised and bureaucratised state, built in large part on the ruins of British rule in Ireland. Significantly, James O'Mara, one of the few authentically bourgeois leaders of the Sinn Féin movement, was utterly disappointed with the polity that emerged and was horrified by the regulatory powers that the civil service accumulated in the first generation after independence.[17] The political autonomy of the lower middle classes may be only relative, but it can also be decisive; Ireland became a nation of shopkeepers, not of tycoons, and until the generation of 1914 grew old and weak, it stayed that way. To quite an extent, it still is that way.

NOTES

Abbreviations

AD CUA	Archives Department, Catholic University of America, Washington, DC
AD UCD	Archives Department, University College, Dublin
FA UCD	Folklore Department, University College, Dublin
IWM	Imperial War Museum, London
LC WDC	Library of Congress, Washington, DC
NA WDC	National Archives, Washington, DC
NLI	National Library of Ireland
NYPL	New York Public Library
PROL	Public Record Office, London
SPO	State Paper Office, Dublin

Chapter 1. Irish Revolutionaries (PAGES 1–12)

1. This is not to suggest that Ireland will not become again the scene of great violence; it is rather to argue that such violence is no longer allied with intellect and has little chance of being translated into political power, unlike seventy years ago. On revolution in general, see Crane Brinton, *The Anatomy of Revolution*, New York: Random House, 1965, 16–20; Chalmers Johnson, *Revolutionary Change*, Stanford, CA: Stanford University Press, 1982, 182–4; Mark Hagopian, *The Phenomenon of Involution*, New York: Harper & Row, 1974, 233–46.

2. J.G.A. Pocock, 'The Case of Ireland Truly Stated: Revolutionary Politics in a Context of Increasing Stabilisation', unpublished TS, Department of History, Georgetown University, 1966.

3. J. Lee, *The Modernisation of Irish Society, 1848–1918*, Dublin: Gill & Macmillan, 1973; Brian Farrell, *The Founding of Dáil Éireann*, Dublin: Gill & Macmillan, 1971. For a recent brilliant empiricist essay on long-term modernisation processes in Ireland, see L.M. Cullen, *The Emergence of Modern Ireland*, Dublin: Gill & Macmillan, 1981. For the standard critique of modernisation theory, see D. Tipps, 'Modernisation Theory and the Comparative Study of Societies: A Critical Perspective', *Comparative Studies in Society and History*, 15 (Mar. 1973), 199–226.

4. E. Larkin, 'The Devotional Revolution in Ireland, 1850–75', *American Historical Review*, 11 (June 1972), 625–52; K. Connell, 'Catholicism and Marriage in the Century after the Famine', in his *Irish Peasant Society*, London: Oxford University Press, 1968, 113–62; D. Miller, 'Irish Catholicism and the Great Famine', *Journal of Social History*, 9/1 (1977), 81–98.

5. Lee, *The Modernisation of Irish Society*, *passim*, and see also his 'The Ribbonmen', in D. Williams (ed.), *Secret Societies in Ireland*, Dublin: Gill & Macmillan, 1973, 26–45. On agrarian social change after the Famine, see S. Clark, *The Social Origins of the Irish Land War*, Princeton, NJ: Princeton University Press, 1979; P. Bew, *Land and the National Question in Ireland, 1858–82*, Dublin: Gill & Macmillan, 1978.

6. George Moore, *Hail and Farewell*, New York: Appleton, 1911–14, vol. iii., 361, 364.

7. Tom Garvin, *The Evolution of Irish Nationalist Politics*, Dublin: Gill & Macmillan, 1981, 69–98.

8. This is particularly true of modernising peasant societies. See J.C. Scott, 'Protest and Profanation: Agrarian Revolt and the Little Tradition, Part I', *Theory and Society*, 4/1 (Spring 1977), 1–38. Cf. his *The Moral Economy of the Peasant*, New Haven, CT: Yale University Press, 1976, 92–8.

9. Barrington Moore, *The Social Origins of Dictatorship and Democracy*, Harmondsworth: Penguin, 1969; Scott, *Moral Economy, passim*.

10. Barrington Moore, *Injustice: The Social Bases of Obedience and Revolt*, London: Macmillan, 1978, 476.

11. Craig Jackson Calhoun, 'The Radicalism of Tradition: Community Strength or Venerable Disguise and Borrowed Language?', *American Journal of Sociology*, 88 (1983), 886–914, at 886–7. Cf. the somewhat similar diagnosis of William I. Thompson, *The Imagination of an Insurrection*, New York: Oxford University Press, 1967, 3–62. Cf. also NA WDC Despatches from Consuls, 841. 00/5–85, 30 Sept. 1916, Queenstown.

12. Calhoun, 'Radicalism of Tradition', pp. 890–2, 897. See also James H. Billington, *Fire in Men's Minds*, New York: Basic Books, 1980, 402–3.

13. Charles Tilly, L. Tilly, *et al.*, *The Rebellious Century*, Cambridge, MA: Harvard University Press, 1975, *passim*.

14. M. Hroch, *Die Vorkämpfer der nationalen Bewegungen bei den kleinen Völkern Europas*, Prague: Universita Karlova, 1968. Quotation from E.J. Hobsbawm, 'Some Reflections on Nationalism', in T.J. Nossiter, A.H. Hanson, *et al.*, *Imagination and Precision in the Social Sciences*, London: Faber & Faber, 1972, 385–406. See also Tom Nairn, 'The Modern Janus', *New Left Review*, 94 (Nov.–Dec. 1975), 3–30; Eric Wolf, *Peasant Wars in the Twentieth Century*, New York: Harper & Row, 1969; and David Fitzpatrick, 'The Geography of Irish Nationalism, 1910–1921', *Past and Present*, 78 (Feb. 1978), 113–44. Hroch states bluntly (*Vorkämpfer der nationalen Bewegungen*, p. 125) that the petty bourgeoisie, defined as artisans, shopkeepers and the like, are the most important 'bearers of the nationalism of the fully developed nation' during the final phase of the movement and are 'a potential source for its ruling class'. He goes on to say that it was in the petty bourgeoisie that the future of the down-trodden nation often lay (my translation and paraphrase).

15. Cf. Wolf, *Peasant Wars*, *passim*.

16. NLI MS 10492. This self-image, propagated by Stephens, prefigures Hroch's diagnosis perfectly.

17. Patrick Pearse, *Political Writings and Speeches*, Dublin: Talbot, 1966, 237.

18 Pearse, *Political Writings*, p. 303.

19. C. Desmond Greaves, *The Life and Times of James Connolly*, New York: International Publishers, 1971, 14, 154. Greaves argues elsewhere that Connolly's father had Marxist politics and that Connolly himself saw the nationalist revolution as a necessary preliminary for socialist revolution. See his 'Connolly and Easter Week: A Rejoinder to John Newsinger', *Science and Society*, 48/2 (Summer 1984), 220–3. The thesis that Connolly's forebears had inherited a Ribbon levelling ideology which could be easily transmuted into either Marxism or nationalism has not been proved but would bear investigation. On Ribbonism and the importance of Ulster border counties such as Monaghan to that tradition, see Garvin, *Evolution*, pp. 34–52.

20. NLI MS 10492.

21. SPO FP Carton 1; *Pilot*, 2 Apr. 1859. But see Munster and Connacht as centres of IRB strength in local representative councils at the end of the century in the aftermath of the Land War, PROL CO 904/184/1. By this time the movement had been transmuted from a revolutionary political organisation into an agrarian league. See Garvin, *Evolution*, pp. 53–68, where this development is charted.

22. Quotation from Daniel Corkery's foreword to F. O'Donoghue, *Tomás MacCurtain*, Tralee: Kerryman, 1958. For other examples of anti-urban nativism, see J. Ambrose, *The Story of Dan Breen*, Cork: Mercier, 1982; U. Mac Eoin, *Survivors*, Dublin: Argenta, 1981, 75–104. As is argued later, the most eloquent proponents of this ideology were priests of the type of Father Peter O'Leary and Canon P.A. Sheehan.

Chapter 2. Men in the Middle (PAGES 13–32)

1. Earlier versions of some of the ideas proposed in this chapter have appeared in my 'The Anatomy of a Nationalist Revolution: Ireland 1858–1928', *Comparative Studies in Society and History*, 28/3 (July 1986), 468–501.

2. Teodor Shanin, *The Awkward Class*, Oxford: Clarendon Press, 1971, *passim*.

3. Lewis S. Feuer, *The Conflict of Generations*, New York and London: Basic Books, 1969, 84, 152–4; Arno J. Mayer, 'The Lower Middle Class as Historical Problem', *Journal of Modern History*, 14 (Sept. 1975), 409–36.

4. J.J. Nossiter, 'Shopkeeper Radicalism in the Nineteenth Century', in T.J. Nossiter, A.H. Hanson, *et al.*, *Imagination and Precision in the Social Sciences*, London: Faber & Faber, 1972, 407–38; M. Hroch, *Die Vorkämpfer der nationalen Bewegungen bei den Kleinen Völkern Europas*, Prague: Universita Karlova, 1968, *passim*.

5. Quoted in Robert Michels, 'On the Sociology of Bohemia and its Connections to the Intellectual Proletariat', *Catalyst*, 15 (1983), 5–25, at 23–4 (first published 1932). Cf. Friedrich Heer, *Challenge of Youth*, Birmingham, AL: University of Alabama, 1974.

6. Duncan Gallie, 'The Agrarian Roots of Working-class Radicalism: An Assessment of the Mann-Giddens Thesis', *British Journal of Political Science*, 12/2 (Apr. 1982), 149–72; M.H. Kater, *The Nazi Party: A Social Profile of Members and Leaders 1919–1945*, Cambridge, MA: Harvard University Press, 1983, 35–6.

7. *Irish Nation and Peasant*, 14 Apr. 1906.

8. Tom Garvin, *The Evolution of Irish Nationalist Politics*, Dublin: Gill & Macmillan, 1981, *passim*; Garvin, 'Anatomy', *passim*.

9. E. Fromm, 'Fascism as Lower-middle-class Psychology', in G. Allardyce, *The Place of Fascism in European History*, Englewood Cliffs, NJ: Prentice-Hall, 1971, 36–48.

10. Hroch, *Vorkämpfer der nationalen Bewegungen*, pp. 123–5.

11. Nossiter, 'Shopkeeper Radicalism', *passim*.

12. Stanley Payne, *Fascism: Comparison and Definition*, Madison, WI: University of Wisconsin Press, 1980, 113–14.

13. R.D. Putnam, *The Comparative Study of Political Élites*, Englewood Cliffs, NJ: Prentice-Hall, 1976, 193.

14. Renzo de Felice, *Interpretations of Fascism*, Cambridge, MA: Harvard University Press, 1977, 51–2.

15. *Minutes of Evidence . . . of the Royal Commission on the Rebellion in Ireland*, London: HMSO, 1916, 83.

16. H. Seton-Watson, *Nations and States*, Boulder, CO: Westview, 1977, 421; de Felice, *Interpretations of Fascism*, p. 52.

17. On some of these ideological themes, cf. R. Ellman, *Yeats: The Man and the Masks*, New York: Macmillan, 1948, 7–24.

18. G.A. Birmingham, *Irishmen All*, London and Edinburgh; Foulis, 1913, 34–5.

19. Ibid., 213–18. Birmingham was a particularly well-placed observer. A Church of Ireland clergyman, he was heavily involved in the Gaelic League during its years of great expansion and knew the west of Ireland well. He was a prolific novelist, and his books are useful humorous commentaries on Irish society and culture of the time. He became a victim of Catholic clerical bigotry because of one comic novel and was forced out of the League by the priests. Hyde did not dare defend him.

20. T.J. O'Connell, *History of the Irish National Teachers' Organisation 1868–1908*, Dublin: Irish National Teachers' Organisation, 1969, 38.

21. G.A. Birmingham, *An Irishman Looks at his World*, London: Hodder & Stoughton, 1919, 240–5; David Neligan, *The Spy in the Castle*, London: MacGibbon & Kee, 1968, 10. Cf. the attraction of Nazism for German

elementary school teachers. Hans Gerth noted: 'The strength of the teachers within the [Nazi] party leadership may partly explain the relentlessness of the fight between the party and the church. The teacher—especially the elementary-school teacher in rural regions—had long resented the supervision of the Protestant ministers who were usually conservative politically, orthodox theologically ... The schoolteachers, being recruited from a somewhat lower stratum than the clergy ever since the end of the eighteenth century, inclined more to a secularised "enlightened" or "historical" philosophy of life but were tied to a church ...' (Gerth, 'The Nazi Party: Its Leadership and Composition', in B. McLaughlin, *Studies in Social Movements*, New York: Free Press, 1969, 258–74, at 264.) Irish teachers' frustrations got a rather different political expression, of course.

22. T. McGrath, *Pictures from Ireland*, London: Kegan, Paul, Trench, 1888, 170–4. But cf. the idealised Fenian schoolmaster in Canon Sheehan's *The Graves at Kilmorna*, discussed in Chapter 4 below.

23. Birmingham, *An Irishman Looks*, pp. 135–6.

24. S. Ó Maoileóin, *B'Fhiú an Braon Fola*, Dublin: Sairséil agus Dill, 1958.

25. Dan Breen, *My Fight for Irish Freedom*, Tralee: Anvil, 1981, 21.

26. U. Mac Eoin, *Survivors*, Dublin: Argenta, 1981, 75.

27. On schoolmasters and revolutionary politics, see E. Hoffer, *Between the Devil and the Dragon*, New York: Harper & Row, 1982, 96–133, 350–94. On Irish schoolmasters, L.M. Cullen, *The Emergence of Modern Ireland*, Dublin: Gill & Macmillan, 1981, 235–7. For an interesting study of hostility to the regime among nineteenth-century teachers, see T. Ó Raifeartaigh, 'Múinteoirí Náisiúnta agus an "Dlísteanas", 1831–1870', *Seanchas Ardmhacha*, 2/1 (1956), 61–77. The Munster ones were by far the most conspicuous.

28. S. O'Casey, *Drums under the Windows*, New York: Macmillan, 1946, 157.

29. Garvin, 'Anatomy', *passim*.

30. NYPL J. Walsh papers, Slipbook. On independent-mindedness of state employees, see M.J. Waters, 'Peasants and Emigrants: Considerations of the Gaelic League as a Social Movement', in D. Casey and R. Rhodes, *Views of the Irish Peasantry, 1800–1916*, Hamden, CN: Archon, 1977, 160–77.

31. AD UCD P17b/100. See also NLI MS 9873, Sherlock memoir.

32. NLI MS 9873. Mathews memoir, 85; for another such quotation, see AD UCD Pl7b/106.

33. Emmet Dalton, Interview, RTÉ Irish Television, 22 Aug. 1978.

34. AD UCD P17b/109.

35. *Forty Years of Dublin Opinion*, Dublin: Dublin Opinion, n.d. (1962), 14.

Chapter 3. The Formation of the Revolutionary Élite (PAGES 33–56)

1. Jaroslav Krejci, *Great Revolutions Compared*, Brighton: Harvester, 1983, 1–21, 191–216.

2. T.W. Moody, *The Fenian Movement*, Cork: Mercier, 1968, *passim*. On Fenian strength in Ireland, see SPO A files A124; *Pilot*, 6 Jan., 3, 17 Feb., 17, 24 Mar., 6, 13 Apr. 1866. Cf. John Newsinger, 'Old Chartists, Fenians and New Socialists', *Éire–Ireland*, 17 (Summer 1982), 2, 19–46.

3. Anonymous ('A Silent Politician'), *On the Future of Ireland, and on its Capacity to Exist as an Independent State*, Dublin: Harding, 1862.

4. Sources: Fenian leaders listed in the *Dictionary of National Biography, the Dictionary of American Biography*, and H. Boylan, *A Dictionary of Irish Biography*, New York: Barnes & Noble, 1978. AD CUA Rossa papers Box 1, Item 4 lists 533 US Fenians of 1865, Cork names being heavily over-represented.

5. *Pilot*, 28 Dec. 1867.

6. NLI MS 7953/6.

7. NLI MS 3041, p. 791 (1 Jan. 1866).

8. Felix Gross, *The Revolutionary Party*, Westport, CN: Greenwood, 1974.

9. S. Clark, *The Social Origins of the Irish Land War*, Princeton, NJ: Princeton University Press, 1979, 246–304.

10. SPO DICS Carton 3; SPO CBS 548/S, 1128/S, 1153/S, 1181/S, 1205/S, 1224/S, 1229/S, 1355/S, 1360/S, 1482/S, 1487/S, 1505/S, 1873/S, 9001/S, 9301/S, 11426/S, 11921/S, 11207/S, 13114/S, 14993/S.

11. Terence Brown, *Ireland: A Social and Cultural History, 1922–79*, London: Fontana, 1980, 24–7; C.M. Arensberg and S. Kimball, *Family and Community in Ireland*, Cambridge, MA: Harvard University Press, 1968; G.A. Birmingham, *Irishmen All*, London and Edinburgh: Foulis, 1913, 213–18.

12. Quoted in S. Levenson, *Maud Gonne*, New York: Reader's Digest, 1976, 113.

13. Vilfredo Pareto, *The Mind and Society*, New York: Dover, 2 vols., 1963, ss. 2025–59; M. Young, *The Rise of the Meritocracy*, Harmondsworth: Penguin, 1961, *passim*; Mark Hagopian, *The Phenomenon of Revolution*, New York, Harper & Row, 1974, 53; Gaetano Mosca, *The Ruling Class*, New York: McGraw-Hill, 1939, 50 and *passim*.

14. House of Commons, *First Report of the Commissioners on University Education (Ireland)*, Cd. 825, 1902, Minutes of Evidence, 25.

15. Ibid.

16. House of Commons, *First Report of the Commissioners on University Education (Ireland)*, Cd. 825, 1902, Minutes of Evidence; 142.

17. Ibid., 195–7.

18. Arland Ussher, *The Face and Mind of Ireland*, London: Gollancz, 1949, 102.

19. D.H. Akenson, *The Irish Education Experiment*, London: Routledge and Kegan Paul, 1970, 316–18.

20. Ibid., 320–2.

21. Cf. witnesses' comments, House of Commons, *First Report of the Commissioners on Higher Education (Ireland)*, C. 9116 and 9117, 1899, Appendix.

22. House of Commons, *First Report of the Commissioners on Higher Education (Ireland)*, Minutes of Evidence, 20.

23. Ibid., 25; cf. *Leader*, 19 Nov. 1904.

24. Francis Hackett, *Ireland: A Study in Nationalism*, New York: Huebsch, 1920, 238–9. Hackett observes: 'From 1878 on, six or seven thousand middle-class youths pushed farther out of illiteracy than ever before. Few decent careers opened for them, but they were the nucleus for the later developments of nationalism—Sinn Féin and the Gaelic League. Anyone who examines the newspapers of that period will discover that Cork, Dublin, Limerick, Waterford, Kilkenny, Athlone, Galway, Ennis, Wexford, were feeding hot nationalism to a flood of romantic, eager youth.'

25. *The Times, The Ireland of Today*, Boston: Small, Maynard, 1913, 139–40.

26. *First Report of the Commissioners on Higher Education*, Minutes of Evidence, 2–4, 24–5, 127, 135, 302–11.

27. Ibid., 127, 142, 302–11.

28. *First Report of the Commissioners on Higher Education (Ireland)*, Minutes of Evidence, 135

29. Ibid., 49.

30. *Leader*, 23 Sept. 1905.

31. *Leader*, 16 Dec. 1911, 24 Feb. 1912.

32. Birmingham, *Irishmen All*, pp. 34–5, 213–18.

33. *Leader*, 21 Oct. 1905. Two pounds was forty shillings.

34. Sources: Data culled from Flynn's *Parliamentary Companion*, Dublin: Stationery Office, 1929, 1932, 1939, 1945; Boylan, *Dictionary of Irish Biography*; P. O'Farrell, *Who's Who in the Irish War of Independence 1916–1921*, Dublin and Cork: Mercier, 1980.

35. R. Putnam, *The Comparative Study of Political Élites*, Englewood Cliffs, NJ: Prentice-Hall, 1976, 195–8.

36. E. O'Malley, *On Another Man's Wound*, Dublin: Anvil, 1979, 144.

37. See the discussion in M. Rejai and K. Phillips, *Leaders of Revolution*, Beverly Hills, CA, and London: Sage, 1979, 24–34, 55–6.

38. *Dáil Debates: Official Report of the Debate on the Treaty Between Great Britain and Ireland*, 14 Dec. 1921–10 Jan. 1922, Dublin: Talbot, n.d., 410–11, 416.

39. Rejai and Phillips, *Leaders of Revolution*, pp. 55, 69–72.

40. *Dáil Debates*, 10 Jan. 1922, 400–1. On the importance of US, London and Munster connections to the IRB, see Anonymous, *Incipient Irish Revolutions: An Expose of Fenianism of Today*, London: 1889 (NLI Eglington 94108 El).

41. NLI MS 11127.

42. AD UCD P48b/374–88.

43. Tom Garvin, 'Decolonisation, Nationalism and Electoral Politics in Ireland 1832–1945', in O. Busch (ed.), *Wählerbewegungen in der Europäischen Geschichte*, Berlin: Colloquium Verlag, 1980, 259–80.
44. *Dáil Debates*, 1 Mar. 1922, 157.

Chapter 4. Priests and Patriots (PAGES 57–77)

1. F.S.L. Lyons, *Culture and Anarchy in Ireland, 1890–1939*, Oxford: Clarendon Press, 1979, 85–112; Tom Garvin, 'The Anatomy of a Nationalist Revolution: Ireland 1858–1928', *Comparative Studies in Society and History*, 28/3 (July 1986), *passim*.
2. See, in general, Terence Brown, *Ireland: A Social and Cultural History*, London: Collins, 1979.
3. Francis Hackett, *Ireland: A Study in Nationalism*, New York: Huebsch, 1920, 238–9; Anonymous, *The Ireland of Today*, Boston: Small, Maynard, 1913, 139–40.
4. James O'Shea, *Priests, Politics and Society in Post-Famine Ireland*, Dublin: Wolfhound, 1983, 317–60; D. Keenan, *The Catholic Church in Nineteenth-Century Ireland*, Dublin: Gill & Macmillan, 1983, 61–6. Hackett, an Americanised Irishman who observed the country closely during the period 1916–18, was struck by the sheer cultural and political might of the Catholic Church. It had much to lose in a secularising world, and penalised dissent: 'The Catholic Church in Ireland resembles Tammany Hall very closely in the manner in which it tries to penalise the independent man. It is said by Sir Horace Plunkett and others that the Catholic Irishman is dreadfully lacking in moral courage. But it takes an extraordinary brand of courage to fight an organisation that has its allies, it dependants, its nurslings in every hole and corner, that has its fingers on the economic pipe-line, and that can punish disobedience by cutting off education from your children, friendship from your household, religious exercise from your soul, and food and drink and revenue and Office from your own isolated self' (Hackett, *Ireland*, pp. 285–6). An overstatement, out not by too much. He omits to mention that the laity had its ways of fighting back.
5. Maurice Goldring, *Faith of Our Fathers*, Dublin: Repsol, 1981, *passim*.
6. F. Boyle, *Canon Sheehan*, Dublin: Gill, 1927, 2–26.
7. P.A. Sheehan, *Literary Life*, Dublin: Phoenix, n.d., 1–34.
8. Ibid., 64.
9. P.A. Sheehan, *Under the Cedars and the Stars*, Dublin: Browne and Nolan, 1903, 292.
10. P.A. Sheehan, *The Graves at Kilmorna*, Dublin: Phoenix, n.d., 66–8.
11. Ibid., 268–70, 339–41.
12. Sheehan, *Under the Cedars*, pp. 322–3.

13. *Irish Ecclesiastical Record*, 15 (Jan.–June 1904), 5–26.

14. Ibid., 22–3.

15. *Irish Rosary*, 1 (1897), 4.

16. *Irish Rosary*, 2 (1898), 185, 235, 281, 320, 377.

17. *Irish Rosary*, 5 (1901), 316–17.

18. *Leader*, 24 Oct. 1903.

19. *Leader*, 29 Apr. 1905.

20. *Leader*, 21 Nov. 1908.

21. Keenan, p. 160.

22. *Leader*, 19 Nov. 1904; P.A. Sheehan, *The Blindness of Dr. Gray*, Dublin: Talbot, 1913, 35.

23. O'Shea, *Priests, Politics and Society*, pp. 17–20.

24. *Leader*, 1 July 1911.

25. *Leader*, 4 June 1910.

26. Keenan, pp. 24–34.

27. Frank O'Connor, *The Big Fellow*, London: Transworld, 1969, 184.

28. Keenan, pp. 152–6,

29. C.S. Andrews, *Man of no Property*, Dublin and Cork: Merrier, 1982, 29.

30. L. O'Flaherty, *The Assassin*, Dublin: Wolfhound, 1983, 107.

31. *Leader*, 28 Oct. 1905.

32. *Leader*, 24 Dec. 1904.

33. *Leader*, 24 Feb. 1906.

34. *Irish Catholic*, 22 Feb. 1896.

35. *Irish Catholic*, 25 Apr. 1896.

36. *Irish Catholic*, 22 Mar. 1902. On Irish Catholic anti-Semitism, see G. Moore, 'Anti-Semitism in Ireland', Ph.D. thesis, Ulster Polytechnic, 1984, and his 'Socio-economic Aspects of Anti-Semitism in Ireland, 1880–1905', *Economic and Social Review*, 12/3 (Apr. 1981), 187–201.

37. *Leader*, 30 Apr., 28 May 1904.

38. *Irish Rosary*, 5 (1901), 478–83, 575–8.

39. *Irish Catholic*, 2 Feb. 1901.

40. *Leader*, 10 June 1905.

41. *Leader*, 23 Sept. 1905.

42. *Leader*, 16 Dec. 1911, 12 Oct. 1912.

43. *Leader*, 1 Sept. 1900, 2 Nov. 1901.

44. *Leader*, 2 Jan. 1904.

45. *Leader*, 30 Apr. 1904.

46. P.J. Gannon, 'Religious Statistics in Ireland', *Irish Ecclesiastical Record*, 17 (1921), 141–57.

47. Trevor Wilson (ed.), *The Political Diaries of C.P. Scott, 1911–1928*, Ithaca, NY: Cornell University Press, 1970, 64–6.

48. Ibid., 66.
49. *Leader*, 18 Jan. 1908.
50. *Leader*, 1 Apr. 1911.
51. *Leader*, 16 Nov. 1912, 13 Dec. 1913.
52. *Catholic Bulletin*, Jan. 1913.
53. Charles J. Kickham, *Knocknagow*, Dublin: Gill & Macmillan, 1978, 220. See R.V. Comerford, *Charles F. Kickham*, Dublin: Wolfhound, 1979, where the novel's status as popular national epic is argued.
54. Fritz Stern, *The Politics of Cultural Despair*, Berkeley and Los Angeles, CA: University of California Press, 1961.
55. Ibid., xii.
56. Ibid., 121–2, 124.
57. *Irish Review*, Jan. 1914.
58. Quoted in Leon Ó Broin, *Dublin Castle and the 1916 Rising*, Dublin: Helicon, 1966, 136.
59. *Catholic Bulletin*, May–June, Aug., Sept. 1916., May, June, July 1917.

Chapter 5. The Politics of Languages and Literatures (PAGES 78–107)

1. This was well understood by many revivalists; see for example Desmond FitzGerald, *Memoirs*, London: Routledge and Kegan Paul, 1968, 13–15, 33. FitzGerald could also see that the language was not just being pushed back by English but slowly becoming impoverished internally, losing its previous richness of vocabulary and expression and becoming more of a patois.
2. L.G. Redmond-Howard, *The New Birth of Ireland*, London: Collins, 1913, 217–18.
3. D. Ó Cobhthaigh, *Douglas Hyde*, Dublin and London: Maunsel, 1917, 37–40.
4. FA UCD, Hyde memoir (unpaginated MS).
5. Ibid. Cf. A.E. Cleary, 'The Gaelic League, 1893–1919', *Studies*, 8 (1919), 398–408, at 401; *United Irishman*, 9 Dec. 1899.
6. M.J. Waters, 'Peasants and Emigrants: Considerations of the Gaelic League as a Social Movement', in D.J. Casey and R.E. Rhodes, *Views of the Irish Peasantry, 1800–1916*, Hamden, CN: Archon, 1977, 160–77.
7. *Irish Ecclesiastical Record*, 12 (1891), 1099–108.
8. *Irish Ecclesiastical Record*, 3 (1898), 551–2.
9. *Irish Catholic*, 25 Jan. 1902.
10. *Leader*, 28 Oct. 1905.
11. James Joyce, *Stephen Hero*, London: New English Library, 1966, 25.
12. *Leader*, 23 Nov. 1907.
13. *Leader*, 21 Nov., 12 Dec. 1908.
14. *Leader*, 9 Jan. 1909.
15. *Leader*, 31 July 1909.

16. Gaelic League Portarlington, *Autobiography of the Ruairi O More Branch*, n.d. [1906] (NLI pamphlets 149162 P8). Cf. Waters, 'Peasants and Emigrants', *passim.*

17. *Belfast Newsletter*, 28 May 1904.

18. FA UCD, Hyde memoir.

19. Cleary, 'Gaelic League', pp. 402–3.

20. *Leader*, 27 July 1901.

21. *Leader*, 12 Mar. 1904, 28 Oct. 1905.

22. Cleary, 'Gaelic League', p. 404.

23. *Claidheamh Soluis*, 8 Apr. 1899.

24. *Leader*, 7 Dec. 1907.

25. House of Commons, *Final Report of the Commissioners on Intermediate Education (Ireland)*, C 9511, 1899, Appendix, 482–3.

26. House of Commons, *Final Report of the Commissioners on Intermediate Education (Ireland)* C9511, 1899, Appendix, 484.

27. *Leader*, 24 May 1902.

28. *Leader*, 1 Sept. 1900, 2 Jan. 1904.

29. *Leader*, 1 June 1912.

30. *Leader*, 8 Sept. 1900.

31. W.P. Ryan, *The Pope's Green Island*, London: Nisbet, 1912, 33.

32. NA WDC, Despatches from Consuls, 841.00/5–85, 30 Sept. 1916.

33. Redmond-Howard, *New Birth of Ireland*, pp. 217–18; *United Irishman*, 5 Mar. 1904.

34. M. Tierney, *Eoin MacNeill*, Oxford: Clarendon Press, 1980, 44.

35. Ibid., 53; *Claidheamh Soluis*, 7 Feb. 1900, 24 May 1902.

36. Tierney, *Eoin MacNeill*, p. 176; Ruth Dudley Edwards, *Patrick Pearse: The Triumph of Failure*, London: Faber & Faber, 1979, 58–63.

37. FA UCD, Hyde Memoir.

38. *Banba*, June 1903; see *Banba*, June 1906 for a ruthless and amusing review in Irish of Pearse's *Poll an Phiobaire*, arguing the essential barbarism of Pearse's beloved Connacht dialect of Irish.

39. FA UCD, Hyde memoir.

40. Ibid.

41. *Leader*, 10 May 1902; *Claidheamh Soluis*, 9 May 1903, 18 June 1904, 18 Aug. 1906, 29 June 1912.

42. *Claidheamh Soluis*, 18 June 1904, 11 Dec. 1906, 24 Aug. 1907, 15 Feb. 1908.

43. *Sinn Féin*, 28 August 1909.

44. S. Brooks, *The New Ireland*, Dublin: Maunsel, 1907, 14.

45. Ó Cobhthaigh, *Douglas Hyde*, pp. 50, 54.

46. *United Irishman*, 26, 29 Apr. 1902.

47. FA UCD, Hyde memoir.

48. *Freeman's Journal*, 31 Aug. 1910.

49. FA UCD, Hyde memoir; *Irish Independent*, 28 Sept. 1911.

50. *Cork Constitution*, 25 Sept. 1911.

51. *Irish Independent*, 3 Sept. 1911.

52. Ibid.

53. Seán T. Ó Ceallaigh, *Seán T.*, Dublin: Foilseacháin Náisiúnta Teoranta, 1963, 50–1.

54. FA UCD, Hyde memoir.

55. *Freeman's Journal*, 5 July 1912.

56. *Claidheamh Soluis*, 16, 23 Aug., 20 Sept. 1913.

57. FA UCD, Hyde memoir.

58. *Claidheamh Soluis*, 8 Nov. 1913.

59. *Claidheamh Soluis*, 29 July 1905.

60. *Claidheamh Soluis*, 14 Oct. 1905.

61. *Claidheamh Soluis*, 7 Oct. 1905.

62. *Claidheamh Soluis*, 18 Jan. 1908.

63. *Claidheamh Soluis*, 15 Feb. 1908.

64. *Claidheamh Soluis*, 23, 30 May 1908.

65. *Claidheamh Soluis*, 26 Aug. 1911.

66. *Irish Independent*, 25 July 1913.

67. *Irish Freedom*, Oct. 1911.

68. FitzGerald, *Memoirs*, pp. 13–15, 32–4.

69. Siobhán Lankford, *The Hope and the Sadness*, Cork: Tower Books, 1980, 124–5.

70. See O'Casey, *Drums Under the Windows*, pp. 346–50, on the characters of the IRB leaders.

71. *Claidheamh Soluis*, 10 Sept. 1910. Cf. E. O'Malley, *On Another Man's Wound*, Dublin: Anvil, 1979, 58: 'The shoneens—those who through snobbery, acquired wealth, inclination or steady bootlicking had acquired an intermediate position, neither food, flesh or good red herring—were held in supreme contempt.'

72. O'Malley, *On Another Man's Wound*, pp. 42, 50, 126.

73. *Leader*, 18 June 1908. 'For similar uncomplimentary assessments of English civilisation, see for example *Leader*, 11 Jan. 1908, 9 Jan. 1909, and especially the views of the influential nationalist writer R. Barry O'Brien in *Irish Ecclesiastical Record*, 25 (1909), 560–68.

74. *Catholic Bulletin*, Apr. 1911.

75. *Catholic Bulletin*, Mar. 1911.

76. *Claidheamh Soluis*, 1 Mar. 1913.

77. *Catholic Bulletin*, Apr. 1911.

78. *Leader*, 9 Mar. 1912.

79. *Catholic Bulletin*, Jan. 1913.

Chapter 6. Ideological Themes of Separatist Nationalism (PAGES 108–41)

1. Karl Marx, 'The Eighteenth Brumaire of Louis Napoleon', in Karl Marx and Friedrich Engels, *Selected Works*, London: Lawrence & Wishart, 1970, 96–7.

2. Hoffer '*The True Believer*' in *Between the Devil and the Dragon*, New York: Harper & Row, 1982, 174–307, at 223–4.

3. AD UCD P17b/122.

4. AD UCD P48c/6/59.

5. K. McDonnell, *There is a Bridge at Bandon*, Cork: Mercier, 1972, 7.

6. NA WDC 841. 00/5–85, 30 Sept. 1916.

7. AD UCD P7/D/14.

8. F. Stern, *The Politics of Cultural Despair*, Berkeley and Los Angeles, CA: University of California Press, 1961, 34.

9. *United Irishman*, 25 July 1903.

10. *Claidheamh Soluis*, 4 Aug. 1906.

11. *Catholic Bulletin*, Dec. 1917, Feb. 1919: *Leader*, 9 Feb. 1906; *Sinn Féin*, 16 Jan., 24 Apr. 1909, 11 Feb. 1910.

12. R. Ellman, *Yeats: The Man and the Masks*, New York: Macmillan, 1948, 22.

13. AD UCD P48c/26b; P48c/106/22.

14. C.P. Scott, *The Political Diaries of C.P. Scott 1911–1928*, Ithaca, NY: Cornell University Press, 1970, 289–90.

15. SPO DE 2/486.

16. Quoted in E. Butler, *Barry's Flying Column*, London: Cooper, 1971, 33.

17. NYPL Maloney papers, Box 7. On emigration, see Tom Garvin, *The Evolution of Irish Nationalist Politics*, Dublin: Gill & Macmillan, 1981, 110–11.

18. NYPL, Maloney paper, Box 5.

19. Scott, *Political Diaries*, p. 349.

20. PROL CO//903/19.

21. *Leader*, 6 Feb. 1904.

22. Robert Wohl, *The Generation of 1914*, Cambridge, MA: Harvard University Press, 1979, 204, 216.

23. *Irish Review*, Jan. 1914, *passim*; *Catholic Bulletin*, Jan. 1915, *passim*.

24. Anonymous ('A Silent Politician'), *On the Future of Ireland*, Dublin: Harding, 1862, *passim*.

25. *Irish Freedom*, Oct. 1911.

26. *Irish Freedom*, Nov. 1911.

27. *Leader*, 5 Aug. 1911; *Catholic Bulletin*, Aug. 1911.

28. AD UCD P17b/100, O'Malley papers.

29. *Irish Freedom*, Feb., Mar. 1913.

30. *Catholic Bulletin*, Apr., May, June, July, Aug. 1920.

31. J.J. Walsh, *Recollections of a Rebel*, Tralee: Kerryman, 1944, 85. Walsh was pleased to describe himself as part of the 'west Cork Mafia', to which so many prominent and successful rebel leaders belonged.

32. S. Levenson, *Maud Gonne*, New York: Reader's Digest, 1976, 94–5, 130, 145–7, 364; Nancy Cardozo, *Lucky Eyes and a High Heart*, Indianapolis, IN and New York: Bobbs-Merril, 1978, 407.

33. Levenson, *Maud Gonne*, p. 152 (on England); Cardozo, *Lucky Eyes*, p. 245 (on MacBride).

34. Levenson, *Maud Gonne*, p. 168.

35. Isaiah Berlin, *Against the Current*, New York: Viking, 1980, 313–16, at 316; cf. J.P. Corrin, *G.K. Chesterton and Hilaire Belloc: The Battle Against Modernity*, Athens, OH and London: Ohio University Press, 1981, *passim*.

36. J.T. Farrell, *On Irish Themes*, Philadelphia, PA: University of Pennsylvania Press, 1982, 20–1 and *passim*.

37. Stephen Gwynne, *Experiences of a Literary Man*, London: Butterworth, 1926, 42–3.

38. *Catholic Bulletin*, Mar. 1917.

39. AD UCD P48a/190.

40. AD UCD P48b/374–88.

41. Ibid.

42. *Irish Peasant*, 27 Feb. 1906.

43. *Irish Nation*, 26 June 1909.

44. NYPL, Maloney papers, Box 5.

45. Ibid.

46. Scott, *Political Diaries*, p. 290.

47. S. Ó Buachalla, 'Education as an Issue in the First and Second Dáil', *Administration*, 25/1 (1977), 57–75.

48. *United Irishman*, 10 June 1899.

49. *Sinn Féin*, 16 Jan., 21 May 1909.

50. *United Irishman*, 28 May 1904.

51. *Leader*, 20 Apr. 1901.

52. Horace Plunkett, *Ireland in the New Century*, London: Murray, 1904, 101.

53. *Catholic Bulletin*, Mar. 1911.

54. *Catholic Bulletin*, Apr. 1911.

55. *Catholic Bulletin*, Aug. 1911.

56. *United Irishman*, 18 Mar. 1899.

57. *Leader*, 27 July 1901.

58. *Irish Review*, Apr. 1911.

59. Ruth Dudley Edwards, *Patrick Pearse: The Triumph of Failure*, London: Faber & Faber, 1979, 257–8.

60. Ruth Dudley Edwards, *Patrick Pearse: The Triumph of Failure*, p. 258.

61. Farrell, *On Irish Themes*, p. 11 and *passim*.

62. *United Irishman*, 18 Mar. 1899.

63. *United Irishman*, 20 Aug. 1904.

64. NYPL, Quinn papers, Letterbook 2, 4 Feb. 1908.

65. Ibid., Letterbook 2, 1908 (n.d., probably Mar. or Apr.).

66. Ibid., Letterbook 3, 12 Nov. 1912.

67. *Irish Freedom*, Apr. 1913.

68. J. Lee, *The Modernisation of Irish Society 1848–1918*, Dublin: Gill & Macmillan, 1973, *passim*.

Chapter 7. The Ideology of Defeat: The Mind of Republicanism after 1922
(PAGES 142–70)

1. NA WDC, Despatches from Consuls, J841.00/86–190, 10 May 1918.

2. IWM, Jeudwine papers, *Record of the Rebellion in Ireland*, vol. ii, Intelligence, 31–2.

3. Ibid.

4. The persistence of non-democratic power structures in western Europe up to 1914 is discussed in Arno Mayer, *The Persistence of the Old Regimes*, London: Croom Helm, 1981.

5. Francis Hackett, *Ireland: A Study in Nationalism*, New York: Huebsch, 1920, 271–2.

6. N. Macready, *Annals of an Active Life*, London: Hutchinson, 2 vols. n.d., ii. 615.

7. PROL PRO 30/59, 1.

8. PROL PRO 30/59, 4; cf. the British assessment of the Dáil delegation and the second Dáil in Lord Birkenhead, *F.E.*, London: Eyre & Spottiswoode, 1959, 373–5, 380. Before meeting the TDs, the British were inclined to underestimate them, but afterward, a note of respect creeps into the comments. Birkenhead was fascinated by Collins, and the feeling was apparently mutual.

9. Warner Moss, *Political Parties in the Irish Free State*, New York: Columbia University Press, 1933, 64.

10. See for example AD UCD P17b/95; Ernie O'Malley, *The Singing Flame*, Dublin: Anvil, 1978, 43.

11. O'Malley, *Singing Flame*, pp. 285–6. Cf. NLI MS 9873, Sherlock memoir, 71, 78–9, 85; J. O'Beirne-Ranalagh, 'The IRB from the Treaty to 1924', *Irish Historical Studies*, 20/77 (1976), 26–39.

12. AD UCD P17b/100.

13. AD UCD P17b/103.

14. Interview with Peadar O'Donnell, RTÉ Television, 9 Oct. 1986.

15. P.S. O'Hegarty, *The Victory of Sinn Féin*, Dublin: Talbot, 1924, 75–7.

16. *Dáil Debates*, 20 Dec. 1921, 59.

17. PROL PRO 30/59, 1–5, 10 Dec. 1921.

18. Sir Ormonde Winter, *Winter's Tale*, London: Richards, 1955, 300.

19. Peter Pyne, 'The Third Sinn Féin Party, 1923–1926', *Economic and Social Review*, 1/1 (1969), 29–50, and 1/2 (1969), 229–57.

20. PROL CO 904/188 (1).

21. AD ACD P17b/123.

22. AD UCD P17b/133.

23. AD UCD P48a/42–3.

24. Ibid.

25. *Dáil Debates*, 21 Dec. 1921, 112.

26. *Dáil Debates*, 3 Jan. 1922, 187–8.

27. *Dáil Debates*, 17 Dec. 1921, 242–43.

28. *Dáil Debates*, 21 Dec. 1921, 112.

29. AD UCD P48a/60.

30. PROL PRO 30/67/56. See E. Butler, *Barry's Flying Column*, London: Cooper, 1971, 33.

31. O'Hegarty, *Victory of Sinn Féin*, pp. 240–43.

32. J. Connolly, typescript memoir in private possession, n.d. (1958–60), 335–6.

33. B. Mazlish, *The Revolutionary Ascetic*, New York: Basic Books, 1976, *passim*.

34. PROL PRO 30/59, 1–5, 16 Feb. 1921.

35. NYPL J. C. Walsh papers, Slipbook; *Dáil Debates*, 21 Dec. 1921, 112.

36. E. Hoffer, *Between the Devil and the Dragon*, New York: Harper & Row, 1982, 182.

37. NLI MS 9873, Mathews memoir, 93.

38. PROL PRO 30/59, 1–5, 17 Aug. 1920.

39. Macready *Annals*, vol. ii, p. 603; PROL PRO 30/59, 1–5, 13 Nov. 1921.

40. M. Tierney, *Eoin MacNeill*, Oxford: Clarendon Press, 1980, 312.

41. LC WDC MS 77 1489, Arthur papers, Container 37.

42. NLI MS 21142.

43. U. Mac Eoin, *Survivors*, Dublin: Argenta, 1981, 340.

44. G. Russell, *The Interpreters*, New York: Macmillan, 1923.

45. LC WDC MS 77 1489, Arthur Papers, Container 37.

46. Daniel Corkery, *Synge and Anglo-Irish Literature*, Cork: Cork University Press, 1947 (first published 1931), *passim*.

47. *United Irishman*, 25 Jan. 1902.

48. *Leader*, 17 Jan. 1914.

49. E. O'Malley, *On Another Man's Wound*, Dublin: Anvil, 1979, 228.

50. NLI MS 15991.

51. Ruth Dudley Edwards, *Patrick Pearse: The Triumph of Failure*, London: Faber & Faber, 1979, 338.

52. NLI MS 21265, Frank Gallagher papers, Robinson TS, 6.

53. *Dáil Debates*, 21 Dec. 1921, 116.

54. NLI MS 10561; see NA WDC, Despatches from Consuls, 841.00/86–190, 10 May 1918.

55. NLI MS 159993.

56. Mac Eoin, *Survivors*, p. 25.

57. K. Griffith and T. O'Grady, *Curious Journey*, London: Hutchinson, 1982, 187.

58. R.J. Lifton, *Revolutionary Immortality*, New York: Random House, 1968.

59. A. Ussher, *The Face and Mind of Ireland*, London: Gollancz, 1949, 25.

Chapter 8. Epilogue (PAGES 171–79)

1. G.A. Birmingham, *Irishmen All*, London and Edinburgh: Foulis, 1913, 9–13.

2. Ronan Fanning, *The Irish Department of Finance, 1922–1958*, Dublin: Institute of Public Administration, 1977, *passim*.

3. Maurice Manning and Moore MacDowell, *Electricity Supply in Ireland*, Dublin: Gill & Macmillan, 1984, 18, 31.

4. Conor Brady, 'Police and Government in the Irish Free State, 1922–1933', MA thesis, Department of Politics, University College, Dublin, 1977, 36.

5. NYPL, Maloney papers, Box 8.

6. J. Newsinger, 'I Bring not Peace but a Sword: The Religious Motif in the Irish War of Independence', *Journal of Contemporary History*, 13/3 (July 1978), 609–28.

7. J. Krejci, *Great Revolutions Compared*, Brighton: Harvester, 1983, 22–69.

8. *Maynooth Union Record*, 1899–1900, *passim*.

9. Thomas Greene, *Comparative Revolutionary Movements*, Englewood Cliffs, NJ: Prentice-Hall, 1974.

10. Rex Hopper, 'The Revolutionary Process', *Social Forces*, 28 (Mar. 1950), 270–79.

11. This is not to denigrate the scholarly achievement of reconstruction of the medieval Gaelic past that was a major by-product of the revolution. There is a major irony in the fact that this reconstruction had the effect of demolishing the revolutionaries' ideas of that past.

12. Hoffer, *Between the Devil and the Dragon*, p. 394.

13. Cf. the discussion in Tom Garvin, 'The Destiny of the Soldiers: Tradition and Modernity in the Politics of de Valera's Ireland', *Political Studies*, 26 (1978), 328–47.

14. S.M. Lipset, *Political Man*, Baltimore, MD: Johns Hopkins University Press, 1981, 127–79.

15. C. Desmond Greaves, *Liam Mellows and the Irish Revolution*, London: Lawrence & Wishart, 1971, 110–11.

16. Greaves, *Liam Mellows*, p. 167.

17. Patricia Lavelle, *James O'Mara*, Dublin: Clonmore & Reynolds, 1961, 307–10.

INDEX